I0742227

THE HUMAN COLLECTIVE

THE HUMAN COLLECTIVE

a novel

Michael Anthony Lang

Overlook Publishing, New York

An Imprint of Overlook Communications, LLC.
1 Colonial Green
Loudonville, New York 12211

First Overlook Publishing paperback edition Janaury 2019
Overlook Publishing and colophon are trademarks of
Overlook Communications, LLC.

For information about special discounts for bulk purchases, please contact Overlook Publishing special sales at www.overlookpublishing.com

The Overlook Publising Speakers Bureau can bring authors to your live event. For more information, or to book an event, visit our website at www.overlookpublishing.com

Inerior and exterior deisgn by Matthew Green

Manufactured in the United States of America

10 9 8 7 6 5 4 3 2 1

Library of Congress Cataloging-in-Publication Data
Names: Lang, Michael 1965 – author
Title: The Human Collective : a noval / Michael Anthony Lang
Description: New York / Overlook Publishing, 2019

ISBN 978-1-7328434-9-3

*To Mom, who calls
me her
"Shining Star"
and Dad who
always called me "Champ".
Thank you for
always telling me
I could do anything in life.*

"The ultimate measure of a man is not where he stands in moments of comfort and convenience, but where he stands at times of challenge and controversy."

- Martin Luther King Jr.

THE HUMAN COLLECTIVE

Chapter One

John Harris's new recruits were not due to start for another half hour, and he sat back in his chair, trying to enjoy the quiet time before the day's media circus. But a voice inside his head said, "Just make the call and get it over with." With a sigh, he sat forward and connected to his phone.

"Hello, Mr. Applegate. It's Dr. Harris…. No, everything is fine, but the most astounding thing happened during the experiment last night at the prison… The baby actually disappeared from the mother's womb for thirty seconds and then reappeared unharmed."

Applegate didn't respond. As the silence became uncomfortable, Harris said, "Mr. Applegate, are you still there?"

"Yes, I'm here," Applegate snapped. "Tell me, Harris, what the hell am I supposed to do with thirty seconds? Is that really the best you can do? You know, I'm beginning to think that I've wasted a lot of time and money on you and your crackpot experiments."

The call dropped.

Dr. Harris put down the phone and tapped his finger on his desk in his dark office. He was relieved the call was over but wondered how he would deal with Mr. Applegate in the future. Staring out the window, he saw that several of the recruits were arriving early.

As the massive medical center rose up in front of her, Jessica Anderson trembled with excitement. She had been looking forward to that day her whole life. A child prodigy, she was on track to become the youngest surgeon in the state. She was also lucky enough to arrive at the medical center on the exact day that Baby X would be born—a monumental occasion because new births were exceedingly rare.

In the private pod her parents had ordered for her, the commute was quicker than she expected, and before she knew it, she was there.

The small, spherical pod landed in the doctors' parking lot, and Jessica took a deep breath, stumbling as she got out.

There were already several other recruits in line for registration, and Jessica filed in behind them. It was hot for late February, and the line seemed barely to move.

As she approached the front of the line, she heard the other recruits asking a lot of questions. Finally, it was her turn.

"Please verify your full name," said the woman processing registrations.

Jessica couldn't tell if the woman was a pure AI or one of the new hybrid AI people. It was getting harder to tell the difference. "Yes, my name is Jessica L. Anderson."

"Kindly step into the room to your right and stand absolutely still on the illuminated circle. All of your information and scans will be verified for accuracy and entered into the system."

As Jessica stood on the circle, the woman said, "I'm just waiting for the last item to clear…" the woman's tone dropped off on the word "clear" so that the rest of her sentence hung in the air. "Don't worry, this won't affect the verification process, but I noticed your eye screen is scrolling slowly. You may want to get that checked out." Jessica exhaled, relieved that it wasn't something serious.

"OK, Dr. Anderson, you're one-hundred percent verified. You can go into the decontamination room now."

It was the first time anyone had called her "Doctor," outside of her friends and family. She took a deep breath, excited and nervous at the same time, and stepped up to the door marked "Decontamination."

An automated voice said, "Please move into the decontamination room." Jessica jumped a little and stepped through the door. The process took thirty seconds and ended with a loud buzzer and an artificial voice that said, "Please exit."

On the other side of the door, Dr. Holland waited for her. As she walked out of the decontamination room, he reached out and shook her hand. If it hadn't been for his nameplate, she might have missed him altogether. He was taller than she'd pictured, and a bit thicker in the middle—an unusual thing for a doctor. His round, metal-rimmed glasses were perched halfway down his nose and Jessica had the strangest urge to push them up.

"So, according to my records, you were at the top of your class. Is that true?"

"Yes, sir, I was."

He looked at her with a slight grin. "Well, good news for you, you're the lucky recruit."

"I am?" she replied.

"Yes. Dr. Harris, the chief of the medical staff, said we should take our top recruit and just throw her in and see what she's got."

Her heart beat a bit faster, and though she tried, she knew she'd failed to keep her expression neutral. "Thank you. I think," she said with a nervous smile. "What do you mean 'just throw me in'? Throw me into what?"

Dr. Holland placed a hand on her back, gently urging her forward. "Walk with me. Let's go into the conference room. Are you hungry? There's plenty of food."

They walked to the conference room, and Jessica reluctantly admitted that she hadn't eaten since the night before.

Dr. Holland led her to a table at the far end of the room, where there were several options for breakfast; mostly plates filled with assortments of fruits, but there were many other options. Jess's stomach growled as she eyed the spread.

The conference room itself was large, but there were many men and women—all in hospital garb—dotting the area. Some stood and chatted, others sat at the small round tables and ate.

"I don't know if you've heard the big news, but the center is delivering a baby today. So that means you are delivering a baby today."

"Really? On my first day?"

"Well, you'll be supervising while the AIs deliver the baby—still a monumental occasion—and of course you're ready. Besides, Harris always does something big or crazy with the first-timers who he feels have potential. It doesn't get bigger than this."

"I do appreciate that, but I thought a high government clearance was required to be present for a delivery these days?"

Dr. Holland waved a hand as though he were batting away a bothersome mosquito. "Well, kind of. Dr. Harris has the highest governmental clearance, and you're his new apprentice, so basically you now have clearance."

"I have to be honest, Dr. Holland; I can't believe this is

happening on my first day. I mean, what if it doesn't go well? What if I screw up and end up on the world feed?"

Dr. Holland took his glasses off and cleaned them as he laughed. Jessica noted that the laughter was kind, fatherly, with no hint of mockery. "Relax. I didn't mean to get you nervous. You'll be fine. You're good under pressure, right?"

She felt a sense of accomplishment for all her years of schooling and training up to that point and answered with as much conviction as possible. "Absolutely."

"Good, because the world feed is setting up outside, and there is talk that this may be one of, if not the last human permitted to be born on earth. The Big Sixteen are considering a moratorium on human babies, then an all-out ban. That would make this baby the last."

"How would they do that? It's already illegal to have children," Jessica asked.

"Well, that's true. Yes, it is illegal. For most. You can obtain a permit, which is how most children have been born in the past few decades. I don't know what the Sixteen have planned, but they will want to further control human reproduction, even though fertility rates among both genders are at all-time lows as it is and despite the consequences of childbearing. I would suspect perhaps enforced sterilization, or mandatory contraception."

Bile burned at the back of her throat, but Jessica swallowed it back. Many knew that pregnancies still occurred on occasion, but the government tended to take no action against women who terminated pregnancies—most often because while the government had made pregnancy illegal, they seemed to only care about children brought to term. If a woman took matters into her own hands, the pregnancy was ignored. Jess had learned in medical school how to care for such women (mostly low-income) who had taken drastic steps to terminate their pregnancies. Many such women died due to complications, and that upset Jess enough. But enforced sterilization…that thought made her physically ill. She didn't want to seem contentious on her first day, so she asked a different question. "How did this family get a permit to have children?"

Dr. Holland hesitated at first then said, "We typically don't talk much about our patients' personal information, but this one is kind of unusual. The mother is actually a prisoner who got pregnant. Obviously without any permits."

Jessica was intrigued by that. "Do they know who the father is? It would have to have been a guard, right?"

"I don't think they know, but I'm not really sure. I do know that somehow the pro-choice and right-to-life folks found out, and there was a battle on what to do with the baby. To further complicate things, the environmentalists are protesting this birth along with all the others, saying more humans are bad for the environment. No one knows it yet, but we were briefed that the Sixteen have decided to have a public bid for the baby. This way, it's fair for everyone, and anyone can bid. Just in case this is the last baby."

Jessica was perplexed but she tried to keep her composure. "Well, I assume the mother has no money, so how can she bid? Can her family bid?"

Holland pushed up his glasses then placed his hand on his chin. "You're right, the mother can't bid. Well, technically she's allowed to, but she has no money. None of that is really your concern. I just wanted you to know what you are walking into with all the media people and bots."

"OK, thanks for the heads-up. I knew my career was going to be exciting, but I never figured it would start like this. Thank you for the cereal."

At 11:05 a.m. the latest AI bots delivered "Baby X" into the world. Jessica was in awe as the AI machines conducted the procedure. She and the other doctors stood patiently in an attached room and observed the delivery through the clear glass. Everyone watched quietly, so she wasn't surprised when Dr. Holland texted her through their eye screens.

"Are you holding up OK?"

"I am. It's amazing to see this in person."

"Did you see this procedure in med school?" the doctor asked.

Jess stared ahead as she thought of her reply and watched as it typed out for her. "Kind of, but I don't remember the table moving as much. It moves so quickly to the different AIs. Do human doctors perform any of the procedure, or do they just oversee?"

"Yes, definitely. The baby was just delivered, so as soon as they move the mother out of the room, it's our turn. Don't be nervous."

Dr. Holland spoke aloud, addressing everyone in the observation bay. "Baby X has officially been delivered and appears to be in good health." The room of doctors applauded, and everyone congratulated each other—shaking hands, smiling, clinking coffee mugs together. Their excitement was infectious. Jessica smoothed the pants of her scrubs and joined in, though she felt a bit shy being so celebratory with people she didn't know well. The occasion felt so enormous, and she was thrilled to have been a part of it.

The temporary hospital room for the new mother was directly behind the doctors, with only a thin wall separating them. When the mother screamed, her voice was crisp and so loud that it was as if they were in the same room.

Jessica, startled by the scream, grabbed Dr. Holland's arm. "Oh my God, what was that?"

Dr. Holland tapped his port and viewed his eye screen. Jessica saw the words of it reflected in his spectacle lenses. She considered trying to read them but thought better of it. "Wow, that was quick."

"Pardon me?" Jessica said.

"They just informed her that the bidding for the baby has started. You'll get clearance soon for your internal eye screen feed, then you'll be able to pull up more information about the hospital; but for now, I'll relay what I've just read. Two pretty big hitters are bidding against each other for the baby."

After a while the mother's screams and cries slowed, and Jessica asked if they'd moved the mother.

Dr. Holland sifted through information on his eye screen. "Let me check. I can get a link to the camera in the room." He scanned a specific page quickly before he answered. "She's still in there. Looks like she's trying to upload a funding source for the public to bid, but the link isn't working."

The door opened, and Dr. Harris walked in wearing a white

decontamination suit. Jessica saw him stiffen as he surveyed the room; likely picking up on the tension within.

He tapped his arm port. "William, soundproof holding room seven." Then he approached Dr. Holland and Jessica, though he didn't look at her. "Good afternoon, Dr. Holland. How are you today?" he asked.

"Very well, doctor. Thank you for asking. I would like to introduce you to our newest recruit, Dr. Jessica Anderson," Dr. Holland said, moving slightly to the left and swinging both hands toward Jessica. Dr. Harris stretched his gloved hand out and Jessica shook it.

"It's nice to meet you. Welcome to the center," he said quickly. He then turned to address the room. "Good afternoon, everyone. I see you all have your decontamination suits on and have been cleared, so let's get started."

Dr. Harris scanned his arm port, the door opened, and the team walked into the brightest, whitest room Jessica had ever seen; so bright, she squinted to relieve the pressure. Holland whispered to her, "Put your eyes on seven."

She did and quietly thanked him; not wanting to bring attention to herself.

In the middle of the small room was a stainless steel table. The baby boy lay in the center of the table, firmly strapped in place. On the baby's head was a strap with small holes so the machines could access the baby's eyes. It looked as if the baby had a mask on. Jessica's heart thundered in her chest. She couldn't remember the last time she'd seen a baby. She felt like she was on an advanced spaceship with all the blinking terminals and screens. Everything was so bright, and no one spoke. Three large vents opened from the ceiling, and black robotic arms descended, their red lasers homing in on the tiny body.

"Robotic testing mode in progress," a voice announced over the loudspeakers. Everyone watched as the robotic arms maneuvered in all directions.

Since all new humans were required to have an arm port and chip installed at birth, this type of medical procedure required the highest government clearance and was like nothing Jessica had seen, though she had experienced it as an infant, herself". Her leg itched, and as she scratched it, she moved a little to the right.

"Please stay in your assigned position," a computerized voice said.

Damn, that was stupid, Jessica thought. I need to focus. You can do this, she told herself.

She moved back to her designated location as Dr. Harris approached the wall terminal from which a scanner emerged, and a robotic voice said, "State your name and kindly look into the brain scanner." Dr. Harris did as directed and a large black box emerged from the wall. He told the others to place their goggles on the highest magnification settings so they could perform the procedure. A light with Jess's name on it glowed on the floor, and she stepped into position. Dr. Harris signaled, and the computerized arms and lasers lowered and moved closer to the baby.

"Dr. Anderson, you are responsible for robotic arm C. If there are any problems, I will ask you to override the system and manually perform that part of the procedure. Don't worry; it's just like what you learned in medical tech school. Do you feel confident that you can perform this task?" asked Dr. Harris.

Everyone looked at Jess for an answer. Her cheeks grew increasingly warmer, and she had to clear her throat before she replied. "Yes, sir—I mean, doctor."

The lasers buzzed and their tips glowed bright red.

At first, the procedure was exactly as Jessica had seen in simulation videos, but soon the baby started screaming in a way Jess hadn't heard before. Her body tensed as the screaming grew louder.

Keep it together, she thought, and her leg twitched, jerking slightly. The baby's screams grew more intense as the laser cut a perfect box into his left forearm. The smell of burning flesh coupled with the screams almost made Jessica faint. She wondered if they had anesthetized the baby enough, but she was afraid to ask. She resisted the urge to clap a hand over her mouth.

"Dr. Anderson, please give the baby another shot of MH-Seven with the small mechanical arm on your right," Dr. Harris said. She did as directed, and the baby's cries subsided.

Dr. Harris opened the black box. Inside was the chip, identical to the chips everyone else had.

Using one of the mechanical arms, Dr. Harris took the chip from the box and carefully placed it inside the main robotics device. Without hesitation, the machine placed the small chip into the incision. With all the robotic machines working in sync, the chip was attached to the baby's sensory nerves, as well as the blood vessels. Jessica watched in amazement.

Finally, Dr. Harris slowly read the chip ID number aloud. A

mechanical arm lowered and scanned the baby's chip for the first time, and the baby's data was uploaded into the collective.

Dr. Holland turned to Jessica and said, "Let's take a little break, and when we return, why don't you start the programming process? You can assist in reviewing the data for future diseases and the probability of unknown diseases that may impact the planet in the future." Jessica smiled, still a bit shaken by the process, but she didn't want to wear her emotions on her sleeve, so she agreed enthusiastically. Together, they left their assigned stations and walked into an adjoining sterile room.

"So, Anderson, what do you think of your first day so far?"

Jessica took a deep breath. "Well, it certainly wasn't what I expected, but I'm happy to be here. I didn't know the collective could calculate potential future diseases and download possible cures."

Dr. Holland clasped his hands together. "Isn't it just amazing?"

Jessica took a sip of her coffee. "It is amazing, but it's also a bit of an invasion of privacy." Jessica paused before she spoke next, knowing that what she said could have negative implications. She chose her words carefully. "I remember as a kid when my friends and I would get messages based on our actions. If we did something a bit mischievous, it was calculated that we could break a law in the future if we continued the treachery of unruliness."

Holland responded, "That's only because it doesn't want you to get into trouble. It's the greatest innovation humans have ever accomplished. I mean, just as it wanted to keep you out of trouble, it has prevented a few wars using similar algorithms. And look what it's done for the medical community."

"That's true, but I've always thought of it as somewhat creepy," Jessica said. One time it told my dad to consider cognitive enhancers because he couldn't find his golf shoes for a few days. My brother and I hid them as a joke. There's no nuance, and that can be cold. And scary."

Dr. Holland looked at her for a moment, then sighed and smiled. "Let's get back and you can start programming. I don't know if anyone told you, but don't be alarmed when you see the small drone cameras. They're just there to make sure everything is done properly and is put on the record. After a while, you won't even notice them." They finished their coffee and returned to the program room.

While the team of AI and human doctors performed tests on Baby X, the public bidding broadcasted on the live feed. The bidding was down to wealthy individuals, medical companies, and private equity firms looking to profit.

After a time, a signal flashed on Jessica's eye screen. It read, "Doctor Anderson, report to the main lobby immediately."

Jessica stopped what she was doing, left the room, and walked toward the main lobby. She noticed that Doctor Harris and Holland were headed the same way and likely received similar messages. As she got closer, she heard a growing commotion. She scanned her port. When the door slid open, room was stuffed with so many people she couldn't get though.

"Excuse me, excuse me," she said as she tried to get past them. "I'm Dr. Anderson." A military guard, armed with a large gold laser gun, must have heard her and moved toward her. The sight of the gun put her slightly off-kilter.

"You're Dr. Anderson?" he yelled over the crowd, his eyes

pinned to hers.

"Yes, I am."

"Step aside!" he yelled, pushing and elbowing his way to Jess. His name tag said Munroe.

"Come with me," he said, his face unflinching, as he sent someone sprawling with a shove.

A reporter tried to push a microphone in Jess's face, and Munroe roared, "Make way now, or I'll have you arrested!"

The reporter quickly stepped out of the way. The crowd parted, leaving a path through the middle of the packed room. As Jess followed Munroe to the center of the crowd, she saw a slightly overweight balding man who seemed to be making a point of not smiling. It was Mr. Applegate, in the flesh, surrounded by fifteen military guards, all of whom stood firm but appeared irritated.

Jess had read about Applegate in med school. He looked even nastier in person.

The room was full of reporters, both human and AI, all looking at Applegate as if he were the last of an all-but-extinct species.

Many of them held their hands up, as if they were asking questions, but all the top media companies utilized a new video-feed technology that was so small it could be implanted in a person's palm. It worked well for the reporters because they could tilt their hand in any direction to get tough angles. Also, streaming was immediate, since the device connected directly to the satellite drones; but the gesture had an odd groupthink feel to it. They looked like the Nazis from the old movies.

Reporters aggressively yelled questions at the doctors: "When will we see the baby? Why is Applegate standing there?" The doctors never had a second to answer because everyone was yelling.

Jess heard people speculate that Applegate would buy the medical center for experimentation. Each time one of the reporters got too close to Applegate, a guard would throw that person to the ground, and the others would move back until the next daring reporter got too close and was also thrown to the ground.

Dr. Harris approached the elevated platform. In the middle stood a glass lectern. He looked anxious as he turned to his assistant. "I am trying to review my speech, but it's hard to concentrate with all of this yelling. Can you quiet these people down?" The assistant stared at him blankly.

The little red dot in the corner of Jess's eye screen caught her attention. A text from Dr. Holland. Normally, her thoughts would be typed quickly on the screen and sent with two slow blinks; but she remembered her professor telling her, "Take your time with your thoughts, especially with your boss. Take your time before sending." As a precaution, she remembered him saying, "Read your response twice and manually send your message."

Surprised when she read the text, she didn't tap her port to manually send her reply. Instead, she blinked.

The text read, "Applegate is the high bidder."

She sent back, "No way, we studied him and his hack experiments in med school."

The guards formed a perimeter to keep the media back, but

reporters jumped in the air trying to get a video shot with their hands. Jess sent a message back to Holland. "I feel like we're at a concert with everyone waving their hands. It doesn't seem to bother Applegate."

It was no surprise that Applegate was used to the limelight. A posse of attorneys and guards were constantly with him. While everyone stood in the mayhem, Jess approached Applegate and reached out to shake his hand.

"It's nice to meet you, Mr. Applegate. I'm Dr. Anderson. I assisted on the medical procedures with Baby X."

Applegate looked at her without responding and nodded. "Get your hand away from my face, or I'll knock you out," he threatened a reporter

A guard promptly grabbed the reporter by the hair, electronically handcuffed the man and escorted him outside. The other reporters moved back once again.

Harris crossed over to the podium with Applegate to his right, and began speaking, but no one listened. The media was focused on Applegate, and since the reporters had Applegate's attention, they bombarded him with questions.

"Are you the high bidder?"

"How did a prisoner get approval for a baby when new, unpermitted humans are banned?"

"Did the president of the World Family Council have to sign off?"

"Are you the high bidder, Mr. Applegate?"

"Will you take the baby to a simulated Disney?"

"Have you named him yet?"

Dr. Harris spoke and grew obviously frustrated that no one was listening. Jess watched as he waved his hands, trying to get everyone's attention to no avail. Applegate walked up to the lectern and signaled to the guards. All at once the guards pointed their guns at the crowd, and everyone ducked. Jessica crouched below the potential line of fire and waited with her heart racing. After five or six seconds, the guards lowered their guns, and the media quieted.

"Go ahead, Doc," Applegate said. "You can talk now."

Dr. Harris adjusted his tie and again stood behind the illuminated glass lectern. Jessica and Holland stood on the far end of the platform. She listened as Dr. Harris introduced himself and the medical team. After a few minutes, he finally got to what everyone wanted to know.

"As you are all aware, the law allows legal bidding if a human baby is permitted to be born. Because the earth's resources are overwhelmed with the current population, more people are deemed an environmental hazard. We do not take this issue lightly, and we expect only qualified and responsible individuals with the ability to mitigate these hazards to bid. We are pleased to announce that the winning bidder, standing next to me, is the distinguished Mr. Sam Applegate. Mr. Applegate is the founder of the Applegate Prison for the Good. Please join me in welcoming Mr. Applegate." There was no applause from the media, only the yelling of questions.

Applegate moved to the lectern, cutting Dr. Harris's speech short. "I will answer a few questions, and then I have work to do." The reporters shouted questions at the same time. Applegate said, "No, no, and no. Number one, it's none of your business what I bid. I have no idea what the family will do, and frankly I don't care. His name is now Chasten Applegate. No more comments, and if one more of you bastards puts your hand in my face, you'll be in my prison." As he left the room, the reporters stayed out of his way. Moments later they followed him outside.

Holland came up to Jess. "I saw you shake Applegate's hand. Do you know him personally? What did you say to him?"

"I've read the medical stories about Applegate like everyone else because of his work, but I kind of know of him in another way."

"How so?" said Dr. Holland.

Jessica sighed, but tried to smile. "Sam Applegate originally founded the Applegate Prison for the Good near my hometown. I think it was the first one in the world. There was a guy in my town named Austin, who was a friend of my brother's. They used to play baseball, and some other sports, before he got in trouble."

"Really?" Dr. Holland pushed his glasses up. A gesture Jessica was thankful for. She couldn't bear to look at those large, wire frames resting on his nostrils. She idly wondered why he hadn't corrected his vision problems.

"Yeah, a guy killed his dog on purpose, and my brother's friend was going through a tough time. He lost it and killed the guy in a fight. He ended up in the Applegate Prison for the Good. My brother would talk to him every now and then, and he would tell him about the experiments the prison would do to raise money. It was pretty crazy."

"I've heard some stories myself," said Dr. Holland. "Why do they say 'for the good' in the name?"

"They use the prisoners as guinea pigs, and every now and then an experiment actually proves that a drug works or a body part can be replaced; but because they are privately owned, they don't have to report the deaths. They also make the prisoners wear a permanent flak jacket, which is basically a magnetic vest they can't take off. The walls and floors are magnetic, and they can stop or slam a prisoner against the wall any time they want. They use the success stories of the experiments as the reason for the name, but I think Applegate put 'for the good' in the prison as a screw you to everyone else."

Dr. Holland was silent for a moment, then pushed his glasses up again. "Obviously they take it off when they finish the sentence? The flak jacket?"

"If they're released, which I've heard is super rare. Surgery is required to remove the jacket. Also, visitors are rarely allowed into Applegate. I'm telling you, Holland, it's awful."

"I guess there are two sides to every story, Jess. I heard Applegate was some kind of hero because his experiments have cured so many diseases."

"Maybe that's true, but he makes insane amounts of money from his experiments, and I personally don't think there is a lot of good going on there."

All the media had left, and Dr. Harris looked exhausted as he approached Jess and Dr. Holland. "Well, that didn't quite go as I thought it would. Take a break and both of you meet me in conference room seven in ten minutes." Dr. Harris turned on his heels the moment he finished speaking. Jess left while Dr. Holland took a call.

Jess was the first to arrive to the conference room. She noticed a half-open door that led to a small room next to the baby's operating room. She hesitated for a minute before she opened the door all the way, then saw a woman standing next to a glass wall.

"Hi, I'm Dr. Jessica Anderson."

"Hello, Jessica. I'm Dr. Rosen, but please call me Nicole."

"I'm new here, but I have to tell you, it's amazing watching all that information scroll across the screens. It looks like it's scrolling at a million miles per hour. Do you know what's being programmed now?"

Nicole adjusted her hair, which was held up in a ponytail. "I do. I know the collective found the Alzheimer gene, so I believe it's programming the baby's chip to modify that gene along with any others to extend the life span."

"Jess smiled as she stared at the baby, but something odd happened, making Jess gasp. "Nicole, did you see that?"

The woman's ponytail bobbed as she shook her head. "No, see what?"

"I was watching the baby, and it looked, for a second, like it was… gone."

"Gone? How so?"

"I'm not sure, just… gone. Almost like a digital flash or something. This is a normal glass, right? Not some sort of digital glass?"

"It's just medical room soundproof glass," Nicole replied. She turned to look back at the baby. That's odd. I'll keep an eye on things." She paused a moment, her eyes staring past Jess. "You'd better go. I heard someone walk into the conference room."

"Oh, thank you. That's for me. It was nice meeting you."

"Likewise," said Nicole. Jess followed her new acquaintance and met Dr. Harris and Dr. Holland in the conference room.

Dr. Harris reached out and shook Jess's hand. "Well, Dr. Anderson, I hope your first day was an interesting one."

"That would be an understatement, Dr. Harris. Thank you again for everything."

Dr. Harris shook his head. "No problem. Have a seat. You too, Dr. Holland." Dr. Harris looked back at Jessica. "We're going to have you wind down for the day. We've had you shadow Dr. Holland today, and we've placed you in some pretty stressful situations. Obviously, we monitor everything and typically start new recruits on Fridays as a precaution."

"I'm not following you, Doctor," Jess said, her eyebrows furrowed.

"Based on the information we received from the collective, it was noted that it would be best to have you take the weekend off, reflect on your day's work, and return on Monday."

Her stomach dropped. "Oh my God, am I getting fired?" Jess couldn't help but feel a bit sad at the news.

"No," Dr. Harris said. "You understand the collective. It uses algorithms for everything, and in this case, it recommends not working Saturday and coming back Monday."

Jess did her best not to tear up at the table, and Holland placed his hand on hers.

"Jess, you did a good job, and the collective's report did not say, 'Don't come back.' It just calculates every situation imaginable and offers guidance. Plus, you're the youngest recruit we've had at this center. You're coming back…unless you don't want to?"

Jess cut him off. "Oh my God, yes, I want to come back. I have dreamed about this career my whole life."

"OK then, let me try to get back on track," said Dr. Harris. I have some good news for both of you. The center and the collective feel that you and Dr. Holland would make a perfect fit to monitor the newborn. You've been assigned to monitor the last human child, from a medical point of view of course. For the foreseeable future, it will be the focus of your medical careers. How do you feel about that?"

The room was silent while Jess and Dr. Holland looked at each other. Almost simultaneously, they answered, "That would be great".

"All right. You can gather your things. Congratulations on this important task."

Dr. Harris got up a bit awkwardly and walked out of the room while Jess and Dr. Holland sat, stunned and unsure what to say. As Dr. Harris walked through the door, he turned around. "Oh, yes. Your instructions will be sent to your chips shortly."

Chapter Two

Baby X, now known as Chase Applegate, grew up in a gated town not too far from where Jess lived. In fact, Jess and another doctor would sometimes visit him at home to do tests. As a child, he had been on the news feed a few times—not only because he was the last legal birth, but also because he had the misfortune of being involved in a fire that almost burned down the entire Applegate estate.

When he was six years old, Chase was playing with a solar beam device he found in the basement of his large estate, and he started a large fire by accident. His mother nearly suffocated as she ran through the flames and inhaled the smoke from the fire while trying to save him.

Chase was disoriented and light-headed from smoke inhalation. He trembled. He couldn't breathe well, and he was ravaged by coughing fits. He cried for his mother when he could; for his father. No one came. While he shook, he felt the air shake along with him. There was a shift, a lightness, a chill. Something in that air altered, then disappeared and there was nothing but blackness. It was as though he were stuck in a vacuum.

Time stopped, and everything was different. It was similar, but he saw his world from another vantage point. Chase wondered if he might be a ghost as he drifted through the air. A strange illumination acted almost as a backlight; everything was engulfed in a glow. Later, he thought that glow must have been from the fire, but at that time, he didn't understand it at all.

Amazed, he glanced below him. There he was. His body. Curled up as he coughed and shook. Chase didn't feel his throat closing anymore. He didn't feel the desperate attempts of his lungs to pump out the smoke and take in fresh air; air that was becoming scarce. He felt nothing. But he could glide. And he understood after a few moments that he could move objects in the world where he'd left his own body. He could see things, and he could physically move them.

He used this ability to stop the smoldering support beams from crashing down on his mother. He parted the fire and the smoke before her so that she had a clear path forward. If he didn't do it; she wouldn't find him. She couldn't save him. He returned to his body once more, out of breath, hot tears stuck in dusted streams down his face; his lungs filled with the urgency to cough, but he couldn't move. He was stuck, momentarily. Time started up again and his mom frantically grabbed him. She had a clear path for a safe escape and Chase could cough. He hated it because it hurt, but he was relieved because he was back in his body again, cradled in his mother's arms.

Chase never told his mother what happened that day. He never told anyone, because he felt responsible for the fire, but more importantly, he felt the immense weight of guilt for almost killing his mother. He wasn't certain of what he experienced, but he was aware that he moved things—that he moved time itself somehow. Even at six years old, he understood that what he'd experienced wasn't something other kids his age would understand. Chase kept his ability to himself.

Seven years had passed, and Jess ultimately became Dr. Holland's work wife. She took the lead on the baby project and enjoyed the challenge.

Jess's eye screen read "incoming". She sighed as she placed her freshly-brewed coffee on her rustic oak end table and connected.

"What now, Holland?"

"Isn't it ridiculous they're making us come in again?" said Dr. Holland.

"Not really," said Jess. "Why are you so upset over it?"

Jess noted a low grunt and pictured that Holland was either adjusting his belt or trying to pull his pants up, so they didn't slide below his ever-increasing belly.   She rolled her eyes at mental image. "I mean, no one goes in to work anymore, but we have the privilege of going to work twice in the same year, rather than doing the work remotely, which by the way, is entirely possible. It's ridiculous. I'm running late anyway."

Jess placed her forehead in the palm of her hand, resisting the urge to bang her head on the coffee table. "How can you be running late? You only have to go to the center twice a year. You need to plan better."

Holland scoffed. "Plan better? Don't give me shit. Almost everyone who works these days, works for AI. The AI don't need to see you in person."

"Oh, you'll live," Jess waved off the rant before changing the subject before he really got to complaining. "Hey, did you see that the boy was completely off-line a little while ago"?

Holland laughed humorlessly, and Jess was glad they weren't in the same room. She had the immediate urge to slap the man. "Jess, that's impossible. Check sensor three, it must be a glitch."

"I did, and it literally went off-line. Look, we'll work on it today. Whenever, you get to work."

Another condescending grunt came from the other end. Jess

wished she had one of those old-fashioned phones that could be held in one's hand and slammed against a wall or a counter, but all she could do was ball her hands into fists as she listened to Holland continue. "Do you know what this is, Jess? It's the man or the government making us come in for some crazy reason. The kid never went off line. I'll tell you right now, I will never go into the center three times a year."

"Sounds great, Holland. I'll see you there," said Jess as she disconnected.

About three hours later, when Dr. Holland arrived at the medical center, Jess was trying to figure out what happened to Chasten Applegate. Chase. It's just Chase now, she corrected herself. As she glanced over her shoulder, she saw Dr. Holland enter the room, wearing a black suit, his name card, and no white coat. The black suit contrasted harshly when viewed against the white walls of the room, all four of which were filled with computer screens.

"Nice that you made an appearance today," Jess said, suppressing a smirk.

"Don't start with me Jess. I'm here, so what do you have?" he said, placing a small bag on one of the rolling chairs and approaching Jess.

Jess spun on her stool to face Holland, leaving all sorts of information up on the screens behind her. "Ok, I spoke with Mrs. Applegate and she thinks that Chasten—um—Chase, was playing with a solar beam device he found in the basement, and he started a large fire by accident. It almost burned down the whole Applegate estate. His mother nearly suffocated. She reports that she ran through the flames and inhaled smoke trying to save him, but she grew lightheaded and was certain she would die. Then, she blacked out.

"Our records show that Chase was in the fire. He was also disoriented and light-headed from smoke inhalation. He trembled and if you look here," Jess turned back to face the nearest screen and pointed, "you can see that he was bent over, panting and coughing. All of his vitals dropped quickly and that's when it happened."

"When what happened?" Holland asked, a knowing look on his face.

"The kid went offline. Basically disappeared."

Holland shook his head. "Well, he didn't disappear, Jess. Something must have malfunctioned."

Jess sat up straighter, thinking that she could refute—or at least try to refute. "That's what I thought, but look, ten seconds later he's back online and Mrs. Applegate and Chase are out of the fire."

"Then someone grabbed them and got them out," said Dr. Holland, who was already walking back towards his bag, as if the case were closed and he could simply leave. Jess wouldn't let that happen. She could probably figure it all out on her own, but Holland was supposed to be her partner, so she decided not to put up with his tendency to brush off similar instances, so he could go home faster.

"Why don't we have a record of that?" Jess asked.

Holland sighed and turned back around to face her. He threw his hands up. "It's a glitch in the system, nothing else. More importantly, Jess, is has to be lunch or dinnertime by now. I'm hungry."

"You're unbelievable," Jess said, and the two worked the rest of the day at the medical center, fulfilling their mandatory appearances.

Jess left the medical center and went outside to meet her pod service. Does it ever cool off anymore? she thought as she left the air-conditioned building. She read on the lower left corner of her eye screen that there was another ozone warning for the rest of that day and the next, so she pulled up her solar hood. She turned around with a few other people and walked back toward the lobby until her pod arrived, descending from road level three. Jess adjusted her ozone hood and got in.

She sat inside the pod and had a drink with the other passengers. The roomy electric maglev pod seated eight and was luxurious with its spacious seats and in-pod service. Almost everyone in Jess's circle of friends used the premier transportation system which was many levels above the public system used by the commoners. Even though people weren't allowed to manually drive or walk on the premier or public highway systems, there were still a few closed-circuit roads where they could drive manual cars for fun or competition, but, of course, that was reserved for the wealthy. Everyone else had to take the public X system, where it wasn't uncommon for sixty or even seventy people to be crammed into a smelly pod with poor ventilation.

When Jess got into her pod, the voice said, "Welcome aboard, Dr. Anderson. It is our pleasure to serve you this evening. Would you like your favorite Pinot Noir and a manicure?"

"No thanks," Jess said as she stretched out on the air-conditioned leather chair. She rehashed her day and quickly changed her mind. "On second thought, I will take the Pinot."

The mechanical arm poured the glass of wine and handed it to her. Jess tapped her arm port to call her brother, and the guy next to her, who she recognized was also a doctor at the medical center, said, "Doc, mind using the silent bubble? I'm planning a nap."

"You got it." Jess tapped the button for the invisible bubble, and as it surrounded her, the sounds from the pod dropped away. "Sean, it's Jess. What's up?"

"Nothing much. What's up with you? Mom told me you got a real job at the medical center? I thought you worked for the government or FBI or something?"

"No, it's just that my project had been classified for all these years. I actually medically monitor the famous baby X, the last human baby boy."

"A real baby? Bullshit," said Sean.

"Yeah. Well, he's six now. It was all over the world feed years ago, if you want to watch it. Guess whose baby it is?" Jess asked. She was so excited to finally discuss it, she didn't wait for Sean's response. "Applegate's! Sam Applegate, from the Applegate prisons."

"Get the fuck out, Jess."

"It's true. I got to meet him in person."

"Really? Is he an asshole like everyone says?"

"Absolutely," replied Jess.

Sean laughed. "What did he say to you?"

"Nothing at all. He's weird. His wife is a little better. So how are you? Mom said you stuck a sword or some knife through your head?"

Sean laughed. "It's not a sword. It's just a large piercing needle through the top right corner of my forehead."

"Let me see it. Show me a live shot," Jess said, more out of medical curiosity than anything else. Sean beamed a five-second live 24-D video to her eye screen. And there he was, as described. A large needle sticking out of his head. His thick, dark hair obscured the entry point, but it was a disturbing sight nonetheless.

"Oh my God, Sean. What part of you thought that was a good idea?"

"Jess, not everyone is like you, living in a gated town in New York, working on celebrity babies. Speaking of which, I thought babies weren't even legal these days."

"He's not a baby anymore, he's a kid now. And hey, you're the one living in LA. A lot of people say you guys should be gated, to keep everyone in, so don't knock our gated towns." Jess paused, waiting for Sean to laugh. There was silence on the other end. Had they grown so far apart that he no longer understood when she was making fun of him? "I'm just messing with you, bro. I'm sure it's a good look for the band. How's that going, by the way?"

"It's fine. You know…sex, drugs, and rock and roll."

Jess laughed. At least she still understood his sense of humor. "Are you coming home for Thanksgiving this year?"

"I don't know. Mom and Dad kind of freak me out now that they've hit a hundred, but Dad does front me money every month, and things are pretty tight for me out here," he said in a lower, serious voice.

"Tight? How is that even possible?" Jess asked. "You fly all over the world with your band."

"True, but things cost money. You know, the drugs and women part." Sean attempted to joke, but Jess wasn't buying it. She knew Sean too well. He often made light of serious situations. Jess wanted to dig deeper, but she didn't want to come across as a nag.

"I hope you're being a good boy out there, Sean."

There was a moment of silence before he replied, "Sure, absolutely."

There was a sudden banging on Sean's door in the background. "Open the fucking door, or I'm taking off. I'm not waiting around all day!" There were two more loud bangs and a louder blast. Jess jumped.

"Sean, what was that? Who's beating down your door?"

"Nobody, Jess. I gotta roll. See you." With the sounds of more banging and yelling, the connection ended.

Jess deleted the temporary bubble and sat back, trying not to worry about Sean.

"Would you like a real apple slice? Excuse me, would you like a slice of real apple, Dr. Anderson?" asked the monotone voice of the AI car servant.

"What?" she asked.

"We have real organic fruit tonight, and I wanted to know if you would like a piece."

"No, thank you," she said, as the other passengers looked at her. The pod had been on an expressway level about six stories above the ground road lanes, flying fast, and before she knew it, her address flashed in her eye screen. The pod lowered and stopped. Jess was home.

She exited the pod and, lost in thought, forgot to scan her arm port to pay. The turbo pod hovered quietly, waiting for payment. Instead of scanning the Pay Now screen, Jess entered a new destination and got back in.

"Where are you going now?" asked a guy who was happily eating the apple she'd refused.

"California," Jess answered. She approached the man. "By the way, I think I will have a slice of that apple. You're sure it's not artificial, right?"

Jess sat and checked the flight schedules. The hydro jets left from New York every half hour, and they were quick flights. Jess sat back and tapped her foot while she enjoyed the sweet taste of the real apple. Trying to keep her mind from wandering back to Sean, she struck up a conversation with the apple guy. Apparently, his great-grandfather was a farmer before everything went to large-scale corporate farming.

"So where did you get those apples from? They're so juicy," Jess inquired. The man covered his mouth while he chewed. He bobbed his head, Jess assumed, to indicate that he'd answer her shortly. He swallowed his food, took a drink of water, and spoke.

"I have three real apple trees. I keep them in a solar bubble on my property on the Livingston estates."

"Very cool," she said.

When Jess arrived at the airport, she bought a carry-on bag and everything she would need at the airport mall. Because the trip was last minute and first class was full, she had to fly coach. No problem, she thought. I'll just get a little sleep.

Jess wasn't used to all the pushing and shoving as people

squeezed into the seats. As she boarded, the small, crowded seats stunned her; she couldn't imagine they would be comfortable, but she squeezed into one and dozed off quickly. It seemed as if her eyes had just closed when a voice over the loudspeaker announced, "Welcome to LAX."

When Jess walked off the plane, she forgot to turn off her digital ID tracker from the hospital, and as a result, people and droids approached her to hawk their goods.

"Doctor, can I interest you in the latest virtual vacation package?"

"Miss, we have face-lifts on sale, hundreds of shapes to choose from."

"No, no thank you," she said as she turned off the setting on her arm port. The ads on the billboard screens changed, along with the music—no longer targeting her.

Jess tried to resume her walk but froze when she remembered that Sean had moved the previous month, and she didn't have his new address. When she tried for the third time to connect with him, the call wouldn't go through. "Damn it," she said, exasperated. She found a chair and sat for a moment to think; to make a plan, but her seat vibrated, stealing her attention.

"Massage, manicure, or pedicure," an AI voice announced. "One simple scan from your chip is all it takes." Jess kicked the chair hard with her heels. "Please don't damage the chair, Jessica Anderson," the voice said. "Rather, love the chair."

Jess decided instead to flee the chair until the voice was no longer audible. She considered her options; one of which was to track the feed Sean sent her earlier that day and pinpoint that location. Hopefully he would still be there or, at least close by. She scanned her feed history; 103 Sixth Avenue, just off Santa Fe. She checked the floating wall screens and saw that the public pods were just down the hall.

The pod she entered was surprisingly spacious, with enough room for sixty people. A thick layer of dirt, and the occasional piece of trash, littered the pod, and it stank like sweat, along with a host of other odors. Maybe even vomit. She tried to ignore it.

The other passengers wore dusty, grimy clothes and their skin was leathery from ozone exposure. One woman had a facial tattoo. With her nice clothes and silky, smooth skin, Jess stood out.

Eventually everyone crammed in, and the trip began. Jess looked outside and couldn't believe the traffic. The public pod had limited maglev capabilities and therefore couldn't rise above level two. Jess was from New York, where there was a minimum of twenty levels and sometimes thirty or more for maglev traffic. Everything back east seemed to move smoother; here the expressways looked like parking lots. She stood on her tip-toes trying to see if there was an accident ahead. She counted ten levels of maglev pods, feeling as if traffic was moving in slow motion.

Jess turned to the woman with the tattoo and said, "Where is the express level?"

The woman looked at Jess without expression. "You're on it, bitch."

Jess ignored the woman and waited for her stop to come up on the pod screen, since she couldn't see it on her eye screen; maybe it wasn't connected. The ride seemed to take forever, and people pushed and shoved one another to get on and off at each stop.

Jess began to doze off, but each time the pod came to a stop, it would jerk back and forth, causing the seated passengers to nearly fall out of their chairs.

"Next stop in five seconds," the screen flashed. Jess almost flew forward as the door opened for a few people to get out. Another quick stop, and everyone slammed into each other again.

"Jesus Christ," Jess said aloud, "shouldn't they fix that? Why does the whole pod jerk like that when it stops?"

"Who are they?" The tattoo woman asked, her eyes scanning Jess from head to toe. "Where the hell are you from, anyway?"

Jess didn't say anything. The tattooed lady shook her head, a look of disgust on her face.

Three and half hours passed, and Jess couldn't believe how long the ride was taking. She tried to shut her eyes and thought, maybe if I fall asleep, it will go faster. Then the pod came to another abrupt stop for a few more people to board.

When Jess had almost fallen asleep, she heard someone lower themselves into the seat next to her. She peeked through one eye and saw a guy next to her; but he wasn't just sitting, he was brazenly sniffing her.

"Did you just fucking sniff me, you sick fuck?" Jess said, snapping out of her exhaustion.

"You smell tasty," the guy said, with a smile that was anything but friendly. He licked his lips.

Jess moved to the other side of the pod. About a minute later, the pod made a stop, and to Jess's surprise, the sniffing guy walked over to sit in the seat next to her again. He gave her a smirk and said, "Hi, it's me again."

Jess stared in shock while she contemplated how to handle him. This guy was much bigger than her. The tattooed lady approached them. Not saying a word, the lady punched the pervert right in his ribs. The man dropped to the ground and curled into the fetal position. The lady held something metal and shiny in her hand to make the punch count; it did.

As the man lay on the floor gasping for breath, the tattooed woman turned to Jess and said, "I got you this time, but be careful out here. You're not in Kansas anymore."

As the man lay on the floor, the other passengers regarded the incident as if it was no big deal. The brakes sounded, and the pod made another stop. The exiting passengers stepped over the man. The pod kept going, and besides Jess, there were only about ten people left.

Jess tried to gain back her composure until the screen displayed "103 Sixth Ave." Five others—most of whom looked like artists—got up, and the door opened. Jess paid and stepped outside.

Holy shit, this place is a dump, she thought. She stood for a second in disbelief, wondering, what the hell is my brother doing here, as the public pod pulled away. Everyone else walked off, and she stood in front of an old, dilapidated warehouse by herself, looking at the broken windows, peeling paint, and garbage lying everywhere. Just to make sure, she double-checked her feed address from Sean; it was correct. The earlier feed had come from inside the old warehouse, straight ahead.

Tapping her foot, she thought, this was a bad idea. The ozone level made it dangerous to be outside at that time of day and she wondered when the next public X would return to pick her up. Walking by the warehouse, she called out, "Sean," but there was no answer.

She slowly opened the door to the warehouse and upon entering the squalid structure, broken glass crunched beneath her feet. Inside, there were discarded liquor and pill bottles. The floor was littered with cups and old food. The air was stale but smelled of dirt—the human kind of dirt. Voices came from one of the other, distant rooms, and she again yelled, "Sean! Sean, are you back there?"

Silence. Not even a person telling her she had the wrong address.

She decided to move forward. The dimly-let warehouse grew darker the farther she walked. The next room she entered looked like a broken-down motel room with a bed, an old piano, and some half-eaten Chinese food. In the next room were vintage motorcycles and what looked like a surgical bed with needles hanging from the ceiling. She wondered how people could live that way.

Garbage—everything from discarded papers and tools to substances that stuck to her shoes— covered the floors. She crept into the next room, which was even darker. A dim light shone from under the door opposite Jess, and she moved in its direction. As she walked toward the light, she felt a slight breeze on the back of her neck.

Maybe I should go back, she thought.

"Hi there."

Jess jumped back and quickly spun around. "Oh shit!" Someone stood behind her in the dark.

"Who are you?" she asked. She could barely make out the silhouette of a man wearing a hoodie. In a trembling voice she asked, "Do you know Sean Anderson?"

The man didn't say anything at first. When he did speak, his words chilled her. "You shouldn't have come here."

"I'm sorry if I bothered you in your home, sir. I didn't mean to offend you."

"Oh, it's no bother. We're going to have a nice long afternoon together, you and I." The man took a few steps closer to Jess, and she could see a little better. The man took his hood off. "Remember me?"

It was the guy from the pod who had smelled her. Jess's leg jerked uncontrollably as she caught the glint of the knife he held in his right hand.

"Here's what's going to happen: first you're going to download your money from your chip, and then we're going to have a fun time, you and me."

He moved closer to her. "Put your arm port against mine and transfer your money…Do it…Do it now!" he yelled. Jess stood frozen as he unbuttoned his pants. "Are you wearing any underwear? Let me see, now. Let me see." Jess couldn't move; she just kept shaking.

"I asked you a question. Are you wearing any underwear?" he yelled at her.

Everything seemed to move in slow motion, and Jess felt numb. Then, behind the man, another faceless person in the dark moved closer to him.

"What are you doing? I said give me your arm and transfer the money, bitch!"

The person behind him continued to approach. The man turned a bit, still yelling at her to transfer the money.

"I'm not going to tell you again. Start transferring the money right now, bitch, or I'm going to rip your clothes off and rape the shit out of you."

With all his yelling, he didn't notice that the other person was now directly behind him. Overwhelmed, tears soaked her face and she tried to block out what was about to happen.

He gripped her arm. Hard. "Look at me, bitch. Look at me!" Right behind him, the small amount of light caught on the cheek of the other person; the face tattoo. It was the woman from the public pod, and she held her index finger over her lips. Jess remained frozen.

The tattooed girl tapped the man's right shoulder. The guy jumped and quickly turned around. As he did, the tattooed girl punched him square in the face, and once again, he hit the ground. She wore a set of brass knuckles and kept punching him in the face.

Blood gushed from him, and the woman yelled, "Take that, you fucking bastard." A massive pool of blood spread across the floor, and the two strangers wrestled. Every time he tried to get up, she punched him in the same spot and he cried out. The lights came on, and three other guys and one girl ran into the room.

"This is the fucker who raped Zaria last week, I know it," the girl said. Others likely heard the commotion and came in to see what was going on.

A guy with a red X tattooed on his face walked in. "What's going on, Kay?"

"Johnny, this is the guy who raped Zaria the other day. I saw him on the pod, and he was about to rape this girl."

Johnny grinned at him. "OK then, now you're mine." The look of fear transferred from Jess to the rapist. Johnny grabbed him by the hair and kicked him in the side a few times with his big black boots. The other guys dragged him out.

Johnny yelled to Kay, "Thanks, Kay. I'll get good money for that arm port once we cut it off, and I'll be able to take care of you."

Jess, still in shock, went over to the tattooed woman and said, "Thank you so much for saving my life! Thank you." She broke down and cried. "Thank you so much!" Trying to regain her composure, she asked, "How did you know I was here?"

"When we got off at the same stop, I heard you yell, 'Sean,'" said the tattooed girl. "There is only one Sean around here, and that's my Sean." Jess's face lit up for the first time when the woman asked, "How do you know him?"

"He's my brother. I'm worried about him. I think he's in trouble."

The woman looked slightly mortified. "Your brother? You must be Jessica."

Jess swiped at her tears. "Yes."

"Wow, what are doing out here? Give me a hug. I'm Kay, Sean's girlfriend." They hugged, and Jess continued to cry, overwhelmed with a sense of relief and happiness.

She took a deep breath, sniffling. Then she almost started to laugh. "Kay, you have a hell of a punch."

"Thanks. I was sort of a pro fighter for a while, plus you don't know what you're gonna find living on the streets, right?"

"On the streets? I thought Sean was in a famous up-and-coming band?"

"Is that what he told you?" She raised her eyebrows. "Let's get you cleaned up. We have a pretty cool room here in the warehouse with some of Sean's motorcycles, and I have a tattoo table."

"I think I walked through that room," Jess said.

"You walked through my room? Damn, I need to put a lock on that door." She smiled at Jess. "Hang in there, it's over."

They walked into the room, and when Kay turned the lights on, Jess recognized some drawings; they were done in Sean's style.

"Jess, sit down wherever, and I'll tell you what Sean's up to these days."

"Thanks, Kay, but is it possible for me to see him now, please?"

"Why don't we just hang for a little while?" she replied.

"I would really like to see him. Please, Kay? I came a long way to see him."

Kay inhaled deeply, ran a hand through her hair and said, "OK then, let's go." Kay took Jess up two floors through a makeshift staircase made of wooden pallets. They stopped at double steel doors with a big padlock on them. After Kay unlocked the doors, they entered another dimly lit room.

"What is this, and what is that smell? Kay, can you turn the lights up more?"

"No, we keep them low for everyone's sake." People were lined up in a straight row, sitting motionless on chairs.

"What is this?" Jess asked again.

"This is where Sean spends most of his time. He's in the second chair; that's his spot. He picked it himself and painted the armrests."

Jess walked closer to him. "Sean, it's me, Jess." Sean didn't move, and Jess saw that his breathing was shallow. His eyes were wide open and pitch black; no iris. "He looks dead. What happened to him?"

"No, he's not dead." Kay looked at her. "I don't know how much your brother told you, but Sean and I do T. We've been doing turbo now for about a year. As you probably have heard, it kind of takes over your life."

"Why would you do that? They say turbo eventually takes control of your brain and your rational thinking."

"I guess…why not?" said Kay. "It's better than living in this fucked-up world."

"Look at him, he's not even breathing right. Who's watching my little brother so no one hurts him while he sits there like a fucking zombie?"

"Look, it might not be perfect, but we stick together and watch over each other. That's why we have the big padlock. We even schedule shifts to check on each other."

"Kay, I know you're a good person, and you probably saved my life. I just love my brother so much and hate to see him and, I guess, you live like this."

"Like what?"

"I mean, look at him. Where is he? He's not even blinking."

"He's alive and on a virtual trip in his mind, somewhere that he chose. The drug gives you a few options at first. I think he picks surfing or something like that before the turbo completely takes over. That's what he tells me when he comes back. He said he was going to sit on a beach while the withdrawal of turbo begins. When you start to come out of it, it's pretty bad for some people."

"Why are his eyes so black?"

"You know how everyone has those small data feeds in the corner of their eyes? Well, when you take the drug, it messes with something in your brain and takes over the eyes through your nervous system or something. Who the hell knows? I'm not a scientist, but I can tell you that the high is like nothing you've ever experienced. It's truly amazing. It's like sex times a thousand. I'm just saying, in case you want to try it sometime."

Jess didn't respond. She just stared at her brother in disbelief. She knew about the drug, but she wanted to know if Kay knew about it. If they were at least practicing harm reduction. "So why is his breathing shallow if the drug is so good?"

"From what I know, the drug overtakes the brain functions, and I guess if you pull so much from one part of your brain for the experience, you have to sacrifice something else. For a lot of people, it's lung functions and breathing."

"Kay, I don't know if Sean told you, but I'm a doctor. I learned in med school that after a while, T will shut down all your body's functions in order to get the experience. Did you know that? It gets worse and worse. It's like termites eating away at your mind. Sooner or later it destroys everything, and you're dead. Do you understand that? It takes control of your brain, and then you're dead."

Kay looked to the ground and shuffled her feet a bit. "I guess that may or may not be true, but if it is; no one knows exactly when it happens. It could be next month or maybe years from when a person starts using. And look, until then, we're not hurting anyone. Who knows? That may never happen, or not for a long time, and really, Jess, don't lecture me. You almost just got raped and killed in one day." Kay paused. "I'm sorry. That wasn't nice, but you don't know what it's like around here. From what Sean told me, you're pretty rich and live in fucking la-la land. I'm sure life is a party for you. Well, not for us."

Emotionally exhausted, Jess started to tear up again looking at Sean. "I can't believe he's doing this to himself." Then she walked up to him and said to Kay, "Wake him up. Wake him up!"

"Are you crazy? Now that can kill him. I saw a girl get woken up from T when her house caught fire, and she was so confused and messed up she thought the fire was part of her trip. At first, she ran into the fire dancing, and when she realized it was real, she had a heart attack. So, I wouldn't wake him up."

"That's terrible. Did the emergency-response droids try to get her to a hospital?" Jess asked.

"No, she burned up in the fire. Look, I know you're not from around here, but the government authorities don't give two shits about people like us. We don't even have a drone fire department. The population in California is in overload, and I think they feel the more people who die, the better it is for all the people left. I heard there are an allowable number of people in each city in America and our population is higher than that number. The cops don't come around here unless some rich person gets robbed or something and they have to track them down. Johnny and those kind of guys, they're our cops. I'll guarantee you that that fucker who tried to rape you is history by now and his left arm and chip is already on the black market."

Jess had to force herself to turn away from her brother, so she could look Kay in the eye, hoping that she would answer her honestly. "So when will I see Sean again, off the drug?"

"I think he took enough T for about a week and a half."

Jess inhaled sharply. "A week and a half. I thought it was expensive to be high on T even for a day."

"It is, but I guess Sean gets money from back east from a trust fund or something like that."

"There is no trust fund; my dad is trying to help him and thinks it helps pay his rent out here." Jess shook her head. "I shouldn't've come out here. I'm going home. Kay, do you know, if I'm willing to pay extra, would a super pod pick me up here?"

"You're kidding, right?"

"OK, I didn't think so, but I'm so pissed off right now, I have to get out of here, quickly."

"I hear you, Jess. I'll schedule the public pod to stop. There will

be one coming by soon. Hopefully your next trip is better than the last.”
They walked out of the turbo room. “Listen, Jess, it’s the same long trip
back, so don’t fall asleep again, and don’t talk to anyone.”

Chapter Three

A few years passed before the drugs caught up with Sean.

Jess was working at the medical center when she got an emergency call from Kay. She immediately connected. "Hi, Kay, what's going on?"

Kay was silent for so long, Jess almost asked if she was still there. Kay took a few shallow breaths, and when her words came out, they were rushed and broken. "I'm sorry to bother you at work, but your brother is on a five-week binge on T. His heartbeat is only fifteen beats per minute, and we can't increase it. I'm scared. I…I think he's going to die. We're trying to plug a program into his port, but I don't think the guy we have knows what he's doing. He's an addict himself, but…um… he also codes a little."

Jess brought a hand to her chest and bent over as pain ripped through her. She crouched on the floor with her back against the wall as she spoke. "Kay, oh my God, call for an emergency drone." Jess listened to Kay sniffle on the other end while Jess's eyes scanned her surroundings.

"They won't come to our neighborhood. They say it's unsafe for the staff."

Jess frantically reached out to all her contacts and eventually connected with her mentor and first boss. She wanted to reach him first, but worried that she would disrupt his retirement, so she saved him for last. Dr. Harris was more than happy to assist Jess.

That night Jess flew to LA in a fully staffed private hydrogen jet offered by Dr. Harris.

When she arrived at the apartment, she found that, at some point between her conversation with Kay and the moment before she entered the apartment, Kay was also exhibiting symptoms of a fatal overdose.

Jess repeatedly asked residents of the apartment how much Turbo Sean and Kay had taken. Once convinced that Jess and her team weren't there to send them to jail, her brother's friends told them the story. Kay was so distraught over Sean's condition that she'd taken more of the drug herself, and also needed to be revived.

Once Jess and Dr. Harris's private team managed to get the two somewhat stabilized, the team brought both Kay and Sean back to New York and placed them in rehab. Jess paid for Sean's rehab because she wanted the best facility for him, and for Kay, too, because while Jess knew Kay was sick, she was important to Sean. And that made her important to Jess.

Jess visited the couple every third day. At first, the center had them lay in white beds with fluffy pillows. The surroundings were clinical, but the décor was soothing. The wall colors were all bright, or grey-blue. Jess supposed those colors were meant to inspire creativity, or comfort. One of the techs she befriended admitted as much one day, when Jess couldn't deal with the symptoms of her brother's withdrawal.

Hooked up to IVs that infused him with nutrients, jabbed with needles that plumped his flesh, and gave the years back to his face that T had stolen from him—Sean was always uncomfortable. For the first few weeks he would scream and rip out the IVs. Luckily most of the attendants were AI. The only humans entered the room were the techs who checked the AIs or the therapists who tried to talk the addiction out.

Sean screamed at Jess and tried to throw things at her so often, the AI attendants bound his arms to his bedside. He cursed her for not leaving him in that squalid place to rot because "that's all that happens to us anyway. Don't you get it?" He repeated that phrase a lot, and Jess always shook her head, holding back tears. Sean would curse his parents as well. Even Kay—who recovered a bit faster than Sean—was often caught in the storm of his rage.

At first, Kay was just as bad. She hated Jess. But Jess urged them to stick with the program, knowing in the back of her mind that her words would fall on deaf ears. That the only way they would get clean would be if they wanted to get clean. And Jess wasn't sure either of them felt that way.

Jess was amazed at the tactics the facility used to encourage T abusers to clean up. The clinic steadily reduced the dosage of T for the abuser while monitoring their vitals very closely, and their brainwaves for any symptoms of catatonia, dementia, or any memory ailment. Jess found it interesting as well as humane that the addicts were still given their drug of choice (which for most, unfortunately, was T).

But that feeling of humanity ebbed when Jess watched the dose reduction process. A therapist sat Jess down behind a window. The therapist was a middle-aged woman with short black hair and big round eyes that made her look youthful. She was soft-spoken, and Jess liked her.

Kay and Sean were on the other side of the window, in a room with only chairs, and similar robotic arms to those Jess saw in the delivery room at the hospital. The arms would drop down from the ceiling and inject the couple with T. Sean's and Kay's faces would freeze, their eyes would either glaze over or close. A second arm would whir around the couple. Then, a second injection. All hell broke loose after that.

Both Sean and Kay were suddenly alert, but unaware of anything. They screamed hellish screams like those you hear from someone who has lost a loved one. The hair on Jess's arms prickled at the sound. The couple suffered in that room, together, but alone. They writhed on the floor, tore at their hair and slapped at their own faces. They cried and screamed.

"Get them out!" Jess yelled.

She approached the door and had placed her hand on the steel doorknob when the therapist gripped her shoulder with a thin hand.

"No, Jess. You have to let them feel it," she said.

Jess spun to face the woman. "Feel what? They're in pain! Why aren't you helping them?" Jess's vision blurred, and she blinked back tears. Instead of allowing herself to grieve for her brother, she grew angry for him. But only for a moment.

The therapist sat Jess back down and told her to breathe, told her she understood her anger, but that this was the only way. The second injection was meant to repel the users from touching the drug by creating a negative association. Each time the user took T, they would also be injected with a powerful hallucinogen which would overwhelm their minds and provide the sensation that insects squirmed within their heads, trying to tunnel their way out by consuming the brain matter of the addicts.

Jess did breathe. She was still angry, but it was best for her not to show that. She smiled at the therapist. "Is it effective?" Jess asked.

The therapist sighed and stared through the window, a blank look on her face.

"Nothing is effective against this drug. The pleasure far outweighs the pain," she said. She stood, read the vital signs of the couple, recorded them in her tablet, and left the room.

Jess couldn't bear to watch her bother and Kay suffer, so she left. She wandered the common area of the rehab where she ran into another patient. An older man—probably in his forties—who looked healthy, likely due to the injections and supplements provided to him. Jess spoke with him and learned that he'd been in and out of the rehab facility for twenty-two years.

"How... how have you survived so long?" Jess asked. The man looked at her, his clear blue irises a reflection of the sky; his pinpoint pupils a reflection of the void he'd fallen into.

"I don't know, darling, but I have. I've had that treatment so many times. Most of the time, us junkies, we either put up with it to get back to using, or the treatment drives us over the edge," he said. He made a motion with his hand as though he were slitting his own throat.

After her talk with the patients, and after three months of watching nearly every patient other than Kay, Sean, and the man with the crystal-blue eyes check themselves out, Jess understood just how impossible it was to stop taking T. She lowered her expectations.

Should she have left them there? Should she have never intervened? She often wondered what would have been better for Sean and Kay, but the couple made it through treatment. Jess, along with her parents, were thrilled to visit the rehab for the last time.

Kay walked out the front door, her few belongings in two plastic bags. She threw her arms around Jess.

"Now we're even, huh?" Kay said.

Jess smiled and shook her head. "How so?" she asked.

Kay gripped Jess tighter. "You saved my life this time."

Sean followed close behind Kay. He'd put on a few pounds, and the treatments he'd been given to restore life to his face and his flesh had worked. He looked like the Sean Jess had always known. He'd even had his piercing removed while he stayed at the center; it was deemed hazardous due to the nature of the treatment and the drug he was taking.

Jess and Sean's parents cried and held their son. Her father shook Kay's hand, but their mother ignored Kay.

"She's a bad influence," Jess's mom whispered to Jess, her eyes pinned on Kay, her arms crossed, and her lips pursed.

"How do you know that, Mom?" Jess asked. "How do you know that Sean wasn't the bad influence?" Her question hung in the air, unanswered, as her stubborn mother refused to open her mind, or her heart, to the wonderful woman her son loved.

The couple would have a rough road ahead, but it had been arranged that they would live off the public draw. Jess was grateful the program existed—not for addicts, but for humans who couldn't find jobs due to the overwhelming number of bots that worked them instead.

A few weeks later, Sean was teaching music lessons to earn a bit of extra cash. He soon graduated to managing bands.

It pained Jess to watch him and Kay struggle with money while she was situated comfortably in the one percent of humans who maintained a job—and she was wealthy. She was the head doctor at the hospital; a job offered to her once Dr. Harris retired. She lived in a gated community near the hospital; a community with a pool, private pod flights at her beck and call, spa treatments that would keep anyone from ever guessing her real age, and real, organic fruit. There was a small orchard that produced the sweetest apples. Like the apple she'd shared with that gentleman on the pod back from her first day at the hospital. All those years ago.

Occasionally, she would still go check on Baby X, who was quickly growing up.

Chapter Four

The Applegates had servants, butlers, chefs, and gardeners. They had plenty of humans to interact with but Chase wanted friends his age, who shared his interests. Eventually, he acquired a small handful of such friends. His parents had bid on them for him, and these friends were all direct descendants of the sixteen families who ruled the world (along with the collective's assistance).

Chase was a trophy of sorts for Sam Applegate, since Chase was the last child born. He enjoyed nature, and although it was rare to see a live animal not in captivity, his parents built a small farm. Chase understood that his father thought he was weird. Sam Applegate had no qualms with making fun of Chase when he was a kid.

"Son," he would say, "animals are for hunting and eating, not staring at." If Mr. Applegate wanted to eat a gourmet meal, he would order the slaughter of one of the farm animals, which made Chase very upset.

He would explain to Chase, "This is what we do to animals; we eat them. That's why God put animals on the planet."

When Chase was about ten years old, his dad wanted rabbit stew. Chase watched as the farm servants killed his favorite rabbit, Snowy (Chase always thought the rabbit's fur looked like fluffy, fresh-fallen snow, so he named his pet after that pure blanket of white). When he refused to eat the stew at dinner, his father hit him. That abuse was the first of several episodes the boy would suffer.

"What is wrong with this boy?" Mr. Applegate asked his wife. "You think he would be happy and more appreciative; I cut off the rabbit's foot for him." He reached out and gave it to Chase. "Here, take it. It's lucky. Rabbit's feet bring you good luck."

Chase, in silent protest, refused, but Applegate hit him until the boy took his rabbit's paw in his hand. He held back the wild sobs his body tried to push out; the wailing of his grief. He knew if he were to cry in front of his father, nothing good would come of it. Chase placed Snowy's paw in his middle dresser drawer and never used that dresser again.

"Mom why does Dad always call me weird?" Chase and his mother sat at the kitchen table one morning, shortly after Chase placed the last piece of his pet in that drawer in hopes of locking the memory of losing his pet away with it. His father had done many things to him that made him believe Sam might not have cared for him, but when his father called him weird, that stung the most. He'd been gathering the courage to ask Mrs. Applegate about just that. He was brave enough, but terrified of her answer.

His mother's face softened. She stood, smoothed her blue dress and knelt by Chase's side. She brushed a hand over his head and kissed his cheek. Her green eyes held a sadness Chase wanted to ignore. He placed his hands in his lap and looked down at them.

"He doesn't mean it, honey," said Mrs. Applegate. The word "weird" would have a special meaning for Chase. He wanted to believe his mother; he believed that she wanted to believe what she'd said and that was enough for him. Then.

Later that afternoon, Mrs. Applegate took Chase over to his friend Phillip's house for a visit. Phil's friend Tucker was also over, and the boys played hide-and-go-seek in Phil's massive house. The kids liked playing there because Phil's mother insisted that the home be built in an older style, with plenty of slanted ceilings and random cubbies.

"Chase, it's your turn. Go hide," said Phil.

Phil tried to whisper to Tucker, but he talked too loudly, and Chase heard them. "When we find him, let's gang up and pound on him a little."

Tucker agreed. "Sure, why not? Two against one. He won't stand a chance. Let's get him."

Chase, trembling, hid in a closet upstairs in the house. He remembered how scared he was during the fire; how he shook then. He didn't want the boys to find him. He didn't want to be beaten up. In fact, he'd come to his friend's house to escape that sort of treatment. Chase tensed and shook harder as he heard the old wooden floors creak with each step Phil and Tucker took closer to him, and with each creak, Chase shook more intensely. He felt as though he were vibrating on a cellular level—that his very composition was separating beneath his skin.

"I think I hear him in the closet," said Tucker.

"Me too," said Phil. "Let's get him."

When Phil pulled opened the door, Chase felt that same feeling from the day of the fire. The air shifted, became light with a chilly undercurrent. This time, white noise blurred the voices of his friends, but he could still hear them, though they sounded far, far away.

"Gotcha!" they yelled out, but the closet was empty except for some shirts on hangers.

Chase could still see the boys; the empty closet. Empty. That was odd. During the fire, his body had stayed behind while his mind went elsewhere. Chase held his hands out in front of him. He could see them. That odd illumination was also present, and this time, Chase knew it wasn't from a fire. Everything had an odd, orange tinge to it, as though the first light of dawn bloomed in that windowless closet.

He was down the hall from the boys, who stood still, their mouths agape, but frozen like a paused show from the stream. While time seemed to stand still for the boys, Chase walked up behind them, noting that the floor did not creak when he stepped on it. The air grew warmer, the orange glow faded, and his ears popped. He abruptly placed one of his hands on each of his friend's shoulders and gripped tightly.

"Here I am," he said. The boys jumped and spun to look at him. Their eyebrows were arched sky-high, and Phil looked a bit pale. Tucker stuttered a bit, but ultimately decided not to speak.

"Wait, how did you do that?" cried Phil. "I heard you in the closet."

"I was," said Chase. "I…um…knew you guys were coming after me, so I moved behind you while you stood there."

Tucker looked at Phil and then said, "What? How? We would have seen you leave. Man, you are so weird. Actually, you might be the weirdest kid I ever met. Tucker grab him. I want to punch him." The three ran down the stairs.

Phil's mom said, "Enough clowning around," and Mrs. Applegate collected Chase and left. When she asked Chase if he had fun, he had no response. The word "weird" rang in his head the whole way home. It seemed he couldn't escape it no matter where he was. He would never be safe from that word.

Chase became of legal working age as the years passed, and it was mandatory that he learn the family business. He spent at least four days per week at the prison owned by Sam Applegate. He followed the employees to learn protocol and made friends with some of the guards. They always got a kick out of him because, being an adversarial teenager, he often said things to his dad others only wished they could say. Applegate grew frustrated with Chase because he refused to help in any way with the medical experiments. Chase simply didn't have the stomach, or the heart, to participate, and the moment he learned what his father was doing to those people, he thought of him as a low-life. He'd long ago lost respect for Sam.

Applegate hired the brightest doctors from the medical center to carry out the experiments, but many were unsuccessful. The prison made huge profits on start-up medical part companies that needed to test new human-droid parts. Because they were just untested start-ups, many of the prisoners would have catastrophic side effects or even die.

Chase didn't have an easy time with such things as his father did; they made him uncomfortable and anxious. He didn't want to hurt people, or to contribute to them being hurt. His father would be angry when Chase refused, and while he had long done what his father asked of him, he was not only older; he was bigger. He had grown at least a full foot taller than his father. The beatings had practically ceased. Chase could fight back. Or, he could disappear.

One sunny morning at 6:30, shortly after Chase had been working beneath his father, Sam and Mrs. Applegate had breakfast together.

"Are things going any better with Chase at the prison, honey?"

Mrs. Applegate asked. Her blond hair hung in loose curls over her strapless sundress. It seemed to Sam that she'd deliberately situated a few of those thick curls over her breasts to conceal them. Sam was annoyed, but so long as she took care of her appearance, he would not complain. He stared at his beautiful, largely untouchable wife and sighed.

"Not really. I'm trying to teach the kid the family business and how to be fiscally reasonable, and he just stands there like an idiot. He doesn't really participate in the experiments or anything I'm trying to teach him. Worse, I know he's made friends with some of the prisoners and actually feels bad for some of them. Can you believe that?" Sam asked, his cheeks growing warm, his fingers tightly coiled about his fork. Those prisoners, to Sam, were sub-human. They were in prison for a reason. Human kindness wasn't something Sam thought should be afforded to those who committed felonies. His own son was out there making him look like a fool, treating those people like they weren't any different from himself.

"Well, I'm sure it will get better," Mrs. Applegate replied, her usually soft eyes appearing a bit vacant as she placed her hand on top of Sam's clenched fist. Sam ignored the look in his wife's eyes. He'd done so for years. She served her purpose in public. That was what mattered most to him.

"I'm not so sure," he said, looking down while eating his eggs Benedict. "You know his biological mom was a nut case, right? Well, we keep tabs on her and she's still in and out of one of my medical health malls. Last week, she almost ended up back in the prison."

"How?" asked Mrs. Applegate.

"She got pissed off and tried to slap one of the guards. They would have already sent her to the prison, but I overruled. I thought it would be…unfavorable for Chasten to see her again…so I told them to give her more drugs to sedate her." Sam smirked a bit. "So far so good." Sam reveled in the torment of the woman for a moment before he spoke again.

"Do you remember many years ago when the team was trying that near-death experiment with her and it appeared as though baby Chasten disappeared for a bit?"

Mrs. Applegate nodded.

"Well, that hasn't happened again, and I'm not sure if it really ever happened. I feel like I need a new strategy."

Sam thought he saw his wife's eyes begin to roll, but instead they stopped halfway around and met his. Her face slackened into a mask of bored curiosity. "Like what, Sam?"

Sam called out to one of his servants. "James, call the head of the medical center, and get her over here to look at Chasten again. I think there's something wrong with his chip, the port, his brain, who the hell knows. Track her down," Sam said to the server.

James sprang into action. "Right away, sir."

Sam Applegate looked at his wife. "Son of a bitch. I wonder if I overbid on this kid."

Chase was headed downstairs for breakfast and overheard his father from the other room. He only caught parts of the conversation but did hear him say "bid" and "Anderson." He didn't know what his father meant by "bid," but he was mainly concerned about being forced to go to work with Sam and hoped his dad would leave for the prison without him, so he turned and went back upstairs. He tapped into some music and contemplated his father's treatment of him.

Chase had become distant from his father. His mom would witness the interactions between Sam and Chase, and she would stand idle, never intervening or disagreeing with her husband. She didn't often defend Chase. Or his father, for that matter.

Chase refused to cut his hair, which annoyed Sam. His dad was mostly bald, and Chase worried about any small aspect of his appearance that could link him to his father. He wanted to look nothing like Sam Applegate, and with his long brown, wavy hair and brown eyes—he didn't. He also looked nothing like his mother. Chase found this a bit odd but knew from biology lessons that brown was the dominant gene as far as eye and hair color were concerned. His dad had blue eyes, too, though…so shouldn't he have blue eyes, he wondered. He didn't remember enough from his lessons for that. His dad could have had brown hair, for all Chase knew; the man had been bald as far back as he could remember.

Chase didn't hear the knock at his bedroom door as he had his music turned up loud enough to drown out a tornado, but when he saw the slender figure of his maid enter his room, he sat straight up in his bed and disconnected from his music program.

"I tried to knock, but…" Maggie said.

"Oh, that's OK. I was listening to music, so I didn't hear you," Chase replied. Maggie approached his laundry basket with a small smile.

"I'm just going to—" she started but Chase leapt out of bed and gently took the basket from her arms.

"Oh no, that's fine, Maggie. I'll clean them," he said. For the past few weeks, he'd felt a bit more nervous around the maid. He'd noticed, even in her genderless uniform, that she was rather attractive with her bronze skin, dark hair and big, brown eyes. They'd shared midnight snacks for the past few years, and Maggie would often come to his room after Chase and his father had disagreements. She never said anything about the fights, but she would smile and point out things in Chase's room, asking him to tell her about them. She especially seemed to like hearing about his physical comic book collection, which his friends often teased him over; but Maggie didn't call him a nerd, and she seemed genuinely interested in superheroes, and the romances that occurred in some of the graphic novels.

Chase often felt bad because he talked a lot while Maggie didn't say much, but she seemed happy. He'd recently realized that he'd been rambling because he had a crush on her. For the past two years, she'd been spending more time simply talking with him, even though she was a bit older than him. Chase didn't mind that at all.

Chase's face heated as he grabbed his dirty laundry. What if it smelled bad? He didn't want her dealing with that. He didn't want to wash his own clothes, but he would rather do it than have her think he wasn't clean.

Maggie eyed him quizzically. "Are you sure, Chase? Do you know how to do laundry?" she asked, then clapped her hand over her mouth. "I didn't…I didn't mean to say that you weren't smart enough. I just…" she trailed off, looking down.

Chase put the basket down, sliding it behind him, and laughed. "Well you'd sort of be right. I'll figure it out, though. You've got enough work to do, but…thanks," Chase said. His neck was warm, and he realized he'd been running his hands through his hair repeatedly. There was a minute of silence before Maggie started to pick up the clutter that surrounded Chase's bed.

"No…no…Maggie, don't do that, either. Look, I'll get it. I just want to listen to music, OK?" he said. He could have slapped himself. He'd basically just told her he didn't want her there. Maggie looked a bit hurt, but she smiled anyway, nodded and turned to leave, but she stopped at the door. She spoke without facing him.

"You know, I've…heard your dad say some things about you. And I just wanted you to know that I don't think any of them are true," she said then dashed out the door before he could reply.

Great, he thought. She's heard all the wonderful endorsements Sam Applegate has made on my behalf, he thought. He couldn't help but be mortified that Maggie had overheard his father calling him an idiot, or even worse, weird. Her words were meant to be comforting, he knew that. He couldn't help but feel mortified anyway.

Chase put his head in the palm of his hands and waited several minutes for his embarrassment to pass before he turned his music back on and forced himself to think of other things.

Chase loved listening to loud music and flying his friends around in Sam Applegate's private jets and ships. The Applegate Prison for the Good opened franchises, and Mr. Applegate couldn't spend all his money if he wanted to. With people doing almost anything for money, legal or illegal, the prison population was bursting at the seams, since the collective eventually caught the criminals. The experiments brought so much money that Sam Applegate became paranoid and dug a moat around his property, complete with guard towers. Neighbors would often joke that it looked like the Applegates lived in a prison much like the one of their own design.

Sam Applegate was never home, which was fine with Chase. Sam spent most of his time at the various prisons, perfecting new experiments. For a fee, a medical or pharmaceutical company could test anything on a prisoner, for the good of everyone else, of course. The daily activities of the prison were hidden from the outside world—mostly. There were likely some who lived in the prison towns who understood, in a small way, what happened there, but it was rarely spoken of. A secret hidden in plain sight.

Chase had plans to spend time with his friends, but he was awoken early.

"Chase, wake up. Wake up, Chase."

Someone gripped his shoulder and shook lightly. Chase rolled over and reluctantly opened his eyes. Lovely brown eyes stared back at him and Chase smiled. "Is it already time to get up, Maggie?"

"Yes, and your parents want you to have breakfast with them."

"Can't you just tell them I'm busy or something?" Chase rubbed his eyes and examined Maggie. He felt bad for having essentially kicked her out of her room, so he thought of something kind to say to her. "You…you look really nice today."

Maggie's cheeks grew red and she couldn't hide her smile, despite the stern tone of her voice. "Come on, Chase, get ready. You don't want me to lose my job, do you? Then who would feed you every day? You would starve to death."

"OK, you've got a point."

"I know I do. Your clothes from the new tailor are on the dressing room table. Here's a virtual photo of what you'll look like," Maggie moved closer as she sent him a photo he didn't even glance at.

Maggie was one of twenty-seven servants, and Chase's personal maid. She was Chase's favorite—and the prettiest. The last time he'd seen her, he knew he was developing a crush on her. And she sometimes acted as though maybe she felt the same. Chase knew his hopes for any sort of romance were far fetched because of the age difference. Fortunately for her, she was born just prior to the population moratorium.

"Tell them I'm coming," Chase said and, worried he'd made her feel like she wasn't helpful to him the last time they'd seen one another, he added, "Maggie, can you please make me eggs benny? They're my favorite."

"I know they're you're favorite. I've already started them," she said with a smile.

"Well, holy shit, is that Chasten Applegate up early in the morning?" said his dad when Chase entered the dining room. "Chase, what the hell is wrong with your hair? It looks like a rat's nest." Chase didn't respond. "Maggie, do we have fresh-squeezed orange juice?"

"Of course we do, Mr. Applegate. I'll get it for you now," Maggie replied. She was much stiffer, much more businesslike in front of his parents. Chase admired her, both for her professionalism and for how she treated him. She was one of the few people who was truly kind to him. He watched as she walked away, but his attention was abruptly snapped back to his father.

"Chase, my boy, I have a surprise for you today. I'm going to let you come back to the prison and learn once more; just like the old days. We have a big meeting with a medical supply company who claims they can replace twenty percent of the right cortex. I want you to be there, you know, instead of sitting home and getting dumber by the day. Besides, this procedure could get bigger and bigger, which means more profit for the company. You know, the money that pays for your lazy lifestyle."

"Wow, how charitable of you. What next, are you going to clean up the man made black slime in the oceans?" said Chase.

"Black slime is a natural occurrence, wiseass. And have some respect, before I come over there and smack you, you little punk. And sit up straight in your chair."

Chase could no longer contain his anger. He no longer respected the man he claimed as his father. He wiped his mouth with a napkin and swallowed his breakfast.

"Dad, I'm happy you're doing brain experiments on people and all that, but I hate going to the prison. You treat the prisoners like shit."

Mr. Applegate slammed his open palm onto the table. "Hey, watch your mouth, you little bastard."

Chase smiled, knowing his father's threats were worthless. Sam Applegate hadn't put his hands on Chase for a couple of years and Chase didn't think he would try it again.

"Come on, boys," Mrs. Applegate said. "Let's have a nice breakfast." She gave her typical fake smile and sipped her mimosa. "Maggie, can you have Chef José warm up my breakfast? It's cold."

"Joe, why is my damn breakfast always cold?" said Sam. "Can you answer me that simple question?"

The chef nodded eagerly. "I will do a better job, Mr. Applegate. I will warm it up right away, sir."

"Dad, the chef's name is José, not Joe. He's fed you every day for three years. Don't you know his name by now?"

Sam looked at Chase as if he wanted to kill him. Chase could see the veins in his neck bulging. They sat at opposite ends of the table, and Sam jumped up, closing that distance with ease, and tried to grab Chase by his hair. Chase jumped back, and his father missed him.

Mrs. Applegate, yelled, "Don't touch him! Don't you dare touch my little boy!" Her mimosa fell, and the glass broke on the floor.

"He's not a little boy. He's a spoiled brat who needs a good old-fashioned beating," said Mr. Applegate, glaring at Chase with a more intense hatred than was typical of him.

"Can't we just have a nice family breakfast?" Chase's mother asked as tears ran down her face.

Chase walked over and hugged his mom. "It's OK, Mom. Don't cry. Sorry to ruin your nice breakfast." Everyone sat back down.

Sam looked at his son and said, "Are you going today or not?" Chase didn't say a word. Sam got up and walked out, slamming the door.

Chase turned to Maggie. "Maggie, does your family fight like this?"

Maggie shrugged. "Sure, we just fight about other things. Do you want more home fries?" she replied, but she was frowning, and her eyes darted to Sam every few seconds. Maggie's glances at his father reminded Chase of small quick stabs from a knife. She lied. Her family didn't fight like that.

"Sure. And could you also please give my mom another mimosa?" He asked, then leaned close enough to Maggie that he could smell the sweet scent of her shampoo and whispered, "Spike it more." In a louder voice, he said, "Mom, don't cry. Have another drink." Chase finished and then got up.

"Where are you going?" Mrs. Applegate asked.

"I'm going to practice a new song with my virtual band. It's called 'My Dad Is an Asshole.'"

"Chase, that's not funny," his mother said, a half-smile on her face. "Plus, it's probably not very original."

Chase laughed, kissed his mom on the cheek and left the house.

Sam Applegate had his own private travel ship—built for one— to go to work. That specific type of ship was illegal for most of the population. The car-pool pod legal minimum was three and preferably twenty or more. Applegate got around the law by saying the ship had an operations staff that exceeded the minimum. Plus, he paid an extra transport fee.

On his way to work, Sam connected with Dr. Jessica Anderson. "Hello, hi, Jessica. It's Applegate."

"Well, hello, Mr. Applegate," the cheery voice at the other end answered.

"Jessica, you remember my son, Chasten, right?"

"Of course. How could I forget? I've been by to check on him a few times. Not lately, though. Your staff has contacted me a few times over the past six months, but we can never confirm an appointment. Is Chasten OK, sir?"

"He's very negative about things, and I'm concerned that something went wrong with the chip you implanted when he was a baby."

"Um…that chip has pretty much been perfected over the last half century, and it is very rare to hear of a defect. It is the model RF-Forty-Five, and the updates are automatic. It is really quite amazing technology. Not to mention, we have checked it before. What types of problems are you having?" asked the doctor.

"He just doesn't listen, and he makes poor decisions. Can you stop by the house and give him a test or something?"

"I could, but the collective does auto testing on the RF-Forty-Five chip on a daily basis. Plus, I've been trying to get over there, and no one ever confirms with our center."

Sam squeezed his eyes closed and pinched the bridge of his nose. "How fucking hard is it to make an appointment with you people? You have an answer for everything. Let me remind you that I own thirty percent of the medical center that employs you. You realize that, don't you?"

"Sure, Mr. Applegate, I realize that, and I can come over today."

"Thank you, and you can call me Sam. You know I'm not the monster people make me out to be."

"I understand, sir. I mean Sam. Good bye," she said before disconnecting.

Sam walked into work and went straight to his office. He called in his first in command, yelling at the top of his lungs, "Frank, get in here, now!" Frank waddled into Applegate's office, his big, round face full of joy, ready for the Monday-morning meeting.

"Why does it take you so damn long to get in here? You know why, Frank? You're too big. Lose some weight! Now what's the latest? And don't beat around the bush. I can't stand when you do that."

Still beaming, Frank replied, "Well, Mr. Applegate, we had a rough weekend. Two prisoners fought with the guards, and one of the guards sprained his ankle."

"Really? I'm not in the mood for this bullshit today. Round up those two. We'll do that new brain-transplant idea to see if it works."

"Sir, the company is scheduled to come in this afternoon to review protocol and begin staff training."

"Screw that, we can do a preliminary test ourselves; get those two ready for surgery in pre-op."

"But, sir, the company—"

"I said now, Frank, or you'll be the third experiment."

Chase was rocking out with the band when the signal on the wall came up, saying, "Damn Tucker Connecting."

"What's up, Tuck?" Chase answered.

"Chase, buddy, we're going big today."

"We are?"

"Yeah, check this out: Philbo found the keys to his dad's antique-sports-car collection, and we're going to drive one of the fast ones, by ourselves. Chase, it's crazy, no scans or computers to control the driving. Philbo researched it and figured out how people drove these things years ago. You manually turn it, speed it up, everything! And the best part is he found out his mom built a special highway years ago with her construction company, but it never got used because those kinds of roads and antique cars got banned. We'll be the first ones to burn rubber."

Chase had only managed to keep two of his childhood friends. Tucker and Phillip had tormented him for many years, but they'd grown to be good friends and often hung out together.

Many people in town thought the boys were out of control. Since babies had been illegal for decades, it was rare to see teenage boys and girls. Tuck and Phil had been permitted to be born a few years before Chase came into the world, since they belonged to wealthy families. Tucker's family had rights to the Mississippi River and dam, which produced power for a good part of the Midwest, as well as controlled the water flow for the downstream towns, residents, and agricultural needs. Chase and Phil called him Damn Tucker. That Damn Tucker, he's no sucker. Of course, Tuck hated it. Phillip's family was in the construction business. His mom had governmental contracts throughout North and South America to build maglev highways. In reality, she was a great programmer and businesswoman, since the AI droids did all the physical work. Ironically, none of the boys were interested in their family businesses. The boys had spent the last few days running about, wreaking havoc together and giving each other shit over their families.

"How will we get the car there? You know you can't drive

that kind of antique on the maglevs without getting arrested," Chase observed.

"Right, Chase, but doesn't your dad have that quantum hydro copter?" Tucker asked.

"Yeah," said Chase, "but I don't even know how to start that crazy thing."

"Dude, my dad owns a dam and energy company; I'll figure that shit out. I'll also grab one of his tech guys to help, and if he thinks of ratting us out, I'll get him fired. Do you have your dad's passcode and scan to start it?"

"Yeah, I copied passcodes to everything years ago," Chase answered.

"OK, meet me later."

Chase waited until his mom left for the day before having Tucker over to the house. They went on top of the garage, where the copter was sitting. Tuck started with Sam Applegate's password and scan, but the computer sensed a variation.

"Tuck, where's the guy you said you were bringing?"

"Relax, I can figure this out myself." Tuck plugged in a program he said he'd found in his port earlier to override the system. The copter sounded a huge bang. The boys looked at each other, mouths agape.

"Shit, did you just break it?" Chase asked, trying hard not to yell at his friend.

"I hope not," said Tuck. "I want to drive that car." After a moment, the system came up with a sound like a fighter jet's. "Hell yeah!" The boys high-fived. "Jump in," Tuck said.

Chase peered down to see Mr. Applegate's outside staff looking up and promptly ignoring the fiasco as they returned to their duties.

"Where to?" Chase asked.

"We're going to Philbo's," Tucker answered as the copter went into flight.

Phil lived on a big equestrian farm. Chase watched as Phil walked out of the main barn, where he'd been waiting. The black copter circled overhead, the wind of it so strong it blew Phil's hair all over. The horses were startled enough to run into the barn. Phil sprinted to the copter as it landed, and it didn't take long for the boys to take off.

"Guys, we have to make one stop first," said Tuck. "I heard about this place on the edge of town where no one really goes. It's basically the underground." Chase and Phil agreed, though Chase was a bit wary. Those two always seemed to find trouble for him.

They flew for a little while, and Tuck pointed excitedly. "Look over there; it's exactly where my dishwasher told me it would be. He said it was pretty crazy and worth it. See the smoke from those buildings on fire? We'll land near there. He told me the people are so poor and drugged out, they'll do anything for a little money, anything. They live like rats." Tucker chuckled. "Yeah, he told me some good stories."

The copter descended near the burning buildings, and Chase noticed that people were standing outside staring up at the sky. At them. It likely wasn't every day they saw a quantum copter in person. When the copter landed, Chase panicked a bit as people approached. The door and ramp opened, and the three boys walked out.

"Wow, Chase, this must be what it's like to be a rock star—well, if the audience were a bunch of zombies," Tuck said, observing the people around him with a look of intrigue. But Chase thought he saw a bit of disgust in his friend's eyes. Which was soon confirmed.

"Look at these degenerates," Tuck said.

Chase did. Most of the people looked depressed, drugged out, and dirty since they weren't allowed much water in that part of town. It just wasn't profitable enough. A lot of people had a reddish tint from ozone burn.

A big guy with muscles everywhere, including his neck, walked up and said, "Who is Damn Fuck?" Chase stifled a giggle as Tuck puffed out his chest, barely tall enough to see over the man's shoulders.

"It's Damn Tuck, and that's me."

"What do you want, Damn Tuck?"

"We want five or six women we can scan for no spreadable diseases and who will do whatever we want. Also, we need some good drugs, anything but B. The good stuff."

Chase was shocked that his friend managed to stay calm, to order such things so authoritatively. He stood back a bit, letting Tuck handle it. Phil looked at Chase, his face red. Chase shrugged and shot him a look that he hoped said "yeah, I know, and I'm sorry".

"All right," the big guy said. "Give me a few minutes."

"Tuck, Tuck," said Phil.

"Not now, Phil. I'm negotiating."

"Tuck—"

"What?" snapped Tuck.

"I'm gay; you always forget. It's either your stupid comments or this kind of shit, and it's starting to piss me off!" Phil was close to Tuck, and Chase prepared himself to separate them if he had to.

"Sorry, Philbo, I didn't mean it. Hey, big guy, throw in two good-looking men for my friend and make sure one of the women has red hair. Oh, and the men better be in great shape. Make sure they're ripped, I guess, like you."

"You guys are pretty picky. You know, it's a good thing you called me and not someone else, because if it were anyone else, you probably would be dead by now and I'd own that copter," said the big guy. "Here's the deal: I go with you guys along with the people you requested, and you owe me two million now, up front."

"Two million? That sounds like a lot for what we're getting." Tuck turned to his friends, laughing. Chase had to keep himself from hanging his head. He was a bit nervous. He wanted to tell Tuck to just do it, but Tuck, of course, would never. He loved to have the upper-hand, but Chase knew that wasn't something that would or could happen where they were standing.

"Was it the red-hair request?" Tuck asked.

With a straight face, the big guy told him, "Two million, or you'll be my red-haired girl for the rest of today."

Tuck quickly lost his smile and held out his arm. "Sounds fair to me." He paid the big guy.

Chase watched as the big guy sent Tuck the options on all the people and his suggestions for a good time via his chip. Tuck scanned his eye screen and made the choices, not consulting Chase or Phil. Chase wasn't too concerned. He wasn't sure he wanted to really be a part of all that. He would have been content walking about the area and talking to people, not selecting humans to buy. The whole idea made him feel uncomfortable. Reminded him of his father's prison, except these people were just in a different kind of prison from which they would likely never escape; poverty.

Shortly after, the selected few came forward.

The others, those who weren't part of the process, but who lived in the area and probably knew the streets and what the boys were up to, started moaning and complaining, and some yelled, "We need this job." Three women started to take their clothes off, and one of them yelled, "Take us with you! We really need the money. We're struggling and sick." Chase's stomach flipped as he watched the desperation of the crowd.

The big guy shut down the selection program and said to the guys, "Just ignore them, or you'll be encouraging more of the crowd, and it could get out of control…. Keep walking."

They loaded into the copter, and the big guy yelled out to the hundred people who were still stood outside. "Go home. Go home, and I will contact you again for the next job opportunity." No one moved; all the people stood there, staring.

The copter took off, and soon the mayhem began. Drinking, grunting, drugging. With music blasting, the drugs kicked in, and Tucker tried to manually drive the copter, which turned out to be a bad idea. One of the women was pouring drinks, and with the copter jerking from side to side, she fell into Tuck. The copter dropped like a rock.

"Come on, Tuck, put the autopilot on and come back here and

have some fun," Chase urged his friend. Though under the influence, he was still worried about getting caught, or hurt. He checked the risk calculation on the dash of the copter. The computer calculated that, with the weight of the antique car, the people, and the supplies, they had exceeded the weight limit and risked crashing. Great, Chase thought. Just what we need. Crashing with hookers, drugs, and a bouncer. Dad will be furious.

When the alert sounded and came on the screen, the boys opened the small escape hatch and threw a few things out, laughing, until the alert went back off. Philbo pretended he was trying to throw Chase out of the cargo hatch. They flew to Phil's dad's secret collection facility and got out quickly. Being high, the boys did the best they could attaching the cables to the antique sports car as the big guy just stood there shaking his head.

Chase asked the big guy, "Do you know how to hook up a car to a hydrogen copter of this size?"

"Sure, if you want me to. I can come up with a price."

"Forget it, we can do it ourselves," Tuck said. "I've given you enough money."

Everyone piled back inside the copter, and Chase checked the straps one more time.

When the copter took off again, they were lopsided, and almost crashed. Finally, they leveled off and headed for the abandoned road. After a while the autopilot brought them closer to the road, and they could see it below.

"There's the mountain road, guys," said Phil. "Wow, isn't that crazy? There are no pods or maglev levels. Program the copter to lower everything down slowly so we don't hurt the car." Once they landed and detached the car, Tuck turned the copter off, took one more hit of the big guy's drugs, and almost fell over.

"This is going to be awesome," Chase said to everyone, now more excited than worried.

Then the big guy said to the boys, "What about us?"

"I don't know," said Tuck. "You're more than welcome to hang in the copter and party a little until the sun goes down. I saw the ozone warnings today; they're not that bad. When it's not peak ozone, just walk home, I guess."

The big guy rolled his eyes but turned back to the copter and the women. "Come on, ladies, we just got a new ride." Phil started his dad's old car with a rumbling from the exhaust pipes.

Chase laughed. It was such an odd thing to see. A manual vehicle, an engine that was only part computerized. "That sound is so cool; I've heard it in the old movies, but it sounds much better in person. And look at the smoke coming out of that pipe. How crazy is that?"

Phil floored it, and they smelled the rubber from the wheels spinning.

"Let me drive, Phil. I've never driven a car before," said Chase.

"OK, we can take turns driving." Phil pulled over, and they switched drivers. After a bit of stop and go, Chase got the hang of it.

"Tuck get that new drug out, the one you take through your eyes." Tuck reached into his bag and removed a powdered substance, some liquid, and a few dropper bottles. After he mixed everything, he handed each of his friends a half-full dropper and instructed them to drip the liquid into their eyes. Chase noticed a slight stinging from the drops, but a few rapid blinks soothed it. A few moments passed before Chase and Phil were complaining to Tuck. "I don't really feel anything," Chase said to Tuck. "Are you sure we did it right?"

"Give it time and request an old antique song that rocks, just like this car." They let Tuck drive while listening to Guns N' Roses' "Welcome to the Jungle."

The drug must have been pure adrenaline. Chase's heart pounded, and every hair on his body felt as though it were electrified. Any concern he had, any worry about being thought of as weird, any reservation—gone. The feeling continued to intensify as the boys found themselves unable to stop talking, full of boundless energy.

Tuck said, "Man, I feel like Superman. Don't you guys feel like you could do anything? I feel like I could lift this fucking car up."

"I do too," said Chase. Phil broke the interior door handle and the rearview mirror off the car, which made everyone laugh and provoked a few smaller but less damaging imitations. They stopped only because Chase spotted a big rock the edge of the road and dared Tuck to pick it up.

They stumbled out of the car and just stood next to the boulder.

A few minutes went by, and finally Phil said, "What are we doing again?"

"I don't remember," said Chase, "but we are high as hell. Get back in the car before we burn up out here."

Once again, Tuck burned rubber, and they sped down the

abandoned road. "Oh shit, look ahead. The road ends," Phil said. "Now what? Screw it, go right and merge with the maglev traffic. We'll just stay on the first level."

"Can we do that?" asked Chase. His mind spun so fast even that thought was difficult to nail down and speak.

"Who cares?" said Tuck.

"Yeah, who cares? We can do anything," said Chase, who felt properly convinced that it would be fine after Tuck's statement. "Floor that shit. Maybe no one will notice us."

They drove as fast as they could and jumped the divider ramp. The car made a huge banging sound as they landed in the middle of the maglev highway. They were going the wrong way and hit 130 as the car rumbled down the maglev highway like a dragster. The computerized car pods darted out of the way, as the computers tried to calculate where the old car would go.

"Pin it, Tuck. Pin it. Go faster," Chase and Phil yelled. They could see people in the pods falling all over each other, and Chase laughed so hard his stomach hurt.

"Oh my God, did you see that lady's face? Do it again, said Phil."

"Tuck, fake that one green pod up ahead of us, and, Phil, give me another hit of that eye stuff. I think it's kicking in," Chase said.

Phil opened the glove box, where he'd lazily placed his stash instead of securing it in his bag, which turned out to be a poor choice because the drugs flew all over the floor. He took off his seat belt and started picking up the drugs while Chase tried to help, though his coordination wasn't as fantastic as he felt it was. Tuck headed for the pod, and as he went to turn at the last second, he clipped the corner of the pod, as it was parked and not moving.

At the exact nanosecond of the impact, with the sound of the car crashing and metal crunching, the car flew high in the air. Chase grabbed the nearest thing he could hold on to. He felt the air shift again. That old, familiar feeling he'd convinced himself so many times he'd dreamed. But this was real. It was happening.

While the car was midair, Chase sat, buckled in, for what seemed like five minutes and looked around. Everything froze, motionless. The life of the world fell away. In his altered state, Chase was scared. He didn't want to be alone, or stuck. And the scene had that odd glow to it. Has to be the drugs, he thought.

He yelled out, "Guys!" But his friends' faces and eyes didn't move; nothing moved.

More time went by. Time Chase couldn't measure because even the clock on his eye screen was frozen. "Guys, can you hear me? What's going on? What kind of drug are we on?"

With a loud bang, everything started again. The car flew higher in the air and crash-landed on its roof. With a huge smash, the car burned as people screamed and the maglev pods came to a halt. The boys lay in shock, upside down with the car on fire. They were so high they thought it wasn't real, and Tucker started to laugh. The fire got too hot, and people got out of the pods to look, but they couldn't help. They just watched and recorded a live feed as the car burned and Chase yelled at them for help. None of them did.

Chase could see the fire reach Phil's body, motionless as he burned. Finally, a fire drone landed on the car, and some of the robotic arms started to cut the car open while the other arms sprayed water and foam on the fire. People cheered as the drone pulled the kids out. Chase and Tucker were in bad shape and a drone flew them to the hospital. Phil wasn't so lucky.

As he was lifted from the car, Chase looked back at his friend, who was still motionless, eyes open and staring; perhaps at the same timeless void Chase had been stuck in moments before.

The incident made the collective's world media feed, as the lead story: "Today all levels of traffic and urban movement in downtown came to a halt as three unidentified young men drove an antique gas-fueled car manually on Central Avenue and Interstate Ten. As you can see in the footage, all three were burned in the fire, and one of the men is presumed dead. We will have more information soon.

"Also, although we cannot confirm as of now, it is rumored that one of the young men may be the infamous Baby X, the last human baby legally permitted to be born on earth, twenty-one years ago. An X-Five fire and rescue drone was mobilized to assist. This accident, although unorthodox, broke the city's seventy-five-year no-accident streak. The mayor said she does not feel the streak should be considered ended, since a real car or ship pod did not cause the accident. She also said that if the one man dies, perhaps there should be a lottery in his name to allow another baby to be born. Environmentalists quickly attacked that idea as 'inhumane' and 'an assault on the environment and humanity in general.' Shortly after, a petition circulated calling for the mayor's resignation."

Tucker's parents, Mrs. Applegate, and Maggie paced in the hospital's waiting room while Sam sat in an uncomfortable chair and fumed. As soon as he got word of the accident, Mr. Applegate became so angry about what had happened that he didn't want to go to the hospital, but for the sake of appearances, he did. The media swarmed the area, but Applegate used his ties and public relations team to make sure only those on his approved list were allowed into the hospital.

Phil's parents were devastated by the loss of their son, and Sam, tying to not explode with rage, listened to their conversation. He tried to sympathize, but he couldn't. In fact, he almost wished it had been Chase instead.

Phil's parent's spoke in low, cracking voices about how they had suspected something like this was coming, because of Phil's young age.

Sam knew immediately what they were discussing. Congress had recently passed a law stipulating that anyone counted in the official population who died before half of his or her life expectancy could be auctioned off in two ways. First, a credit would be given to the family who bid the highest for that specific population spot, since the spot was now vacant. This would guarantee a spot for the high bidder, in the event new babies were permitted in the future. Second, the body parts, if not destroyed, would be auctioned piece by piece, to replace body parts for older people. This auction would be conducted once the parts were merged with AI devices for improvements. The body part auction was often gut-wrenching for the family of the deceased, since it was always broadcast live over the collective feed. Because there were not a lot of young people in general, young deaths were rare. The auction was expected to garner top dollar. Phil's parents spoke more about the worth of the parts of their son than they did his worth as a person. Sam understood this. Those damn kids were worthless.

Later that night Chase and Tucker were released. Chase got a new leg, spleen, and three ribs, while Tucker got an arm, a left ear, and new lungs. Both boys received the latest skin grafts for their burns. Phil's parents said their good-byes from a special window, since Phil's body had to be kept in an airtight refrigerator to preserve his organs for the auction.

As Chase, his mom, and Maggie walked into the kitchen, there was an uncomfortable silence. The staff silently lined up, looking at Chase.

Finally, one servant said, "Mr. Chase, are you OK? I'm so sorry about what happened to you. We all saw the crash and fire on the feed."

"I'm banged up, but I'll be OK." He shook his head. "I just can't believe Phil is gone." Chase broke down and started to sob. "It was also the strangest thing; it felt like time stood still on the moment of impact."

Maggie was rubbing Chase's back when Mr. Applegate stormed through the door.

"What is wrong with you, Chasten, you stupid bastard?" Chase didn't say anything. "They found drugs and who knows what else in my smashed-up copter. My copter is ruined. Do you know how much a hydrogen copter costs? We're the laughingstocks of the town! You're lucky I've hidden your identity from the feed. Do you know what people would think? I'm a man in the public eye as it is. What do you have to say for yourself?"

Chase remained silent.

"Nothing? Nothing to say? What do you think, life is a party while I work my ass off so you can play with your retard friends?"

Two human guards and single AI guard walked in. Mr. Applegate nodded, and the guards began beating Chase with nightsticks while the AI held him in place. Maggie and his mom screamed, and Applegate told them he would have the guards attack them if they interfered with his discipline.

"Dad, make them stop. Stop!" Chase yelled.

Finally, the guards stopped, and Maggie ran over and wiped the blood off Chase's face. With a good-sized gash on his chin, Chase said, "I lost my friend, Dad, and that's something I'll never forget and always have to deal with. Those 'retards,' as you call them, were like family to me."

"Family?" Sam scoffed. "I can't believe you're even part of this family." Mr. Applegate continued to rant. "I've brought you up right, showed you my accomplishments, and even offered you a job at the prison, and this is how you repay me; with embarrassment."

"I don't want to be part of your fucking Frankenstein prison."

Mr. Applegate slapped Chase in the face, and the two wrestled and punched each other as the guards watched, waiting for Mr. Applegate's direction to intervene. Fighting, father and son fell on the kitchen table; the china went crashing to the floor. Chase punched his dad with all his might. Mr. Applegate grabbed a carving knife off the floor and tried to stab him.

Maggie yelled, "Don't stab him. Look out, Chase!" The two struggled for control of the knife, and when they rolled again on the floor, Chase's stomach got sliced.

Applegate yelled, "Staff! Staff, grab him and get him off me." Three staff members reluctantly grabbed Chase and pulled him off his father.

"Chase, listen to me." Sam wiped blood off his clothes. "I could have just had my guards intervene and you would be dead. If that's what I wanted. So listen to me for a change, you shit, you're twenty-one years old. You're an adult, so that means that if I tell you to get the fuck out of my house, you have to do it. Pack up and by tomorrow, you better be gone."

Mrs. Applegate screamed "no" as Sam stormed off. His lip and ear were bleeding severely, and just before he walked into the bathroom, he yelled, "Someone make me some Goddamn dinner. Oh, and one more thing…Maggie, you're fired!"

Maggie's face dropped. "Oh no, no."

Chase kicked the garbage can out of his way and went outside. He looked up at the stars and said to himself, "What a fucked-up life. I wonder where Phil is right now."

Maggie joined him shortly, a small bag of meager personal belongings in hand. "Chase, are you OK? I can't believe your dad had his guards attack you, or that you two had a fistfight."

Chase clenched his fists. "I don't care about that; he's an asshole. I can't believe he fired you. Don't worry, I'll fix that. I'll talk to my mom at the right time."

As Maggie hugged him, she started to cry. Then Chase teared up.

"I can't believe Phil's gone. I feel like he's still around; here with me right now." He felt reckless enough to state something to Maggie that he'd wanted to tell her for many years. "Thanks for being here, Maggie; you're the best thing in my life."

Chase went back in the house, and his mom asked the chef to make something warm.

"Chase," his mom asked, "was this your idea?"

"What idea? Mom, please talk to Dad. There is no fucking way Maggie is fired. What did she do wrong? Dad just knows I like her, so that asshole's punishing her for it. It's not right."

Mrs. Applegate stood with her arms crossed, frowning. She looked older than she had the day before, and Chase recognized that the entire ordeal probably hurt her, as well. "Chase, watch your mouth in this house. You know you're on thin ice."

"Mom, I'm sorry for what happened today. I am. I didn't intend to hurt you. But dad's a piece of crap for firing Maggie and I swear to God, if she goes, I go. I swear."

His mother slouched a bit and her arms hung at her sides. "Calm down, Chase. And I'm asking you if this whole thing was your idea."

"Was what my idea?"

His mother tucked a lock of hair behind her ear. Chase noticed a white strand or two in that lock. And her face seemed gaunt; ashen. "Was causing havoc with your friends and wrecking your father's copter your idea?"

Chase shrugged. "I don't know. We just wanted to have some fun, and it got out of control. I guess it was everyone's idea." He swallowed a lump that had formed in his throat. He didn't want to think about it. He felt the guilt build. Maybe it wasn't his idea, but maybe part of it was his fault. He could have stopped them. He could have…

"Well, I just spoke to Tucker's mom, and they think it was your idea and that you're a bad influence on poor little Tucker. He is a good boy," Chase's mother interrupted his thoughts.

Chase scoffed as he fought back yet more tears. "Oh really? Did Tucker say that everything was my idea?"

"No, his mom did, and she thinks Phillip was also a bad influence on Tucker."

"Great, Mom. I'm going to bed!" As Chase walked to the elevator, he said, "Mom, Maggie's not going anywhere. Please? Talk to Dad."

His mother nodded. "I'll talk to your father when the time is right, and he calms down a little."

The next morning the incident was still all over the feed. Overnight, quantum copters and antique Pontiac GTOs tripled in value on the exchange. It seemed the incident was so unusual that everyone wanted a collector's item or a gift for the holidays. The Applegates sat at the dining room table, and no one said a word as the feed was broadcast on their eye screens. They all watched the same feed, which was unusual, when Maggie walked in to clean the table.

"What is she doing here?" said Mr. Applegate.

"Sam, I told her she could stay until I had a chance to talk to you," Mrs. Applegate replied.

"There's nothing to talk about. I fired her. Now get out, Maggie, before I call the authorities and you'll end up like the rest of your family." Chase sat at the far end of the table turning red with anger as Maggie took off her apron and walked out. Before Chase could say anything, the feed announced that the auction of Phil's body parts would be held that day and the bid for a baby credit would begin the next.

"Jesus Christ, he died yesterday," said Chase.

"You can't let those body parts go too long or they can't transplant them successfully. Didn't you learn anything at the prison?" Sam said.

Chase looked at his father but didn't say anything. He finished his breakfast, took off, and spent the day looking for Maggie. She wouldn't connect the signal when Chase tried, and as the day went on, he grew more frustrated. He found Sanchez, another of his father's servants who lived on the other end of town, and asked if he know where she lived.

"Chase, you don't want to go down there, my man. They kill and eat up little skippys like you."

"Come on, Sanchez, help me find her."

"If I do, you have to agree that, if something happens to you, I'm not responsible and that I warned you. Deal?" Chase agreed. "All right, but you're going to have to change those clothes and wear a hat so nobody sees that haircut." Chase laughed. "I'm not kidding. You're going to get your ass kicked again, and these aren't Daddy's guards; they're real killers."

"OK, should we grab one of my dad's turbo pods to drive down?"

"Are you nuts? We'll definitely get raped and cut up showing up in one of those. I don't think you understand. You and your dad's pod would be on the black market by the end of the day." Frustrated, he said, "Just shut up and come with me on the public pod and don't talk to anyone. Here, wear my hat."

They left the Applegate estate, and once they got outside the town gates, they jumped on a public pod. When the pod split off for the ninth time, Chase rolled his eyes. He wasn't used to the slow pace of public transportation. Whenever Chase wanted to go anywhere, his private pod would go directly from A to B.

Public pods started out very long to accommodate as many people as possible. Once en route, these maglev vehicles split off three or four times into various sections of the city. Maggie lived so deep in the hood that it kept splitting and joining other long pods.

"Sanchez, are we going to be able to get a pod out of here? I thought I knew the city, but I don't even know where we are. I can't believe Maggie goes through this every day."

Finally, the pod stopped. "Here you go, buddy," said Sanchez. I'll see you when I see you."

"Thanks, man." Chase stepped out of the pod into an old warehouse district that more resembled a war zone. He walked to the main warehouse's steel door, where about ten people were, just standing around. "Hey, does anyone know the way to Maggie Jacob's place?"

"Are you a friend of Maggie's?" a woman asked.

"Yeah, she's a good friend of mine," he said with a smile.

"You look a little like a government person or a defective AI droid. You know we cut up government people around here and feed them to the dogs."

"I'm not with the government," Chase said. He hoped not too quickly. He frowned.

There was an uncomfortable silence, then she said, "I'm just messing with you, kid. Third door down the long hall. Keep walking; you'll find it."

Chase practically ran to the door and knocked. An older man answered.

"Can I help you?"

"Yes, I'm here to see Maggie."

"Who are you?"

"Me? Well, I'm…"

Chase caught sight of Maggie as she peered out from the back room. "Oh my God, Chase, what are you doing here? Come in."

Chase rushed towards her. "I came to see you," he said. Luckily, Maggie seemed happy to see him and they embraced like old friends. "So, this is where you live."

She quickly tried to tidy up. "Yeah, it's a little different from the Applegate estate."

Chase gently gripped her arm to stop her from cleaning. "It's fine. Are you having a party or something? Who are all these people?"

Maggie smiled the way a person would smile at a puppy. "No, there's no party. This is my family and some are my friends. I'm the only one in my neighborhood who makes any money—or was, besides the government draw. I mean, some people here make money on the black market, but I'm the only one with a steady legal job. Well, I guess I should say I used to have a real job."

Chase looked around. "How many people live here?"

Maggie shrugged. "It ranges, but about thirty, thirty-five these days."

Chase saw no possibly way for more than ten people to fit in the space. "Thirty-five people in this small place? That's nuts!"

"I know, right? Your bedroom is bigger than our entire part of the warehouse." They walked into a small bedroom, and the people who were inside the room immediately walked out.

Chase took a deep breath. He was worried that what he had to say would sound absurd to her, but after losing one of his best friends, he couldn't imagine not telling her how he felt. "Maggie, I want you to know something that you probably already know, but I'm going to say it anyway. I have always had a crush on you since the first day I met you. I don't care where you come from; I want to be with you."

Maggie started to cry. "Chase, I feel the same. I can't believe it took so long for one of us to say it." The two kissed for a while. Shortly after, Maggie walked out of the bedroom to get something to show Chase, and he heard the people who were standing around waiting ask who he was. It was obvious that he was not from around there. He didn't blame them for being curious.

Maggie said to everyone, "I'm fine, guys. Everything is cool. Now go somewhere." She seemed giddy as she shut the door, and Maggie and Chase made love for the first time.

Later that night, everyone was talking about the auction. One of

Maggie's friends projected the feed in the middle of the street. Since it was dark, it looked like an old-school drive-in, minus car pods. People filled the street, prepared for the unique event.

"We are going to start the bidding at fifty million dollars for the first foot, and then we will work our way up the body. Everyone is eligible to vote," said the auctioneer.

A girl standing near Maggie said, "Sure anyone can bid. What a joke! I've never met or known a person who had fifty million dollars." Little did she know, Chase, who was standing right next to her, did have that much.

The auctioneer came back on. "Hold on, a private equity company has just bid twenty-five billion, that's billion with a B, American dollars for the whole body. Since this is not customary, the collective and the senior human representatives from the sixteen families must consult with each other. Please hold." A commercial for the new and improved waterless spray shower came on the feed.

People started to boo because the senior reps were made up of the sixteen elected families who controlled industry and all the wealth in the world.

"Come on," a woman yelled out, "not another commercial for AI porn. We already know they can make house visits. And yes, it is still cheating on your wife or husband. I don't buy 'If it's not human, you're not cheating.' And I don't trust any of the Sixteen."

The history of the sixteen families was well documented. In the beginning, all kinds of people had been elected to represent the human race in order to amalgamate with the AI and other collective technology. Once more and more of the sixteen families had been elected, they changed the minimum financial requirements, and it wasn't long before no one in 99.9 percent of the population had enough money to run.

The booing continued, and the live auction came back on with a cheer from the street crowd. Maggie reached over and held Chase's hand. The auctioneer returned to the feed.

"Members of the senior sixteen families have officially voted to allow the body to be sold in its entirety to the highest bidder, winner take all."

Again, the people booed. Divided up properly, the body could help hundreds—if not thousands—of needy people. Unfortunately, most people felt that with one company or family controlling every part of the body, profit would override compassion for others. The bidding went back and forth with the bids highlighted. The feed started to flash, and everyone was glued to the excitement.

"A five-hundred-billion-dollar bid has just been submitted, almost double all the other bids! The bid has come in from EGI Pharmaceuticals of China, so that takes us down to only two bidders." There was a pause in the feed, followed by a commercial for Nike's latest titanium feet, allowing people to jump "even higher."

The feed came back on live. "Update, folks: a five-hundred-fifty-billion-dollar bid had been submitted from a private bidder. Then five hundred seventy billion from EGI." There was another pause on the feed, then the announcer said, "Eight hundred billion, ladies and gentlemen. Eight hundred billion dollars on a body for which the starting bid was fifty million, from an anonymous private investor."

"Anonymous?" someone said. Immediately, the feed got millions of requests for the collective's supercomputers to find out who was bidding. It took the collective a nanosecond to narrow down the world's possibilities of families with that kind of bidding power. Everyone watched the eye screens for an answer, but there was some sort of block on the collective for this request. Because people from around the world were requesting the same information, there was a possibility the collective feed would crash, which had never happened.

"Come on," someone said next to Chase. "How can something be blocked on the collective? I thought it was the world's public system of information."

Chase looked down and thought, Poor Phil. Is someone going to use his face or his eyes? It just doesn't seem right. Do they get his chip and all his memories?

"Eight hundred billion going once, eight hundred billion going twice, sold to Sam Applegate from the United States of America for eight hundred billion dollars."

Chase and Maggie looked at each other, dumbfounded. "Are you fucking kidding me?" said Chase.

Maggie's friends and family saw her face. "Maggie isn't that the guy you used to work for?" Maggie just shook her head as she held her hand in front of her mouth in shock.

"Let's go, Maggie. I'm going home," Chase said, grabbing her hand.

Maggie tensed. "I can't go there, remember? Your dad fired me."

"Well, you're with me now; you don't work for him anymore. That doesn't mean we can't hang out. Please?" She agreed.

After a couple of hours, their public pod made its final split and stopped in front of the town's main gate.

The security guard scanned the pod. "Can I help you?" Chase opened the door and walked out.

"Frankie, what's up?" he said to the guard.

"Chase, my friend, what are you doing? Where's your pimped-out ride?"

"My dad has it."

"Really? So what's your next toy? By the way, your dad is the man! I couldn't believe he beat that big China company in a bidding war. Hey, by the way, get your chip looked at."

"Why?"

"When I scanned you, it came up unauthorized."

Chase was surprised but didn't give the issue much thought. "I will, Frankie, thanks."

Soon the pod entered the town's most secure perimeter. When they pulled up to the house, it was swarming with reporters trying to interview Mr. Applegate. Media drones circled the estate overhead. Chase and Maggie got out and started walking. One reporter recognized Chase.

"Look! That's Applegate's son." The swarm of reporters and video bees flew over to him. "Chase, Chase, how does it feel to be the winner of the youngest dead person in years? How is your family going to celebrate? What are your plans with the body?"

"Celebrate what? That was my friend," Chase said, clearly

irritated.

"Do you plan to keep a part as a memento? If so, Chase, which part? We did a survey on what you would keep, and a locket of hair won at sixty-two percent. Will you keep a locket of hair?"

AI reporters were also yelling out questions. "Yes or no, were you one of the other two in the accident? It was reported earlier that Baby X was one of those involved."

Chase was puzzled by that, but simply replied "No it wasn't me."

"You must be real proud of your father, Chase. Can we get a comment on that?"

"Yeah, he's amazing." Chase turned to a human reporter and angrily asked him, "Have you ever had anyone close to you die?"

The human reporter replied, "Sure, kid, I've had friends die."

"Then how would you like it if I cut your friends' balls off and hung them from the mirror on my private pod?"

The reporter turned to his video guy. "You'd think that kid would be more excited. Rich punk."

Chase and Maggie made their way into the house. Mr. Applegate was occupied with the media, and Chase was sure his father hadn't noticed them. They went to talk to Mrs. Applegate.

"Mom, how could Dad have done this? Phil was one of my best friends."

His mom didn't respond. She said hi to Maggie as she looked down at their clasped hands. Chase stood there for a minute but couldn't take it anymore. He walked over and interrupted Mr. Applegate from his press conference.

"How could you do it?"

"Do what, Chase?" Sam said, not looking at his son.

"Bid on Phil. That's fucked up."

"Chase, watch what you say; the media is recording everything." With a fake smile, he moved to the side with Chase, turning their backs to the reporters. "Look, I bid fair and square like everyone else, and I'm sick and tired of your attitude toward this family. Besides, it's just business. Someone has to buy the body parts." Then Applegate looked over at Maggie. "What's that Spanish rat doing here again?" He motioned a servant over. "Call the head staff member to escort her out of here quickly or have her arrested for trespassing, I don't care."

Chase had had enough. "She's no rat, Dad. And do you really a need to be a racist asshole?" He tried to grab Applegate to punch him, but one of the media security guards grabbed Chase by the arm.

"That's it, Chase. I'm disowning you."

Chase laughed. "You're disowning me? I can't even believe I'm your kid, you freak."

"Get out and don't contact me again and say good-bye to your trust fund." Applegate yelled at his wife, who was standing on the porch, "Delete the funds in his chip. Do it now. Delete all the funds, every damn cent!"

Mrs. Applegate watched the episode with tears streaming down her face. She made no move to do what her husband asked. The media moved in. One reporter said to another, "Make sure you're getting all of this!"

Chase, Maria, and Mrs. Applegate watched and followed as Mr. Applegate's public relations team stepped in, moved the media outside, confiscated all the recorded feeds one by one, and deleted the footage and signals.

Chase reluctantly went back into the house. He wasn't surprised his father would do such a thing. He would be in a world of hurt without his chip, but Chase felt a small sense of freedom all the same. He'd never have to look at his father again.

"Put the code in and delete that little bastard…now, or so help me, I'll lock him up!" Mrs. Applegate met Chase's eyes. The look in hers was helplessness. Chase shook his head, but his mother continued. She shook as she put in her password and deleted Chase's funds. He now had less money than Maggie.

Disgusted, Chase nodded and left. He and Maggie walked out together, and she grabbed his hand as they ignored the barrage of questions from the media.

"Chase, you're better than this," Maggie said.

She summoned a public pod, and they waited together outside, just across the property line. Sam Applegate went back to his interviews as the PR firm reviewed and modified the footage that would eventually end up on the feed.

The freedom Chase felt earlier had vanished. It was replaced with an anxiety that left him nearly unable to breathe.

Finally, the pod came, and Chase looked at Maggie. "Maggie, where am I? I feel like I'm lost."

Maggie gripped his hand and held his gaze. "You're stepping into your new life. But you're not alone."

Chapter Five

Chase moved in with Maggie, and it was indeed a new life. Without funds, he literally went from feast to famine. He stood in line and applied for the draw like everyone else in the ninety-nine point ninety-ninth percentile. The draw was a government family program wherein they deposited money remotely into most of the population's chip twice a month. He used to spend more in one day than the draw provided in a year. In the beginning, Chase kept to himself. However, word got around quickly about who he was, and Chase felt more like a circus animal. Because so many people lived at Maggie's place, someone was always coming or going. Even though Maggie wasn't working anymore, she was much better off than those who had never had a paying job. Maggie's sister had brought her friend Violet over to hang out.

"Aren't you the misfit kid from the Big Sixteen? I heard about you. Someone said you were related to the late president and you had a real lion and a white Bengal tiger. Is that true?"

"Well, sort of. My family is one of the Sixteen, so I did meet the past president of the council before, but he died. And no, I never had a lion or a tiger."

"Don't you guys own all the prisons?"

"Most of them, but that's my dad, not me."

"Do you know if Maggie will ever get a job again? People are worried. I mean, her money fed a lot of people," Violet said.

Chase got up and tried to find a quiet spot in the warehouse where no one would bother him. He climbed up to the third level and saw some multicolored lights under the door at the end of the hall. He walked down the hall and slowly opened the door. It was bright, and he saw screens projecting everywhere and programs flashing.

As he stood in the doorway, he heard, "Hey, what do you want?"

"Um, nothing. I was trying to get away from everyone."

"That's cool. Come on in and shut and lock that door." In the middle of the room was a skinny, nerdy-looking kid with purple hair.

"Hi, I'm Chase."

"I'm Julian. What's up?"

"Nothing really, just getting sick of answering the same questions over and over again from everyone."

"I get it. You're from the Big Sixteen, right? I guess they're just curious."

Chase nodded. "Yeah. I probably would be, too." He pointed at the equipment. "So, what is all this?"

Julian's eyes lit up as he explained to Chase, "It's a network I made over the past few years."

"What kind of network?" Chase asked, examining the programs.

"Basically, I track everything on the collective as well as monitor the chips in people's forearms," he said, smiling.

"That's pretty crazy. Like how many?"

"I'm over two million now," said Julian.

"Wow, two million? Why are you doing it?"

"Everyone in the world gets the collective and all the feeds, right? But I don't think the feed is real."

Chase scoffed. "How could the feed not be real? That doesn't make sense."

Julian wiped his hands on his pants and stood up. Chase noticed that while he spoke, Julian used a lot of gestures. "Well, the feed you view may be real in the sense that you are actually getting it, but I think the feed is manipulated by either the collective or the Big Sixteen. I've been trying for years to intercept the data before it goes out to everyone in the feed."

"So you're a hacker?"

"I prefer 'truth seeker'. Did you know today about six percent of people use the collective to control their lung functions? So if the collective or the Big Sixteen wanted, they could stop your breathing."

"Wow. That's fucked up," said Chase. "I didn't know that."

Before long, Chase and Julian became good friends. Julian was the first new person he met who didn't treat him like a circus animal. They would spend hours together brainstorming ideas. Chase wanted to hear all the things Julian was working on, and Julian was fascinated by what it was like to live the life of one of the Sixteen.

Chase would meet Julian in the mornings and talk about the things they'd heard on the feed. Julian uploaded the latest technology on Chase's eye screen and increased its capacity a hundredfold. Julian was also paranoid that the collective would find him, and he sometimes wore disguises, which made Chase laugh. Julian loved to show his friend his latest findings. He uploaded a program that allowed the two of them to interpret every language on earth. This program was only available to the highest council on the Big Sixteen. Julian also found a way to display an eye screen on the corners of both eyes instead of just one. It initially made him dizzy, but Chase got used to it after a few days. The amount of information they would receive boggled Chase's mind.

Chase joked, "Jules, you're going to turn into a giant pile of data. I hope no one deletes you or makes a copy of you." He laughed, then remembered a story he'd seen earlier and quickly switched topics. "Hey, did you hear that a drone war is about to start in Africa over water rights?"

"I heard that," Julian said, "and I also heard actual human soldiers are fighting, trying to shoot down the drones. They say they just can't sit back and watch the drones go at it while their families have no water."

"Really? Is it working?"

"Of course not. The drones have programs to sense organic living matter. They're called organic snipers, and they kick ass against people. They're picking the soldiers off nonstop, like shooting fish in a barre; but I broke into one of the drones last night to review the data through the collective. One of the drones killed seven hundred twenty-two soldiers so far."

"Jules, I set up my screens the other day to have one eye based on your collective feed and the other eye from the public feed. The public feed said that the drones are programmed not to kill any humans since the population is almost in balance for the earth's capacity."

"That's the kind of stuff I'm talking about; someone is changing the public feed. Now you can see it for yourself. Chase, remember when you let me plug into your port the other day to scan your chip?"

Chase nodded.

"Well, your chip isn't like any chip I've ever seen."

"What do you mean?"

"You have so many more programs that you have access to."

"Are they things you did?"

Julian shook his head. "No, they're programs I haven't even heard of, and I have access to at least two million chips, plus I've studied the collective for years. The weirdest thing is your data isn't coming from your chip port. Your entire body is receiving and projecting information. It's crazy. It's like your whole body is a receiver or some kind of antenna? I have no idea how that's possible. I think, because you're one of the sixteen families, that your whole network system is different."

"Really?"

"Yes, really, but I also found that some of your programs have been blocked for access."

"When was it blocked?"

"It looks like about thirty percent of the things I've never seen before were blocked just this year."

"That must be when my family kicked me out. Julian, what do you think those programs did?"

"I don't know, but I'd love to find out. I'm not even sure how you receive information, to be honest."

"Maybe I'm a monster." They both shrugged. "Let's go eat."

Later that night, before Maggie and Chase went to bed, the

public feed broadcasted breaking news on the fighting. Heavy drone

conflicts were escalating over the Nile River Dam between North and

South Africa in an increasing battle over the water rights. The drones

from the south had been firing into the dam, attempting to penetrate it,

while the north employed thousands of mechanical bots to plug up the

damaged holes. A small human army kept a safe distance from the war

zone, but three humans had been killed in the fighting. There was no

word on whether Africa would have a human baby auction, as the rest of

the world was lobbying for new legal human births.

In other news, the Pearson Group, who controlled eighty-five

percent of the world's food supply, said that because of unforeseen ozone

depletion, animals would be allowed only one hour of sunlight exposure

in order to keep toxic meat levels to a minimum. Pearson said there

should be no significant change in the health of the animals, although

they did anticipate an increase in meat prices in the next quarter. The

collective and the Sixteen were reviewing the data.

Chase scoffed. "Three killed. What a joke."

When Chase woke up the next morning, Maggie had already

left for the day to find work. Chase would have to start doing the same

soon. He felt badly that he hadn't begun the search for a job yet, but he

wasn't used to the area, to the people there. Everyone knew that he was

different, so he figured it would be even less likely he would find work.

Everyone knew his parents were loaded.

He looked out the window at the overcast day before he heard

a commotion in the street. He jumped off the bed, slid on a pair of

weathered sandals, and walked out toward the noise. Tons of people

gathered around an old makeshift flying pod that was loaded with bottles of brown water. The pilot landed the pod in the street and offered each bottle at an outrageous price. It was the same price the shiny metal supermarket drone ships charged in the nicer areas of the city, but those shiny ships didn't land in such neighborhoods. People ran up to the ship, excited to get water for their families.

The crowd started yelling things like, "Come on, you know no one has that kind of money here. Lower the price. Why did the price of water go up again?"

A few banged on the side of the pod as the guy yelled, "Don't touch the pod!"

Chase pushed his way to the front of the crowd. He knew in the past he could have easily bought the entire pod and ended the crisis right away, but that wasn't a possibility anymore. The crowd was getting angrier, as no one could afford a single bottle. No one had had a clear cup of water to drink in a long time, and it was hot.

Chase yelled, "At the price you're charging, where's the clear water? I've never seen water that brown. You're kidding, right?"

Someone yelled out, "Look, even Richie Rich doesn't believe crap water should be that price."

Chase didn't say anything to the crowd. Instead he told the man, "I'm just saying, that water doesn't look too good. You know that."

A burly, bald guy shoved Chase and said, "Nobody cares what you think, rich boy. I haven't had a good glass of water in a long time. One more word out of you and I'll punch you in the fucking face."

Chase knew he was only alive in the district because Maggie was well liked, but she wasn't around. The bald guy walked up to the flying water pod and told the guy, "Lower the price now, or else."

"I'm selling this water well below market value. Maybe you're not aware that the prices went up today, and…"

Before he finished his sentence, the bald guy pulled him out of the pod and nearly beat him to death while everyone watched.

Chase ran and grabbed the bald man's arm, saying, "Don't kill him."

The burly guy turned and punched Chase in the stomach. He fell to the pavement curled in a ball as the people stepped over him to loot the water. Once the water was gone, the crowd took the flying pod apart, most likely to sell the parts later. The water salesman lay in a pool of blood and finally got up.

"Thanks for saving my life, man. I think that guy would have killed me."

"You got it," said Chase.

The salesman was missing two teeth. "For a second I thought they hated you more than me. Well, my pod is gone. I have no way to fly out of here. What should I do now?"

"Start walking, I guess, and hope for the best."

Chase was in the largest area of the small warehouse, which was naked of furniture, minus a few crates and pallets the occupants had stolen. Dirty cushions from old patio furniture adorned a few of the pallets, turning them into makeshift couches and chairs. Another two pallets nailed together served as a coffee table that was lined with dirty dishes and recently, dozens of bottles of brown water. Chase sat on one of the dusty couches while he gathered the dishes into a neat pile. The sound of Julian's many screens floated through the area; bouncing off the walls. The others sat in similar chairs, laughing, or planning how they would get their next meal, or bottle of real water. Chase listened to the noises of his new home. A dripping pipe in the hall. The low hum of the generators whirring with electricity.

Maggie returned to the warehouse and Chase half-heartedly waved at her. It had been a difficult day for him, and he was still having trouble coming to terms with his new life, which Maggie was very patient and understanding about. She surveyed the area and Chase assumed she'd seen the bottles.

"Why is everyone so quiet?" Maggie asked.

"No reason, really," one of their housemates, Clio, said. "We got some water today." Clio smiled, but her blue eyes didn't reflect any kind of happiness. Chase had only had a few conversations with the woman, but he understood that she was unhappy with her lot in life; thirty-five years old and completely impoverished. She was over five-foot ten, and rail thin. Clothes hung from her body like the tarps people wore to protect them from the chemicals in the rain, and she shaved her head, she said, because it was too hot. She was often quiet, with a faraway look on her face, but she helped people out whenever she had the opportunity. Chase liked her, though he felt sorry for her.

"Oh? Where did you get that?" Maggie asked, eyeing the brown sludge in the bottles. Chase noted that she did not reach for one.

"Some guy was selling it this afternoon," Clio replied.

"Oh, that's great…Chase? Are you OK?" Maggie asked. Chase got up and went into one of the bedrooms, beckoning her to follow. When they reached the room, Chase turned to face her, worried what she would think of his bumps and bruises. Maggie covered her mouth, shook her head, and hugged him. "Chase, you have to stop saying things like, 'This is wrong,' or 'That is not fit to eat.' This is how most people live when you're a 'sewer rat' or whatever your dad called me. Everyone is in same boat. You know that, right?"

Chase sighed. "Maggie, that's not really why I got…well, sort of. But it shouldn't be like this. It is wrong—plain and simple. I can see how the things I've said have offended people, and I should stop saying them. But look, I'm exposed to a world I've never even known existed. Not even vaguely." He tried to keep himself from clenching his fists but failed. Adrenaline thrummed and built throughout his body and he wanted a physical outlet for it; to throw something, to punch a wall. But he couldn't. Not in front of Maggie. He took a deep breath. "The way the Sixteen treat people, the fucking collective. No one's working, so no one has money to live on except from the shitty draw. It's wrong." Chase spoke quietly but with emphasis. He wondered how someone who had lived that way her entire life failed to see the wrongness in it.

Maggie sighed. "Great, Chase. What do you plan to do about it?"

"I don't know, Mag, but…something."

"Well, while you're sitting pissing and moaning about everything, I'll be going out again tomorrow, like every other day, to try to find work. Maybe you should do the same instead of getting beat up every day. You know that's the third time someone's hit you this week?"

Chase felt his cheeks flush. She was right. But he wouldn't admit that. "Thanks, Maggie, for your concern. And that's great advice. I'll try not to get beat up next week. That will be my goal in life. Along with maybe looking for a job." Maggie's posture shifted. She slouched and crossed her arms over her chest. Chase though he heard her sniffle. I'm being an asshole. Again, he thought. He grabbed one of her hands. "There's no reason you should be the only one working. I'll try to find a job."

Maggie smiled and kissed his forehead, which had a soothing effect on Chase. Her affection still made him feel as though everything was right in the world.

The next day Chase tapped his port to connect with his mother. No response. Chase was upset by this. She had barely defended him the night his dad kicked him out. She'd always been that way; never involving herself in the fights between Chase and Sam. Never sticking up for Chase when his father insulted him, and now she wouldn't even take a call from him.

A sharp pain jabbed at his chest, nearly taking his breath away. He recalled that when he was a child, his mother would hold him and tell him that she was sorry. That she loved him. That no one could take him away from her. So much for that, Chase thought. He tried to shake his bitterness as he sent a direct message to her. "I know you're getting my messages, Mom. Please connect." Twenty minutes later, his mom answered.

"Chase, you know you're not supposed to call here. Are you ok?" Her voice was quiet, but her tone was tinged with concern.

"Yeah. I'm hanging in there, but things are pretty crazy out here, Mom. But Dad would think it was perfect for a weirdo like me, so I'm sure he'd be thrilled with the whole situation."

"You know, Chase, I have been talking to your father, and I'm trying to convince him that this all started when that Maggie came into our house. I realize now that she's no good, Chase. She's toxic."

Chase planted his forehead in the palm of his hand. "Mom, Maggie is fine. She's kind and has helped me so much. Without her, I might be dead. I actually think I'm in love with her." It was the first time that word had entered his mind when he thought about Maggie. Love. He couldn't stop himself from smiling at that, at the word, the possibility of something soft and tender growing around the jagged edges of his home life; of their current life.

"Oh, no, Chase, she changed you. You…weren't always this way. Listen to your mother; I know these things. She is why you're in this mess."

Chase suppressed a laugh at his mother's dramatics. She's trying to blame someone for this. Someone she doesn't love, he thought. He didn't believe that she believed the words she said, but she was trying to. "Mom, I don't want to fight with you. I wanted to ask if I could get some things out of my room."

"Chase, you know you're not allowed in this house.

"Come on, please? I can't even take my own stuff that was given to me? Gifts? If Dad doesn't go near that area, there's no way he'd find out, right?" There was a pause.

"Chase, it breaks my heart what this girl did to you."

Chase groaned. "Mom, please drop it about Maggie. I'm trying hard to not argue with you." He wished he wouldn't blame Maggie, especially because the two had something in common; they both grew up living in terrible conditions. He wasn't certain if she had money, but Chase did know for sure that her family was nowhere near as wealthy as his dad was. They also treated her terribly. He couldn't believe his mother didn't have more empathy for Maggie.

Mrs. Applegate sighed and was silent a moment longer. "OK, your father is going on a conference for a few days. Did you know he's getting an award for his exceptional experimental work? He has had the least deaths per experiment: three to one."

Chase laughed. "Mom, who's doing the counting, a blind guy? You know as well as I do that he would come home and say the nineteenth prisoner died in one of his experiments, but now the overall number is only three? Sounds like bullshit to me."

"Chase, I'm trying to help you, so don't talk about your father like that. He works very hard to give us a wonderful life. He leaves Thursday, so you can come then, but listen to me: please don't bring that girl. Be ready at ten in the morning and send me your coordinates."

Chase wanted to argue, but he didn't want to press his luck. He'd gotten what he wanted. "Fine. Thanks, Mom."

With that, she disconnected.

Two days later a sleek top of the line cargo pod traveled to the south side to pick up Chase and Julian while Maggie was out looking for work again. Chase hadn't told Maggie that he was going back. He didn't want to have to explain why she wasn't allowed with him, though somehow, he knew she would understand. She'd lived with the Applegates for a very long time, herself. The only thing she may be upset about would be the fancy pod.

Inside the big pod were two of Sam Applegate's guards who worked in the prison. They were muscled meatheads, and both sported the bald look. They were similar except one guard was much bigger and wore a patch on his shirt that said "Tiny."

When Chase and Julian entered the pod, the guard said, "Let me scan your arm to make sure you're who you say you are." Chase and Julian held their arms out and waited for the men to check the scans.

Tiny said, "OK, we're good. It's Chase Applegate, and the other punk is Thomas Smith."

Chase looked at Julian but was smart enough to not comment on the false name. Applegate's cargo pods flew instead of using maglev, so when the rocket thrusters blasted, Chase looked outside and could see that all the neighbors on the block ran to their windows to peek at the pod.

"So you guys work for my dad?" Chase asked, attempting to sound casual.

"We do," said Tiny. "Mr. Applegate is a good boss and treats us with fairness."

"Yes," the other guard said. "He's a pleasure to work for."

Chase rolled his eyes and laughed. "Ok, you can cut the shit, guys. My dad is an asshole."

Nothing was said for the rest of the trip. The pod landed at the town gate entrance pad, and the door opened so the gate guard could investigate who was attempting to enter with a large cargo pod. Chase figured the gate guard saw the Applegate logos on the men's uniforms and the Applegate Prison for the Good insignia on the pod.

"What's up, guys?" said Frank, the gate guard.

"Mrs. Applegate asked us to escort these two to her residence."

Frank walked into the cargo and conducted a quick inspection, probably for contraband.

"OK, let me scan them…oh my God, is that you, Chase? It's me, Frankie."

Chase smiled. "Yeah, it's me. I didn't recognize you with that white hair. A lot of people would get a different color, but you know what? I like it."

"Hey, thanks, man. The ladies seem to like it, too, so I didn't opt to get a blonde transplant. But Jesus Christ, Chase, you look like shit. Don't you eat anymore? You're skinny, man." Frankie looked Chase over and folded his arms, almost the same way Chase's mother would have done.

"Yeah, I eat a little. It's not that bad."

"Damn, I almost didn't recognize you. You look sick."

Chase felt like lashing out, but he knew better. Frankie wasn't trying to upset him, after all. "No, I'm not sick. How's it going, Frankie?"

"You know, doing good, just keeping the bad guys out. So I'll let you through. And, guys, give my friend Chase a piece of cheese or something. You can just fly out when you leave but go over the ship scanner." The pod went through. As Chase looked back at the checkpoint, he saw Frankie and everyone inside talking while the other guards pointed at the pod and squeezed their faces up to the window, staring in Chase's direction.

When the cargo pod arrived, Chase and Julian walked into his house. His mother was waiting in the kitchen.

"Oh my God, Chase! Look at you. You have to take better care of yourself," she said, her voice high-pitched and almost frantic. "Staff, make him and his friend something to eat." His mother indeed crossed her arms in the same way Frankie had as she observed her son. Chase may have imagined it, but he thought he'd seen her eyes slightly glaze.

"I am, Mom. You don't know what it's like out there."

For whatever reason, his mother chose not to address his statement, instead asking who his friend was.

Chase looked at the prison guards, then back at Julian and said, "Tom."

"Well, Tommy, it's nice to meet you, dear."

"It's nice to meet you, Mrs. Applegate," Julian replied. He gently shook her hand and winked at her. For a shut-in, Chase recognized that Julian could actually be charming, if the slight blush on his mother's cheeks meant anything.

"Chase, once you're done getting your things, I want to have a chat with you about that girl. I really think she's the problem with your behavior."

"Mom, please. Can you either drop it or mind your own business? Please?" Chase said, trying to keep his tone neutral. Mrs. Applegate opened her mouth to speak, but then clamped her lips together.

Chase stormed up the winding staircase while Julian followed. Julian's eyes roamed over everything in the house, his jaw practically on the floor.

"Man, you really lived in the lap of luxury. I mean, I know it was true, but I never imagined this kind of thing; winding stairwells and sheer size of everything. This is a mansion, man. Your room is like twice the size of the house I grew up in. Your bed is massive, probably with like, twenty-four karat gold sheets. Shit. I'd be having trouble adapting to the warehouse too. This is, this is—"

"I know, Ju—Tom. Look, let's just grab a few things and get outta here. I need some clothes and my graphic novels," Chase interrupted as he rifled through his dresser and the piles of clothes on the floor.

"Ok, I'll help. I'll grab as many suits as I can. You've got some nice luggage in here, too. Man, this stuff would be worth so much on the black market," Julian said. Chase was too busy sifting through his bookshelf. The boys hauled the luggage out of Chase's closet and stuffed it full of clothes, shoes, cufflinks, tie clips and other trinkets.

Chase remembered that he had an antique music player that ran on solar power and also had a flashlight and a universal charger. If it was dark, there was a crank that could be turned to somehow power it. Chase wasn't sure how that worked, but he figured it could come in handy.

As he reached into his dresser drawer for spare socks, Chase's hand brushed against something soft. Without thinking, he gripped the item and pulled it out. He tried not to panic as he recognized the rabbit's foot. I'm sorry, Snowy, he thought as he held the paw close to his heart. His eyes stung, but he fought back tears. He couldn't think about that now.

Chase placed the rabbit's foot back inside the drawer and turned to Julian. "Well, I've had enough. Let's get some things out of the kitchen and get out of here." Julian agreed, and the two struggled to close the luggage. They'd grabbed anything that could be worth money.

They loaded the pod, and Chase kissed his mother good-bye as the guards loaded everything Chase and Julian had spent so much time packing into a different container with a a security system.

"What about that talk? Can we please talk about Maggie?" Mrs. Applegate asked.

Chase laughed. "That's not going to happen, Mom. I love you, but you're wrong about her, and I think you know that. I'm sorry, but I have to go."

Chase and Julian flew back to the south side. They landed on the top of the warehouse, as Chase had requested. The guards piloted the ship carefully as to not allow the thrusters to start the old warehouse on fire. The roof supports cracked with the weight of the cargo pod. The guards unhitched the container quickly and left it on the roof, then gave Chase the passcode and shook his hand.

As Applegate's guards got back in the craft, Tiny looked at them and said, "Good luck, kids."

When Chase and Julian climbed down off the roof, Julian got a message: "We're under attack, Julian, please help us," he read. Chase was about to question him, but Julian, looking panicked, didn't give him the chance.

"Shit, let's go. We need to get into my room fast."

"What's going on?" Chase asked.

"I'll tell you in a second. Seriously, run."

The two ran until they reached Julian's room and locked the door behind them. The screens were all blinking and flashing with images of people running in the streets in every direction.

"Holy shit, Julian, what's going on?" Chase asked. The chaos that swirled around him was something new. He'd heard of such things, but never had he seem them.

Julian typed code between a series of screens. "This is the fourth time I've seen something like this. Generally, the Sixteen keep these things quiet. All the reporters work for the collective now. Independent journalism once existed, but it died a long time ago,"

A voice sounded, which Chase thought sounded like Clio, but he couldn't be certain. "Julian, quick, do something. They're everywhere and shooting innocent people. Oh my God, a lady and her three kids just got mowed down by the bees. Julian, do something!"

Julian typed as quickly as he could, both by hand, and—Chase could tell by the way Julian's jaw tensed and released— through the thought cap he had plugged directly into his port, which remotely connected to the main terminal.

"What kind of bee shoots people?" Chase asked. His stomach sank as he wondered if Maggie was still out there. "Jules…can you see Maggie? Is she out there? Can you ask Clio if she knows where Maggie is?"

Julian didn't answer as he kept typing. Finally, he hacked into what must have been the secure government cameras in the street, and the live feed came up on the walls.

They looked like real bees, but they were actually small drones with sensors and laser guns. Although the laser guns were small, they could synchronize for precision blasts. A big black cloud of bees swarmed the buildings in packs. The cloud of drones moved to an abandoned building on the street and kept hovering.

"What are they doing?" Chase asked Julian. That time, Julian responded.

"They're scanning the building to see if there are any criminals inside." All at once a stream of two- or three-hundred drones went through a broken window. Civilians screamed as shots went off, and a big flash overtook the screens. Even though it was only an image on the wall screens, Chase ducked instinctively to avoid the explosion.

"The building's on fire. Can they do that? I…I thought the law said enforcement drones can never harm innocent people. Wasn't… that written into law a long time ago?" Chase stammered. He was having a hard time catching his breath, and he searched for Maggie on the screens, relieved at every face that didn't belong to her, but also panicked and enraged at what the government was doing to them.

Julian kept typing. A man and a woman with a dog ran out, and Chase's heart dropped again. He couldn't handle seeing that dog harmed. He still loved animals, and it broke his heart to think that an innocent, oblivious animal could be so spitefully attacked. But that's what the people were; innocent animals, and the government took no issue harming them.

A small line of drones chased them. More and more small drones streamed out as the building burned. Within a few seconds, a whole cloud of them flew out and circled the couple and their dog. Eventually, there were so many, all Chase could see was a black wall. The swarming bees drowned out the people's screams and the crying dog. Chase pressed his fingers into his ears. The terrified desperate screams coming from both humans and animals alike unnerved him. He was still on edge wondering about Maggie, too. Where was she?

Julian moved screens in the air, running back and forth between multiple displays.

There was silence for a moment as the drones stopped, turned upward, and hovered. Julian zeroed in on one screen and plugged his arm port directly into it. As he did, the drones shot up quickly in the air, paused for a minute, then took off.

Huge flames licked the skyline as hysterical people rushed into the streets, some of them on fire. Not knowing what to do, most people stood in shock, looking at the blood-stained street and burning flesh. Some used blankets to help others who were alive and burning. All that remained of the people chased by the bees was some jewelry and the dog's metal tag.

Chase examined the faces again, looking for Maggie. Most were so badly burnt, he couldn't make out their gender.

Clio's voice came back on: "Thank you, Julian." She wept. "My mom was in that building."

"Man, I'm so sorry," he said. "I tried to hack in as fast as I could, but they kept coming up with new blockers. I'm so sorry for all of you, Clio."

"You did the best you could, and if it weren't for you, even more people would have died. We need more people like you on our side. Don't give up. Please don't give up. We're going to get that fucking collective!"

"I won't." He tapped his port, and most of the screens turned off, vanishing from the room.

That night, aside from Clio, who wanted to be alone to mourn her mother, the group watched the collective feed. Chase tried to stay calm as he listened, but Maggie had yet to return. He worried even though she often didn't return early. Had he been with her, looking for a job as he'd promised…. He tried to tune out his anxiety and guilt by listening to the feed, but it was a useless attempt and only caused him more anguish.

"As the African Water War continues, the south is employing larger drone missiles to attack the Nile Dam. Newly improved dual-purpose flying and sailing cruise ships are gaining popularity across the world as the cruise companies are further expanding into the airline industry. Improved eye lenses are going to be offered at only a thirty percent increase in cost next year. Also, if you are of reproductive age, don't forget to see your doctor who will recommend options for you. It is required that all males living beneath the poverty line are sterilized and all females are placed on birth control." The newscaster barely took a breath, moving from tragic topics to advertisements, to inane subject, then back to tragedy. Chase listened, despite this. The reporter continued, "In other news, a fire broke out today in Chicago in an illegal housing complex, when two men attacked enforcement drones during routine safety surveillance. Both men were detained and could face up to one-hundred-fifty years at the Applegate Prison for the Good if convicted, which is likely."

"Julian, who controls the feed?" Chase asked.

"The collective and the Sixteen, I assume, but you know what they say: 'Is the tail wagging the dog?'"

"How did you stop the killer bee drones, and where are the videos from the people we saw burning in that fire?"

Julian turned away from the feed and took a deep breath. "The killer bees have a VL-Seven geo field around them individually as well as around the entire swarm. All outside video gets scrambled. You'll never see them kill people on the collective feed. My dad invented the VL-Seven for the military. He also studied living killer bees for twenty years with sensors to learn the traits that enabled their survival for millions of years in nature. He took that information and wrote programs with algorithms for the military drones. As you saw, they're deadly, but once my dad learned that the sixteen families were using them against humans, he spoke out. He's in Applegate now."

Chase shook his head in shock and embarrassment. "I'm… sorry." He didn't know what else to say Then he looked up at Julian. "I can't believe you'd even want to be friends with me, knowing who I am. I mean, if the tables were turned, I don't know how I would handle that."

Julian shook his head and smiled. "You didn't put my dad in prison. Plus, Maggie's been telling me about you for years. Like that you used to go along with what your dad wanted, until you were old enough to tell him no. I respected that about you before I even saw you in person, and I could tell when I met you that you weren't like them. Even when I met your mom, I could tell…no offense."

"None taken."

"I have to tell you, though, there's a lot of talk that because you're from one of the Big Sixteen families, you're here to, in some way, set up the people of this community so that everyone will end up in Applegate. They think you're some sort of plant. That's why you've been beaten up so many times, and I think they're planning something against you. They also know about the stuff in your container on the roof, and a few people have already tried to break into it."

"Really?" Chase asked, stunned. He thought he'd proven that he wasn't a traitor simply by having not yet betrayed anyone, but all he'd really done was to stick around. Nothing special. Of course they were wary of him.

"I have been asked at least ten times to hack the code and get in. I said no, and a few guys are getting pissed off at me because their families are so poor and hurting and they know I could hack it if I wanted to. I'm not sure what to do. Sorry to tell you all this." He paused. "And…that's not all. Another guy grabbed Maggie yesterday and ripped her shirt. He told her if she didn't get the passcode from you soon, he would be back to see her. And it wouldn't be pretty."

Chapter Six

Chase couldn't believe someone would threaten Maggie, when she'd helped so many in the community. He still wasn't sure if she was alive, though Julian had assured him after his initial freak out that she wasn't anywhere near the deadliest part of the attack but Chase was still worried. He closed his eyes, and there was silence.

After a long pause, he said, "Julian, could you tell everyone in the community to meet me on the roof where the container is? If the people can't get on the roof, would you please ask them to go to the street and look up toward the roof?" Julian raised his eyebrows. At that, Chase sighed.

"They trust you, Jules. They don't trust me."

After a moment, Julian agreed to do as Chase had asked.

Chase searched until he found Maggie. He pulled her into his arms and inhaled her scent, happy that she was okay.

"Where were you? I was so scared, Maggie…I thought I could have lost you," Chase said. Maggie's arms tightened around him— surprising Chase with her physical strength. He could barely breathe, but he didn't mind. All that mattered was that she was there. In his arms. In one piece.

"I'm fine. I was looking for work when I received that notification about the hormone-controlling implant. I guess it's required for women to get them so that we don't get pregnant. So I went to the nearest building that offered the chip implant." Maggie paused, and the couple parted, though Chase held on to his girlfriend's hand. Maggie continued, "They'd given me a numbing shot, and I was in the room, on the table with those creepy robot arms ready to cut me open. They didn't even sedate me, just a local anesthetic. I felt intense heat. That's when the alarms sounded, and I smelled something burning. The building was on fire. Nothing crazy like what happened a block over, but it was still burning. I grabbed my clothes, put them on, and ran. I didn't know then that all hell had broken loose. I heard the screams, but screams aren't uncommon around here, so I just continued looking for work." Maggie inhaled sharply. She had spoken the words in a swift meter, probably to discourage Chase from interrupting and asking if she'd been hurt.

"You didn't get the chip, then?" he asked. Maggie shook her head. "You're one hell of a person, Maggie, you know that, right? Looking for work after you almost died."

Maggie chuckled. "That's a bit dramatic. I'm fine," she said. The two embraced again for a moment. Chase didn't want to let go of her. He wanted to tell her that he loved her, but the words caught in his throat. Fear of them not being returned pushed them back down. He settled for being thrilled that she'd lived through her experience.

"You know, Chase, you're lucky. I mean, I know you've given up a lot, but you're lucky that the government doesn't go digging in your body, deciding whether you can have kids. I know, most of us are infertile anyway, but…it feels like a complete violation, being robbed of your choice like that," Maggie said.

"I know, Maggie. I'm sorry. So sorry," he said, wrapping his arms around her.

All that was left was for him to deal with the threats she'd been getting. After ttalking a while longer, they headed up to the roof, which was filling fast. People were mumbling, things Chase tried to ignore like, "I knew this kid was up to no good." Others thought Chase was turning everyone in for something and took the opportunity to run before the police could arrest them.

Looking down from the roof, Chase watched people run off in the streets with whatever belongings they could carry as others pushed and shoved to get onto the roof.

Chase climbed up and stood on top of the container, so everyone could see him. He was both excited and nervous, as he knew he could be in danger. The crowd gathered, and eventually there was no room left on the roof. Everyone else looked up from the street as Chase began to speak.

"You all know who I am—well, you think you know." More people in the street started to run.

"My name is Chasten Applegate, and I'm not your enemy. You know who my family is.

"I grew up disagreeing with my father and the Applegate Prison for the Good, for everything he and his friends stood for; and I've paid the price with my family. I saw what goes on in those prisons, and you know as well as I do that no one visits, and no one gets released.

"I've also had the best of everything that money can buy, and yeah, I grew up privileged. I've had servants, butlers, drone jets, you name it. But I've also seen the pain of the common person firsthand from the prisoners who have been wrongfully accused and have been used in, basically, experiments not fit for animals. Because I rebelled against my father, he disowned me. I'm the first Big Sixteen family member ever to be disavowed. Mr. Applegate told me that I was no good, that I was weird, a loser, and I would never live a meaningful life. Well, he was wrong. I met Maggie, her friends and family, Julian, and all you guys, and I can say to all of you right now that I feel alive for the first time." About ten people in the crowd cheered.

"You're the real people. The people who struggle and still try, still hope for something better, even when the odds are stacked against you.

"There's no fucking jobs left, and you look for work or ways to make ends meet for your families. Most importantly, there's love here that I've never experienced before. Real love."

Chase looked down to his left and heard murmurs of acceptance. Some members of the crowd nodded along with the things he'd said. He felt like a massive weight had been lifted from his chest, like he could breathe. But he still needed to prove that he was there to help, not to harm them.

He took another deep breath and as he spoke, the crowd quieted a bit faster than they had upon their reluctant arrival. "Everyone here helps each other instead of trying to screw the next guy. This, my friends, is how the world should be. It's never been fair for the average person, but these days the deck is really, really stacked against you. There are forces, powerful forces, keeping you down, and someone has to rise up and do something about it.

"I want to be that person, and I vow to you today that I will fight this injustice, even if it kills me."

The crowd burst into a roar. The people in the streets cheered and banged anything they had that made noise.

"There's been talk about what's in the container. Well, it's time for everyone to see. Maggie, would you please put in the passcode." Everyone moved back a little. Maggie wasn't even told what was in the large thirty-foot long container, but she must have known that it was important to Chase. She hadn't even asked.

Chase felt it was do or die and with the pressure of the crowd, he needed to be gracious about what he did next. He stepped aside as Maggie opened the case, revealing all the items Chase had taken from his home. He'd even managed to swipe a few pieces of artwork that could be worth millions on the black market.

There was nice clothing in his size and his father's and mother's sizes. Jewelry, old-fashioned watches, silverware, blankets, pillows, shoes and even a water filtration system, which he set aside.

"This," Chase said, indicating the water filter, "will be located inside the warehouse, but you are all free to come by at any time for fresh water." He rifled through the back of the trunk, producing a few torches and canned goods. "These should help some of you to heat your food. I've brought non-perishable items that I found in the pantry of the Applegate Estate. It isn't much, but it's enough to keep some of us healthy for a time without having to spend Draw money on terrible food." Chase reached for a bunch of K bars he'd managed to grab. These he gently tossed into the crowd, but not before warning that if anyone fought over the items, he would take them all back. The crowd grunted their approval.

He overheard someone down below, daydreaming of a different life. It was an elderly man whose liver-spotted hands shook as he spoke:

"You know, maybe with all this we could buy ourselves a one-way ticket to the moon. Anything goes there. It's complete anarchy and far that is better than this," the man said. Chase had heard the same rumors about the moon; a massive biodome constructed around all sides of the satellite so that people could do as they wish, and it was completely outside the jurisdiction of the Sixteen. It was a novel thought, but Chase knew that even a short stay on the moon for one would cost much more than the total of the items he had with him.

After he'd unloaded a few packages of biodegradable toilet paper and feminine products, he moved on to the non-essentials. No one fought. The clothes were given based on whom they would fit; the jewelry was easily broken down and divided up evenly, as was the silverware. There were only about ten pairs of shoes, but no one argued over who would get them; in fact, the members of the crowd examined their feet, deciding based on the current condition of their footwear who would benefit most from a new set, but ultimately deciding that it would be best to sell the shoes. They lived in a dangerous neighborhood, and the items were likely to be stolen. The clothing would suffer the same fate. Most of the items would end up sold on the black market. The neighborhood collectively agreed that any money would be pooled together and then divvied up amongst everyone.

"Look, I did this because it was all I could do to help. The filter won't last forever, and neither will the money, but it will improve our quality of life so that, if we must fight, we'll be able to do so. Do whatever you want with the items, but if you can get money for them and collect your Draw, maybe you'll have enough to live off for a little while. Maybe you'll be more comfortable. Happy, even. That's what you deserve," Chase said. He turned and looked at Maggie, who had tears in her eyes.

"What about you?" someone said. Chase turned around. An elderly woman in the crowd, wearing only a tee-shirt about five sizes too large for her was standing on her tiptoes. "The case is empty. What do you get?" she asked.

Chase grabbed Maggie's hand. "Well, we get clean water for a bit, and I saved both Maggie and me each one decent outfit for job hunting. But look, I've lived my whole life surrounded by shit. Nice shit, yeah, but shit nonetheless. I have Maggie, I have friends, I have all of you. I don't want the shit anymore because the shit isn't what matters. We matter," Chase said.

Maggie nudged him. "That was eloquent," she said, grinning. "And sweet. I don't know any person in your position who would give their possessions to the poor. Most people are selfish."

"That's why the world is in this condition. Greed and apathy. I want to change that, Maggie. Do you think I can?" he asked. The crowd had hollered "thank-you's" and was dispersing.

She laughed. "If you can change their minds," she said, indicating the receding crowd, "I think you might be able to."

"Maybe," Chase replied. "But not without help."

"I think you've earned yourself a few fans tonight. Hopefully, you won't have to do anything alone," Maggie replied, her brilliant smile on full display.

When Chase and Maggie walked into her place, it was empty.

"Where is everyone, Mag?"

A puzzled look caused slight wrinkles in Maggie's smooth skin as she surveyed the area. "I don't know."

They looked around the corner and there were their friends and family, peeking from another room and into the hallway. There was a long line.

"What are you guys doing back there?" Chase asked.

A man Chase recognized as Maggie's uncle replied, "Chase, after what you've done for us, we think it's fair that you and Maggie live in the big room, and the rest of us will live in the smaller back rooms."

"Thank you anyway, but the back room is fine for us," Maggie replied.

After Julian and Maggie had hooked up the water filter, everyone who lived in the warehouse trickled back in.

Chase peeked outside and saw several lines of people, standing with jugs in hand. Julian had already rigged their water system to provide much more than the standard amount for any given household, and he'd expressed concern to Chase that someone could notice that their water usage jumped up by five-hundred percent.

"Can't you do something about that?" Chase asked Julian, as the people efficiently entered and exited the front room, happily strolling away and drinking clean water for the first time in years. Julian was silent, and Chase saw that he was watching the influx of desperate people as well as calculating a solution to that problem.

"Yeah, man. I could probably mask it, but only for a week or so," Julian said. That was good enough for Chase.

It took three hours to get water to all the folks who waited, but Julian, Chase, and Maggie happily helped them all fill their jugs. Once the crowd had thinned for the night, Julian asked Chase to grab a drink. Everyone sat on the couch, except Julian, who sat in an old rocking chair, holding a diary. It was an old-fashioned physical diary and it was handwritten.

"Chase, my dad sneaked this out of prison for me to have because he worried he would die quickly in there. My dad was brilliant, and the people who ran the prison knew it. Dad was the only prisoner with his own lab to continue his work. Before he died in there, he was working on his biggest experiment. It tapped into the collective's influence of space-time and quantum physics. He felt it was possible to utilize this knowledge and disrupt the entire collective with a rogue malware spider program."

"I don't understand what all of that means," said Chase.

"My dad knew that if it worked on a human, it could stop time temporarily. However, he calculated that there was a good chance that the person infected would be killed instantly. His diary said Sam Applegate made him finish the experiments and keep testing it through a test chip. Applegate told my dad that he wanted to use the technology to profit from the collective and maybe take over the world someday with an army of people programmed with the infected spider program. Dad refused to do the experiment on humans, and the diary says Applegate came in one day fuming that his wife may have had an affair. He summoned my dad to the operating room. When my dad walked in, there was a one-year-old boy strapped down for the experiment. They tortured my dad and shot him up with drugs until he did the experiment.

"He went back to his cell and later wrote these last words in the diary: 'Applegate may be having a breakdown. He made me experiment on a child. He said his wife cheated on him and the boy was his bastard child that he won in a lottery.'

"Chase, that child was you. That spider program may be inside you."

Chase took a deep breath and looked at Maggie. There was an uncomfortable pause. He'd always known he was different, that he could bend and manipulate time, that he wasn't wanted in his own home, that his father didn't like him let alone love him; and most of all, Chase had always known that he was, in his father's words "weird." He'd heard bits of his parents' conversations while he was growing up, where words like "auction" and "bidding" were spoken at night in hushed voices. He ignored those words because he knew that if he examined them too closely, he wouldn't like what he found.

"So I'm just some…experiment?" Chase asked.

Julian shook his head. "I'm sorry, man."

Chase's eyes stung, and he turned away from Julian and Maggie, briefly pulling himself together. He refused to cry over Sam Applegate. "If I'm not an Applegate, I don't know who I am," Chase said. "That was me."

Maggie grabbed his hand again and said, "It still is you. Nothing can erase your family history. You're still the same person. It shouldn't matter."

Chase tried not to show that he was upset. He knew what type of man his father was, but he'd still thought that man was his father. He thought he would be grateful to learn otherwise. Why would such news hurt him? He shook it off. "I think I'm going to sleep. Thanks for coming by, Julian."

It didn't take long for word to get around about what happened the day before, and suddenly Chase and Maggie had volunteers scheduled in shifts to watch the perimeter of the warehouse, as people would come by at all hours to thank Chase or use the water filter. Otherwise, they stood around, likely being nosy.

Maggie paced her bedroom wondering about Chase, wondering if there was someone she could call. She wanted more information. She remembered the name of the woman who used to visit to check Chase's chip. After much poking and prodding, Julian assisted in finding a way for Maggie to connect with Dr. Anderson, who was surprisingly friendly and more than willing to to stop by to talk.

A few days later, Maggie watched as a shiny new private pod pulled up and came to a stop. Everyone moved out of the way. Maggie hadn't met Dr. Anderson, but she'd seen her a few times on the feed, so when a short, thin woman with brownish-blonde hair worn in a bun stepped off the pod, Maggie felt her stomach flutter. She couldn't believe the woman had come. She watched as Dr. Anderson and a man close to her age exited the pod.

"Hi. I'm looking for Chase Applegate and someone named Maggie. I'm Dr. Jessica Anderson," she said to Maggie, who had opened her door.

"There are so many people standing outside," Dr. Anderson said. "Do they know how dangerous it is to just stand outside without protection?"

Maggie agreed. "You're right, doctor, but I doubt they care. By the way, Dr. Anderson, I'm Maggie. Chase is expecting you. I'll take you to him, if that's alright?"

Maggie gently urged some of the bystanders to move aside. Maggie, Dr. Anderson, and the man with her entered the warehouse, where Julian had set up his own custom scanning procedure.

"Would you mind waiting here for just a moment, Doctor? We have to verify the scan," said Maggie.

"You're scanning me?" the doctor asked, her head slightly cocked to the side.

"Yes," Maggie said, looking at her feet. She didn't feel comfortable asking for a scan from such a high-profile doctor, but she knew she had to. For Chase's safety at the very least if not for that of everyone else. "We scan everyone. We're always concerned that the government will send someone to hurt Chase. Rumors are rampant these days about him."

"How will you know what to scan for?"

"Don't worry, Doctor; we have someone who's knowledgeable with this stuff."

With a mixture of amusement and curiosity, she looked at the man with her, then back at Maggie and said, "OK, scan away."

"We already did. This room is a scanner. You two are all clear, so come this way, and you can see Chase."

As they passed through the dimly lit hallway, Dr. Anderson briskly walked ahead of everyone, and Maggie could see that there was a bounce in her step. She'd never met the doctor, despite having been at the Applegate residence nearly every time Dr. Anderson had stopped by. It was nice to see someone who seemed to care about Chase after Maggie had spent years watching Chase's mother stand by while Sam tried as hard as he could to break his son's spirit.

Good, Maggie thought, at least he's had one consistent person in his life who did something for him.

"Hi, Dr. Anderson," Chase said as Doctor Anderson entered his and Maggie's room.

"Hey Chase. Here to check the chip again," the doctor said.

Chase stood still while she scanned him. After a moment he asked, "Everything Okay?"

The doctor smiled. "Right as rain." She leaned in close to him and whispered "I think your dad's going a bit off the rails. He already mentioned something about me coming back next month."

"So…he thinks something's wrong?" Chase asked.

"He always thinks something is wrong or that someone is out to get him." Then Dr. Anderson motioned for someone to come into the room.

"This is my brother, Sean.

"Nice to meet you, Chase." said Sean, extending his arm, which was tattoo-covered and had tally marks on it. A lot of tally marks. "They're for the number of days I've been clean," Sean said, having noticed that Chase was staring.

"Oh, that's awesome, congratulations. It's tough. We've got a lot of issues with drugs in the area, so I've seen a bit of what it can do." Chase said, then looked at Dr. Anderson. Well, the doc says I'm doing fine."

"That's good news, right Jess?" Sean said. Jessica nodded.

"If that's all, we'd better get going. Sean's got some work to do, and well, so do I, nice as it was to see you again. I wish it were under better circumstances. Is there anything else I can do for you, Chase? Maggie?" Jess said, staring straight instead of at the couple, likely scanning her eye screen, or entering information into her records from the scan.

Chase cleared his throat. He didn't want to ask, but he had to. "I actually did want to ask you a question," Chase said. Jessica's eyes shifted slightly, but just enough that Chase felt her attention on him. It took a moment for him to get out the words he had to say. "Do you know if my father experimented with my chip when I was a baby?"

Jess's face paled, and Chase felt like he would be ill from that alone. That cannot be good news, he thought, waiting for her to explain.

Jessica shuffled her feet; dark red heels scraped against the pavement, and Chase wondered if she was more used to tennis shoes. Thinking of simple things in times of stress helped to calm him.

"I know that he did something with quantum physics, but that was a long time ago, plus, I was new to my career. I had just started in medical technology, and I wasn't that close to your family in the beginning."

"Right," Chase said, shaking his head. "Yeah, I remember Dad— uh, Sam—calling you in a rage because, according to him, either my chip was malfunctioning, or I was a reject as a person. Just because I disagreed with him. That was annoying."

Maggie grabbed Chase's hand and squeezed it. "Chase, it made you feel like you didn't matter, like you weren't a part of the family. I have a good memory, and I remember you always being locked in your room away from them. That's why I tried to always be pleasant around you."

Chase's eyes stung again, but he held back the tears. "Maggie, you were the best part of my life there, and even though Dr. Anderson's visits were irritating, she was always kind to me, too," he said, smiling at both women.

"It was irritating for me too. There was never anything wrong with your chip or port. Or you, for that matter," Jess said.

"I know. He really just didn't like me. I guess, even today, you can't program someone to like you."

Jess sighed. "For what it's worth, I was there when he bid on you. He did it without emotion. His was not the demeanor of a happy new parent. Sam has never been the kind of man to care about other people. He only cares about himself. It's not your fault that he didn't like you; it was his fault, and he'll never change," Jess said. Her blue eyes revealed a strange, decades-long anger that Chase had never seen in them.

"There is something you should know. Sam did go through with some crazy experiments in a rage," said Dr. Anderson.

"Really?" Chase asked as he glanced over at Julian, who had entered the room with his portable devices.

"Yes, when you were a baby, I visited your house with the late Dr. Holland, my mentor, to do some normal postnatal tests. I remember the night vividly because your dad threw us out as soon as we got there, and it was obvious he was upset about something. Dr. Holland and I walked outside, and we could hear your parents arguing. Sam thought your mom was fooling around with a neighbor because he found a note from the neighbor thanking her for some vegetables. He said he didn't like the way it was written and how the man signed his name, saying, 'Love—' whatever his name was."

Chase groaned. "That's ridiculous. I know the guy you're talking about. Mr. Diaz. He had the best vegetable garden in town. He was senile and spent all his time in that garden. I don't think he even had time to cheat; and if they ever did, I wouldn't blame my mom. I remember when Mr. Diaz died; he insisted that his ashes be used to fertilize his garden. Nice guy."

Jess sighed. "I wouldn't blame her, either, to be honest. Anyway, Dr. Holland and I stood outside waiting for our pod and we couldn't help but overhear your dad threatening to give you up for adoption unless your mom admitted to the affair. She insisted she never had one, then he started hitting her. We weren't sure what to do, so we left. I do know that, from that point forward, when we did future tests, your IQ numbers went off the charts."

Chase tried not to visibly react to the news. It wasn't a surprise to him, anyway, having known Sam for two decades. "Well, thanks, Jess. It appears I've somehow gotten directly connected to the collective, which I know is weird since the collective is not human. But if he hated my mom and me so much, you wouldn't think he would do something to benefit us. Unless, of course, it benefitted him in some way."

Everyone was quiet for a few moments. Jess and Sean both looked like they were ready to leave, but Chase had to ask the doctor about his ability, no matter how crazy he sounded. Best to just…spit it out, I guess, he thought.

"Dr. Anderson, before you go…I have something I need to ask you. Something that's been happening to me for years." Julian and Maggie sat down, both looking up at Chase with confusion. I haven't told anyone this, even you, Maggie. I'm sorry, but I know no one will believe me, and that's OK. I just want to ask Doctor Anderson about it, in case she knows anything."

"Chase, I would never judge you. You can tell me anything, you know that," Maggie said. Julian nodded along.

"Thanks guys." Chase turned back to Jess. "I wanted to tell you that something happens, um, sometimes. When I'm really nervous or in danger." He paused and took a deep breath. "Believe it or not, I can move as time stops." He looked down as he finished his explanation, but not in time to avoid seeing the wide-eyed shock on Maggie's face.

"Time…stops? Are you entirely sure that's what happens?" Jessica asked. "Time never stops, Chase."

"I know you think that, but it actually can stop. Well, technically speaking, when it happens to me, time moves in super slow motion, but that doesn't matter."

Jess looked puzzled. "How can that be?" She sat on one of the crate chairs for a couple of minutes in complete silence.

"Yes, really." Chase stood and explained everything from the beginning; the fire, hiding from his friends, the accident that killed Phil— every story he recalled where the world faded away and he floated above it.

Jessica held a hand to her mouth. The room was silent once more until Jessica spoke. "Chase…after you were born, I could have sworn I saw you just disappear. It was less than a second, but…I knew what I saw. It was my first day, and I knew that if I mentioned it to any of my superiors, they would think I was insane. There was a nurse in the room, but she didn't see anything. I started to feel like I was crazy after that event, but then there was the report about your chip inexplicably going offline during the fire." Sean placed a hand on Jessica's shoulder to calm her shaking, and she quickly composed herself.

"Chase?" Maggie's voice was small and somewhat sad, and her face matched it. She didn't need to say any more. Chase knew what her question was. Her brown eyes reflected the closest thing to betrayal Chase had ever seen in them, and it hurt him to know that he'd done that to her.

"I'm sorry, Maggie. I didn't know if you would believe me. I didn't know anything, Okay? I should have told you. I should have looked for work while you did. I should have told you that I loved you a long time ago, but I was stupid. Some things are hard to say, and they come with the possibility of pain and rejection. I didn't want to risk losing you. After all, not many people could say that they shift dimensions and be taken seriously. Hell, most people would be locked away in an institution. I figured that at some point it would happen around you. That you could see if for yourself and that way I wouldn't have to explain. Can you forgive me?" He'd blurted out everything so fast, he didn't realize he'd said it. He'd told her he loved her. He wobbled a bit on his feet, then steadied himself against the wall.

Tears rolled down Maggie's cheeks and she uncrossed her arms and wrapped them around Chase. The gesture made his stomach flutter. Her touch was pure warmth. Maggie's tears soaked into the shoulder of Chase's shirt, and he gently pulled away from her to look at her. "Are you all right?" he asked.

"I'm fine, it's just…you've been through so much. I could have helped you; but of course I forgive you," Maggie said. She moved toward him, closing up every inch of space between them. She stood on her tiptoes and gently wrapped her arms around Chase's neck, leaning into him so that their foreheads touched, clearly not concerned with who was watching them. "I love you, too," she said.

Chase felt lightheaded again, but he allowed Maggie to help steady him. They fused together for a few moments before someone coughed.

Jess approached slowly. "Chase, do you want me to set up time at U Med? It's by far the best hospital in North America."

"Thanks, Dr. Anderson, but I just wanted to see what you remembered from back then, when I was a little kid. It really helps to know that I wasn't crazy. I don't need to go to the hospital. I have so many things I want to do. I've been spending my time helping people, people whom the collective and the Sixteen are oppressing."

"Good for you, man," said Sean. "Those fuckers are killing everyone!" He looked from Chase to Jess. "I'm sorry. I didn't mean to interrupt your meeting."

"Well, I think Maggie and I already did that," Chase said, smiling at Maggie, whose cheeks turned red as she returned his smile. "No, Sean, you're right. They're literally killing people, no bullshit. You are absolutely right."

Sean became animated, gesturing with his hands while he spoke. "Did you know there was a riot in Toronto last night because their energy got rationed?" Sean asked. "The family in charge—I think it's the fourth or twelfth family—raised the rates again to make more money, and people can't pay more money because the draw they get sucks. You can't pay what you don't have."

Sean went on. "I mean, the draw is barely enough for people to eat. Everything goes up, except the draw. And now it costs more money for energy, which means some people can't even afford heat. Imagine living in Canada, where it's cold, and these pricks charge so much for heat, you can't even keep your family warm."

"I hear you, Sean," said Chase. "Do you have any ties to Toronto, like with the underground?"

Sean paused for a moment and rubbed his chin. "I actually do. One of my good friends, who I was in rehab with a long time ago, organizes up there and is lobbying the twelfth family of the Sixteen to lower the heating and energy prices. They've been working on this for a few years now. An entire family was found yesterday frozen in their house."

Chase shook his head. He couldn't help but think of incidents like that as murder; nothing less. "I know the twelfth family. A guy named Francisco is the head of it. And you're right; he's a real prick. His cousin is part of the fourth family, who controls Eastern Europe. He even controls part of Russia, and over there, they know cold."

"He probably got the idea from his cousin to freeze out whomever he doesn't like as well as make more money," Sean said, while veins pulsed on either side of his neck.

"I haven't heard about this yet. Is what Sean is saying true?" Chase asked.

Julian tapped his port, and the wall shifted as 3-D screens appeared midair and slipped closer to the couch where he sat. A digital wheel floated down from the ceiling, and Julian turned it to make changes to all the screens.

Chase watched as Sean and Jessica quickly ducked in their seats, likely to avoid being whacked by one of Julian's screens.

"It's true, Chase. Look," said Julian. "Here are the numbers on the homes that turned their heat down to one-point-one degree Celsius—just above freezing. The forecast says another arctic blast is coming soon, so it doesn't look good for that city. Here we go; look at this." He paused, and Chase saw a look of concern on his friend's face before Julian spoke again. "I just picked up bots that are going through Ontario's power grid. That's odd."

"Why are they doing that?" asked Sean.

"I'm not sure yet, but something's up."

"Check out the feed," Chase suggested.

"The feed? The world-feed update doesn't come on for another half-hour," said Jess.

"We can see it before that. There's another feed, the real feed. Jess, the feed you see is the modified version." Julian pulled up the feed and a bar indicating a download appeared in the bottom corner of the screens.

"What did it say about Toronto?" asked Sean.

"It said there's no notable news in the upcoming public feed from the province of Ontario."

Sean yelled out, "Liars!"

Julian looked over at him. "Sean, everything is a lie."

Sean's face was red, and Chase told him that he and Julian and the rest of them would do what they could to make sure that lies didn't dominate the world forever.

Chase noted that the man seemed neither convinced nor comforted. Chase didn't know himself if the words he said were true, but he hoped they were He smiled at Jessica. "Thank you for coming over and talking to me about all this."

"It was no trouble at all," Jess said. They all got up. Jess hugged Chase once again and asked, "What's next for you?"

Chase glanced at his girlfriend. "Well, I'm going to spend a little time with Maggie, then I think I'll be in Toronto to see if I can help the people up there."

Jess furrowed her brow. "Be careful, I'm sure word has spread to the Sixteen. Everyone is talking, saying you could be the voice that no one has anymore. A disavowed member of the Sixteen is a public danger as far as the Sixteen are concerned."

"I'm going, too," said Sean, taking a step closer to Chase. Chase liked the determination and ease with which Sean made his choice. "I'm going with you to Toronto."

Jess looked at her brother. "Stop it, you're not going anywhere."

"Jess, I'm going. I'm not going to sit around and watch people die because they can't afford basic heat. That's bullshit."

The room grew quiet as Sean teared up a little, which made Chase feel slightly less embarrassed about almost crying in front of them before. Human. It was a human reaction.

"Jess, I've struggled my whole life, and I can't even explain how it bothers me to see other people struggle because someone else is intentionally trying to keep them down. Going out of their way to keep people down! I'm going. I mean, if it's OK with you guys?" Sean looked at the group.

No one said anything.

Jess sighed. "Okay, I see why it's so important to you. I understand, I get it." She turned back to Chase. "What do you think? Do you have room for one more?"

Chase was quiet for a moment, then after consulting with Julian, said, "Absolutely. Sean, get some warm clothes and meet us back here at ten tonight. We're leaving then, and you're more than welcome to come."

Once everyone left, Chase asked Julian, "What do think, honestly?"

"Uh… what about? So much shit just happened, but I think I'll put the PDA and time-traveling shit on the back burner for now." Chase laughed, and Julian continued. "I think Sean seems like a bit of a hothead, but he may have some good contacts up there, and that should help. He's just fed up like everyone else."

Chase smiled. "Thanks for your opinion on Sean, but I was talking about what you think is going on up in Toronto."

Julian's eyes widened. "Well, shit, man, eight different things just happened here. Be specific. Toronto? Something is definitely going on with the power grid. I've seen these bots before, and I'm certain they belong to terrorists, but I can't identify what organization they're from. If they attack that grid, they'll move on to others. It's just a matter of time. That's how these wars always start, but I'm not sure who would want to start a war with Canada. Or why."

Chase spent the rest of the evening with Maggie and got his things ready. At ten o'clock, Jess's private hydrogen pod landed in the street. Chase heard Maggie's eye screen indicate the alert.

"Chase, your doctor friend Jessica just came back, probably to drop off her brother. They just landed," she informed him.

As the heat from the ship charred the street, the door opened, and Sean was alone inside. Maggie walked out and saw that Clio was standing outside at a safe distance, and she walked up to meet Sean as the ship settled.

"Hi, Sean. Nice night tonight with the ozone and everything," Clio said.

Sean got out, and they started walking as Maggie looked back at the pod. "Your pod isn't moving yet. Is the autopilot working right?"

"No, everything works fine. My sister gave it to me for the trip," Sean replied.

"Really? Those new ships are pretty costly. That was nice of her," Clio said. She took another look at it. "The black also looks really cool. I'll tell Julian because he may want to change a few things to protect you guys."

"How many of us do you think will go?" Sean asked.

"I would say probably just a handful," Maggie answered.

Chase had just finished packing a small bag of his meager belongings when his eye screen displayed an incoming call from Julian, which he picked up. "Chase, it's me," Julian said. Chase rolled his eyes. With how technologically adept Julian was, it annoyed Chase just a bit that his friend felt the need to announce who he was when he called. "Sean came back; he has Jess's ship. Said she gave it to him for the trip."

Chase was stunned but delighted at the donation. Though it could prove problematic for the group if things didn't go well. "Oh, Okay. Well, does he know it could get damaged? Once the Sixteen figure out this ship is involved with anything detrimental to them, they'll try to destroy it. Hopefully without us being inside."

"Yep, he seems to understand that. I'm in the pod, doing some work so the pod can't be detected by laser, radar, or GP zone."

"Is there enough room in it for those modifications?" Chase asked.

"I'm not completely sure, but I'll make it work."

"Okay, Julian sounds good."

While everyone was getting ready, Chase walked into Julian's room. All the screens in the air were flashing, and Chase gathered from the information displayed that Julian was researching the Toronto infrastructure and how the twelfth family made their money on energy and politics.

Chase wanted to talk to his friend about something personal, but the timing wasn't right with Julian being in research mode. And though

Chase regretted it when he kept things from Maggie, he didn't know how to articulate to her that he didn't only have an ability to stop time; he'd been experiencing other oddities. For days, he had a tingling feeling all through his body; some unfamiliar sort of energy. It was as if he was gaining knowledge from somewhere in the universe. He could easily look at and solve advanced math algorithms and understand biological mechanisms of which he knew he had no prior knowledge. He stood in the doorway and looked over at Clio, who had practically transformed into a different woman.

"Hi, guys. Look at you, Clio; you're all dressed up," Chase said. He'd only seen Clio in ripped up jeans and old t-shirts, but she wore a white cotton dress with a light floral pattern. He wondered if it was one of his mother's dresses but resisted the urge to ask her.

"Well, I wasn't sure if you wanted me to go, so I packed a few things. I'm almost done packing for Julian, too."

"That's what I wanted to talk to you about, both of you," Chase said.

Julian looked up from what he was doing.

Chase cleared his throat. "I think…I think it's better off if you guys stay here. Especially you, Julian."

"Really?" Julian said.

"Yes. It's not practical to dismantle and reprogram all your networks then make them mobile. We have a direct link to you, so I think it's better if this is always our home base. I also think you need to invent new ways to protect what you've built. People are going to come after us and try to destroy us, and we can't let them know where your network is based."

Julian examined his screens and equipment. Chase wondered if Julian wasn't trying to think of a way to make it all mobile, but Chase knew that would be impossible, so he assumed Julian would know it as well. "Okay, Chase. I want to go, but if you think this is the best way, then I'll stay." He looked at Clio in disappointment.

"I do," Chase replied. "Plus," he said, smiling, "who's going to take care of Clio and Maggie?"

"Why aren't we going?" Clio asked.

Chase sighed. "Well, I want some people here at home, and honestly, it could get dangerous and really cold. I just don't want to risk your lives. And I know it's not my decision, but there are so many things you're needed for here, and that I'll need you for in the future."

Clio pouted a bit but didn't argue. Julian pointed out that it wasn't just the women who were staying, and she seemed to perk up a bit.

Soon after, the pod was modified, and the group took off. With the ship's speed, the flight was pretty short, and before long, they could see Toronto below. It had always been a cool city with lots of culture.

As they flew in, the city lights came into view and steam blew everywhere in the cold. There were pitch-black pockets of the city, with no lights at all. Sean was in contact with his friend, and he directed them to land in a remote park the authorities rarely patrolled. As the hydrogen ship landed, a slightly overweight man approached, his parka bubbled around him.

"Hey, I'm Brian," the man said to Chase, who introduced himself as well.

"Nice ship, Sean. Now use those coordinates I sent earlier to hide it before the government family confiscates it," Brian said.

Brian appeared to be in quite the hurry. "Don't waste any time, just come with me." He looked over his shoulder. In a land pod that looked like a bullet, Brian transported everyone through a series of underground tunnels to his place.

"I think we're safe now," Brian said as they entered his home. He took a deep breath. "Sean, it's so good to see you, and nice to meet you, Chase. Didn't get a chance to shake your hand earlier," Brian said, holding his arm out to Chase, who immediately shook his hand. Brian's skin was cold, Chase noticed, despite having been wrapped up in warm gear. As they all walked down the steps, a large roar came from a room to the left. It sounded as if they were on their way into some sort of arena or stadium.

"Wow, sounds like fun," Sean said. "What's all that noise about?"

"See for yourself," Brian said as he swung open the door.

When they walked in, a big party was going on…a hockey party. All four walls in the room displayed live coverage of the Toronto Maple Leafs' hockey game. With virtual censors beaming, it seemed as if the guests were in the middle of the hockey rink. The seating area for the party looked like it was in the center of the game itself.

"Sit. Sit down, everyone," Brian said.

Chase and Sean found a couple empty seats off to the side. Sean went to sit and quickly ducked. "Shit, I almost got hit in the head by the puck." He gasped for air.

Chase laughed. "Dude, relax. It's not the real puck."

"I know," said Sean, "but this has to be the coolest VR I've seen in a room this size."

The Canadians were having quite the party, with plenty of beers and drugs to go around. When the hockey game wasn't in play, the sounds of the newest bands were rocking and shaking the walls.

"Brian," Chase said, "is there a place we can talk?"

"Absolutely." Brian looked over at his friend, and the friend tapped his port.

Four smaller glass walls lowered from the ceiling around them as the sound of the game and music died.

Sean looked around as the walls lowered. "I like this, Brian."

"Yeah, we found these super glass fiber optics that are so clear, you can hardly see them. Plus, it's a much better way to watch the game."

"Nice touch," said Sean.

"So, Brian, what's going on up here? How are you Canucks doing, generally speaking?" said Chase.

"You wouldn't know from, well, all this," Brian said, waving his arms to indicate the buoyant crowd. "But, people are dying. It started about eight years ago, when the prime minister was assassinated with about a year to go on his term. The twelfth family made up most of the government and decided to pass a new law that in order to run for prime minister you had to pay a political tax to make sure you were qualified."

"I thought Canada had public financing for elections," said Sean.

"We technically still have it. The public election money is supposed to come from the tax, but no one can afford the tax. At this point, the twelfth family controls the entire country's finances. The family also owns the tar sands, and the entire country buys the oil. What isn't used gets purchased back by the family at a discount for future sales. It's like printing money for the family.

"It got worse a couple years ago when Emma Roy came on the scene and everyone was behind her to run for prime minister. Sean, you would have liked her; she was smart and progressive. Emma had some good ideas for the people, and it was so cool because the everyday person got behind her, and people from all over the country contributed what they could afford, even if it was a dollar. When the family controlling the government realized that Emma may actually be able to pay the tax and run, they quickly raised the tax. She never raised enough money to run, and the war against the citizens increased.

"Lately, the family decided to pass the Energy First bill, which basically increases spending on the tar fields and completely cuts public financing for anyone running for any office. That bill basically took away our right to vote, and the family became our government.

"We have the Luke, which is like your American draw. It's a very minimal amount of money the government pays the people to live, since there's little work. About six months ago, they passed another bill to lower the Luke and increase oil spending."

Brian looked around the room. "People struggled to make ends meet on the old Luke, but the new one has caused more stealing, violence, and addiction. I mean, if you don't have enough money to live and your family might die, you resort to all kinds of horrible things.

"That was the summer and of course it gets cold in the winter. They don't call us the Great White North for nothing. The shit hit the fan about two weeks ago, when they passed a new bill to increase heating costs because they say the tar fields need more revenue for safety upgrades. There's not enough money in the Luke for people to pay the increased costs, even if they wanted to. I think they're using the collective to determine how much they can take from the people before they kill them—death by poverty. They think the people are just a burden; an inconvenience."

Brian looked directly at Chase. "Now the choice for the citizens of our country is: Do you want to starve or freeze to death?"

Chase sighed. "Look, I personally know Francisco. Let me think about this a little bit."

Brian gasped. "You know Francisco? Literally the head of the twelfth family?"

"I do." The screens on Chase's eyes scrolled as he scanned the collective for heating or warming solutions for the people.

Chase tapped the port on his forearm. "Julian."

"I'm here," Julian replied.

"I'm sure this isn't the case, but can you check if the Canadian tar fields are running low on supply or if there are any safety violations with the world energy council?"

"Okay, one second," Julian said. But it was probably less than a second before he answered. "Here you go…no safety issues, and there's a supply which will last for seven-hundred-sixty-five years."

"OK, thanks," Chase said. He disconnected from Julian and turned to Brian.

"Brian, can you please show me an area of the city where people are going without heat?"

Brian frowned, but nodded. "We won't have to go far. Come on."

As the clear walls rose up, Chase heard the roar of the game again. As he walked out of the room with Brian, the two were confronted with many subterranean entrances and exits. Brian had impressively mastered the tunnel system and had secret doors set up in the underground, and they didn't surface until they reached their destination. They walked up the street, on which heavy snow and ice made even the maglev pods move slowly. A pod went by them, packed from top to bottom with people.

Chase said to Brian, "I can't believe how many people you guys put in a pod. It looks like they're stacked on top of each other."

"They are, Chase. There are some families who rotate and share seats with each other to ride the pod because it has a little heat, and with the body heat of the people, they can survive the nighttime cold. They refuse to get out when they reach their final destination, and eventually the door shuts, and they start over. There is talk the twelfth family might find a way to shut that down, which would not be good for these people. They're only trying to survive."

Chase didn't say anything as they walked another two blocks. They turned a corner, and Chase spotted a mass of metal across the street.

"We're almost there, Chase."

Chase looked back at the object. "What is that?" he asked Brian.

"Looks like a broken-down pod." Brian kept walking, but Chase gripped his shoulder.

"I think we should check it out, don't you?" Chase said.

"Yeah, you're right. Okay, let's see what's going on with it," Brian agreed. Chase appreciated Brian's patience. Both of them spoke through chattering teeth, their bodies shivering.

The two ran across the street. When they reached the other side, they saw that the pod's door was stuck open and the vehicle had no power. Chase saw that the first two people closest to the open door were very pale, and likely unconscious.

"What happened? Did you crash?" Chase asked a woman farther into the pod who seemed cognizant of her surroundings, at least.

"No, when the door opened for the destination, it never closed, and eventually the power shut down," she said, shivering. "A group of us huddled together, but I don't know if the people on the outside got enough heat. They…they blocked the wind for us." The other occupants of the pod shook, and ice had formed everywhere.

"Please help us," another person said.

Chase, on an instinct he didn't know he had, reached his port over the pod's motherboard and scanned the collective for maglev pod power. At first the pod's lights flickered, and immediately the power and heat turned on. Tears came from the passengers' eyes as they shook from the cold. Everyone who could speak thanked him.

A voice sounded. "Welcome to your destination. Please exit. The door will close in exactly one minute."

Chase exited the pod and joined Brian, who was watching from outside.

"How did you do that?"

Chase didn't know the answer. Instead, he said, "Can you please take me to one of the families you were talking about?"

Brian lowered his eyebrows and looked around a bit. "Okay, we're pretty close. I know one maybe another block from here." They kept walking while the Toronto pods with their foggy windows buzzed by.

"Here it is, eleven-eleven Swan," Brian announced, stopping in front of a small, one-storey home. Chase noted the house's peeling paint, frosted windows and detached gutters, which were pushed by the wind into producing a rhythmic, metallic creaking sound. The two walked up the steps from the street. By this time, they were covered in snow, and no one had shoveled the steps. Chase took a step and almost fell as he grabbed the railing. Brian grabbed the other railing, made his way up through the snow and knocked on the door. There was no answer.

"I know this is the right address." Brian banged on the door harder. A few freezing minutes went by, as they waited for an answer. Finally, much to Chase's surprise, Brian pulled a screwdriver from his coat pocket and pried open the door with it.

"Brian, isn't this breaking and entering? Should we be doing this?" Chase asked.

Brian shrugged. "You live in sub-zero temperatures like we do, and people don't always answer their doors right away. If waiting for forever, risking hypothermia or going to jail are our options—a lot of us will risk jail. Come on, let's go."

As they walked inside, the temperature was almost the same as it was outside, but Chase was grateful there was no wind, and that at least they had shelter from the snow. It was dark, and it appeared as though no one was home.

"Hello? It's me, Brian."

When Brian received no reply, they cautiously walked into the empty kitchen. To their right, in the family room, were two people huddled together in a corner, trying to stay warm. Chase and Brian approached them, and Brian tapped a man on his shoulder.

"William? William, it's me, Brian. Get up."

The man was shaking, and he moved very slowly, turning his head. He said in a low, shaky voice, "I'm not sure if I can."

Brian and Chase grabbed his arms and helped lift him.

"I'm so cold." William's face was pale, and icicles had formed in his gray beard. "I think he's dying," the man sputtered through chattering teeth, his breathing irregular.

"Who's dying?" Brian asked.

William pointed down to a woman, who was curled into a ball. She was pretty stiff, so Chase took her by the legs and Brian held her by her shoulders, and they tried to lift her. William was too weak to help. They didn't want to hurt her, but they finally lifted her up.

Underneath, to Chase's surprise, was a young boy about seven years old. Chase found it odd to see a child in person; how small and helpless they were, especially this boy who was shivering. "He's a child," Chase said, unable to hide his shock.

"He is. This little boy was born completely in the underground since new births are illegal here as well. In Canada, the offense is punishable by death."

The boy was wrapped in a blanket, his face blue, and his eyes closed. After a few minutes, his mom stood up, shivering just as much as her husband and son. She said to Brian, "You have to get him warm. We need heat, Brian." Her cold hands grabbed Chase by the arm, then she gripped Brian. "We're dying."

"I know, I know, and I'm doing everything I can," Brian replied, but Chase caught him staring mournfully at the kid. That child was probably the last one on Earth, and he would likely be dead within the hour.

William yelled, "What are you doing to help us? We will die like frozen animals left in the cold."

While everyone else was frantic, Chase was calm as his eye scans found a possible match. He spoke over the hysteria. "There's a new technology from the collective in China that can raise the body temperature of animals by five degrees. They've already begun testing on humans, and it's going well. Without heat, it may be enough to save you two and your child. It will give us time to figure this all out."

"Figure what out?" the mom yelled. "You don't understand; we don't have time to figure things out. We are dying now. My baby is dying!" She slapped Chase. "My boy is dying!" She screamed, "Look at him! Look at him. He is dying!"

Brian grabbed the woman's arm, then he turned to Chase. "No, I don't think that's a good idea. Listen to me; the collective is bad. You can't trust anything the collective says. I know for a fact the family up here uses the collective and its programs to hurt and trick people."

Chase remained calm. "The collective is what you make of it, good or bad. Trust me." He looked at the mom. "Believe me, I want to help you. You're freezing to death, and it's only going to get colder."

The mom stopped trying to hit him and began to cry as William held her. "Hey," he said, "we'll get through this."

Then Brian spoke. "Chase, I just want you to understand that up here, the collective has been used to kill a lot of people."

"I understand what you're talking about, Brian."

"It doesn't matter anyway," Brian said. "We're wasting time. We need to get them warm now."

Chase sighed. He didn't want to feel as helpless as he did at that moment. "Look, even if I find a way to generate heat in here, it will only be temporarily warm, since you can't afford to pay the rate. So as soon as it gets colder, you'll be in the same predicament. I may not be able to solve your heating issue, but I'm doing my best to try to save your boy. He's almost at the end of his life. His body temperature needs to be raised, and this is the only program worldwide. I can try what I found on the collective, but it's in a trial phase and hasn't been tested very long on humans. Like I said, it looks promising, but on the other hand, it could hurt or even kill you and your boy."

Brian glanced at Chase. "I'm telling you, it's a trick to kill more people."

Chase turned his attention back to the mom. "I want to save your boy, I really do, but I don't want to try this on him if it will hurt him. It's your decision."

The mom cried out, "What choice do we have? He's dying right in front of us. Look at him. He's blue."

William turned to Chase. "Do it on me first. We'll see if it works."

"William, didn't you hear him? He said it can kill you. I mean, raising your body temperature through a program; that's not even possible," Brian said.

"What's our alternative, to just let our boy die?" He looked at Chase. "Do it."

Chase stood next to him. "Give me your forearm so our ports are touching." William did, and Chase pulled up the procedure on his eye scan. He downloaded the program into William's port.

"Something is happening," said William. Chase observed William as his flesh grew clammy and he started sweating profusely. He grabbed his chest and fell to his knees.

"I think he's dying," said Brian.

Chase shook his head, but his heart sped up. "No, I can see his vitals on my screen. Wait a second. William, do you have a heart condition? Your profile says you were due for a heart replacement six years ago. Did you do it?"

William whispered, "I didn't have the money to do that. I'm having pains in my chest. I can't take a deep breath." He held his right hand over his heart. His wife took his other hand and told him she loved him.

Brian yelled out, "He's dying. Try to stop it. I told you, the collective is killing him!"

Chase was nearly panicking. His voice shook. "I'm trying to slow the program so he doesn't get shocked to death when it turns off."

William's body shook violently for a few seconds, then it stopped as he gasped his last breath. His wife cried out "No! No!"

Brian yelled at Chase, and Chase remained silent, holding his head. He still thought the program would work on the boy, but he didn't dare say so. He felt responsible for William's death. Chase held back tears as Brian continued to scream at him. Chase tried to apologize to the woman and her child for not having the foresight to ask about William's medical conditions. The words wouldn't come out. All he could mutter were broken "sorries".

The mom interrupted after a moment. "Look how blue he is, and he's barely breathing. I can't lose him, too!"

Brian shook his head. "I'm so sorry. I don't know what to do. I'm so sorry."

Chase reluctantly spoke up. "The program didn't work because your husband had a defective heart, but your son doesn't. He's freezing to death, no heart conditions. I've scanned him. I should have scanned William…but…if we don't do this, he will be dead in less than ten minutes."

"Oh my God." She put her hands over her face. "What do I do?"

Chase grabbed her hand. "You have to do it to try to save him."

She nodded and kept her hands over her face.

Chase picked up the boy, who was wrapped in blankets. The boy's lip quivered.

"He's still alive," Brian said. He placed the child's forearm on Chase's chip and read all the information on his eye screen. "Who put this chip in? It's all wrong," Chase observed, reading the information onscreen.

"He was born without government technology or a hospital," said Brian. "We had no choice; they would have killed him. He was the first child born in Canada in thirty years. We didn't know it was that way here, too. We'd just moved from London. We had a doctor modify a deceased person's chip and implant it in him. We thought it would work. She's a top doctor here and she risked her life to help us."

Chase held the boy's arm tightly to try for maximum connection.

"I'm trying to repair some of the entry points and functions to allow for the technology, but there are lots of miscalculations on the circuits in the boy's chip. He's barely alive. Wrap him in all the blankets you have again but keep his arm out."

Chase took a deep breath and went blindly into the procedure for a second time.

Chapter Seven

Chase tapped his port. "Julian."

"Yes?"

"Can you connect?"

"I'm connected. Chase, what are you scanning? The data I'm getting is all jumbled."

"It's a child who was born illegally up here. A doctor tried to make her own chip for the child, but…he's dying." Julian was silent for a moment.

"Hmmm, give me a second. I'm looking at it now and trying to figure it out. Okay, I can see that the B-Thirty-Four connection to the nervous system was connected backward," said Julian.

"Right, looks like you can repair or download a temporary repair quickly because he is dying from hypothermia right now."

"I'll try. Chase, what have you done for the boy thus far?"

Chase scrambled to recall. His mind was a jumbled mess. "I…I…found a new technology on the collective that raises body heat, and I just tried it on his dad, but unfortunately he…died. But I think it was because he had a heart condition. I'm trying to use the same technology on the child, but I didn't know his chip was messed up."

"Got it," said Julian. "Let me send you a new nervous system program. Hold on a second while I pull it up."

The boy shook more vigorously. The mom yelled to Brian, "Look at him! What's happening?"

"Julian, move quickly. The boy is shaking. Is that from the download?" Chase asked, his words running together so that even he could barely understand them.

"Hold on, let me check. It's a big program," Julian said, obviously able to understand. "Wait, I keep getting an error message. Who is John McEwen?"

Chase shook his head, trying to think through the panic. "I think that's the chip from the guy who died, the…the one they used." Chase looked at Brian for confirmation. Brian nodded, and Chase asked Julian, "Is that why he's dying?"

"No, it's the hypothermia. It's killing him, and his resistance is nearly non-functional. It doesn't look good, buddy," Julian replied.

Chase's heart sank upon seeing the display on his screen. "My main screen says he only has a minute or two left."

"Chase, repeat it. Did you just say a minute or two and he dies?"

The mom screamed, "Oh my God, do something! Do something!"

"Julian, work quicker. We can't let him die." The boy's chin was blue, and the discoloration had spread up to his nose.

The mom cried out, "Please do something." She grabbed Chase's other arm and almost knocked him over.

"Chase, it's not working. I'm sorry," said Julian.

The mom again yelled, now only indistinguishable screams of grief and fear. The boy's forehead turned blue, and his breathing became shallow, almost nonexistent.

Chase stood for a moment, speechless. He let the mother's fingernails dig into his arm, barely registering the pain.

The little boy's body went limp.

Chase picked up the boy, who was pale blue, as the mom cried out, "My baby! Oh God, he's dead. My baby's dead."

Chase pulled up a program in his eye screen and placed one of his hands on each side of the boy's head.

The mom barely responded as she rocked with the child in her arms.

Chase held the boy, and the program flowed through Chase into the boy's body. He continued to hold the boy by his head as his tiny legs kicked in the air. The blueness slowly faded, and the boy opened his eyes.

"Oh my God, it's a miracle," the mom cried out, the tears of her grief mixing with those of her sudden joy. "He's breathing!"

They wrapped the child up again with blankets, turning him away from the corpse of his father. Chase assumed she didn't want that to be the first thing the boy saw. "I'm warm now," the boy said.

As the mom and Brian celebrated, Chase asked, "What's his name?"

"William Jr., but his nickname is Nine."

"Nine?"

"Yes. He almost died in childbirth and again when the chip was implanted, so we call him Nine—like he has nine lives."

Chase chuckled. Thrilled but still shaken, he tried to hide his trembling limbs. "Excellent name for him." Chase spoke his next words in a whisper, hoping that Nine would not overhear. "I'm so sorry your husband didn't make it, but I want you to know that, although he had a heart issue, that information allowed the program to modify and correct itself so that it could work on your son."

The boy's mom hugged Chase and asked him, "How can we ever pay you for this?"

Chase hugged her back without saying anything, and he and Brian walked out the door, gripping the railing as they went down the stairs.

They didn't walk far before Brian turned to Chase. "Man, I'm really sorry. I kind of lost it in there. It was just so crazy, and I thought we were going to lose what may be our last Canadian child ever."

"Don't worry about it, Brian. These are your people, I get it. I'm just glad we were able to save the boy and his mom."

The wind picked up as they walked, and Brian said, "I think I might know a shortcut—that is, if the door still works in this cold. It will get us underground where it's warmer." He paused for a moment. "So, how did you download that program when his chip was messed up? And how did you transfer the information by just putting your hands on his head?"

Chase raised his eyebrows and answered honestly. "Not really sure. I'm just happy it worked."

As they walked down the street, the wind became more intense, and snow was piling up. They went two blocks, then Brian turned around. "Sorry, I think it's the other way."

"Is the GPS in your chip not working right?"

"No, it's not that," he said. "This address won't come up on any GPS. Plus, it's a camouflaged door next to a storefront window, but with the snow, they all look the same. Did you see an old building with a storefront that said Gilhooley's Meats?"

"Yeah," Chase said, "we passed it on the last block." They turned around and went back as a big public pod flew by and kicked up more snow.

"The snow is picking up even more. Is this lake-effect snow?"

"No, it's just snow." They both laughed.

Up ahead, they saw the storefront they were looking for. Brian approached first.

"It uses an old-fashioned fingerprint scan." Brian scanned the lock, and the two went inside, out of the snow and cold. They walked down the stairs into the abandoned subway tunnel. It was damp and cold but warmer than ground level. Brian went first, and slowed down before he got to the next corner. He raised his index finger at Chase to signal for him to wait.

"What's wrong?" Chase asked.

"Nothing," Brian said. "Everything is fine, I just want to respect their home." As they turned the corner, there were about fifty people lined up on the old subway platform.

"Walk quietly," Brian said in a low voice, "a lot of them are sleeping. These are the fortunate ones because they have warmth and don't have to worry about heating costs. On the other hand, they have to search for food. I wish there was more room, but we're restricted by the size of the subway when it was built years and years ago."

"How did these people get these spots?" Chase asked.

Brian smiled. "I run an underground lottery that the family government doesn't know about. It's free. We can fit fifty people on this platform at Seventh and Church, and I pick fifty numbers every week. Some people trade for other things they need or barter in order to have other family members come with them for the week. Once a number is picked, they work out the details. It goes pretty smoothly for the most part."

As they walked back into Brian's place, he immediately bragged to everyone. "Hey guys, guess what? You should have seen it; Chase saved a bunch of people in a pod. That was amazing, but then he saved a kid's life, right, Chase?"

Chase didn't say anything at first.

As if Brian could tell Chase didn't really want to talk about it, he said, "Okay, let's sit down and make a plan."

As they watched a replay of the last game, the group seemed optimistic with the news of the help Chase had provided. The volume from the hockey game was low, and the music was loud and jamming. The crew was drinking and having a good time when one guy—who they called "the goof"—got everyone's attention by standing on his head and playing a virtual-reality video game on the ceiling. He made it to the top level then stood up, and everyone cheered.

He said, "I have a surprise for everyone. I went in the time vault and found a song from an old-school band from more than a hundred years ago. Rush, 'Tom Sawyer.' This song's kicks ass even after all these years."

They turned the volume up to ten, and everyone started jumping up and down. Sean said to Chase and Brian, "They sure are having fun!"

"What?"

Yelling at the top of his lungs, Sean replied, "I said they are sure having fun."

Brian nodded, then his face turned more serious as he looked down a bit. "We've all been so beaten down by the twelfth, and as time goes on, you just get tired of fighting. In the beginning when they would screw us, we would fight back out of principle. Now it's really more about surviving. I never thought I would see things come to this. Chase, do you think you can raise everyone's body temperature and get us through the winter?"

Chase had to think for a moment. It only worked as a desperate attempt one time, with one person. A small person, at that. "I don't know how that would be feasible. I mean, how many people live in Toronto right now?"

"Around seventy million."

"How am I going to meet with that many people? I don't know if that technology will even work for everyone. That one man died today, so it's really only worked half the time so far. Let me think about it. I'm going to check on Maggie."

Chase found a semi-quiet area where he talked to Maggie and Julian for about an hour. When he was done, Chase returned to the group and they all sat down to watch the final period of the hockey game.

"Brian, thank you for inviting Sean and me," Chase said when the game was over. "He was right; you're doing a good thing here. We're going to leave in the morning."

Brain shuffled around so he stood in front of Chase. "Wait, Chase, where are you going? Why are you leaving so soon? There are so many things I want to show you."

Chase put his head down and ran a hand through his hair. "Well, I thought about it, and the only way to help this number of people is to talk to the family directly. I'll talk to Francisco and try to work something out."

Wide-eyed, Brain placed a hand on Chase's shoulder. "Chase, are you crazy? Francisco doesn't meet with just anyone. He doesn't give a shit what you or anybody else thinks." Brian looked around and leaned in closer. "In fact, it's very possible he won't like you. And people he doesn't like…they end up missing."

Chase smiled a weary, exhausted smile, but he tried to maintain an optimistic outlook. "Well, we'll have to see what happens. He's in Brazil right now, so nothing can be done tonight. I'll leave for Brazil tomorrow." He turned to Sean. "You go back and take care of Kay and keep an eye on Maggie for me while I'm gone, okay?"

Brian gripped Chase's shoulder and spun him so that the two were facing each other again. "Chase, you're making a big mistake. Your plan might not work, and there are people tonight, right now, who might die from the cold! We should be out there raising the temperature of as many families as we can, just like you did today. If you could stay for a month or two, I know it would make a difference."

Sean looked at Brian and placed his hand on his shoulder. "Hang in there. I trust Chase. He's looking at the big picture—looking out for your best interests. With this plan, he could save millions of your people."

Chase noticed Brian's pale cheeks grow red. "No, Sean, you fuckin' hang in there. I have people all around this city, lots of people, and families who depend on me, and I'm their only hope. I'm letting them down!"

Sean remained calm. Chase noticed his sympathetic expression as he spoke to Brian. "You're not letting them down. You're doing all you can, but some things are out of your control."

"Okay," Chase said, "I'm going to leave now. Brian, I promise I'll do everything I can for you and your people." Brian stood, arms crossed and momentarily silent. Chase shifted his attention to Sean. "Sean, get everyone ready to leave in the morning."

"Where are you going?" Sean asked.

"I'm going to walk back to the platform and stay there tonight."

"That's another bad idea," said Brian. "Look, they don't have the security and safety checks that we have here."

"I know. I appreciate you looking out for me, but I'll be fine. Thank you again." And out the door he walked.

Chase approached the platform after a moment. He entered quietly, and there was one spot left next to a frail, older woman who looked about sixty-five, but could easily have been twenty years younger than that after suffering from exposure to the elements or a tough life. She was skinny and weak, her eyes were sunken, and the lines on her face were deep. She was lying on the concrete with a blanket covering her meager frame.

She looked up at him. "You know, you're lucky no one ever came for this spot."

"I guess I am. My name is Chase. Can I sit next to you, then?"

The woman jumped a bit, as though she were startled and placed a hand over her heart. Her eyes glistened, but she smiled a large toothless grin. "You sure can, honey." She scooted forward and smoothed her hair. "Cuddle right up in here, young man. It's warmer that way, you know?"

"I know it is," said Chase. "I like your blue dress. Does it keep you warm?"

"It does with my long underwear underneath." She pulled her dress up a little to show him. "I got them from my Lindsey. You know she is a wonderful niece; she won the lottery and gave this spot to me. Want to hear about my younger years as a go-go dancer?"

"Tell me about it," Chase said and spent the rest of the night talking to the woman until the last lottery winner fell asleep at Seventh and Church.

Chapter Eight

Chase and Sean left the next morning after saying a quick good-bye. Brian was visibly upset, and Chase apologized once again, but tried to assure him that he would do what he could to help.

"Come on, gentlemen," one of the crew said, indicating Chase and Sean. "We have to go now. Another storm is blowing in."

They took off in the ship and headed back to the warehouse. When they landed, Maggie and Kay were waiting. Kay grabbed Sean's hand, and they left to take a walk together.

Maggie ran into Chase's arms, hugging and kissing him. "I missed you, and I have some good news."

"I missed you too. What's this good news?" Chase asked as they walked into the warehouse and entered their room.

Maggie turned to Chase and clasped her hands together. With a wide smile and a flip of her black hair, she said, "I got a new job!"

Chase was stunned. "No kidding? How did you do that?"

"You know me; I'm always looking."

"Where, Mag?" he said, too excited to wait for the entire story.

"At the zoological society."

"Wow, I thought everything there was automated and only a few AI droids worked in management."

"That's true, but they were having a problem with the AI moving the animals from cage to cage and section to section in the facility, and they weren't sure why. Turns out, the animals sense a certain smell from the AI and won't listen to them. I guess a rhino smashed eight or ten AIs up and stacked them in a pile. They've tried all sorts of AI variations, but the animals boycott. It's a mess. So they posted the job for two people. Twelve thousand applications, and I got one of the jobs!"

Chase pulled Maggie to him and gripped her tightly. "Maggie, that's awesome. I'm so proud of you. I'll get a job, too…after I fix everything," he said, cringing at how insane his own words sounded, but Maggie didn't flinch at them. She only nodded against his shoulder, then pulled away and looked at him, a hint of sadness, or anger—or maybe a mixture of the two—in her brown eyes. "Chase, you should see this place. Seventy percent of all the animals—like that rhino, giraffes, elephants—are extinct. This zoo has the last of them. I love it," she said with a smile. She sighed, and her eyes widened. She playfully shoved Chase. "How was Canada? Tell me all about it."

"The people are suffering there just like everywhere else. It's a mess."

Maggie's happy expression faded into one of concern. "Really?"

"Yeah, the family government there is practically freezing the people to death in order to squeeze every penny out of them."

"That's terrible," said Maggie. Her eyes misted when Chase told her he had to go on another trip to try to help the Canadians. "Chase, no. You just got home. Don't turn around and leave again. Please?"

Chase sighed. "I know, but I'm not leaving again until the morning."

"Well, in that case," Maggie said through tears and a few slight sniffles, "we have the rest of tonight to get some other business done."

"Oh really? What kind of business do you have in mind, Mag?"

She said nothing as she got up and shut their bedroom door.

The next morning, word had gotten around that Chase was back at the warehouse and that he had saved the life of a child in Canada. Families from all over began gathering at three o'clock in the morning to see if Chase could help a loved one. As Chase sat at the kitchen table, the room filled with friends and family wanting to hang out with him.

Clio said to Chase, "That must be irritating for you. It sure is for me."

"No, it's fine," he said. In fact, he was dumbfounded by it. He couldn't fathom what was going on. He'd only saved that boy because it was the right thing to do. He'd only given these people his belongings because they needed them. And maybe also because he thought it was the only way to keep them from potentially killing him. Now, suddenly they all thought he was…what? A magician? It was too much. He tried not to think about it. "They're just desperate and looking to get some help."

Julian sat next to Chase. "I'm sorry I couldn't get that program uploaded for that kid in Canada. The problem was the chip the boy has is from a dead guy, and they connected it wrong. I tried to fix it. I'm sorry, man; I just ran out of time."

"It's okay," said Chase. "It all worked out."

"I know. I just felt bad and didn't want you mad at me."

Chase observed his friend. "Come on, when am I ever mad at you?"

"Okay, cool," Julian said. "Hey, did you hear about Sean's

Kay?"

"No, hear what?"

"She organized the entire neighborhood."

"Organized, how?"

"Well, everyone has questions; everyone wants to see you. So she organized a system where people can put in a request, and she lists them by topic. She wants to surprise you with it later."

As Chase listened, he glanced at the doorway to the kitchen. There was a line of people trying to get a look at the table, and Sean and Kay were the first two in that line. Chase asked them, "Sean, Kay, why are you guys standing there? Come over here."

They both walked in and came over to the table. "We didn't want to interrupt your breakfast."

Chase grimaced, then chuckled. "It's fine; I'm not eating anyway. What's up?"

"Well," Sean said, "thanks for taking me to Canada. I think you made a difference."

"Sure, and hopefully we're really only just getting started. In fact, we're leaving today to find the family. If you're still interested, get your things together, because we're going in a few hours."

Sean's face brightened. "Really? That's great."

Chase could tell Kay wanted to say something. "Kay, what's up?"

"Chase, I wanted to tell you that I organized the people's requests and I tried to categorize them in order of importance—well, really the life-or-death sort of things."

"I appreciate it," Chase said. He tried to project confidence, but he wasn't fully certain he had any healing capabilities.

"One more thing. I want to ask you because Sean is uncomfortable about it. Would you mind if we move to the warehouse neighborhood?"

"Not to the warehouse neighborhood." Chase watched her smile fade away. He gripped her hand loosely. "No, not to the neighborhood. You guys will move into the warehouse with us."

Her smile instantly came back. "But there's no room."

"We'll make room. And one more thing." He stood up from the table and spoke louder. Everyone turned toward him. "I know a lot of you have questions and want to talk to me. Also, there are people in the street wanting to see me, and I'll do my best. But from now on, starting right now, any requests or concerns you have will go through Kay. Kay is in charge of all personal organization and visits."

Kay looked at Chase. "Really?"

"Is that okay with you?"

"Definitely, thank you." Kay turned around as everyone chatted with each other and masterfully lead them all away to form organized lines. "As the people got into their designated lines, Kay asked Chase, "Is that alright?"

"Perfect. I'll come down in an hour or so. Good job, Kay, and while I'm gone, make sure you and Sean get a good spot in the warehouse."

Chase, Maggie, Julian and Clio sat at the table, and Clio said, "There are so many rumors out there about you, Chase. It's crazy. Some people think you're working for the government family and you're going to arrest everybody any day, and other people think you're a god. It's nuts."

A god? That seemed insane to Chase. He shook his head. "Well," Chase said, "I know what everyone in the line will be asking about."

"What?" asked Clio.

"Either they're sick and can't afford the hospital visits or they can't feed themselves because of the low draw."

Julian chimed in, "That's what I wanted to tell you, Chase. I've been working on a program to help people get more of the draw. I may be able to work something out."

"But that's impossible," said Maggie. "The draw only comes from the government, and the family decides how much, since they run the government. People have tried for years to break that code. It's the most secure in the world."

"Well, I'm experimenting with a couple of ideas. I'm not there yet, but I'm getting closer."

The head crew chief, who was working to get the hydrogen ship ready, connected with Chase. "Where are we going, boss?"

"Brazil, my friend."

"Why there?"

Chase said, "That's where the Francisco family lives in the winter months."

As the crew chief went back to his work, one of the other guys glanced out the window and said, "Wow, look at the line on the street."

"Look, I'm late. I have to get going," Chase said. "Could you please go to the back of the line, Kay, and take the last five people. Bring them in. That's all I'm going to see today. Unfortunately, I don't have time to see many." Kay went to the back of the line, and as she took the last five, everyone ran to start a new line behind them. Some people started to push others. Chase watched and listened, worried that things could get hairy.

"It's too late," Kay told everyone else. "You ruined the line, and now he is only going to see these five."

One guy grabbed her by the arm.

Chase stood, ready to intervene, but that turned out to be unnecessary.

"Get your hand off me." She punched him in the face. The man immediately dropped to the ground, and everyone stepped back as Kay brought the five inside.

"Kay what do we have here?" Chase asked with false confidence.

"These three haven't eaten in nine days, and these two have the new virus that makes it feel like something is eating them from the inside."

"Let me see those two first." Chase gestured for the two with the virus to approach him. He scanned their bodies. "The virus is stationed in your feet, on both of you. That is where it usually starts. Sit here and put your leg up so I can hold your right foot. This is going to hurt, but tomorrow you'll start to feel better." Chase took a deep breath, terrified he was some sort of imposter, but he had a feeling that he could help. A small feeling that wouldn't allow him to not at least try.

The man's foot was rotting, and Chase stuck his finger and thumb into it. The man cried out in pain as Chase pulled out a three-inch worm that was hidden from the preliminary scan.

"This is the problem. Where are your shoes?"

"They wore out, so I walk in my socks or bare feet."

"You can't do that," said Chase. "When your body's breaking down due to a virus, like it is, and you have no shoes, you're stepping on micro worms that formed after the world war. Once they get inside of you, it's absolute hell. Kay, could you please get them both a pair of sneakers, and some food and fresh water for the other three." To the woman who stood with no socks or shoes, he said, "Let me see your feet."

Soon after, Chase and his team were on their way to Brazil. The ship blasted off, and the small group talked and told stories on the flight. Logan was in charge of the crew, and when he wasn't serious, he had some good jokes. The temperature began to warm just south of Miami. The winds died down a little, and the ride was pretty smooth. Finally, the flying pod made its decent to Rio, and as it was landing, they looked out the window at a line of military vehicles.

Sean told Logan, "That doesn't look good!"

On the tarmac was a row of military fighters with laser guns and full body gear. The fighters wore red helmets and huge black boots. Once the plane landed, they could see that half the soldiers were human, and the other half were the latest M6 android warriors.

Chase got out first, and his friends looked at each other as if wondering what they had gotten themselves into. Chase didn't have time to soothe their worries.

A smaller, one-man rocket flew by low and landed between the row of soldiers and the five. The door on the rocket opened, and out came Chase's cousin Randal, who they had nicknamed Rad when he was a kid.

"Chase! Cuz, what's up?" Rad yelled.

Chase just smiled, and Rad yelled to everyone, "Move, it's going to blow!" Everyone hid behind something, and there was a loud boom as the small rocket blew up.

"Chase, how about that, my man?" Rad said. "Let's blow some shit up! How have you been?"

Chase gave his cousin a hug. "Rad, these are my guys." Chase introduced Rad to Sean and Logan. Everyone seemed to be in a decent mood and receptive to each other, which eased Chase's nerves a bit. He felt awkward bringing his old world and his new one together, but it was more seamless than he thought; and for that, he was grateful.

"Great. Chase, these are my guys. Watch this." The androids ran down the runway and formed two lines. Then the soldiers started shooting their lasers at each other and quickly blew each other up, until there was nothing except a cloud of smoke.

"Seriously, these are my guys, minus the ones we just blew up. Chase, look at you. You're too skinny. Let's go eat. I just got a new turbo pod with missiles attached right over here. We can take that to my place. Come on, guys."

They all jumped in. The turbo pod was plush, with midair

screens and tons of gadgets.

"Rad, is your dad around? I want to talk with him later."

"No, he's in Africa. Did I tell you we bought South Africa about a year ago?"

"No, I didn't know that," Chase replied.

"Yeah, he made a deal with another family, and we picked up Brazil here as well as South Africa."

"I heard there was a war starting over the Nile Dam," said Chase.

Rad sighed. "Well, when they drew the line for the sale, that bitch from the second family said the dam was on her side, and my dad said, 'Screw you.' So we keep sending drones to blow up part of it. It's awesome! I guess the family council is upset because the families aren't supposed to fight with each other, but they'll get over it."

The turbo pod landed.

"Where are we?" Chase asked.

Rad said, "Everyone, get out, and let's have some fun. This is the casino that I built for my friends and myself. It's the largest casino in South America. I get all the players here, and we make so much money. Do you gamble, Chase?"

Chase swallowed. He didn't gamble. He also didn't have much money with which to gamble. "Sure, a little."

"Great. Well, I told them to give you and your friends as much money as you want, and everything is on the house. Now, Chase, old buddy, don't get alarmed when you hear shots or people screaming. It's the best."

"Really?" asked Chase.

"Yeah, I let the commons in who bitch about the draw and everything you could imagine. I let them play one roulette table that pays pretty good, but for one lucky winner, they could win what equals to about five years of the draw money. Wait until you see it. They line up like zombies. This is the best part. Here's the catch: If they roll the green double zero, we blow their fucking head off! It's great. We have a magnet under the double zero, so if it doesn't hit for a while, the dealer can click a button, and the next roll…boom, blood everywhere. You have to see it. Now, you would think they would stop playing, right? But no, they are so stupid, they just stand there…Next. Place your bet. Joey, tell the dealer to click the double zero so Chase can see how it works."

"No," Chase said with a fake laugh while his stomach churned. "I believe you. I'm going to go over to the craps table with my guys. I love craps."

Chase tried to be friendly, and they played craps for a while. As they played, beautiful women would come over and offer them things to eat and drink or anything else they wanted. His team members were all in relationships, but it was hard for them to resist the girls, as they would rub up against them when offering the drinks. Of course, they were following Rad's orders.

Chase rolled the dice and bet heavy on number eight. He rolled a hard eight, winner again.

He looked at Sean. "There goes Logan. I guess he couldn't resist," he said as two women escorted Logan behind the curtain. The dealer was paying Chase his money for the hard eights, and suddenly he heard a loud boom, a single shot. Everyone looked over. It was the roulette table. Some people cried out in horror as two men were arguing over chips and one guy shot the other. The worst part, as far as Chase could tell, was that most of the people laughed. Everyone turned again as people yelled over the loud music, "Look up at the chandelier."

Chase looked and saw Rad swinging from the chandelier. "Whoa!"

Rad yelled down, "Chase, are we having fun yet?" He jumped down and said, to no one in particular; "Turn up the music, and someone clean all that blood off my new floor."

This went on all night at Casino Rad.

Chapter Nine

By morning, people were passed out all over the casino. The place was covered in money, naked men and women, and blood. Some people even slept soundly in those pools of blood—something that unnerved Chase.

A disheveled Rad approached him. "Chase it's been some night, huh? I'm going to turn in. These androids will show you to your suite."

Not wanting to insult his cousin, Chase said, "It was definitely a night I won't forget."

Rad ran a hand through his mussed hair. His brown eyes were bloodshot and beneath them rested the deep purple circles of drug-induced insomnia. "Good, Chase. Let's walk a little." The androids picked up his bags. "Are you married or in a relationship or something?"

Chase was reluctant to discuss Maggie. He decided he'd only provide as much information as was necessary. "Yes, in a relationship."

Rad stopped walking and slapped a hand on Chase's shoulder. It took everything Chase had not to physically remove that hand. "Chase, seriously? Why on earth would you ever be in a relationship with someone? The world is a candy store for us. So whatcha got? Is it a woman or trans-droid, or can't you tell?"

"Why does that matter?" Chase asked, his agitation surfacing. When Rad crossed his arms and stared at Chase, he gave in. "She's a human woman, and yes, I can tell."

"Look at these women." Rad swung his arms out, indicating the mass of bodies, mostly comatose, on the floor. Sure, some of the women were attractive, but Chase wasn't concerned with them. "You must be straight-up crazy. I don't know where you've been lately or who you've been hanging out with, but I can't help you. I mean, I'll take care of you later, but I've been on a three-day binge with my dad gone, and he'll be back tomorrow. Good night, Chase." And with that, a seemingly annoyed Rad stormed off.

Chase went back to his five-bedroom luxury suite. After being away from such extravagance for so long, it felt strange to be living, even temporarily, in a four-thousand square foot room. Inside there were organic fruits, vegetables, and a large gourmet kitchen. A chef was on call for him whenever he was hungry. Chase didn't feel comfortable. He didn't know that he'd ever ease back into that sort of lifestyle, and that was fine with him. He missed his small, messy room that he shared with so many people. He missed Maggie.

In the afternoon, before going to the pool, Chase had the crew come by for a meeting. When they walked into his room, Chase saw that Logan's hair was a mess, and he had lipstick on his face and neck.

Chase sighed. "Guys, sit down. Sean, you're in charge. Keep an eye on everyone."

Sean scoffed. "I'm trying to, but some people don't listen." He glared at Logan, and Chase followed suit.

"Come on, Logan, we're here on business. I need to talk to Francisco. Remember, we're here trying to help those people in Canada. Come on, straighten up." With his vacant stare and poor posture, Chase didn't feel that Logan was listening. He tried again as he raised his voice. "Logan, I'm not sure you understand, but let me help you out. Rad will blow your head off in two seconds for fun if you look at him the wrong way. Do you understand that this isn't a game?"

Logan sat up straight and ran his palm over his shirt, but the makeup and lipstick were stubborn. He heaved a sigh. "I know, Chase. I'm sorry, but I couldn't resist. The things those women do… it's something I've never experienced, and the new trans-droids are unbelievable"

"Logan, worry about your cumulative life experiences later. I don't want to hear about this. Right now, I need you guys to have my back, understand?"

Sean piped up. "Yes, we understand." He slapped Logan on the back of the head. Logan jerked quickly and ducked, trying to avoid another slap. Sean demanded, "What are you going to do about it, Logan?"

There was silence.

"Yeah, that's what I thought. Maybe I'll have a chat with your wife."

That got Logan's attention.

"What, Logan? Did you say something? What's the matter, Logan? Cat got your tongue? Don't worry, Chase; I'll take care of old Logan here," Sean said, smiling triumphantly at Logan.

Chase clapped his hands. "Let's go to the pool. Rad says he has some new jet skis that fly pretty fast."

But they never saw or heard from Rad. Chase could only assume he was sleeping off his days-long binge. Later that night, after a big dinner, Chase and the crew went back to their suites.

Chase was scanning the collective for the latest on The African Water War, when he heard a knock on the door.

A woman with an Asian accent asked, "Chase, are you in there?" Three more light knocks.

Chase opened the door to find that there were multiple women waiting in the hall. He turned away, took a sharp breath then smiled at them. He didn't order these women. He didn't want them, but he couldn't be rude. He didn't have it in him.

"Chase? Rad asked us to stop by to see how you were doing. Can we come in?" the Asian woman said. Chase couldn't help but notice her perfect skin and hair. She was dark-featured, and her eyes were the color of amber. He knew that whatever was about to happen, he was in for a struggle.

"Sure, come in."

And with that, four beautiful women entered his room. The Asian girl introduced her friends. Each of them was of a different nationality, but they all wore tight dresses. Chase tried to keep his gaze eye-level. He didn't know what to do about the situation, but he would work something out. He figured, worst-case scenario, maybe he could become panicked enough to stop time and flee the room. He'd never wished more for control over his ability than he did at that moment.

"Come in and sit in the living room, girls," he said, indicating the modern chairs and couches that furnished the sparse room.

The Asian girl did not sit. She stood next to Chase and rubbed his arm. She said, "My name is Lucky. I met you briefly in the casino. Rad told me you spent some time in Tokyo."

Chase did not recall having met her the night before. "Yes, I have been to Tokyo. I traveled there a lot with my family."

The woman appeared to be pleased by this information, but Chase couldn't tell if it was genuine or not. He scooted away and sat on the couch so that he wasn't touching her anymore. She followed. "Are you having fun at the resort? There should be a lot to do," she said as she persisted rubbing his arm. She moved her other hand to his leg.

The other three women sat on the couch across from Chase, and when the black woman moved to reach for a pillow, he could see that she had no panties on. She looked at Chase and the other girls before asking him, "Do you want me to take my clothes off now?"

Chase sat for a moment, shaking his head. His mind raced, and so did his heart. When he thought of what something like that would do to Maggie, he felt a pain in his chest. Finally, he said, "Ladies, I app reciate you coming up here, and you are all very beautiful, but I'm not interested." Lucky took her hand off Chase's leg.

"Are you not attracted to us? We can send for other women. Or men. What are you interested in?"

Chase laughed. "No, I have a girlfriend back home, and I'm not that kind of person." Then Chase sat in silence, hoping they would take no offense. Smiles appeared on all their faces, but Chase could sense that something was bothering Lucky. Her smile didn't reach her eyes. "What's the matter?" he asked her.

"When Rad finds out that we didn't entertain you, he'll be pissed, and believe me, when he's angry, he gets violent. I've seen him kill people he doesn't like, it's crazy. Others who have known him a lot longer than I have say he gets his mean streak from his father, who is even worse."

Chase's stomach dropped. He didn't want anyone to be hurt

because of him. "Don't worry," he said. "We'll figure this out." He wanted this to be over. "So how did all of you get here?" It was all he could think of to say.

No one answered.

"What about you?" He looked at the pale white woman. She had silver hair cut into a bob and nearly transparent green eyes.

"I'm from South Africa. Francisco liked me, so he took me and all the other pretty women in my town for himself and his friends. My father tried to stop him, so Francisco took a knife and stabbed him in the stomach and let him bleed to death. I watched it." The girl cried as she spoke those last few words.

"I'm sorry to hear that. I didn't mean to get you upset." Chase grabbed and held her hand. "What's your name? Your real name?"

"Abuta," she responded, wiping her tears with the index finger of her free hand.

"Nice to meet you, Abuta." He shifted his gaze to Lucky. "And you? Your name can't really be Lucky."

"Tenshi." She spoke her name as if it were something far away and without meaning. It disturbed Chase. He was still thinking of ways to make sure the girls got through the night unharmed. He'd already planned on lying to Rad, but he doubted the women would be capable of doing the same.

"How does this normally go with Rad and his friends?"

Abuta said, "Normally we would be here all night, doing all kinds of things. When he finds out we went back in a half-hour, he'll know this didn't go like he wanted, and things will get ugly."

"I have an idea," Chase said. "Why don't you just not go back in a half-hour?"

"What do you mean?" Tenshi asked.

"Is it possible for you to invite all the girls here, but none of Rad's guards or people?"

Tenshi twirled a lock of shiny black hair around her finger. She looked at the other women, each of whom sat leaning forward with their heads inclined. "Sure. He told us to do whatever you wanted us to do."

Chase stood. "OK then, I'll page the chef to make some serious food since you deserve a good meal, and you can go ahead and invite as many girls as you think can fit in the suite. You have the night off, ladies."

"Really?" asked Tenshi.

"Absolutely. It's only Rad's money, right?" Chase asked, trying to suppress a smile.

That night the staff and casino workers got to have their own party, and it was a blowout.

The next day Rad connected to Chase's eye screen.

"Chase, my man, how's it going?" Rad said, a little too loudly.

Chase muted his end for a moment so that his cousin wouldn't hear him groan. "Good, Rad. I was a little tired, but I feel better now. How are you?"

"I'm great, as usual. I heard that you had a pretty wild night."

"That I did," Chase said, relieved that he didn't have to lie to Rad.

"My security guy told me you had sixty-eight of my party girls and guys in your suite. Good for you. I figured it would take you a few days to get into the groove. My dad flew in last night, and I told him you were here. He agreed to meet with your crew on our new yacht. Chase, wait until you see this thing. It's insane. It's five-thousand meters long, and it can lift itself out of the water to park, with hydro jets. We just built a new marina for it. I'll get the details to your crew chief, Sean."

When it was time, Chase assembled the crew, and they walked toward the ocean marina. The water was murky, and the marina was so large, they felt as if they'd walked ten city blocks.

"This must be it," said Logan, pointing at a custom pier that stretched from the boat to the marina. As they approached the pier, they realized the immense size of the yacht.

Sean looked at the other guys and said, "Man, I hope it floats."

As they climbed on, Sean said, "No screw-ups, guys. Don't do anything stupid, especially you, Logan." Logan looked down, shaking his head.

As they stepped on to the yacht, five heavily armed soldiers met them.

"What's this?" Logan said to one soldier.

"We need to scan you as a precaution. Mr. Francisco is on the boat today."

"OK, no problem," Logan said as he looked around. "Where's the arm or eye scanner?"

"We don't use those. We only use the brain scanner. It's the most accurate these days." There were four vertical posts making a square with rods sticking out of them in various positions. The structure glowed and formed a virtual security box that the crew or anyone else would enter. The rods were set up based on the heights of the human race as well as various types of AI, big and small. The rods were glowing, and red and green beams shot across the box in virtually every imaginable angle. It appeared that the box was on fire.

"Stand in the middle and remain still," said one of the soldiers.

"Um, I've never seen one of these before," said Sean. "I'm not standing in that thing."

"Then you're not getting on, boy," said the muscular soldier.

The other soldier said, "If you'd like, I can do a full body scan… from the inside." He laughed.

Sean looked at the soldier and said, "Let me see you stand in there first." With a look of disgust, the soldier stopped laughing and didn't answer.

Logan looked at Chase, and Chase nodded. Logan told the soldiers, "No problem."

One by one, they walked into the box and stood inside. Sean closed his eyes when he entered. Chase went last. When he was scanned, Chase heard one soldier say to the others, "This one is Applegate."

The head soldier approached Chase. "It's nice to meet you, Mr. Applegate. Right this way," he said, leading Chase and the rest of the group toward the yacht.

As they walked on the deck of the yacht, a booming noise above grew louder and louder. Everyone looked for the source of the sound.

"Right this way to the center court of the yacht, Mr. Applegate," a soldier said, apparently ignorant of the sound, as the others followed him. Once they all got into the center court, the sound became noticeably louder. As they spotted the nuclear jet, someone jumped out of it, flares alight all over his body.

Sean pointed. "Check out this guy on fire." And then boom, the jet exploded into a million pieces, falling into the ocean as Sean yelled, "Holy shit, did you see that?"

Of course, the man jumping from the explosion was Rad, yelling, "Whoa!" He landed in center court. Logan, Chase, and Sean ran over to him. Chase was more annoyed than impressed, though he didn't dare show it.

"Rad, you're crazy, man, but that was awesome," said Logan.

"Center court—bull's-eye, bitches! I told you guys, enjoy your life while you can."

"I would say so," Sean said. "I'm not sure if you noticed, but some of that shrapnel almost sliced your head in half. A big piece flew right by your head."

"Rad, that jet must've cost a pretty penny," said Logan. "Is that the new Fresco A-Fourteen fighter jet?"

"Well, it was the A-Fourteen." Rad laughed. "Money is meant to be spent and wasted. Plus, what are going to do with it anyway?" He put his arm around Chase and said, "Cuz, I don't know if you heard, but my dad launched three solar satellites, and we have clearance from the family council to send three more up next month."

Chase wasn't too excited.

"Are you familiar with them, cuz?"

"A little," said Chase.

"Yeah, they're huge solar displays. I think they look like big pool covers connected and put in place by satellites. It's a big moneymaker. You should look into them. They're much closer to the sun, and the energy they generate is awesome. We funnel it down to whatever city and make mad money off the energy. My dad's giving me one for my allowance because he's sick of me spending his money. Go figure. Do you or your family have any solar satellites?"

"No, I don't." Chase wondered how he was going to talk to these guys about how much the average person was suffering when they were so far detached from it themselves.

As Chase looked at the remains of the nuclear jet burning in the water, he heard a commotion behind him. He turned around, and there was Mr. Ronald Francisco. He was a large, overweight man, at least four hundred pounds, with a bald head and a triple chin. At six-foot-three, he was quite a dominating figure.

"Is that my nephew, Chase?" he yelled, his deep voice booming. He was Chase's fourth cousin on his dad's side. "Get over here and give me a hug," Francisco roared.

Chase reluctantly allowed the wobbly arms of his bulbous uncle to nearly suffocate him. "Good to see you, Mr. Francisco."

The man slapped Chase's back and broke their friendly embrace. He stared at Chase, his thick, black eyebrows raised so high his forehead resembled that of a wrinkly dog. "Who are you calling Mr. Francisco? Don't let these asswipe soldiers intimidate you. Call me Ron."

Chase did his best to smile. "Sure, Ron, it's great to see you."

"Good to see you, too, son. So, has my boy been taking care of you while you've been down here? Don't say no, because I'll kick his ass right here in front of everyone." He laughed.

"Yes, Ron, he definitely has."

"You know, Chase, the family council started divvying up countries about five years ago. I now own Canada, Brazil, and I thought I had Africa all wrapped up, but we had to split it with the eleventh family from Russia. They want Africa for the diamonds and mineral money, those greedy bastards." He laughed again. "Don't worry, we won't let them win. They tried to cut off the water, so I'm blowing the entire Nile River Dam up next week. Stick that in your pipe and smoke it." He looked at the soldiers, who were silent but laughed in unison as Francisco's elephantine neck swiveled in their direction.

"Has your dad taken any of that fortune of his from the prisons to buy a county or some US? Isn't that what you guys do in the States? You can only buy a city or state, right?"

Chase shook his head. "I'm really not sure. My dad and I had a falling-out a couple years ago, and we don't talk anymore."

"That's a shame. Your dad's a nice guy. So where do you live now?"

"I'm in the States and kind of here and there. Actually, believe it or not, I've been living among the population."

A look of disgust passed over Ron's features and he tucked his head back so that instead of his normal triple chin, he had endless folds. "Why on God's earth would you want to do that? The population is a group of slackers and losers who bitch and moan about everything. They live off us. You think the draw comes from thin air? Personally, I'd like to crush them like the termites they are. Here's a question for you: Do you know what happens when you get too many termites in your house?"

"No, Ron, what happens?"

"They eat the whole fucking house." He laughed. "What do you think happens?"

Ron continued talking at an impressive speed for a man who could scarcely take twenty steps without panting. Chase wondered if Ron and Rad were on the same sort of uppers. "Chase, Chase, come here. Look at that piece of ass right over there on the upper deck. Is that a work of art or what? Actually, hold that thought. I'll be back in little while," Ron said as he walked toward the yacht's elevator.

"The girls waved at him from the top deck, where they tanned half-naked. Tanning was a luxury only possible due to a chemical wealthy people could add to their shower water. The chemical was expensive and left an invisible film, but it protected against the harmful aspects of the sun, and instead, allowed the wealthy a glowing, bronzed complexion.

Rad told the staff, "Let's get drinks for my friends, and make them strong." Then he told everyone, "My dad got this new boner program uploaded where he can stay hard for three days straight, and today is the third day, so he's on the prowl. It's kind of disgusting and funny at the same time, but then he's sort of out of it for a few days, and I don't have to deal with him." Rad paused and looked at Chase. "By the way, you gotta take it easy with all your goodwill hippie stuff with my dad. He hates that crap. We've hung out since we were kids at the family reunions, and you don't need to worry about anything right now. Just enjoy life. You're sitting outside and not wearing any special clothing. Come on, you're an Applegate.

"Chase, don't live like the common people. I mean, why choose that lifestyle? Honestly, my biggest problem is that I have everything, so I have to keep coming up with things to entertain myself. Do you want me to ask my dad to call your dad?"

"No, that's OK," said Chase. "Look, I live with the common population. You can't believe how they are suffering. It's bad."

Rad placed his hand on his forehead. "There you go again with that crap. They deserve it. They put themselves in that situation and deserve what they get. Go get a job or start a business; do something to help yourself. And, in my opinion, it's disgusting how they live. I heard about a guy in Arizona that ate part of a dead person once."

Chase snapped; he couldn't help it. "Maybe that's because he had nothing to eat."

Rad looked at Chase as though he was crazy. Maybe he was. He didn't care. There were people suffering in so many places.

"Bullshit. My dad's right; I think they're tuning into society's termites. Come on, enough of this crap." And with a big, bright smile, Rad changed the subject. "So, check this out. Did you know I'm starting an entertainment division?" There was a short, uncomfortable pause between them.

"No, I didn't know that. What kind?" asked Chase.

"We're going into arenas and inviting a hundred people who haven't eaten in a few weeks, with a chance to eat a huge feast. Or whatever they've been deprived of, that we'll find out in pre-interviews. I'll have them fight each other, and the winners gets to eat something like a month's worth of food or whatever their greatest wish is. I'm going to have brackets, and as the winners go through eliminations, we introduce props, like swords or a chainsaw, for the next round. The farther they get, the better the props. I want to have some crazy props to really get the crowd into it. I'm thinking maybe a blowtorch or an old-school nail gun to shoot the other people. What do you think? Seriously, what do you think?"

Chase shook his head as his stomach churned. He thought it was horrifying. "I don't know."

"OK, well, my dad thinks we should have a spin-off with naked people and the contestants have to fight each other to get in the main cage, which would have the best girls and guys; but when they do, the most beautiful girls kick everyone's ass. What do you think? I think it's his boner program talking." Chase forced a laugh with Rad. "I don't really like that one, but of course he thinks it's a winner. Which one do you like better?"

Chase shrugged, saying nothing. He looked around, but Sean and Logan were busy examining the yacht and the women. Chase said nothing as Rad continued his manic rant.

"I know the food one will work, and maybe I'll let the crowds decide at the end who wins. There are so many ways to go. Maybe the crowd decides who gets the chainsaw or who gets a shotgun? I'm halfway through the family council, and they're almost on board. When it's approved, we'll start with a ten-city tour. I'm pretty excited, and you can join us if you want." Rad smiled and put a hand on Chase's shoulder.

"You can be a judge in your city.

"Let's go swimming in the jet pool. If you swim to the bottom through the tunnel, it leads to a bar. It's pretty cool." Rad looked around. "Come on, guys, let's party." He ran off with three girls and two guys. Chase didn't know what to think, but he knew his cousin, who was clearly on some sort of speed and had a sadistic streak, would never listen to him. Neither would Ron.

Chase walked to the pool and said to Sean, "This isn't going well for the people in Canada, is it?"

Sean said, "Look, you can only do your best, Chase. Maybe this isn't the time? It looked to me like they were getting irritated with you."

Chase sighed. "You're probably right. I don't know if we'll even see Ron anymore, since he's out screwing everyone on the boat. He did get fatter than I remember."

"Is he close to your dad?" Sean asked.

"They went to Sunday school together before the big drone war. Ron got into energy a long time ago. He was one of the first to build a combination fusion-oil reactor, and when he found out another guy, who wasn't in the Sixteen, had already built one better, he blew it up. They barely contained the explosion. It was almost a worldwide environmental disaster. It fried about five hundred people in the town. My father helped him show some bogus information saying that it was the owner's fault due to faulty design, and Ron and my dad sold the ten thousand credits to have children. Those baby credits got bid up to crazy money. It worked, and after that, Ron was the only one who could build that type of energy plant. He made so much money from the first one that the council let him buy Canada because of the tar fields, which increased his energy monopoly. I guess that's when he got fat and became more of an asshole than I remember, but I can't be sure."

Frustrated and half kidding, Chase said, "I don't know, guys. Is this worth it? Maybe I should just buy cities and go back to having servants and step all over everyone, like these guys."

"Chase, that's not you," Sean said.

"I know." Deflated, Chase told the guys that he was going to connect with Maggie. He walked a few yards from his crew and tapped his wrist. "Hi, Mag, it's me."

She replied immediately. "How's it going down there, Chase?"

"Well, not good. These guys are really in their own world."

"Do you think Francisco will go easier on the people in Canada? Did you tell him they're freezing and dying up there and he needs to do something about it?"

"Honestly, I think there's a chance that if he does anything it will be to intentionally make things worse."

"Worse? How's that even possible?" she asked.

Chase sighed. "You can't even imagine, Mag."

"Wow, ummm OK, Chase. Did you hear what happened in Miami today?"

"No, what?"

"They had a beauty contest for new model openings for guys and girls. Four thousand people signed up, and when it got to the top twenty-five men and women, the authorities arrested them and put them in containers for shipping somewhere."

"What did they arrest them for?"

"They made up some line that the people in the contest owed money on the draw and never paid it back. It's definitely human trafficking, but that's never happened with the help of the authorities."

"That's insane." Chase was angry. He felt impotent in the face of this massive power. He had to talk about something else. Anything else. "How's your new job?" he asked.

"I love it. I feel like I can look into the animals' eyes and understand what they're thinking."

That made Chase smile. He remembered the farm he had as a kid and playing with the animals. He missed having animals around and he was a bit jealous. "What are they thinking, Mag?"

"They're thinking, Is it good or bad that I'm locked up?"

"What do you tell them?"

"I tell them that right now it's better to be locked up." They laughed, talked a little more and disconnected.

"Logan," Chase said, "summon the pod to fire up, and just have it fly out here and hover over the water next to the boat for a while. I think it's time to leave soon."

A few soldiers stood around the pool where Chase's team sat. Sean asked one big guy with no neck, "How many people are on the yacht right now?"

The soldier replied, "There are one hundred and ten people on board right now."

"Really? It doesn't look like that many. It looks empty."

"That's because the ship is so large, but there are people all over the boat."

The team swam for a little while, and the bar had everything they wanted. The four sat in their chairs after getting out of the pool, and customized dryers in the chairs blew for twenty seconds to dry them off.

"Chase!" a deep voice sounded. "There you are. I didn't know if you left yet." Ron and eight of his soldiers came over to Chase and the crew. For the first time, Ron Francisco sat next to him, and they had a little privacy. "Chase, Rad told me that you might want me to call Sam and patch things up a little between you both. Is that true?"

Chase suppressed a bitter laugh. "No, Ron, that's okay. I don't know if I'm cut out for all of this anymore."

"All of what?" Francisco replied.

"You know…this. I've been out of the Promised Land since my dad threw me out, and now I live like everyone else. When I see almost all the people and their families in pain, it's tough for me to ignore that." Chase began to sweat a little and saw his blood pressure elevate on his eye screen, but he knew this might be his only chance to talk to Ron.

He went on. "I was in Toronto the other day, and people are dying up there from the cold."

Francisco's face changed immediately, and his eyebrows rose. "Why were you in Toronto?"

"A friend of mine told me some of his friends needed help." Chase glanced down and saw that the zipper on Francisco's fly was down and wet. He kept talking. "They're in tough shape, literally freezing to death."

"Chase, how many times have you been told you to stay out of other people's business, especially mine? You don't know the people up there anyway. They get what they need and what they deserve."

"Ron, they can't pay the energy rates anymore, and—"

Francisco cut him off. "Are you retarded or something kid? Because you're not listening." Everyone turned and looked at Mr. Francisco as he raised his voice.

"You know, your old man is probably right; you're really an outcast. It's amazing you're a descendant of one of the Sixteen. Is that why you came down here, to ask me to lower the rates in my fucking country? I'll tell you what, you get your own country, then you can control the rates, you little bastard." He raised his voice even more and got the attention of the guards.

Chase didn't care anymore. He wasn't afraid of Francisco. "Look, Ron, all I'm saying is I know you want to make a lot of money off the people, but at a certain point, they can't pay what they don't have, and they'll die."

Francisco yelled, "I don't give a shit, and I just told you to drop it, or I promise you, you won't make it off this boat." The soldiers moved closer.

Chase couldn't help but look again at Francisco's underwear and the buttons all undone, and Francisco noticed.

"What are you looking at, you son of a bitch? Go ahead, Chase, say one more thing about Toronto, and I'm going to have my friend Ned here blow your fucking head clear off with his laser gun." Ned moved next to Francisco. He stared at Chase.

Chase stared back at him, closed his eyes and then reopened them. Francisco peered at him as Ned raised his gun and pointed it at Chase's head.

"Go ahead, say one fucking thing about Toronto. Go ahead." Ned firmed up his scope between Chase's eyes.

The boat was silent. Someone turned the music off, and everyone stared at the commotion by the pool.

"Okay," Francisco said, "now I'm going back to my business." He turned to one of his other soldiers. "Get me something or someone."

The soldier whistled, and to his right, another soldier brought out a girl. To Chase's surprise, it was Abuta from his party. Her face was expressionless, except there were tears in her eyes. Francisco was the one who had killed her father. Chase's lips curled in disgust as he itched the side of his neck.

He looked at Francisco. "You know, Ron, your fly has been undone since you walked over here."

"What's that supposed to mean?" he replied. Ned adjusted the sight on his gun again.

Chase glanced over at Abuta again and got madder. He pulled up Francisco's sex program in his eye screen, and it scrolled until it found a match.

"Nothing, Ron, I just wanted to let you know in case you were concerned about how you look in front of everyone and that your floppy dong is hanging out, right there, in full view of whoever wants an eyeful, which I can assure you is no one. Looks like that program isn't working too well, huh? It's like a deflated balloon animal, to be honest."

"Are you crazy or something, kid?" Ned looked at Francisco, waiting for a signal to shoot.

Chase had the program up in his eye as he looked at the port in Ron Francisco's arm. Chase sent a digital virus to block the program.

Francisco stumbled a bit, and bent over, clutching at his abdomen and groin. After a few minutes of groaning in pain, Francisco pointed his bloated index finger at Chase. "It's him," he said. "He's doing something to me. Guards, grab him and put him by the edge, and, Ned when he gets there, blow his fucking head off. And don't get his blood all over my deck."

Many people yelled "no," or gasped in horror, as they dragged Chase to the edge.

Rad came running up the stairs. "Dad, what the fuck is going on?"

"I think Chase somehow corrupted my new program, that son of a bitch. That's what's going on. That kid is evil."

"Dad, you can't kill him. He's one of the Sixteen!"

"You're wrong son. He's a reject."

To Chase's surprise, Rad begged his father. "Dad, please don't shoot him."

"You're right, son. Guards, tie him up and kick the shit out of him, then throw him over so he drowns."

Two guards held Chase while another guard grabbed some electronic lock straps. They beat and kicked him in the head and ribs repeatedly, as Chase yelled out in pain, blow after blow.

Abuta screamed, "No!" She ran over and grabbed one of the

soldier's arms. "You're killing him." His head pressed against the deck, Chase watched Abuta's stark white heels as they clacked against the ground. The gold bracelet looped around her smooth, dark ankle jingled as she grew closer.

Francisco yelled, "What are you doing? Is he your boyfriend or something, you little whore?" She turned and spit in Francisco's face. She went to slap him, but Ned was faster. Before she could gain forward momentum, he had shot her in the head. Blood spewed everywhere.

The two members left of Chase's crew stood, open-mouthed in shock. They didn't move an inch. The guards tied Chase tight, secured the locks, and kicked away.

"Dad, don't do it," Chase heard Rad plead once more. The pain from the beatings was making it difficult for him to process information.

"Rad, he deserves what he gets." Francisco yelled to the guards, "Keep kicking and get that railing down so you can throw him overboard." They unlatched the cables, and Francisco yelled out, "Not yet, wait. Let me give the final kick." Sean and Logan took a few steps back. Chase could barely see his friends, but he could make out the spatter pattern of Abuta's blood on their pant legs.

Francisco warned them, "Don't move again," and the other soldiers pointed their guns at the crewmates' heads. It was the last thing Chase would see for a while. Francisco walked over and, with a big kick, shoved Chase overboard, sending him splashing into the waves of the ocean.

Chase was in pain, struggling against the salty water as he finally went under.

Running, Sean and Logan got off the deck and grabbed the latch to their ship when they heard two laser shots blast. They turned around quickly and looked back at the boat. Abuta had been shot point-blank, and now, so had someone else, likely Chase.

Sean couldn't help but envision how Abuta's head had split in pieces and fallen into the ocean, not leaving a bloody mess on Francisco's boat. The soldiers picked up the rest of her body and tossed it overboard. Sean felt terrible that he and Logan had run the moment the guards and Francisco shoved Chase into the water. Still, they were shocked and selfishly happy they'd made it off the boat alive. Their relief was short-lived as the adrenaline subsided and their loss of Chase sunk in. Sean leaned back against the pod, covering his face with his palms.

"He'd understand," Logan said to Sean. "He'd want us to do exactly what we did. Our only other choice was to needlessly die."

Sean nodded as tears ran down his face. "I know, but who's going to tell Maggie?"

They fell into a silence filled with grief and uncertainty.

As Chase gasped for air, his body sank deeper into the ocean. He felt he'd been sinking long enough to reach the bottom when time stopped. He looked around, saw that the water was still, and he quickly moved towards the pod, which was backlit by the sun, giving it an orange glow. Or was it the same orange glow Chase always saw when he traversed time?

Sean yelled out to Logan, "Quick, quick, scan the door, so we can get in." They jumped in the pod as fast as they could, Sean tripped and banged his leg, and it started bleeding. Logan grabbed him by the arm to help him in and then shut the door as quickly as they could.

As they jumped in and turned around, they were taken aback to see Chase sitting in the pilot's seat, getting the ship ready for takeoff.

"Oh my God, where did you come from? How did you make it out of the water alive?" Logan scanned his port so the ship would fire up and start.

"Go, go, go. Take off with full thrusters," said Sean.

The three of them took off at Mach eleven. As they looked down at the yacht, people had begun to dance and party again. As the ship raised up from the ocean, the three friends looked down in amazement. The flight was a quiet one, and for the first hour, no one even said a word.

Finally, Logan spoke. "Chase, we are so happy you're alive."

"Me too. I'm happy you made it out of there," said Sean. "We're sorry we left you behind."

"How did you get those locks off before you drowned?" asked Logan. "And look at you, man. You have cuts everywhere, and your ribs must be broken. Those guards kicked you really hard. It's amazing that you made it."

Chase had a far-off look in his eyes and it took a moment for him to speak. "When I was drowning, I felt like I went into another dimension and this dimension is sort of blurry, but I can move around. I went to the pod and moved back in this dimension and then I'm back in my body.

Logan shook his head. "How is that possible, Chase?"

"I don't know, Logan. It just is," Chase replied matter-of-factly. "And don't feel bad about saving your own lives. There's no reason for you to apologize for that," he added.

Logan and Sean stared at each other for a moment before Logan said, "Okay, man. Well, I'm just glad you made it."

They were mostly silent again for the ride, but Sean noticed Chase's glossy eyes. His long hair was still wet, and so was his face, but Sean knew that some of that water wasn't from Chase's attempted murder. He'd been crying. No one said anything, but they were all broken up about what had happened, and Sean thought Chase was sad about Abuta. It made sense; if he really had the ability to slow time to save himself, Chase was probably blaming himself for their losses.

They landed at the warehouse, and Maggie, Clio, Logan's wife, and Kay met them as they got off the ship. Logan got off first, and Sean held Chase as he hobbled with his broken bones.

Maggie screamed, "Chase, look at you! You're bleeding and bruised everywhere, and why are you limping like that? What happened to you guys?" Chase pulled Maggie to him and held her for a moment. She continued to ask questions, but they deemed so unimportant compared to the knowledge that he could've died without seeing her again.

"Clio," said Chase, "can you tell Julian that I need to meet him later? We need a new strategy."

"With what?"

Chase opened his mouth, then closed it. After a few more attempts, he said, "Just tell him, 'Everything.'"

Chase spent the day with Maggie, and as night fell, he said, "I need a drink."

"Do you want me to grab you some water?" she offered.

"That would be really nice of you. Thank you," he replied.

Chase went to Julian's screen room after drinking two massive glasses of fresh water. On his way, he passed two people and noticed something strange about them, but his mind was set elsewhere so he brushed it off. When he saw it again, he stopped a girl walking in the hall. "Hey, what's that black dot in your eye? Did you hit it or something?"

"No," the girl said.

"Does it hurt?" he asked.

"No," she replied.

Chase immediately felt bad. What if it was a physical defect? "Okay, I…just thought maybe if something was wrong that I could help, but that was intrusive of me. I apologize." He kept walking. Once he got to Julian's room, he knocked twice and walked in.

"Chase, look at you. I didn't think you could get much darker. Looks like you caught some sun in Rio, huh?" They laughed. "I heard things got pretty crazy in Rio."

Chase's heart pounded, and he found it difficult to breathe, but he forced a smile. "You wouldn't believe it if I told you. Things are changing pretty quickly."

"Really?" Julian kept working on his screens, reviewing feeds and data. "You mean in Rio?"

"No, I mean throughout the world. As I see it, the Sixteen are out of touch with the entire population. Which I should have known before we even left. I used to be one of them. I was out of touch. But I don't think I was that out of it. Not like them."

"How? Why? Do they not see the reports or feeds on what's going on with the people?"

"No, that's not the problem. They see everything. Hell, they even cause some of it for fun. They just don't care."

"So did you have a chance to talk to Francisco about the people suffering in Canada?"

Chase clenched his fist and tried to control his breathing. He was glad Julian wasn't looking at him. "Sure, I met with him. I brought it up a few times."

"Well, what did he say?"

"Well, he mostly tried to kill me. Actually, he probably thinks I'm dead, and that's probably a good thing."

Julian looked at him then. "Holy shit, Chase. Why? Because you asked him to stop hurting people?"

Chase ran a hand through his hair, idly noting how long it had grown. Anything to keep his mind off Vic and Abuta. "Yeah. I'm not sure what the best plan is from here on out. There's a vacant seat on the council, and I'm a member of the Sixteen, so I could actually run and maybe have a voice that way."

Julian raised his eyebrows. "Do you think that would work? I mean, you just said one of them tried to kill you."

"I don't know."

"Did you hear the latest on the feed?" Julian asked. "The main power supply got damaged or cut somehow in Toronto, and there are literally millions of people without power and heat."

Chase dug his fingernails into the flesh of his palm. He didn't know how much more he could take. But he had to take it and probably much worse. "How did it get cut, Jules?"

Julian shook his head. "They don't know. They said it was a fluke and they don't know how to fix it."

"It's no fluke," Chase said. "I know what's going on, and believe me, it won't get fixed. I feel like he's punishing the people because I was trying to help them. Do you know when it got cut?"

"Let me pull up the info…looks like it was while you were flying home. I'd say it happened twelve hours and twenty-eight minutes ago."

Chase paused for a minute deep in thought and then tapped his port. "Clio, get the hydrogen pod warmed up. I'm going on a short trip."

"Where are you going so soon?" she asked.

"I'm leaving for Toronto in ten minutes."

"I'm not sure if I can get everyone ready in ten minutes," she said.

"No need, I'm going by myself."

"Chase, that's not a good idea, in fact it's a really bad idea. You should never go on missions by yourself."

Against Maggie's and Clio's pleading, Chase took off by himself. He felt solely responsible for the chaos those people suffered. The sense of guilt was killing him. As he got closer to Toronto, he paged Brian.

"Hey, Brian. It's Chase."

"Chase, oh my God, I'm so glad to hear from you. Did you hear what happened? We have no power."

"I did. I'm on my way to you right now."

"Wow, Chase, that's great news, because this is a disaster."

"I know, I heard all about it. Hey man, could you please find a spot for my hydro pod where I can fly back out when I need to? Somewhere discreet?" Chase asked.

"Sure, I'll send your pod the coordinates and meet you when you land."

Chase thanked Brian and tapped his port to disconnect.

When he touched down, Brian met him at the landing site. "Man, I can't tell you how good it is to see you. I heard you went to Rio to meet Francisco. How did that go?"

Chase felt like he might be ill. He had to tell him that it was his fault. "Brian, I have some bad news, and I wanted to tell you in person. Things are going to get worse for your people."

Brian, taken aback, asked, "Why? What do you mean, worse? How? I thought you were going to see if he could lower the rates and give everyone some relief."

Chase looked at his feet. "Francisco is a monster, and he wants to make the people suffer."

Brian shook his head. "What do you mean 'suffer'? We're already suffering. What should we do?"

"You need to get weapons and fight," Chase said. It was the only solution.

"Fight? Are you crazy? Against the government family, the collective…they'll destroy us."

"Listen, I'm just here to tell you that it's going to get worse, and you're going to have to organize a fight. It's really not a choice."

"You came all the way up here to tell me to fight?"

"Yes."

"Well, can you at least look at our power-grid problem? We don't even have power to turn on the lights."

Chase agreed. It was the least he could do. "Sure, I can take a look, but I'm not sure what I can do." The quiet of the night was broken as another of Brian's pods pulled up. There were two people on board, and Brian waved to them. He ushered Chase into the pod.

"Chase, this is Ava. She works at the power grid," Brian said, indicating an older woman. She actually had wrinkles, which surprised Chase. Most people chose not to visibly age with all the options available.

"This kid's gonna help with the power grid?" the woman asked. She didn't look convinced. Brian affirmed that was what was happening while Chase fought the urge to say that he probably couldn't do anything.

"So what's going on?" Chase asked, knowing it was something Francisco had likely done remotely. He doubted he could do anything to help these people. He'd already failed them. He didn't want to fail them twice.

Ava explained, "The main cable that connects Burlington to Toronto has been damaged or possibly cut. The grid supervisors are looking at it, but they can't figure out a remedy or tell what happened."

"Okay," Chase said, "let's go take a look."

On the way to the grid, Brian asked Chase, "do you think you could talk to Mr. Francisco again? See if he'd reconsider?"

Chase glanced at Brian, who had begun to look defeated. "I don't think so. In fact, I think he cut the grid on purpose."

"Why would someone do that?"

"Because, in his twisted mind, he has so much money that he thinks the people are starting to get in his way."

"In the way of what?"

"I don't know. His enjoyment, his money? Maybe owning a country is more of a burden to him now."

Ava interrupted. "See that big fire? That's it."

Chase saw the brilliant orange and the smoke rolling away. It reminded him of when he was young. When he'd helped his mother save him from the house fire. He shook off the memory. "Can you get me close?"

"Yes, let me put my uniform back on," she said as the pod pulled up closer. The woman donned a full-body suit with a badge and a hardhat. When they exited, hundreds of people were standing behind the electronic barriers, watching the fire.

"Chase, see this screen?" Ava said. "It shows the damage is affecting three quadrants. The north quadrant is the city of Toronto, and that's where the largest population of people live and are freezing without power. The Canadian feed estimates seven thousand people have frozen to death so far."

Chase looked at it, unsure what to do. "So, what needs to be done?"

"Well, what should be done is the whole grid in this providence should be shut down, the repair should be made, and the grid should be turned back on."

"So why don't you do that?"

"The family controls the energy in this country, of course, and they're the only ones authorized—and the only ones who have all the codes—to shut it down. We have our best coders trying to hack the system but it's not working. We've repeatedly tried to reach the family council. They're shockingly unavailable. Those two main power lines flashing and sparking need to be fused back together, but without shutting it off, it's a hundred million live volts."

Chase was stunned. He wasn't a master electrician. In fact, Ava was one, and she didn't know how to fix it. He sighed, exasperated. "How long would it take for the live cables to fuse back together if they touched?"

"We thought of that. Technically, two or three minutes if they were held together somehow, but that would blow up any machine that tried. Plus, there isn't a machine I'm aware of that could do that."

Chase walked closer to the live cables.

"Watch out," Ava yelled. "Don't get too close, or you'll get fried."

Chase looked back at Ava, and signaled Brian to come over.

"Brian, have one of your guys do something on the other side to distract the police and fire officials so they don't stop me."

"What are you going to do?"

Chase didn't respond.

"Okay, when do you want me to distract them?"

"Right now."

Brian had two of his guys jump the barrier, screaming to get the attention of the police. As the police went to see what was going on, Chase carefully approached the sparking cables. He reached down to grab each one, and Ava let out a loud scream.

"Chase, you'll be electrocuted!"

Chase grabbed one cable in each hand. Sparks flashed and his body appeared as though it was on fire. He pulled the cables together, and a loud blast sounded, but Chase held the cables together. Sparks and flames burst everywhere, and after a few minutes, he dropped the cables and took a few steps backwards before turning around. Ava held her hands in front of her mouth, along with the others, who appeared stunned.

Brian scrolled through all his screens, a confused expression on his face. "Look, all the quadrants are back on line."

Chase tried to look but grew lightheaded and fell to the ground. With the blast and fire, the police and fire officials ran toward the commotion.

When Chase dropped, he heard someone yell, "I think he's dead."

Chase was shaking and breathing shallowly. He could barely perceive what was going on around him but felt someone pick him up. There was a ringing in his ears, but he could hear the people who were close to him.

"Quick," Brian said, "get him in our pod and rush him to the hospital."

"Stay behind the barriers and let them through," a police officer yelled.

Brian held him by his shoulder, but Chase hobbled into the pod on his own, and they took off.

In the pod, Ava said, "How did you do that without dying or getting electrocuted? You were on fire. How did you do that?"

Chase sat with burns on his face and arms, recognizing that the woman was in shock, but also that he likely shared the affliction. "Did it work?" he asked.

"Um, yes, it did. That was amazing." Then she said, "we're moving fast and should be at the hospital in about fifteen minutes."

Chase blinked a few times and shook his head. The ringing in his ears had subsided, and though he still felt warm and shaky, he didn't have time for the hospital. "I'm not going there. Just drop me off a few blocks from my pod."

"Why, where are you going?" Brain asked.

"I'm going to check on someone I met here last time. Please do as I ask."

The pod landed on a side street, and Chase got out.

"Are you sure you're going to be OK with us just leaving you here? I really don't want to do this. Are you sure?" Brian asked.

"I'll be just fine. Brian, remember what I told you; this is only the beginning. So you need to prepare to fight."

Ava looked at Brian. "Fight? What is he talking about?"

Brian didn't say anything to her, instead responding to Chase. "Thanks again, man, and be careful."

Chase walked a few blocks to where most of the homeless people lived. He didn't stand out there with his burned and ripped clothes. Once he arrived, he walked through the crowd and found the elderly homeless woman whom he'd taken a liking to the last time he was in Canada.

"Hello, remember me?" he asked her.

She smiled immediately and spread her arms open for a hug. "I sure do, you handsome young man. You're Chase."

"Come, walk with me," he said after briefly wrapping his arms around the woman.

"Okay," she said.

"Why aren't you staying in the underground shelter or the public auditorium?" Chase asked.

She was quiet for a moment, and as they walked, she grasped his hand. Chase didn't mind. Maybe he could provide her some sort of warmth. "They said the power went out, so we all went into the street. There are hundreds of us."

He put his arm around her and got a good look at her. She had icicles coming out of her nose, and her stringy gray hair was frozen.

"Tell your friends there is power again," Chase said as they walked another block. The lights in most of the buildings flickered on.

He walked her into the auditorium, where cots for the homeless were set up and the heat was kicking in. The room filled up quickly with crowds of people coming in from the streets.

"You'd better get your spot quick before someone else does."

The woman's voice shook as she spoke. "Are you going to stay here with us again tonight, Chase?"

"No, I'm going to take off, but I'm sure I'll see you again."

"I told my daughter about you, and she said she would like to meet you sometime."

Chase smiled. "That sounds great." He said good-bye and wove through the maze of cots toward the exit.

After he walked out the front door, he stood on the stoop for a moment, then he walked about ten steps and turned around to gaze at the shelter. Peering through a window, he was surprised how quickly the large building had filled up with the homeless.

The ringing returned to his ears and grew into a loud hum. It took him a moment to recognize that the noise was external, and by the time the realization dawned, it was nearly too late. Julian had been tracking Chase from a hacked satellite feed and sent an urgent message to his eye screens and port, "LOOK OUT!"

Behind Chase, a drone hovered over the street and fired two missiles at him. In one single motion, Chase dropped to the ground as the missiles flashed by, missing his head by inches. He hit the concrete as the missiles smashed into the shelter with a massive explosion, blasting it to pieces. A great ball of fire mushroomed into the sky. The blast blew him back into the middle of the street, and Chase's first thought was that everyone inside was dead and though his life was still at risk, he was almost ready to give up himself.

The drone took off, probably to reload, Chase thought. Survival instinct kicked in and he stood and ran as fast as he could to a door to the underground, heading toward the old abandoned subway station.

The old woman cupped her hands over her mouth and exhaled in short bursts, attempting to warm her frigid hands. The fingerless gloves, full of holes, didn't do much to protect her against the raging cold, but her heart was warm.

She'd just seen her son again, and even though her tears nearly froze the moment they left her eyes, she allowed herself to cry them. She wanted nothing more than to take the boy—man…he's a man now, she thought—into her arms and tell him everything, but she couldn't do that. She turned and watched as he walked away, his back to her.

He'd been kind. Offered her conversation, hope, and shown her to the homeless shelter. There was electricity there, and she even had her own cot. It was such a kind thing Andrew had done for her—they called him Chasten, but she'd named him Andrew the moment she knew she was pregnant. She was happy to learn that her baby had grown into a caring, human being who disregarded the wealth of the Sixteen and decided to live amongst the poor of the world. She was proud of him.

All those years locked up in prisons for the pregnancy, and the years she'd spent doped up on sedatives before she was tossed into the streets due to the overpopulation of such facilities—all those experiences had been worth it for the moment her grown baby walked back into her life.

The first time she'd seen him; she had known her was her

boy. She felt tethered to him, and she knew he felt something similar. Otherwise, he wouldn't have listened to her talk for hours. The woman understood that she wasn't sane. He may not believe her if she had told him of his origins.

She was content to learn that he wanted to help others. People like her. He might not have had a penny to his name, and that made the woman cry even harder. He'd given up everything. She had always thought she'd made the right choice to not terminate her pregnancy, and seeing the soft, kindness reflected in the boy's eyes only validated that choice.

Screams interrupted her thoughts. "Get down!" someone yelled. The woman heeded the advice, but she knelt too slowly; her old bones were arthritic, and she couldn't dive for cover as nimbly as she once had. The boom came almost at the exact second the light burst from the building behind her. She felt a slight pinprick in her abdomen and the hot flow of blood seeping from the wound. She reached down to feel the thick piece of metal that had lodged itself into her body. The blood poured and poured.

As the white light from the explosion overtook her vision, and her ears rang, she felt only warmth. Warmth and peace.

Running, Chase connected with Julian. "Are you there? It's me."

"Yeah, thank god you got my message"

"Julian, you have to scramble my port or something. They know where I am somehow."

"Okay, I'll put in some false coordinates on your GPS to throw them off. How much time do I have? Are you being followed right now, or do you think they just found you from a camera?"

As Julian spoke, a pack of bee-sized drones were headed for Chase, their low hum growing into a roar. "You hear that, Jules? They're after me right now. Come on, man, please help," Chase begged as he ran from the machines.

"Shit! Hide behind something. I'll make the tracker go back up on the street. I can see where you are now."

Chase found a bathroom door and hid behind it as the drones grew so loud he had to cover his ears to muffle the noise. He stood in silence, barely breathing hoping to avoid their sound sensors. Finally, he heard the drone pack fly away.

"Chase, go the other way and get out of there, quick. Run fast, and about thirty meters to your right, there will be a stairway that goes back up to the street. It should get you pretty close to your pod. I know they're looking for it, so I keep changing the coordinates and cameras, but they're trying to scramble my signal."

He did exactly what Julian told him, and sure enough, when he opened the door to the street, his pod was around the corner. He heard a lot of drone sirens, which he knew were after him. He quickly climbed into his pod and took off. As the ship gained altitude, he looked down and saw the fifteen-story homeless shelter engulfed in flames. In time, the building would be reduced to a pile of rubble, with everyone inside incinerated. Chase hung his head.

As Chase flew back, the feed played breaking news regarding an unidentified man who had sabotaged the grid and caused the blackout as well as the deaths of innocent people. The footage captured a quick shot of Chase being loaded into Brian's pod, but it was dark, and the image wasn't crisp. No one was identified, likely because Julian had scrambled the chips. Chase thought, Boy, Francisco has some spin machine here. It looks like everything was my fault. It appeared that the public may not have seen his face, but he figured Francisco knew.

Chase connected with Julian again. "Jules, how's the scrambling going? Because I have a feeling they're still after me, and I don't have any weapons on board this pod. I'm kind of a sitting target if they find me."

"I'm working on it right now, and I have your ship's signal going in another direction."

After a moment, Julian asked, "You don't see anything following you, do you, Chase?"

Chase checked all the windows and screens. "No, I don't, but I also don't think I should risk going back to the warehouse district and placing all of you in danger. What do you think?"

"Well, I've been scrambling a ton of programs all day, and it will make it hard for anyone to find you, but you know the collective can decode almost anything over time. I'm trying every trick in the book."

Then Sean chimed in. "Chase, go to LA. I still have friends in the underground. Kay and I can take off soon and meet you there."

Maggie came on the signal. "Chase, go. I'll meet you there. I just heard a rumor on another unofficial feed that they're about to post false information about you being a terrorist. I don't want you to be by yourself."

Chase shook his head. "No, Mag, stay with everyone else."

"Why?" she asked.

"I hope they don't, but there's a possibility that they might catch me, and I don't want anything to happen to you, to any of you, for that matter. Just stay there right now. Julian, can Francisco come after me outside of Canada and cross family jurisdictions into other countries?"

"I'm not sure, but I'll find out. I'd assume that if he claims there's a threat and gets cooperation from the US family…I really don't know yet. Wait a second." Julian paused. "I just hacked into the feed that's going to go live in five minutes. Bad news, buddy. The feed is going to say they just identified you as the person who sabotaged the Canadian grid and caused thousands of deaths. They're posting a worldwide all-points bulletin to apprehend you at any cost."

Chase was in the pod by himself and not sure if any place on Earth was safe enough for him to live there. He didn't know what to say. That little voice that told him earlier to just give up was back, and louder, but when he thought of letting them falsely accuse him when all he'd wanted was to help people, he knew he couldn't give up. He also couldn't put his friends in danger. He'd caused enough suffering.

"Chase, just come back here, and we will hide you," said Maggie.

"Mag, you don't understand. A drone just fired missiles at me and killed hundreds of people. I'm not going to risk coming back until Julian is ninety-nine percent sure he can scramble my chip so they can't find me. Obviously they're going crazy tracking me right now." Chase paused for a second and then said, "I have an idea."

"What's your idea?" Julian asked.

"Give me some time, and I'll connect with you all soon."

Chase tapped his arm port. "Connect me to Randal Francisco." The connection was made. "Rad, hi. It's me, Chase."

"Chase, how the hell are you cuz? Man, when I saw you on the feed and my dad freaking out, I said to myself 'holy shit.' I thought you drowned to death. Cuz, you're one hell of a swimmer! I can't believe you're alive."

"Yeah I made it out alive and I was trying to help the people in Canada, but, long story short, your dad found me and now is chasing me down."

"I know, my dad's and asshole sometimes. I'll help you out, but don't tell him it was me helping you, if he catches you."

"Rad, he's trying to kill me, so I think you're okay. Can you get me somewhere safe without your dad or the collective catching me?"

"Let me figure something out on my dad's terminal. I have to be careful because I don't want him to know it's coming from the inside.

"Where are you anyway? I'm on my dad's terminal now and he can't find you."

Chase paused and didn't answer, as this was the moment of truth. He was deciding whether to give Rad his coordinates and trust him. He could see on his eye screen equations displaying the probability of his capture if he gave Rad his coordinates. That probability was at 50.1%.

"Chase are you still there? What's the closest airport near you that you can get to quickly without getting caught?"

Chase thought for a moment. "Uh…O'Hare in Chicago would be the closest. I'm minutes away."

"Okay, good. I own a launching pad and I have a ship that

leaves there every hour, direct to the moon. Look for the big ship that has a big Dark Side of the Moon Casino logo on the side. Ditch your pod and autopilot it back to Canada. When my dad's government eventually blows it up, it will take some time to figure out if you were in it or not. I can't wait to see my dad gloat when he thinks he killed you again. When you find my casino ship, walk up to it and ask for Vinnie. I'll connect with Vinnie right now, and he'll get you on without getting scanned by the collective. How far away are you?"

Chase checked the pod's map display. "I can be there in about twenty minutes."

"Hold on." The line went silent. After a moment, Rad returned. "OK, I just talked to Vin. You're all set. When you're in line, go to the left side of the ship. Vinnie will have an Elvis costume on. It's all part of the show."

"Thanks so much, Rad. I really appreciate it. Do you think they'll find me up there?"

"Are you crazy? There are no rules or laws up there now that the moon is pretty much just a really big casino. My partner runs everything, and you know the laws on Earth don't apply. Plus, I'll mess up any of the requests for information that come in. And you know what, Chase? The people love it. Even though they spend money they really can't afford to lose, but hell, that's not my problem."

"I've head your commercials down here, Rad. It seems like your casino is getting bigger every year."

"I am getting bigger, really ever since Mars had all those problems. For so long, it was 'Mars is great, Mars is this, and Mars is that.' That all sounded good, until the third disaster when the dome blew up and killed five hundred people. Then the pressure blew people's heads off. Plus the travel time and money they charge to get there. While all that bullshit was going on, we developed five big craters on the dark side of the moon and built those casinos and hotels. Today, we are on both sides of the moon. Remember in your history books when they called Las Vegas 'Sin City'?"

"Yeah," said Chase, anxiously waiting for his cousin to stop talking so that he could find some measure of peace and quiet. So that he could flee. He thought of disconnecting from Rad, but Rad was the one doing him a favor, so Chase sat and panicked while he listened to Rad talk about how amazing all his toys were.

"What a crock of shit that used to be. Sin City? Come to the Dark Side of the Moon Casinos; we don't even have laws to break. Do you like orgies, Chase, you never answered me when I asked you last?"

Chase paused, not wanting to insult the man who was saving him. "I mean, not really, but I don't really know a lot about them."

"What's there to know? A lot of people screw. Okay, let's worry about all that if you make it here. Look for Vinny. Over and out."

Chase, relieved to no longer be speaking to his cousin, entered his new coordinates and hoped he would get there before the collective caught him. When he arrived at O'Hare and found the ship, there was a long line of people dressed in all sorts of costumes. Most of them were singing and cheering. They were excited, and when Chase scanned the line, he spotted at least thirty Elvis costumes. He tried to blend into the line in case any police with collective scanners walked by.

When he felt the timing was right, Chase approached two Elvises standing next to each other. "Are you Vinny?" he asked, not really directing the question at one particular Elvis.

"Who's Vinny?" one said, and the other asked, "Are you the guy with the stuff?"

"No, never mind," Chase said as the line grew longer. Since he didn't have a ticket, he got out of the line and walked to the side of the ship.

One lady yelled out, "Don't even think of cutting the line." Then she yelled, "I see you."

When she shouted, Chase was taken aback for a second, hoping she hadn't recognized him from a recent most wanted post. At the same time, he couldn't remember if Rad had said to go to the right side or the left. The ship was much larger than he'd imagined. Walking along the left side of the ship, he saw two guys who looked as if they were making a drug deal or doing some other sort of illegal activity. Chase slowly approached them. He figured this would be his best chance to not startle them, in the event that they had weapons.

As he got close, a skinny red-haired guy in an Elvis suit spun around. "Who are you?"

Chase answered, "Are you Vinny?"

"I don't know. Who are you?"

"I'm Chase."

"Oh, good, I thought you were a cop. Yeah, I'm Vinnie. You want some PLG for the ride?"

"I'm not really sure what that is," said Chase, "so I'm going to say no."

"Okay, fine, more for us. Go through that door." He pointed at a hatch near the back of the vessel. "Go to the right. The party will start a few minutes after we take off."

"Thanks." Chase felt a wave of relief and took a deep breath as soon as he stepped onto the ship.

Shortly after, the casino ship took off with a blast, and it didn't take long for the party to begin. The pilot announced that the flight was going to be quick and told the guests to party hard.

As the ship approached the moon, Chase looked out the window to the left, and all the space was pitch black. To the right was the raging glow of casino lights, blinking on and off. Rad and his partner owned two massive solar satellites that orbited the moon, facing the sun. He collected enough solar energy to power two small cities, and they used this energy to line every hotel and landscape with the brightest lights at the highest intensity.

The oversized ship landed on an enormous mechanical track. There was no trace of the earth, since they had landed on the dark side of the moon. The ship was divided between out-of-control guests on one level and food, water, and other supplies on a second level. The track transported the ship from the landing pad directly through a glass tunnel that headed for the casino. The escalator moved the beast of a ship inside a retractable door, as it got closer to the casino. As it picked up speed, the passengers began to cheer. They made it through one last large glass doorway, and the cheering grew louder as the ship moved into the center of the main casino. When the doors simultaneously opened, a huge crowd of people yelled, "Surprise! You're here, fuckers!"

The new guests cheered at the top of their lungs, and when they got off, the mayhem began.

Chase walked off the ship and watched in amazement as one woman threw a man with a cowboy hat on top of the blackjack table. They started having sex, and the crowd hooted and hollered while pouring drinks all over them. Then the blackjack table broke, and everyone laughed as they landed on the floor. The blackjack dealer said, "Don't worry; there are plenty more we can break."

"Remember, everything here is free, except the gambling," a waitress told Chase. Then she asked, "Can I get you some of the latest drinks, drugs, or sex programs?"

Chase was a bit overwhelmed with everything going on and now this mayhem. He didn't want his mind altered; he wanted something familiar. "I'm good right now. Do you know where Rad's partner Jared is?"

"I'm sorry, sir. He doesn't party with a lot of the guests, but I can get a manager if you have a certain fantasy in mind. I'm confident we can accommodate you either physically or virtually."

"No, he told me to ask for him once I got here."

Realizing that Chase was talking about the Jared, she connected with the man, and he told her to immediately put a pack on Chase's back. She told him to hold on a minute, as two men came over and strapped a flight pack to his back.

"What's this for?" Chase asked.

"Jared is on the ninth floor, and he prefers that Rad's friends fly to him and not use the elevator. I will send you to that floor from our main lobby. Don't worry; they will throw you a line once you're at the top near the ceiling." As she tightened one of his straps, she asked him, "You're not afraid of heights, right?"

"Well, I—"

They pushed the button, and Chase rocketed speedily into the air.

A loud voice sounded over the main lobby speaker. "Please do not shoot the flying guest in the main lobby. If you would like to shoot someone, go to the shooting gallery on the eighth floor and select a volunteer."

Chase glanced at the crowd and saw that a bunch of people had guns of all kinds. Suddenly, someone shot a round up in the air, just to scare him, as the people in the lobby laughed. Chase overshot the ninth floor and floated near the ceiling until he saw an opening where a party was going on. He did his best to move toward the opening but was having problems maneuvering the rocket pack. Then he saw a girl in the opening looking at him.

She yelled over the music, "Is that him? Does he have messy hair?"

"I think so," someone else yelled. She raised a funny-looking gun and pointed it at Chase, who at this point was moving around in circles. She aimed, shot, and hit him in the rocket pack. It was a cable gun that retracted him into the opening.

Chase's body squeezed through the opening, and as soon as he got in and found his footing, he fell down. He stood back up and grabbed the side of the wall to get his composure.

"How are you, Chase? Rad told me you were coming," Jared asked.

The room spun, and his stomach lurched as he swallowed back pure pile. "I'm dizzy."

"Are you having fun?"

Chase answered, "Sure."

"Then that's all that matters. Sit down. Do you need anything? And you know I mean 'anything' when I say it." Jared was a tall man with a ZZ Top beard. Throughout all the years Chase had heard about Jared and some of the stories, but he could never figure out how he stayed so positive. Maybe it was the way he was born, or maybe it was the drugs.

"So Rad told me you're having problems with Ronnie Boy, eh? You know Rad really doesn't get along with his dad? I haven't seen him in a long time. Is he still fat?" Jared combed his fingers through his beard.

Chase laughed. "Yeah, he is."

"Did you know that if Ronnie was here right now, you could shoot his ass, and it would be totally legal. Hell, you could chop him up and cook him like a big fat steak." Chase smiled, and Jared laughed. "Damn, I probably have some sick bastards here that would do it and then eat him for a snack. That is, if you threw on some barbecue sauce. Get over here and hug me, you crazy bastard. I'm a hugger. I hear you're trying to save the world. Let me give you some advice: Stop trying and start enjoying. Life's too short."

After a quick hug, Chase said seriously, "Jer, you heard right. I'm living with the population these days, and I do try to help out the common guy."

"And how is that going, Chaser?"

"To be honest, not too good, but I'm still working on a few things. Did you know there's a vacant spot on the council?"

"Okay…so what?"

"Well, if I had a recommendation from two other family members, I could ask for a vote. Would you recommend me?" Chase asked.

"Hell no!"

"Why not?" Chase asked, surprised.

"Are you kidding me? I love you already and all, but I could care less about the sixteen families and all their bullshit. I wouldn't want to be involved. Seriously, as time goes on, I don't even want to know what goes on down there on earth. Sorry, Chaser, no vote here, but you can live here as long as you like. Although right now you're too serious and making me too serious. You're kind of freaking me out a little. Check out the suite I have for you and meet me whenever you settle down and relax a little."

"How do I get back down the nine floors?"

"Take the elevator."

"I thought you didn't have an elevator to your floor?"

"I do. We don't like to use it, but you can."

Chase felt better knowing that the collective and thanks to Rad, Fransisco probably wouldn't track him on the moon. He decided to stay put, recharge and make a new game plan. He needed more of a break than he thought, and the days flew by.

The parties at the casino were epic. Each night brought the mayhem to a new level. Chase met plenty of fun people, but he was surprised that the suicide rate of all casino guests was about fifteen percent. At first, he thought it was because people lost all their money, but as time went by, he realized that most of the suicides were people sick of life on earth and just didn't want to go back. The most common suicide methods were either to overdose on drugs or to simply walk outside the protective structure and die from lack of oxygen. The casino kept the suicides low-key and only the casino's video footage was allowed.

Chase learned all of this when he met a casino worker who lived in the suite next door. They became friends, and instead of knocking on the door, Mike would knock on the wall.

"Chase, you in there?"

Chase knocked back twice, walked out the front door, and met Mike in the hall. "Mike, how come you never knock on the door?"

"I like the wall better. Do you want to go see some dead people tonight?"

Chase had gotten accustomed to all sorts of bizarre activities. He shrugged. "Where are we going?"

"I have to install a larger net for the suicides, and I need another guy to hold the straps." They took the elevator to the top floor.

"OK, I'm in. I'm trying to limit my time in the main casino." The two walked onto the roof in a special air-transfer room.

"Put your helmet on so your eyes don't blow out and mess up my uniform."

"Mike, don't worry about me. Look at you. You look like you're drugged out of your mind. Did you just take something?"

Mike smiled. His pupils were enormous. "I did. It's a new Chinese program that makes you high but gives you like ten times the amount of energy for a while. I mean, I feel like busting up shit right now." He yelled, "Come on, Chase, let's put up a net!"

"Great," said Chase. "Just tell me where to hold this big thing." He heard someone trying to open the lock on the air-transfer room. He signaled to Mike to look at the door. It was moving back and forth a little, and someone or something was pulling on it. Then it cracked open, and out walked a middle-aged woman with long hair. Her face was beet red, and she had a purple streak in her hair.

Mike yelled out, "Go back in, quick," but she couldn't hear him because Mike had his helmet on. The woman opened the door all the way, took a deep breath, and started to walk on the moon. She looked up at the stars and then turned to look at the blinking casino lights. She made it about twenty steps before her mouth opened as she gasped for air and her eyes rolled to white. She started to float, and Mike moved the net as fast as he could to try to catch her.

The woman's foot got caught in the net, and Chase raced to grab her. He caught her arm and one of her legs. Chase made sure her body was secure in the net and went back to the air room, where he and Mike took off their helmets.

"It's too bad that girl thought it was better to end her life," said Chase.

"It's happening practically every night now. That's why I needed your help to install the larger net."

Chase made his way to the main lobby. He had come to know the lobby girl pretty well from all his visits.

"Good evening, Mr. Chase. Would you like to use the elevator again tonight?"

"Not tonight, Sally Girl. Strap the flight suit on me, and I'll have an old-school liquid vodka club in a glass."

As Chase flew in, Jared ran over to greet him.

"It's my boy Chaser. Get your ass over here. I love this guy," he said to everyone. "Do you know why I call him Chaser? Look at him; he always has a drink in hand. I love this guy. Chaser, are you ready to have fun tonight?"

Chase sat next to Jared, and the cocktail waitress asked him if he was ready for another drink. He stared into space, thinking about the woman who had committed suicide. Then he looked at the waitress and said, "Sure, why not?"

"Chaser, do you want to do some Squad with me tonight?"

Chase was a bit tired. The constant partying was thrilling, and he was still young enough to enjoy it, but he couldn't keep up with the moon people. And he wasn't afraid to admit that. To himself, anyway. "I don't know. What is it?"

" If I told you, it would take all the fun out of it." Jared reached into his pocket and pulled out two little silver packets that would plug into the arm port. "It's a virtual-reality drug, but it's a short-lived one."

Chase wasn't paying attention. He was still thinking about the dead girl's face.

"Hello, Chaser. Moon to Chaser, are you still there?"

Chase snapped out of his daydream. "Yes, I am. Sure, bring it on."

"Awesome. Take one of these and plug it into your port. I'll do the other one." They sat for a second as the music got louder, with another guitar solo breaking out.

"I'll do it, but you do yours first," said Chase.

Jared looked at him. "Fair enough." He placed the silver packet on his arm port, and his eyes closed as he sank back into his chair. About twenty minutes went by, and Chase had a couple more drinks while he watched the band.

Jared jumped out of his seat, his eyes opened wide. "Wow, what a rush!" He shook his head a couple of times. "That is my eighth or ninth time, and it's still awesome. Here you go, Chase. Enjoy."

He put the packet over Chase's port, and Chase closed his eyes. His eye screen downloaded and scrolled through information very quickly.

Then everything went black, and Chase couldn't see or hear anything. There was complete silence, void of everything. "Am I dead?" he wondered. He had no sense of time or space. A beautiful purple light shone in front of him with a waterfall in the middle. He could hear birds humming, and a beautiful girl was riding a horse naked. The horse was white and had huge wings. The girl rode closer, and as she galloped faster, the horse spread its wings and flew off into the sunset.

Suddenly, something grabbed him from the back and yanked him hard. A bag came over his head.

"Hey, who are you? What is going on?" he cried out.

Everything went black again. He felt his body being lifted and carried.

"Hey, I can't see anything. What is going on?" Chase felt helpless. He heard branches cracking and breaking, and knew he was being carried to another place. Then the movement stopped, and he heard more people, or creatures, walking toward him.

"Tie him to the post," someone with a deep voice in an old English accent said. "Tie him up good."

Chase felt the rope being tied tight around his arms and legs. A hand pulled on his hair, and the bag was yanked from his head. He was tied to a wooden post, and in front of him were twenty men dressed in robes and cloaks. A crowd of people was looking on. They all looked like people from ancient England.

A man with a pointed hat stood next to him as another man yelled, "How does your criminal plea?"

"Plea for what?" Chase yelled out. "I didn't do anything."

There was a rumble in the crowd. "Let the king speak."

"Admit what you've done," said the king, who wore a large gold crown and a bright red robe. He pounded the ground with an ostentatious gold scepter.

"I didn't do anything," Chase replied.

A person in the crowd shouted back, "Yes, you did. You had sex with the king's virgin daughter riding the white horse."

"No, no, that's not true. I saw her, but I didn't do anything."

"Liar! That's what they all say." Everyone yelled at the same time, "Guilty! Guilty! Guilty!"

The king said, "Assemble the firing squad." The firing squad filed in with their long rifles at their sides. They formed a line and stood firm, awaiting their command.

The king spoke again. "Raise your weapons." Chase watched the row of the king's soldiers as they raised their rifles, aiming at his head.

"Soldiers, prepare to fire. Ready, set…" Chase closed his eyes, and the king yelled out, "Fire!"

The shots came at the same time, and Chase heard the loud blast. He immediately felt fire on his face and the pain of bullets penetrating his skull. Then suddenly, wham! He was lying on the floor at the Dark Side of the Moon Casino.

Jared and everyone around him was laughing hysterically.

"Holy shit, Chase, you jumped out of your chair at least six feet. How was the squad? Did they shoot you with the firing squad? How fucking cool was that?"

Chase looked at everyone in the room, stunned. He rubbed his eyes to try to compose himself. "Yeah, I thought I was dead," he said. "That was so crazy. I felt the bullets hit my face. How did the drug do that?"

Jared said, "I know, right? I have done Squad almost ten times now, and it still hurts a little, even though I know it's coming. I guess the drug taps into the brain's pain function."

"Chaser, does Squad kick ass or not?" asked a waiter who was looking down at him on the floor.

"Yes, it was definitely nuts, but I'm a history buff. Did you ever hear about the old-time drugs like cocaine?" asked Chase. It was a long time ago, but people would snort it into their nose and get all amped up."

The waiter asked, "Then what would happen? They would get eaten by a lion or a dinosaur?"

"No, they would just be high and feel all pumped up."

The waiter said, "Really? That just sounds pointless." He started to walk away.

Chase sat back in his chair. "Wait," he said to the waiter. "Can I get another vodka club?" Then he looked over at Jared, who gave him a wink.

Chase had had his fill at the casino. He found a quiet corner to connect with Maggie on his port. Hearing her voice would remind him of home and he desired that comfort more than anything.

"Hey Chase," Maggie said. She sounded down, but her voice made him feel much better. Somehow less alone.

"Maggie, how are you?"

"I'm fine, but everyone down here is going crazy and freaking out."

Chapter Ten

"Why is everyone freaking out?" Chase asked.

"The Sixteen just made it official. They claim that, due to tight budgets, they need more money so they're modifying the draw and currency system worldwide. They've already cut the draw by fifty percent. Crime has ramped up., and it's not safe down here without a weapon. And…" Maggie trailed off, sounding far away and tired.

Chase was worried for her. He was also upset. Not because of what the Sixteen had done, but because he wasn't in the least surprised by it. "I'm so sorry, Maggie. I didn't know that was going on. Jared blocks the feeds up here because he doesn't want the gamblers sidetracked by earth news. As soon as this group of gamblers finishes, I'll hitch a ride with them back to Earth. I can't leave you down there."

He paced, heaving deep breaths that felt empty of oxygen. He didn't have a plan. He had nothing. Everything he had attempted trying help others had failed. Hell, maybe he'd even made things worse. All he could do was sit, hands balled into fists and yell into a void. He tried to keep his voice level. "I'll see you as soon as I can. Could you please put Julian on?"

The couple said their goodbyes, and Chase felt his throat tighten. He liked the moon, but he needed to go home. When Julian came on, Chase managed a few words. "It sounds pretty crazy down there."

"It is. People can't make it on half of their draw, so they're out stealing and killing to survive. The government drone force has swarm packs everywhere, arresting or shooting the people. When the grocery-store pod flew in yesterday, hundreds of people attacked it. Broke it open and stole everything."

"Really?" asked Chase, trying to contain his anger.

"Another drone pack flew in and opened fire on the people. Blood everywhere. Same thing's happening in Europe and Asia.

"We can't just let them open fire and kill people like that. We have to do something," said Chase, but without the optimism he'd had months ago. Were they beyond the point of no return? When the government kills civilians in the streets instead of through legislation, when they aren't even hiding it anymore, is there a point, he wondered.

"The people around the world; they've been beaten down for so long, most of them aren't fighters. Or if they used to be, they don't have the strength anymore," Julian said. Chase couldn't help but detect the same note of defeatism in his friend that existed in his own heart.

"Well, maybe we can convince them to fight," he said. His anger was reaching a boiling point. There had to be something. "I'm so sick of this. Yes, this will be a battle." Chase thought as adrenaline finally took over his rage. "We need a command center, but a lot of people know about you, Jules. They know you have a ton of high-tech hacking equipment, and the government will find out. We need to move your equipment to a secret place. Now."

Maggie interrupted. "I know the perfect place."

Chase jumped. He hadn't realized she was still listening. "Where?"

"The zoological society had to fight off poachers a couple hundred years ago, so they moved into a nuclear fallout shelter. They only use part of it, and the largest part is under the zoo. They made sure it was big enough to hide the animals in case of an attack. I have all the codes and everything."

"Will that work,?" Chase asked.

"I guess it would, but I have a lot of things to move," Julian said.

Chase was feeling a bit better. "Okay, I'll help you as soon as I get there. Hopefully no one sees us."

No one spoke for a moment, then Julian cleared his throat. "That's…going to be a little harder now."

"Why?"

"The collective has sent thousands of AI into the streets and air to secure the looters, but I'm working on something. I'll show you when you get here."

"Sounds good." Chase disconnected. There was a lot he needed to figure out. Quickly.

When Chase returned to Earth, he was surprised by the amount of violence. People were looting everything they could, searching for food, water— anything of value. Even the public transit system was down, with all the destruction in the roadways.

When Chase walked into Julian's room, it was empty. The room looked so big without all the equipment. Where is everything? he wondered. "Hello," he cried out, but all he heard was his echo.

Maggie connected to his port. "Chase, where are you?"

"I'm in Julian's room. Where is everyone?"

"We're all upstairs. "

He ran upstairs, and everyone was waiting for him. He greeted them but was most thrilled to see Maggie. Not being certain that he'd see her again was a worry that had taken its toll. They embraced for a while, forgetting about everyone else until Julian interrupted them.

"How was the casino?" Julian asked.

"Good and crazy as usual. All the stories you've heard are true."

"We figured as much. Hey, sit down. I have a surprise for you," Julian said.

"Okay, what is it?" Chase asked but did as he was told.

"Are you hungry?"

"Sure."

"Here you go." Julian reached under the table and handed Chase a dish with organically grown apples and fresh shrimp.

Chase's eyes bulged, and his stomach grumbled. "How did you get this type of food instead of the pills?"

Julian grinned. "I had one of the government patrol soldiers go to the supermarket pod and get it for us."

"Why would a soldier want to help us eat a nice meal? Out of the goodness of his heart?" Chase asked, incredulous.

"No, he wouldn't," Julian answered. "I found a way to hack into the port chip. If I get close enough to someone to scan my new program into their port, I can go back to my computer lab and control the chip. Maggie said you like real shrimp."

"Really, Jules, and have them buy us shrimp?" Chase said with a smirk.

Julian shrugged. "Hey, I had to test it somehow."

Chase knew the significance of such power over another person.

Then Jules said, "Everyone, close your eyes. I'm serious. Are your eyes shut? Sean, close your eyes."

Chase watched the others reluctantly close their eyes and did the same. A door opened slowly, and he heard someone walk in and then stop.

"Open your eyes."

Standing by the door was a man about five foot seven dressed in a German Nazi uniform. He looked like Adolf Hitler, complete with the mustache. No one said a word. They all just stared at him with his large gun and perfectly shined black shoes.

Finally, Chase broke the silence, saying to Julian, "Uh…is…is he an AI you built, or is he a real person? I can't tell."

"He's real. Look at him closely; you can see him breathing. His name is Sven," Julian said. He was practically bursting with excitement. Everyone continued staring.

Clio walked around the figure, keeping a good distance before she asked, "Is he dangerous? He looks really mean. He's not going to kill us, is he?"

Julian shook his head emphatically. "No, I just wanted to show you guys that I think I can control anyone's chip with my new program." He turned to Chase. "You said we need to go to war against the government, so I wanted to surprise you with a government guard who is now on our side, as a Nazi. I can make him into any kind of soldier, that's the important part. Our fight isn't just about greed and oppression, it's about technology and who controls it. That's all the collective really is. The real question is, who controls it? The people? Or the Sixteen?"

Maggie spoke out. "He's giving me the willies. Why is he standing there and not blinking? He looks like a zombie."

Chase had about a million questions, but Julian seemed so excited, he figured he'd skip over the most obvious of them; most notably, how a Hitler clone would be of any assistance to them. They wanted to make a good impression on people, and generally, Nazis didn't tend to produce good impressions.

Finally, Chase asked, "How many of these guys do you have right now?"

Julian paced and spoke emphatically. "Right now, I have scanned ten government soldiers, who will do whatever I program. They already moved all my stuff to the zoo." He laughed. "I didn't have to do anything."

Everyone in the room seemed to lighten up. Sean ate one of the pieces of shrimp. "Wow, if this is real shrimp, the synthetic version of shrimp really sucks." A few members of the group agreed. Chase didn't want to mention that he'd eaten real shrimp before. He couldn't imagine their excitement and felt guilty that he'd taken the luxury he'd lived in for years for granted.

Another soldier entered, a taller, more youthful-looking man with dark brown hair and green eyes. He stood with perfect posture in the center of the room. Clio circled the new addition to the group. "Did you say they will do anything, Jules?" she asked.

"Yes, I believe so. Why?"

"Well, this one's kind of cute."

"Stop. Clio, is that all you think about?" Maggie said, but she was laughing. Everyone seemed in such good spirits.

Chase asked, "How long will the control program last?"

"So far it's been forty-eight hours. I've scrambled the program twice because the collective somehow caught on that the chips are being manipulated. Naturally, they're trying to undo my program, so I just keep changing it, just like they do to me."

"Can you have them go buy more food and bring it back so we can help out some of the families in this neighborhood?" asked Chase.

"Sure." Julian programmed a few things in his port and, Chase assumed, beamed it to the guards. The original Nazi soldier moved abruptly, turned toward the door and walked out.

"He still gives me the willies," said Maggie.

Sean and Kay were organizing and signing people up to join their effort. Gangs had already formed to protect each neighborhood from attack drones or other desperate people. Sean spotted a supermarket pod landing about two blocks from the warehouse district. About one hundred mini drone gunners accompanied the ship to fight off looters. Sean and Kay walked in the ship's direction.

"They didn't have those gunners a few days ago," said Kay.

"I know," said Sean, "but there will be a lot of people gathering, so maybe I can sign up a bunch of recruits for our cause."

As they turned the corner, they saw the supermarket pod sitting in the middle of the street. A long line of people went up to scan their ports and make their selections. When the first woman scanned her port, and checked the display screen, she became agitated. "Wait," she said, "these prices are almost double what they were a few days ago."

A man standing near her said, "Let me take a look." Then he yelled out, "These fuckers are trying to starve us to death." He banged on the pod, and five others followed suit.

Within a few minutes, many people crowded the pod, kicking and smashing it with rocks or whatever they could get their hands on.

Sean and Kay tried to point out the hovering drones, weapons at the ready. Sean grabbed the arm of one of the guys. "Don't do that. The drones are right above you!" The guy turned and pushed Sean to the ground. Sean got up, shaking his head, and walked back to Kay.

The bottom lights on the drones blinked red, and a voice sounded. "We are police enforcement modules. Do not—we repeat, do not—damage the government food supply."

The crowd ignored the warning, and again it sounded.

Sean yelled, "Everyone stop, before they shoot or do something worse." The lights flashed faster and brighter. He grabbed Kay's hand and said, "Run."

After the fifth warning, the announcement stopped. The drones lowered from the sky, about fifteen feet above the crowd. Mechanical arms from two of the larger drones attached to each side of the pod and began to lift it off the ground.

"Hey," one guy yelled, "they're taking our food back!" He jumped up on the pod and climbed the drone's mechanical arms.

Again, the warning began. "Do not damage the government food supply."

As the guy climbed the drone's arm, laser guns lowered from the drones.

Multiple blasts shot from many directions, and the man on the pod was cut in half as his blood sprayed the crowd. The group scrambled to get away, with people tripping over each other. Sean yelled, "Keep running!"

While the two large drones lifted the pod off the ground, the smaller drones lowered and started picking people off with precise laser shots.

Within five minutes, the drones and the food pod were gone, and about seventy people lay dead on the sidewalk. The rest of the crowd wailed and kneeled in their bloodstained clothes.

Kay shakily climbed up onto a small building so everyone could see her. "Don't kneel. Stand. Now is the time to fight. We need to join together and fight the government sixteen, the collective and these fucking drones. If you're with me, get your friends and families and meet me back here in one hour."

Shortly thereafter, Chase learned of the drone massacre in the streets and sat with Maggie on the couch. "I'm not sure what to do, Mag. How are you feeling today? I know you were sick."

She had an odd, blank look on her face when she looked at him. "I feel okay," she said. "My stomach's upset, but it's nothing. Nothing compared to this."

Chase was pleased that Sean and Kay signed up a small army of volunteers, though none of them knew exactly what the plan was. Chase and Maggie spent the next few weeks making contacts with family members to try to get a recommendation for Chase, but nothing came of it.

Word got around to the other family members, and most of them felt Chase was a disappointment and a reject. Most of them originally thought he would take over his father's prisons when it was time for Sam Applegate to retire and live the good life.

Chase knew the annual council meeting was scheduled soon in the New Mexico nuclear bunker, where most of the collective computer brains were located. His focus was on the council, but he enjoyed being back at the warehouse and listening to the group brainstorm about how to fight the family drones.

Chase busied himself with the idea of making it onto the council, but it was a tough task. He couldn't even risk going outside without being targeted.

"I bet they lure you there to try to murder you," Maggie said. She sat next to him on the couch with her arms crossed. Chase closed the program on his eye screen and turned to her. He couldn't remember the last time he'd looked at her without something in the way and he immediately felt guilty for that. He grabbed her hand. "They can't, it's precedent. I promise, it will be fine. Besides, I need two votes from sitting members and they all hate me."

Maggie snatched her hand from him. "Precedent? Since when has the government cared about that?"

Anger colored her cheeks, which were unusually pale. She stood abruptly, covering her mouth as she ran across the room to the trash can. Chase followed, rubbing her back as she knelt, heaving. He brought her water when she was finished.

"Mags, you might need to see a doctor. I know it's expensive, but I'll find the money. You've been sick so long."

"No doctors," she said, her words fast and her eyes wide.

Chase leaned away from her. "What's wrong? Something's going on. I need to know what it is," he said. He tried to take her hand again, but she pulled away.

"I don't know what to do," she said. Tears fell from her eyelashes onto the floor as she held her head in her hands.

"I'll help you. Please tell me what it is so I can help you. You know I'd do anything—"

"Don't!" Maggie practically screamed the word. "Don't say it. I know you love me, and I love you, but I also know you have a priority and an obligation that's bigger than us."

Chase couldn't deny that, so he settled for something less. "We're a team, even if the collective and the Sixteen stuff is important to me. So are you."

Maggie stood and stared at him with what he could only interpret as hatred. She left the room. He supposed he'd upset her, but it was always just an unspoken thing between them. Life was important. Freedom was important. He would have to make sacrifices, and so would she. They'd agreed on that without speaking a word. At least, he thought they had.

She rushed back into the room and held her closed fist out to him. "Take it," she demanded, dropping a smooth object into his palm. "I would send it through our ports, but Julian's helping me hide it."

Chase felt the blood drain from his head as he looked down at the item in his hand. A white piece of plastic, with a little window and a deep red plus sign in the middle of the window.

"Th…where did you get this? They still…still make…" he stammered.

"Black market," she answered, "and yes, they still make pregnancy tests."

"Julian knew?" Chase's voice dipped and squeaked, as though he were experiencing a second puberty.

"I needed help. They'll find out, eventually. You'll have nothing to protect," she spat, but her features had smoothed, and she wrapped her arms around him. He held her tightly.

"How?" he asked.

"I didn't get the implant. You weren't given anything, since you were one of the Sixteen. They probably planned to do it after your dad kicked you out, but you've been on the run. I'm one of the lucky women, to still be fertile," Maggie said through sobs that left her gasping for air.

"Oh God. Why weren't we careful? Why…" Chase trailed off, trying to think of how the impossible could become possible. His thoughts raced. "Most people can't have kids. They know that, and they still take extreme measures to control the population." He was rambling. He was terrified.

"I have no idea what to do," Maggie said.

"That's alright," Chase said, attempting to stay calm for her sake. "We'll not know what to do together, and we'll get through this."

They stood together for a long moment, until an emergency alert came through Chase's port. Maggie paled even more. It ordered him to connect.

With trembling fingers, he tapped his port. "Hello, this is Chase," he answered.

"Please report tomorrow morning to the Family Council Meeting in New Mexico at nine o'clock. You will be given the exact coordinates once you are in the state of New Mexico. Prior to your appointment, you will receive proper conduct requirements. Failure to adhere to these codes of conduct will result in your removal and/or arrest."

"Chase, this time I'm coming with you," Maggie said. Her eyes were warm, bright, excited.

Chase deflated. He wanted her with him always, but he couldn't live with himself if he were to bring her harm. He drew her to him. "Mag, we go through this every time. You know I don't want you in any danger. And now, especially since, you know…"

Maggie scoffed and pulled away from Chase. "I'm always in danger. You see that, right? Everyone is in danger these days. I'm not staying back. This is your biggest meeting, and you might be able to fix everything. It's everyone's biggest meeting, and I want to be there with you. What's wrong with that?"

Chase smiled. She was right. Maggie was strong. Had always been strong. Living in poverty without a safety net her entire life—she was stronger than he was. Still, he didn't want to be responsible for any harm that came to her. What if they somehow knew about her condition? But if something were to happen while he was gone…wouldn't that be his fault, as well? "Can I talk you out of this?"

"No."

"Okay, fine then. Start packing, and let's go."

Sean walked in and slapped Chase on the back. "I heard you might be on the council. That's huge. Maybe you can be the voice of reason for those crazy fucks. Take the hydrogen ship; it's the fastest. Do you want me to come with you?"

Chase thanked him for his offer. "They definitely won't let anyone in the chambers except me, but Maggie is insistent on going, so why don't you grab Kay, and you guys can come along in case we get separated. Then at least you guys can stay together as a group."

"Sounds like a plan. Let me find Kay. We'll pack up and meet you on the ship."

There was a lot to be done. Chase was wearing a standard black tee-shirt and tattered jeans. His sneakers were filthy. Julian surprised him with a white suit and polished shoes, all courtesy of his cloned soldiers. "Everything went according to plan, except I asked for a black suit and shoes. Somehow the program screwed up. Sorry about that, Chase."

"You know what? I really like that it's white. I'll stand out more that way."

"Hey, that black dot we've seen in some people's eyes on the street?" Julian said as Kay helped tie Chase's tie, and Clio ran a lint brush over his suit. Chase nodded.

"Well, it's a side effect of that crazy new drug," Julian said.

Chase was having a hard time focusing. "Shit. Well, if you guys could look into that while I'm gone, I would appreciate the help," he said.

"Sure," Julian replied. Maggie fluttered in and out of the room.

"Hey man," Julian said, lightly grasping Chase's shoulder. "She's going to be fine. So will you."

Chase wanted badly to believe it.

Chapter Eleven

The group of four blasted off in the high-speed ship. On the way to New Mexico, they passed over many cities, and many of them had large fires burning, Chase knew, because of the violence. Maggie sat close to Chase and held his hand.

Looking down at the fires, she asked, "Do you think we can really help to stop this?"

"Maybe," he answered.

As she rubbed his back, she whispered in his ear, "I am so proud and love you for everything you are trying to do. I understand why you do it."

He smiled and lowered the interior lights so everyone could catch up on some sleep. Chase was dozing off and thought he was dreaming when his eye screen blinked. Mom calling. He sat up straight, jerking Maggie a little. He hesitated a moment, but he tapped his port.

"Mom, is that you?"

"Yes, Chase, it's me. Are you on your way to the meeting?"

"I'm on my way. You heard about it?"

"Yes, your father is very upset. He won't even speak to me."

"Why?"

"A lot of reasons, but you're my son, and no matter what, I love you."

"Thanks, Mom. I love you too. I'm sorry we don't see each other, but I think of you all the time. I miss you."

"I miss you too, Chase, and that's why, against your father's wishes, I signed the recommendation order for you to speak your piece at the council meeting."

Chase's throat closed as he fought back tears. He hadn't expected his mother to sacrifice her marriage, ridicule from peers and perhaps her way of life, to help him. "Mom, I…I don't know what to say. Thank you." He paused to gather himself and swiped at his eyes, worried he'd be seen crying. "Do you know who the other recommendation is from?"

"I don't, honey, but I was just calling to tell you good luck and be careful. You know, dear, most of the people in the family council don't agree with your type."

Chase was about to say, "What type?" but he decided not to argue with her. She'd done him the biggest favor of his life.

"Well, thanks, Mom, and maybe after everything calms down, we can get together again. Maggie is here with me."

There was no response. Perhaps his mom was also doing her best not to argue with him. They said their good-byes, and Chase disconnected.

A yellow light illuminated in the ship, and a voice sounded. "We are landing in T minus five minutes, per the inputted coordinates." The passengers perked up and had something to drink. Chase adjusted his white suit with Maggie's help. How odd it was to wear that suit. He had long ago stopped feeling comfortable dressing like the rest of the Sixteen.

As the ship's altitude declined, the interior screens showed that there were many objects below. As they continued to lower, they could see hundreds of military drones and other war machines. There were flashing lights everywhere, and two large gunships positioned themselves on each side of their private hydro ship.

Sean seemed a bit frantic, looking in every direction. "I guess they knew we were coming." No one responded. As the ship landed, larger round ships quickly surrounded them, with enormous laser guns protruding. They looked like big wheels with large spokes sticking out, but instead of spokes there were weapons. Both AI and human soldiers secured the perimeter of their landing pad.

"OK, I guess this is it." Chase said his good-byes, and Maggie gave him a prolonged hug and kiss. He reluctantly let her go as the door opened.

When the door was fully opened, one human and nine AI soldiers immediately said in loud, firm voices, "Identify yourself. Which one of you is Chasten Applegate?"

When he answered, they grabbed him by the arms and pulled him onto the tarmac before letting him stand on his own.

No one in the ship said anything except Sean. "Give them hell, Chase. Good luck!"

Chase acknowledged Sean before the soldiers directed him into one of the military ships. They all held their ears as the ship took off with a sonic boom.

Inside the military ship, soldiers surrounded Chase. "Applegate, put a blindfold on. We don't want you looking at our equipment or seeing our coordinates."

He complied and put the blindfold on. Once he closed his eyes, his eye screen showed him exactly where they were and where they were going.

Once they landed, they took off his blindfold, and a new set of soldiers conducted a security check. Before they got off the ship, everyone was scanned until only Chase and the human soldier remained.

"It's just you and me left. We need you to put these on. They are—"

"I know what they are. Magnetic wrist and ankle cuffs . My father invented them," Chase said, looking at the objects.

"That's right; I forgot they're called the Applegate cuffs. I'll keep the power on low, unless you do something stupid, then I'll turn it up high and kill you. Sound good?"

"Sounds great," Chase answered.

Once Chase had the magnetic cuffs on, the soldier signaled the others. Chase walked out of the ship and down the stairs with the human soldier behind him. When he got to the last step, the soldier said firmly, "Stop!" Two AI soldiers approached him and detached both of their arms, forming a body scanner. They proceeded to scan Chase from head to toe.

"Take three steps forward." He did. "Take one more step and stand in the middle of the blue circle on the ground." Once Chase did as he was told, the soldier stepped on a second blue circle and yelled out, "Clear!"

Chase and the soldier dropped into the ground. The circles morphed into high-speed elevator shafts traveling into the earth. Chase held on to the inside of the tube until the drop was over. He looked at his eye screens, and they estimated he was fifteen hundred feet below the surface.

The door opened into a large bright room, and Chase stood still while his eyes adjusted to the lights. After he was scanned again by another soldier, he took a few steps out of the elevator tube. Standing next to the AI soldier was a woman dressed in plain clothes.

"So you're Chase Applegate?" she asked.

"Yes, I am," he said.

"I've heard so much about you. You don't look like I thought you would. You're shorter. For some reason I thought you'd be really tall."

"Thanks, I guess," he said, as her face was expressionless.

"Come right this way and follow me." They walked down a long hallway, lined with soldiers on each side. As they walked, the soldiers turned slightly to keep a keen eye on him.

"Are you on the council?" he asked her. She had no response. At the end of the hallway, he saw a large scanner.

"How many times are you guys going to scan me?"

"We really only scanned you a few times. These are invisible doors. They can only be opened when a member of the Sixteen gets scanned."

"Oh, so you're a member of one of the sixteen families?"

"No, idiot, you are. That's how the invisible doors keep opening."

Chase felt his face heat. "Sorry, I have never been here."

The woman laughed. "From what I hear, you never will be again, either."

They reached the end of the hall, and she pointed, indicating that Chase continue walking by himself. He knew that to open the main door to the council, a person had to be in the Sixteen. He got there and looked around, but there was no door handle to get in.

He looked back at her. "How do I open the door?"

"Put your port over the fake keyhole." He did, and the door slowly opened.

Chase walked into a brightly lit semicircular room. Up on a stage, behind a long continuous desk, were sixteen seats. Behind each seat was a flag representing the governmental family as well the country represented. In front of the large desk were two smaller tables for anyone addressing the council.

When Chase entered the room, a soldier directed him to sit at the smaller desk up front. He sat and watched as family members filed in and sat in their respective seats. He recognized a few members he hadn't seen in person in a long time. There was complete silence, and finally the lead family member, Wang from China, started.

"State your name and your purpose to the World Council."

Chase cleared his throat. "Your Honor, my name is Chasten Applegate, and I wish to speak to the council in hopes of gaining the seat that I understand has recently been vacated on the board ."

"Prior to this council allowing you to present, I must first ask the members if there are any objections to you speaking today."

Immediately, the flag behind one of the members began to glow. "Let the record show that Ronald Francisco of the Francisco family has filed an objection. You may speak, Mr. Francisco."

Francisco appeared to be quite confident. He was dressed well, and clearly sober. A fake version of the man, not the actual person. Chase took a deep breath as Francisco began to speak.

"Thank you, Mr. Chairman and fellow council family members. The World Council law clearly states that family members, descendants or offspring not in good standing may not at any time speak to the council, unless they have two member recommendations. Now, I realize that his mother recommended him, but unfortunately, he would need one more. If there is no second recommendation, this person should be removed, and I believe I can demonstrate why he should be arrested for breaking the law."

A large screen appeared in the room. Looking at the screen, Mr. Wang spoke. "I respectfully request that the collective produce and confirm or deny a second official recommendation."

Chase swallowed and sweat formed on his upper lip and the back of his neck as Ron Francisco stared directly at him with a frown. Information on the screen was scrolling, and the collective voice sounded as an official document was displayed on the screen.

"Our records confirm that the document displayed is the second recommendation received yesterday from Mr. Randal Francisco." Lead Councilman Wang looked over at Ron.

"It appears your son Randal has legally recommended Mr. Applegate to proceed. Perhaps you should consider alternate means of control over your own family as well as your family business matters,

Mr. Francisco." Francisco didn't say a word, just slammed his fist on the table as he tried to contain his anger. There was a brief silence and then the chairman spoke. "Thank you to the collective. Mr. Applegate, you may begin."

Chase took a deep breath. "Thank you, Your Honor and fellow family council members. My name is Chase Applegate, and many of you know my family, but you may not know that I had a falling-out with my father and no longer enjoy many of the privileges of the Sixteen. Once I was renounced from the family, I began living with the common population. My goal here today is not to air my family's dirty laundry but to shine a light on today's society. The common people, which make up over ninety-nine percent of the world's population, are struggling and are enduring tremendous adversity."

"Why are you voicing this opinion of yours to this council, Mr. Applegate?"

"Respectfully, Your Honor, it is not simply my opinion but a fact of life. First of all, the people have little to no money for basic necessities or the means to contribute to society. Technology has also evolved over the past couple of centuries to the point where advanced AI systems have replaced most, if not all of, their jobs. There is no opportunity for them to earn any money outside of the draw."

"Perhaps, Mr. Applegate, they should focus their energy on finding work that technology cannot accomplish," said the lead councilman. "I'm sure you're aware that the family members around the world have graciously paid a draw to help these so-called common people, where they are not obligated to do so. The draw was never meant to provide all of the living needs of the people."

Chase nodded. "Your Honor, I understand and appreciate that fact, but the draw barely covers basic necessities, and some members have recently decreased this small amount of income."

"Let me remind you again that the draw was never intended to be the sole source of income but simply as a supplement to enhance earned income. Member families are also not obligated to supply any draw if they do not desire to do so."

"Again, Your Honor, with all due respect, the draw is what most people do live on because their jobs have been replaced. Just this winter there was a dramatic increase in Canadian energy expenses. This new energy cost alone is more than the draw. People are freezing to death because they can't afford basic heat to survive."

The lead councilman again looked over to his right. "This is your country, Mr. Francisco. Is that true?"

"No, it is not true, Your Honor. We did have a slight break in our power grid, but I believe Chase Applegate was the cause of that failure. Furthermore, even with that slight disruption, only a handful of people died, Your Honor. We are also overpopulated by a hundred and eighty percent, so a few deaths are not a problem."

"That's not true," said Chase.

The lead councilman interrupted. "Mr. Applegate, you are a guest here today. Do not interrupt a sitting council member in these chambers, or you will be removed. Mr. Francisco owns the country to which you are referring. At such time as you purchase your own country, you can do as you see fit to manage the population. Are there any other comments you would like this council to hear before we consider your request for a vote regarding the vacant seat?"

Chase sat silently for about twenty seconds. This was his big opportunity and both of his eye screens scrolled at rapid speed.

"Yes, Your Honor. I believe if voted in, I could be the voice of reason and offer a point of view for the common people."

"Are you suggesting that this council is not reasonable, Mr. Applegate?" All the family council members stared at him simultaneously.

"Not at all, Your Honor, but let me give you another example. Recently in my hometown in America, the draw, which I believe is very small to begin with, has been further reduced. At this point, the common people are having a hard time buying the basics, such as food and water. A crowd protested this reduction, and gunner drones attacked and killed many of them in cold blood."

The lead councilman looked over at the collective screen. "Is what Mr. Applegate described true? Please supply the report from that zone."

A video appeared, and the collective voice said, "According to this police security video, individuals unlawfully climbed the transport food pod in an attempt to damage government property. Police drones intervened and took reasonable measures to control the crowd. The food pod was then moved to an alternate location to avoid further violence."

The lead councilman said thank you and then asked Chase, "Did you realize there was a riot and they were attacking government property? You understand this is illegal?"

"I do realize that, Your Honor, but they rioted because they could not afford food for themselves or their families."

"Mr. Applegate, a society needs laws, and these laws must be enforced. You of all people should be aware of this concept, since your family business is prisoner rehabilitation. In normal circumstances, we would have limited your comments prior to this point. However, since you are a descendent of the original sixteen, we extended this hearing as a courtesy. I believe that I can speak for the entire council when I say we have heard enough to cast a vote. Before we do vote, is there anyone who would like to make a comment on Mr. Applegate's request to fill the vacant council seat?"

The chief security representative spoke up. "We do, Your Honor. She is an elderly member of the council who is in poor health and could not be here today. With all due respect and in light of her health, she has requested that we connect in order for her to make a statement."

The lead councilman glanced at the other members, and they all nodded with approval. He responded, "Let the record show that such request has been accepted." The elderly lady appeared on the screen.

Chase was stunned, as he hadn't seen her face in years.

"My name is Eleanor Sanford of the fourth family. I would like to personally express my extreme disappointment in the fact that this individual has even been given the right to speak in front of this pristine group. The man sitting in front of you, Chasten Applegate, killed my son with his reckless and wicked decisions. My boy Phillip was destined for greatness and was a wonderful and important part of our family. He was being groomed, and successfully, I might say, to walk in his father's footsteps. That was before this monster took it all away. He should have ended up in his father's prison."

Chase spoke up. "It was an accident, Mrs. Sanford."

She yelled, "Don't you ever speak to me!"

The lead council member reprimanded him. "Mr. Applegate, this will be your second and final warning. If you interrupt a sitting family member one more time, you will be removed and subjected to our council court for punishment. Do you understand?"

"Yes, Your Honor, I do."

"Mrs. Sanford, you may continue."

"Thank you. He took everything from me, and his own family disowned him. He speaks of the common people and their struggles, which are now his struggles. They are struggles he deserves. He has had every opportunity to live among the Sixteen and instead has ruined it for himself and hurt other families along the way. Now he has the audacity to interfere with other wonderful families, like the Franciscos, while you all sit there and listen to his lies. If I were not so old, I would beat him myself."

The lead councilman piped back in. "Thank you very much for your comments, Eleanor. I believe we understand your position of disapproval and appreciate your time to speak today. I feel as though we have heard enough from our council members as well as Mr. Applegate, and I make a motion to commence a vote. Would anyone like to make a motion to second?"

"I would, Your Honor," said the European member from the eleventh family.

"All in favor of Mr. Applegate filling the vacant seat, say aye." There was a pause for a moment, and no one voted. The lead councilman looked to his right and then his left.

"All opposed?" Each member uttered a "nay" as the lead councilman took a count.

"We have no members in favor, three who have abstained, and thirteen opposed. I'm sorry, Mr. Applegate; your request has been officially denied."

Chase put his head down.

The councilman moved on to the next topic on the agenda. "We will proceed with normal business and ask Mr. Applegate to be removed from the council chambers."

At the far end of the council was the family member from Russia who had abstained from voting. "Your Honor, on behalf of the Russian family, perhaps it would be relevant for Applegate to sit in for a few more moments as we discuss the next item on the agenda. In an unofficial manner of course. Applegate does seem to vigorously defend the commons."

"That is a bit unorthodox, but I can put it to a vote if you would like to second it, Mr. Popov?"

"I would, Your Honor."

"OK, all in favor of letting Mr. Applegate stay for a short time while we discuss a matter of the commons, say aye." There were ten in agreement and six opposed. "Very good. Then we will proceed. Mr. Applegate, you may remain for a short period of time, but let me remind you that you may not interrupt."

"Let's begin. This portion of the meeting will be an open forum. The matter at hand today is the common populace that Applegate referred to in his speech." The lead councilman continued. "I see that a few members would like to speak, so I will start with the Kim family. Please proceed."

"We are at a point today where we control all the technology, the money, the collective, and the land territories. We continue to have these meetings on how to support this portion of the population that seems to myself and my family to be worthless."

The member sitting next to him spoke up. "I have to agree with him. We spend most of our time managing the population and the problems they cause. They sit around and consume our goods and services like termites. They eat the food we produce, drink our water, use our energy then they have nerve to complain about it. The best thing this council did years ago was to make new births illegal." Chase's pulse sped rapidly at the mention of illegal births. His pulse seemed to beat in a manner that screamed, "Maggie. Maggie."

"Ironically, Mr. Applegate was the last legal birth. It is becoming impossible to monitor billions of these commoners. Also, you know as well as I do that they are probably having illegal babies to pollute the planet. The planet just can't fit any more of these takers!"

Another family member spoke up. "I have to agree, especially in light of the new version of AI droid. They can do almost anything the commons used to do for us. I have a gardener now who shows up at the exact start time, never complains, and never asks for a raise. My favorite waiter at my restaurant is an AI droid. We named him Billy." He turned and smiled to the member next to him. "Billy is also an excellent cook."

"Very good comments," said the lead council member. "Thank you. Now, Mr. Applegate, you may speak in a moment to answer this question or comment in general. It seems that these common people you defend appear to have no purpose on this planet anymore. Would you agree?"

He paused, as he was lost for words at such a question. "I would say that I respectfully disagree, sir. These are good people you all speak of, with few options. They don't want to drain your society. They want to work and support their families like they have for the entire history of human existence. These are the people who built our cities alongside AI, who contributed to society and built up our economy."

The family member from Australia interrupted. "That may or may not be true, but that was the past. For the past century, they have been nothing but a drain on everyone here, and they don't even try to support themselves. At fifteen billion, there just isn't enough food, water, energy and space to go around. Furthermore, they don't help themselves by protesting and not contributing, except eating and trying to have illegal babies! My God, think about it. Half of them look like the walking dead. How do you defend these commoners? You disgust me!"

Chase wanted to say something immediately, but he feared getting thrown out or arrested, so he treaded lightly with his comments. "May I speak?"

"No, not yet," said the lead councilman.

The Australian family member asked Chase, "Can you tell me one good thing the commoners provide the family members that we can't accomplish without them? I would like you to answer that simple question."

"May I answer, Council Leader?"

"You may."

"They are good, smart people, and many of them are talented in their own right. Some are artists, others are builders, doctors, service providers, and musicians, just to name few."

Another council member answered him, "We don't need any artists, and we have the collective and complex machines for building and medical needs. You didn't answer the question, or do you have no plausible answer?" The member looked at the others and continued in a serious voice. "I believe the time has come to consider a sort of phase-out program for the common human population. We should be focusing our concerns and efforts with our own population, not the common population. I bet if you look at the sixteen families around the world and all of their blood relatives, it's a mighty number."

The lead councilman tapped into the collective, and the number 1,127,138 was displayed.

"There you go," the member said. "We have over one million family members, and we already control everything worth controlling. That also doesn't include all the AI droids each family owns. My last point is that not even Applegate, the defender of the commoners, could answer the one question to my satisfaction." He turned to his right. "Come on, Francisco, you and I have spoken about this, and we have a solid proposal. Let's move this thing along."

Ron Francisco spoke. "I would like to make a motion to continue the meeting in confidence without Applegate, who is not a council member and who was declined on his vote."

"Ronald is correct," said the lead councilman. "Mr. Applegate, best of luck to you. Guards, please remove him from our council."

Two soldiers picked up Chase and walked him out through the

big electronic door that slammed shut behind him. He walked down the hall to the elevator tube in silence, thinking about the meeting. He got in the tube with two new soldiers, and it led him back to the surface. Before the elevator door opened, the larger soldier grabbed Chase by the hair and threw him against the wall.

"Hey, let me give you some advice." He made a fist with some of Chase's hair still in his hand. "Don't fuck up. Look at me, punk!" Chase turned a little bit, and the soldier grasped his head with both hands. "Look into my eyes so you know who I am. My name is Gio, and I would love nothing more than to torture you for fun. I listened to you in there and all your bullshit about the maggot population. You're no good. So again, my advice to you is; don't fuck up." A smile came across his face. "Because if you do, I'll volunteer to be the one to catch you. What's my name?"

Chase didn't say anything. Gio punched him in the stomach and, when he keeled over, kicked him in the side. As Chase lay there in pain, the soldier yelled, "What's my name?"

In a pained, spiteful voice, Chase said, "Gio."

"Good. It's nice to meet you too." He said to the other soldier, "Blindfold him." At the exit, Chase was scanned and thrown to the ground. Gio picked him up and threw him into the military battleship for departure.

Soon he was back on his own pod, and they took off as quickly as possible.

Maggie hugged him, her body shaking and her eyes glossy. "You were gone for a really long time. I thought something happened to you. Are you OK?"

"I'm OK," he said and tapped his port for Julian. "Are you there, Jules?"

"I am. How did it go?"

"Look, Julian, I know Francisco and others will be coming after me. Can you scramble my chip as well the rest of us on the ship right now?"

"Of course I can. I did it as soon as you boarded, but let me track you now, the same way they would, just to make sure. Yes, the collective tracker shows you are going in three directions right now. Obviously, they know what I'm doing."

"Good. Jules, you're the best. Listen, make sure your chip and Clio's are also scrambled; I don't want the collective or the council to know where our home base is located. We need a safe zone."

"You got it, my friend. Okay, here's the plan. In twelve minutes, your ship will land in the Arizona desert and we have a black market mini ship for your guys to get on but do it fast, Chase."

Maggie answered. "Don't worry about that, we'll be ready."

"Stay safe. Over and out."

"So how did it go with the council, sounds like no good, since we're running?" Kay asked.

Chase shook his head. "It didn't go well. It didn't go well at all."

Sean asked, "Does that mean you're not going to be on the council and fill the vacant seat?"

"Are you crazy? Not a chance. Do you know who spoke out

against me?"

"Who?"

"Phillip's mom, Mrs. Sanford. She blames me for Phil's death."

"Wow, I can't believe she was there."

"No, she came in on a feed, but it didn't really matter. They never would have voted me in."

"Did you get to tell them how people are suffering since they reduced the draw?"

"Forget about the draw. Forget everything," he said.

"What do you mean, 'forget about the draw,' Chase, and why are you being so negative?"

Chase tried to rein in his anger. He wanted to snap at his friends, and he knew they didn't deserve such treatment after all they'd done for him. "The council doesn't care about the draw. They don't even care about the common population as a whole."

"Why?" Maggie asked.

Chase held her hand. "It doesn't really matter. I need a little bit of time to think."

"Well, I'm glad you're alright," said Kay. "Chase, since we have to hide and we're so close to the West Coast, we can hide in my LA neighborhood. Plus, a friend of Sean's and mine is pretty sick."

He agreed, and once they switched ships, they put in the coordinates and Chase filled everyone in on what had happened. By the time they descended near Kay's old neighborhood, it was dark. There were fires in the streets, and some of the buildings were also engulfed in flames. Because they were located in the no-rescue zone, there were no fire drones in sight.

"Kay, where are we landing?" Sean asked.

"On top of the number four warehouse. It's safer there."

It was a warm, clear night as they landed and got out. Four of their old friends met them on the rooftop. Sean did all the introductions and asked about his old friend.

"So where is the Zank man?" Sean asked.

"Dude, Zank is pretty much shot at this point." They all went inside.

"Do you mean more shot than usual?" Sean laughed.

"No, seriously, Sean, he is pretty much gone from B." They walked into Kay and Sean's old warehouse. There were some paintings on the walls and a few new sculptures, scant furniture and a few dead plants, but that was about it. One girl asked Kay if the gangs in the east were in control yet. Kay told her that they were not as organized on the East Coast but were growing every day.

The girl explained to the group, "Here, we basically have three gangs now that control everything in Los Angeles. For the first time, they started working together and have broken into the water supply, so we at least have water. The other gang is working on food, but that's much harder."

"What about the drone fighters? They're killing a lot of people back home," Kay said.

"Well, we have a guy out here that bought a fusion blaster on the black market. It can shoot a number seven drone right out of the sky.

We feel like we're making strides, but we just found out that the fucking council and collective might be poisoning us with B. Look at my eye."

They all looked, and there was a black dot in the corner of her eye.

Chase said, "I've been noticing that dot in a lot of people's eyes back east. Is everyone just doing the drug B these days to escape reality?"

"Yes and no," she said. "There definitely are a lot of people who are just giving up and taking B, but most people are still fighting the fight and don't take B. Somehow, they are getting it anyway."

"Where is Zank?" Kay asked.

"Do you really want to see him, Kay?"

"Yes. Where is he?"

"He's in the next room."

They all got up. Sean opened the door slowly, and there was Zank, sitting in a chair. His eyes were both open but completely black. He was so skinny that his facial bones were protruding, covered only by a thin layer of skin.

"Shit, he looks like a zombie or something," Sean said.

"His mind is spinning, and he's barely breathing. Eventually, he'll be dead. There is nothing we can do at this point, except let him die. I know the sixteen are responsible for this, and I'll show you how I know. Let's take a ride," said their friend Angelina.

They got in her small pod and flew about ten blocks. They landed in the street, where a bunch of people were walking around, dazed.

Kay said to Maggie and Chase, "Wow, these people are beyond high. Look, some of them are walking into each other."

Chase was viewing his eye screens to gather as much information on the drug as he could, but it was transforming itself so quickly that he didn't trust the information.

He asked Kay, "What is the latest version of B doing to people today?"

"Like any drug, it is an escape, right? These days, when you take B for the first time, it programs your eye screen and your mind to crave whatever your greatest desires are and then delivers. You feel like you are literally living that experience. It is the greatest high because it is your personal greatest desire, whatever that means to you. When the drug and experience end, people are generally pissed off and want to go back as quickly as possible. The dealers also sell it inexpensively, so people can afford it on the draw." She went on to explain, "Everything is wonderful for a while, but then the door shows up."

"What door?" Chase asked.

"In the beginning when you take Black, the first thing you see is a door. You open it and go through it, and your fantasy starts. But the longer you take B, additional doors appear, and some are hard to open. Some doors lead to circular hallways and force addicts to start over again with a new door, but the new doors have windows that give you a peek into the fantasy. Sometimes the doors open, sometimes they don't.

"At this stage of the drug, when addicts come off the high, they go crazy to take more Black and try to find the correct door. The fantasies get shorter and shorter, and more hallways and doors appear. The brain's desire for more of the drug grows exponentially. Once the addicts' eyes are completely black, they are in some sort of endless loop with millions of doors and visions of their fantasies. The fantasies are behind distant doors that get slammed when they get close. They stop eating and drinking and eventually they die. It's fucked up, Chase. I want to show you guys something," she said. They walked around the corner to a huge abandoned airport hangar.

"What is this?" Kay asked.

"You'll see." Angelina opened a side door, and they entered the massive hangar. It was dark, so it took Chase's eyes a minute to adjust. A repugnant smell of urine and feces filled the space. Hundreds of people were lined up in a standing position in long rows. They were propped up with makeshift wooden braces under their armpits to hold them upright. Many of the people had candles next to them for light.

Chase fought the urge to gag or scream. These people weren't simply left to live that way; it was beginning to seem more and more as though they were encouraged to live that way.

"This is unbelievable," said Sean.

Angelina agreed. "This is what we call a B hive. It's where our addicts go when they want to stay on B permanently and leave reality. They're all at or near the loop stage, and their minds are pretty much fried. Some loving family members come here and scan in more funds if they are getting low, so that their loved one doesn't get stuck in a hallway loop or a doorway. They make these arrangements and reserve either a stand-up spot or chair once the person is hooked."

Chase looked around and couldn't believe the rows and rows of people in the large airport hangar, just propped up in a vegetative state. To his left he saw an IV hooked up to one of the addicts.

When Angelina noticed Chase looking at the IV, she said, "Some families don't want to say good-bye, so they hook up IVs for food. It basically prolongs the inevitable."

Sean said, "Let's get out of here. I can't take this anymore."

Everyone walked out except Chase, who was still scanning the room and downloading data from the addicts' chips. He was sending the data back to Julian.

He finally stepped out, and as the group walked away from the airport hangar, six new addicts walked toward it with their loved ones.

"That sucks," said Kay.

They all looked up when they heard a drone gunner ship firing close by. Sean grabbed Kay's arm and said to everyone, "Quick, get in the pod. The gunner ships move fast, but this is actually the safest place these days. We can fly straight up and get above the gunners before they track us."

They took off and hovered above the gunner drone, staying in a safe zone. Chase watched the gunner ships and noticed they were targeting certain neighborhoods while avoiding others.

"Angelina," Chase asked, "are there any new airport hangars or large spaces being prepared for new Black addicts?"

"Absolutely, there are so many new addicts every day that we are preparing seven new sites in this part of the city alone. I know of eight others that are planned for the west side."

"Could you give me two or three of those addresses?" She did, and Chase tracked the gunner ships in comparison to the addresses.

Sean asked, "Chase, what are you thinking?"

"The data on the drug B reveals that it is worldwide at this point. That large gunner drone just blew up most of the neighborhood below, except the hangar that we were just in. It also missed the new addresses." He paused for a second. "These aren't drug houses; they're concentration camps. They're trying to exterminate the common people."

Chapter Twelve

The four decided to stay in LA for a while. Kay set up a meeting with a gang called the Correctors. They were brutal fighters, but they were happy to see Kay, who spent that whole day tattooing the Correctors' necks with war eagles and swords. The Correctors were experts at stealing food pods and destroying drones.

Chase and Julian stayed in contact, trying to figure out how the collective and the families were integrating B into the people's systems. Julian suggested that it had to be through a common method, so they sent food and S water samples to a local underground chemist in Santa Monica. S water, which was originally called Super Water, was developed with a harmless chemical additive to basically increase the water supply to the population. The Sixteen claimed it was four-parts additive and one-part water, but many didn't believe it. It was still clear, it had no distinctive smell, and no one really had a choice.

While Chase was collecting the samples, he noticed Angelina's black dot was getting larger.

Julian connected. "Chase, are you available?"

"Sure," Chase said. He picked up a commotion on Julian's end. "Wait. What's that noise in the background? Did they find out where I am?"

"No it's just some people yelling about something. I'm in the warehouse," Julian answered.

"Why? I thought we moved everything to the zoo bunker for safety."

"I did, and all our important networks are there, but going to and from the bunker is getting more dangerous. The drones and gangs are blowing up everything. I'm trying to work remotely, but we need to figure out a better long-term plan."

"I understand," Chase replied.

"Anyway, I wanted to tell you I found the drone attack schedule for your location, and you were right. They avoided all the addresses you listed. It appears they are driving the users to certain locations, like ant traps."

"OK, I'll let you know if I find out anything from the chemist."

The next day, Chase and Sean went to Santa Monica to meet the chemist. Sandra was a science whiz kid who had rebelled a few times from her family. She'd heard about Chase from her friends. The community was gated; therefore, she met them at the guard station.

Chase and Sean landed in a secluded area and walked to the guard station. As they walked, Chase immediately noticed the government family emblem on the guards' uniforms and quickly scanned their chips from a distance to review their personal histories. They approached the guard station cautiously.

"Don't worry," Sandra said. She was petite, with short black hair and dark eyes. Her pale complexion was youthfully smooth, so Chase was surprised to find grey strands scattered throughout her thick dark hair. She wore a white lab coat over a pair of white pants, looking more like a doctor than a scientist. "These guys are my friends. Come on, I have a secret tunnel to my lab. So, Chase, is Kay your girlfriend?"

"No, we're just friends. This is Sean. He's her boyfriend."

"Cool, I like her; she's a fighter. I'm Sandra, for those who don't know my name, and I've been working on your samples. My dad is a cousin of the Sanford family, and they control the S water supply in America. There has always been something strange with the new water, but no one has really detected anything illegal."

"I know them too," said Chase. "My friend Phil was in that family..." Chase trailed off, choking on his words unexpectedly. He cleared his throat. "But he…uh, he died. A long time ago."

Sandra cocked her head to the side and drew her eyebrows together. "I'm sorry to hear that," she said.

They entered Sandra's vast lab, which was filled with shiny, stainless equipment and plenty of AIs for assistance. She showed them some of her experiments and she had a special area set up for her work on B.

"I've been researching B for a while now, trying to find a cure and a malware virus to contaminate the program. I also overheard a family member joke that it's a good thing the family personally doesn't drink S water, which made me suspicious. So for the past two weeks I've been testing this water and have found a chlorine molecule that is masked within it. The additive is also nine parts to one-part water, not four to one. More importantly, the molecule is not chlorine; it's a high concentration of Black."

"Good work discovering that," Chase said. "Do you think you can find—" He was cut off by a message.

"Chase, it's Julian. Emergency. Connect now!"

"I'm here. What's going on?"

"I've been scrambling your chip tracker since you got out there, but somehow the collective must have figured it out. Sixty gunner ships just detoured to go to Six Seventy-Four Jay Boulevard, Santa Monica. Is that where you are?"

"Yes."

Julian yelled. "Run. Now! You're about to get hit!"

Chase spun and ran to the basement window of the lab. A level nine drone gunner ship hovered above the property. It lowered and turned to face the basement section of the estate where they were standing. Chase watched as the two large laser blasters pointed directly at him. Feeling like a caged animal, he looked both ways and out the window again. He saw a flash on the tip of a laser gun, and then…he stopped time.

Everything froze. Chase noticed that he could move more freely. Time had completely stopped for the others. In the past, when this phenomenon occurred, time would continue, very slowly, for everyone else. He thought that perhaps parallel dimensions in the universe actually did overlap. He remembered learning about multiverses in school, but that was so long ago. He thought for a while, ultimately deciding to move the chemist to a safe place and take off in his small ship with Sean, who was oblivious. He knew that when time started again the collective would simply track him then, so he needed a plan. While time wasn't moving in the earth's dimension, he picked up Maggie and Kay—being extra careful carrying Maggie—so he could fly to LAX. He was fascinated that he could move about while everyone else stood still in time.

Inside the gunner ship, Lieutenant Harrison was excited to get the order to move immediately to 674 Jay Boulevard in Santa Monica. It was his lucky day, since he'd already been patrolling California and his warship was the closest to the address. His team had been tracking Chase for a long time, and this would be a feather in his cap.

They arrived quickly, and the large level nine-gunner ship lowered on the target. The crew warmed up the laser blasters.

"Lieutenant Harrison reporting from drone gunner ship two-two-one-seven-MB. We have arrived and have the target in sight. Requesting permission to fire."

"Ten-four, Lieutenant Harrison. This mission is of the utmost importance. Prepare to fire all laser blasters on board at my command. Do you read?"

"Affirmative. Our lasers are warmed up and ready to fire."

"Ten-four, Lieutenant Harrison. Prepare to fire. Four, three, two, one, fire!"

The power of the blasters shook the ship as it fired repeatedly at the target. A massive cloud rose from the spot where the estate once stood.

"Lieutenant Harrison to base, direct hit."

"Ten-four, Lieutenant Harrison. Fire all remaining ammunition at the target, then raise your ship to allow backup gunner ships to fire. Because of the target's unconventional defense, the collective has directed the annihilation of all objects in a ten-kilometer zone of the target. Fire your remaining weapons and proceed upward accordingly."

The lieutenant did as directed, and the other ships moved in, continuing to fire from every angle in the zone. Within seconds, Santa

Monica was in flames.

"Lieutenant Harrison, is it possible you missed your initial shot on the target? The collective has picked up a signal from the subject's chip at LAX at the exact moment of impact. Did you miss the target?"

"Absolutely not. I had a direct, unobstructed hit and killed the target. It's probably a decoy like all the others. Our ship's scanner made a positive match seconds before impact. I'm looking below, and there's a crater from what used to be the city of Santa Monica. There's no way we missed him or that he escaped. I promise you that!"

"Very good, Lieutenant. Over and out."

Inside Chase's ship, which was now sitting on the tarmac of LAX, time began again as the ground shook from the large explosion in Santa Monica. Maggie, Kay, and Sean came to and immediately grabbed the closest thing they could.

Maggie said, "Where am I? What just happened?" The others were pale, and swiveling their heads rapidly, likely trying to understand their new surroundings.

Chase quickly said, "They found me, and just as Sean and I were about to get killed, I stopped time."

Kay hugged Sean. "Did we die, Sean? Do you think were in heaven? Sean shook his head as he looked out the ship's window. "That's crazy. Look how big those flames are over there."

"What now, Chase?" Sean asked still hugging Kay.

"It won't be long before the collective figures out I'm alive. I'm sure they're scanning for remains right now, and there are none. If we can get off the planet, it's possible the collective will determine that I'm dead and stop blowing things up and sending so many people to look for me."

"How are we going to do that?" Maggie asked.

"Follow me." Chase hurried outside, where their ship was parked right next to the Dark Side of the Moon Casino ship. He used his contacts to get them on board. The ship headed off to the moon, and the passengers began partying as usual. The flight manager connected with Jared, and the four were immediately moved into first class to avoid the cameras and scanners in general.

When the ship landed on the moon, Jared was there to greet Chase and the others.

"Chase, you're a crazy bastard! I don't even follow the news down there very much, but you're all over the feed. I heard you were the number one most wanted, but they killed you in Santa Monica." Jared went on, laughing. "My passenger guests are so high that, out of three hundred people, no one recognized you. Amazing. You can stay as long as you want, but you should consider a disguise or something, in case someone recognizes you."

"I will think about that, and thank you for letting us hide out," said Chase.

Over the upcoming weeks, Chase stayed in contact with Julian and monitored the feeds from Earth. In time, it seemed the families believed Chase was killed in Santa Monica. The attacks on the population decreased, and Chase and Julian believed the families were letting the people die a slow death from the drug in the new water supply.

When they felt it was safe, they asked Jared to put them on

the next ship back to Earth. Chase didn't want to go back to LAX, so they prepared to board the Chicago O'Hare returning ship. Julian was having problems finding a ship to infiltrate the airport space without the collective detecting something out of the ordinary. Waiting for the ship to board, Jared met the four and hugged Chase.

"Chase, I'm not real big on good-byes, but I have a feeling I might not see you for a while. I don't agree with everything you're doing, but at least it's from the heart. Sometimes I think you're a little naïve on what you're up against, my friend. Be careful. All right, I feel like I'm getting too emotional here. Look, when you land in O'Hare, I'll have my private jet pod fueled up and ready to go. Take the jet as my gift. And remember this: If you're going to go down, go down in flames!" Then he turned and walked back toward the casino.

Chase yelled, "You're the best, Jared. Thank you." Jared kept walking and raised his arm with his thumb up.

Chapter Thirteen

Flying back to Earth in the luxury casino liner, Chase knew they were headed for turmoil. Maggie, Sean, and Kay seemed to know it as well, but they were enjoying the last bit of the calm before the storm.

Maggie asked Chase, "Should we tell them?" He nodded. "OK, Sean and Kay, we have something to tell you."

"What?" they both asked.

"We're… expecting," Maggie said with a glow on her face. Chase knew she feared for her future, but she was determined to be as positive about the situation as she could be. "We're so excited!"

"Oh my God, yeah. It's scary, but we're happy for you guys," said Kay, looking at her feet. "We actually have something to tell you guys."

"Really?" Maggie asked with a smirk on her face.

"I'm pregnant, too," Kay said. The group fell silent.

Maggie said to Sean, "I knew it." Sean laughed.

"How far along are you guys?" Kay asked.

"Twelve weeks," said Sean.

"We think we're about five weeks," said Chase.

Kay explained how they would keep the pregnancy low-key, so that no one would notice and turn them in to the collective. At that point, though, she wasn't sure if it mattered.

Maggie agreed and said that, while Julian already knew, they were only planning to tell Clio. Then Chase turned to Sean.

"Sean, do you think your sister will do our exams and the checkups?"

"Absolutely, I already asked her. She loves you guys, she'll totally do it."

For the rest of the flight, they laughed at their situations, though the dark threat of arrest remained, the group tried to stay upbeat. Chase felt better just knowing that someone else was going through the same thing. With all the excitement, the flight seemed to go by very fast. Shortly thereafter, the program let them know that the destination was just ahead, and the excitement died down.

Once they landed and exited the ship, Chase looked for Jared's private jet. As promised, the jet was warmed up and ready to go. They boarded and took off for New York. Jared's ship was fast, and they were descending toward New York within minutes. Looking out the window, Chase could see fires and the destruction from the resistance of the common people and their gangs.

Sean glanced at Chase. "It looks more like a war zone, doesn't it?"

Chase nodded and tapped his port to connect with Julian. "Jules, what's going on down there? We're getting close to home."

"Nothing major. There have been a couple of skirmishes, a bunch of people got killed, and they're burning buildings in protest. Land at Central and Pine and go to that back alley we used in the past."

"You got it, Jules. See you in a few," Chase said before disconnecting.

They landed, and when the door opened, they could feel the heat from a nearby burning building. They ran down the alley and into the back of the warehouse. They were eager to get inside, so they ran down the hall and banged on the door.

Everyone yelled, "Let us in!"

Julian yelled back, "It's open, come in. It's so great to see you guys," he said. "I have something huge to tell you, and, Chase, I wanted to tell you this in person."

"Well, wait. Jules, where's Clio?"

"I don't know. She's around here somewhere." They encouraged Julian to tell them his news.

"I hacked the Code," he said with a big smile. With excitement apparent in his voice, he repeated, "The Code." Chase went silent, as did the rest of the group. Chase didn't know what Julian was talking about, and he was certain the others didn't, either.

"What does that mean?" Sean asked.

"Okay, guys, you might want to sit down for this one. Over the years, I've hacked into so many of the collective's codes, I can't even keep track anymore, but many of them led to dead ends. Finally, I found the most important code to fight against the collective and the Sixteen: I cracked the code that controls and launches the collective's mass-destruction weapons. Right now, I could launch the biggest fusion bombs myself. At any target on earth."

"That's amazing," said Chase. "And you can aim them anywhere?"

Julian grinned and clasped his hands together. "I can launch a fusion X-Five bomb right now and blow up an entire country. I can target an F-Ninety-Nine drone fighter ship the size of a football stadium and blow it out of the sky." The group was silent, and Chase observed that they were all taken aback by this information, just as he was.

"This may be exactly what we need to level the playing field in our own war efforts," said Chase.

"That's amazing," Sean said. "How did you figure that out?"

"Listen, no one knows. I haven't even told Clio yet, because I just cracked it about an hour ago. Chase, I want you to have the code. I started a sequence program to put the code in your—"

The room started shaking, and an accompanying rumbling sound grew louder and louder. Chase grabbed on to the closest thing he could find, as did the others.

"It's an earthquake!" Kay said, as the entire warehouse shook, and parts of the ceiling fell down. They tried to get to the door to go outside, but the building shook again, the force of which slammed everyone into the walls.

Another wall smashed open from a large explosion. The group dropped to the floor to try to take cover. When the smoke cleared, there was Clio with ten heavily armed soldiers, whose weapons were pointed at the group. They moved the debris out of the way and stood up.

Julian shook his head at Clio. Within seconds, thirty more soldiers beat down the remaining walls, and Chase heard fighter drones above. A tall commander with a several medals on his uniform entered and approached Clio.

"Thank you, Clio. Your cooperation will be noted in the history log."

Chase's jaw dropped.

Julian raised his voice, which had more anger in it than Chase had ever heard. "Clio, how could you turn us in? Why would you do this?"

She shook her head frantically. "No. No, you have it all wrong. This is a good thing for us. They told me we'll be rewarded beyond our wildest dreams by one of the sixteen families, and we'll live a good life from now on, all of us. No more struggling. Isn't that wonderful?" Clio was pleading, and Chase watched as Julian dropped his head, shaking it as though he were trying to dislodge the idea altogether.

Julian looked up at her. "I can't believe you did this to us. To our friends."

Clio tried to grab Julian's hand, but he shook her off. "Julian, I thought you would be happy. They told me that you wouldn't be arrested and that you can come with us. Come on, let's go."

Julian lowered his head again. The soldiers circled the five with their laser guns pointed, ready to shoot.

A gap opened between the guards, and in walked a muscular soldier who appeared to be in charge. He had a square jaw and a mean look on his face. He walked directly up to Chase, their faces just inches apart. Chase recognized him immediately.

"Remember me, boy? What's my name?"

Chase looked away, and the soldier punched him in the stomach. As Chase fell to the ground, the soldier said, "It's Gio, motherfucker." He grabbed Chase by the hair and pulled him to his feet. "Alright, let's get this over with."

Gio tapped his port and said, "I have the suspects. Applegate is in my custody. Permission to kill him?" There was a slight pause as Chase was trying to stop time, and the arrogance on Gio's face turned to disappointment. "Ten-four. I'll bring him in."

He walked back over and knocked Chase down again. "You just got lucky, but I have bad news for you. Now that you're mine, things aren't looking too good for you. When we got the tip that you were close by, I rushed over here so fast with my gunner that I almost blew this whole shitty place up. I was hoping to see you again," he said with a grin, right before he shoved Kay to the floor as well. When Sean ran to try to help her up, another guard kicked Sean in the ribs.

"Hey," Clio yelled out, "you said you weren't going to hurt any of them."

Gio looked at the other soldiers. "Shut that bitch up before I shoot her." The soldier standing next to her slammed his gunstock against Clio's head, sending her sprawling, bleeding, perhaps even unconscious, onto the floor. And Chase could only watch.

The transport ship Gio placed the traitors onto had been custom made for prisoners. Inside the ship were massive metal cylinders that were about seven feet tall. Next to the cylinders was a robotic scanner into which they strapped and secured Chase. Red beams of light scanned his body from head to toe.

Once the scanner moved to his feet, the screens on the ship lit up with calculations and body images. After about three minutes, the data was complete, and two robotic laser devices surrounded the cylinders and started cutting. Soon, the metal block was an exact mold of Chase's body, and he was placed in the middle, with only his head sticking out. The robotic lasers melted the openings shut so that it would be impossible for him to escape. Gio directed the soldiers to turn on the charge and test the metal block.

Gio enjoyed torture. "Now you're a living magnet. Watch this." He cranked up the charge, and Chase's block of metal smashed against a high-powered magnetic wall, and Chase screamed out in pain. After some more tormenting, Gio said, "Let's move them all out."

Once everyone was secured in the metal blocks, the AI soldiers used a portable crane to move the prisoners to the gunner ship for transport. A crowd of people had assembled outside the large F-99 fighter drone. When the door opened, and the crowd saw the crane move the metal blocks toward the F-99, someone yelled out, "Look, that's Chase Applegate!"

The crowd gasped when they saw Chase, his head sticking out of the metal cylinder. Some people fell to their knees. Gio shook his head. That kid really had those people hoodwinked.

Finally, they were all loaded into the big ship. The thrusters fired up, and the ground shook again. Gio sat at the helm of the ship, very proud, and connected to the lead councilman.

"Lead Councilman, sir, I would like to report mission accomplished on Project Applegate. Everyone can sleep well tonight because I'm looking at Applegate and his crew and they are in metal blocks, with nowhere to run."

"Good job, Commander. I will send out a press release. Keep an eye out for the update on the feed, and again, good work."

While the flight was in progress, many of the human soldiers walked by Chase, just to have a look at the person they had heard so much about. Gio was telling some jokes when he noticed on the big screen the words "Breaking News." He yelled out, "Quiet, everyone. Look!"

"We have breaking news. Worldwide criminal and America's most wanted, Chasten Applegate, was captured today just outside of New York City. The most wanted terrorist the world has ever seen was responsible for thousands of deaths in multiple countries. His crew was also captured, including a master hacker who is still unnamed. Decorated Commander Gio Rinehart and the four-hundred-fifty soldiers of the forty-fourth battalion were instrumental in the capture."

As the soldiers on the ship erupted with cheers, the report continued.

"Ironically, Chasten Applegate will be housed at one of the Applegate Prisons for the Good. Applegate was once a member of the Applegate family but was later disowned with no connection other than his name." The newscaster paused to smile, then continued with reports Gio couldn't care less about, but even as he basked in the glory of his own genius, the words still floated through his mind. "In other news, a mysterious plague is spreading and has killed hundreds of thousands around the world. Top researchers are working to find the cause, and a source with some authority has said there is no cause for alarm. Markets today were unchanged, while energy prices climbed substantially, and water prices are at a fifty-two-week low."

Gio turned the ship's feed volume down and told everyone to applaud again. He continued to speak.

"To all the human soldiers on this ship, as well as the AI soldiers;: good job! It is your courage and determination that will win the new war. Because of your hard work, I have been informed that we will be the lead battalion in Operation Francisco. I prefer to call it what it is: human purification. Let's get rid of the weak so the strong like you can enjoy the fruits of our planet." Once again, everyone cheered.

The lights flashed as the big ship began its descent over an island in the Atlantic Ocean. Chase recognized it immediately as the largest maximum-security Applegate prison, two-hundred miles off the coast of Hatteras Island, North Carolina. Unlike Alcatraz from centuries past, no one had ever escaped Applegate One.

When the ship landed, fifty heavily armored guards welcomed the most famous prisoner. The ship's ramp and a hydraulic mobile crane moved into position to pick up Chase.

Gio approached Chase. The man's chest was exaggeratedly puffed, Chase observed. "In case you were wondering, I'll be visiting you in the prison later for some quality time."

Chase didn't respond, and the crane picked him up and moved him into the prison. The others were also attached to cranes and were lowered in after Chase. He moved the best he could to look into Maggie's eyes. He felt sadness for the pain he had bestowed on her and now his unborn child. Desperation. He wanted to remember the joy that was in them not so long ago. There was nothing he could do to help her now.

As the steel doors slammed shut, fifty guards lined up in two rows on each side of Chase. In the shadow, a man was approaching from the far end. Shadows nearly obscured the bald head of the small man. Hatred stirred inside Chase, but he willed himself to hold back. He wasn't in a position where he had any leverage.

"Hello, Chasten," said Sam Applegate.

Chase didn't say anything. The guards stood at attention with their hands firmly affixed to their weapons.

"For years now, you have been an embarrassment to our family, to your mother and me. I'm so sick and tired of being asked, 'where did we go wrong?' What happened to you? We have had to spend countless hours with Eleanor Sanford, who is still devastated that you killed poor Phil. She's been begging me to discover a cure for death. We have him packed in ice in the other room, in case a cure is discovered."

Chase's interest piqued when he heard Phil's name, and he moved his head a little in the metal block. Sam Applegate continued.

"For someone who had the world in his hands, you're the poster child of disgrace. Look at you and your sorry friends, all prisoners. How do you think this makes me look? I own all the prisoners, and now my bastard son is the most famous prisoner. What do you have to say for yourself?"

Chase was silent.

"Fine then. From this point on, you are simply a number and will be treated like every other maximum-security prisoner. Your mother begged me not to kill you in the prison." He turned to the row of guards and spoke in an angry tone.

"Guards, listen up. I don't want this specific prisoner or any of the new prisoners to be treated any differently than the general population."

He looked back at Chase. "You may be surprised, but I'm going to let you out of the magnet block for now. But understand, Applegate

One's walls are all made of the same material as the cylinder. The only difference is that the magnification is greater. Now I promised your mother that I wouldn't kill you, but I can't be responsible for what my guards might do to an unruly prisoner. So don't get any bright ideas. Maybe you remember the guards' credo from when you visited here as a little kid? 'Shoot first and ask questions later!'"

Sam Applegate ordered the prison's tech team into the holding area. The team was headed by one human man and six AI droids. The human was skinny and tall and wore glasses. The team scanned Chase many times, until Sam Applegate yelled out, "Enough! Give me a report!"

"Chasten Applegate, prisoner number nine-seven-three-eight-four-nine, has some sort of scrambler in his chip that we have never seen before." For the first time since the capture, Julian had a slight grin on his face.

"Can you unscramble it?" Mr. Applegate asked.

"Not at this time, sir, but we will figure out a way."

Applegate looked at his son. "Well, it seems that you're not as stupid as you look. Fortunately for us, our magnetic jackets and cuffs have built-in trackers."

He directed the guards to remove the metal cylinders. Chase had difficulty breathing. Once he caught his breath, he began itching all over. The guards changed him into his prison uniform and attached the flak jacket and electronic cuffs.

Sam Applegate stood and watched. He yelled, "Make everything tighter." The guards did, and Chase screamed out in pain.

Once the other four prisoners had their flak jackets installed, they were placed in a line in the middle of the room. The head guard pulled a device out of his holster. He held his finger on a button until Sam Applegate gave him the go-ahead for the test. When the guard pressed the button, all five flew into the air and smashed against the closest magnetic wall. They stuck to the wall until the guard pressed the button again; then they fell to the floor. Maggie's head jerked from whiplash.

Chase, worried about her and the baby, yelled over, "Maggie, are you all right?" He wanted badly to stop time and get himself and everyone out of that hell,but that might only be possible when his own life was on the line.

"Silence!" the guard yelled. He pressed the button again, and Chase flew up to the ceiling. "When I say silence, I mean silence."

Months passed, and with no unified opposition, the Sixteen and the collective continued their human extermination. With the water-contamination process in full swing, it was a slow and steady death around the world.

Back at Applegate One, the guards took a liking to the five new prisoners, especially Chase. They all wanted to know what Sam Applegate was like as a father or any other gossip they could learn about their boss. Chase also got reacquainted with some of the old-timers who were still guards from when he was a child.

One evening, an old-timer named Billy opened Chase's cell door and walked in. Chase looked up from his cot, happy to have a visitor.

"Hi, Billy," he said. "How's it going? Is everyone behaving?"

"Good," he answered as he shut the door. They moved to the

back of the cell.

"Billy, I wanted to thank you for keeping an eye on Maggie and Kay. How are they?"

"They're fine. I keep rotating them to the friendly guards; but, Chase, I have to tell you, Maggie's getting bigger and bigger, and I don't know how long I can keep her out of sight and away from the other guards."

"Can you give her a larger uniform?"

"What do you think I've been doing? She's getting too big."

Chase smiled and said, "Thanks again for your help." Then he asked, "Billy, why have you stayed here all these years?"

He shrugged. "What else can I do? My wife died fourteen years ago, and it's all I know. Plus, it's a job. Not a lot of people have a real job. I know some bad things happen here, but with the years, you get used to it."

Chase could no longer hold in the question he'd wanted to ask for months. "So where is my father keeping Phil's body?"

Billy frowned. "You know I can't tell you that. I'd get fired, or worse."

"All my father's prisons have the same design. He has to be in a cold-storage place, and there are only two. One is on platform three, and the other is on platform seven. He's a gambler, so I would guess seven. What do you think, Billy?"

Billy grinned and looked at the ground quickly. Chase laughed. "Billy why are you looking at the ground?" Then they both laughed.

"Chase don't get me in trouble."

"I'm just messing with you. I know a lot about his prisons. Too much. I know there's a place in every one of his prisons with dead bodies or at least body parts. He always wins those bogus awards for doing all these experiments, with so few prisoner deaths. What a crock of shit. I bet more than half die and he just tosses the bodies and cuts out the chips. Where are the bodies located? And don't tell me platform three, because that's where you guys store the food."

Again they laughed. There was a pause.

Then Billy said quietly, "It's the holiday, and we're short on staff, so I'm going to take you for a walk."

"Hide-and-seek, like when I was a kid?" They laughed, and Billy scanned the cell door before they walked out. He motioned Chase to be quiet.

Billy escorted him with his laser gun and magnetic gun out to make it appear official. They kept walking, and Billy looked both ways to make sure no one was around. Then he scanned a lock to enter a private door. He whispered to Chase that he'd disconnected the video scanners earlier in the day. Apparently, he'd planned to help Chase all along.

They walked to a private wing of the prison, and Billy put his guns away. "No one can hear us over here."

"Cool. Is this new?"

"Not really. They just rebuilt this section. It's the old zone six, if you remember? The big hallway is just ahead."

"Oh, right, I know where we are," Chase said.

They continued down a hall, then Billy stopped and took Chase's arm. "Do not—and I repeat, do not—tell anyone that I showed you this room." He scanned the door lock, and it opened.

They walked in, and a block of cold air hit their faces. Billy scanned the terminal, and a set of lights turned on. The smell was repugnant, and Chase pinched his nose. When the lights got brighter, Chase could see a large circular saw in the middle of the room with bloodstains everywhere.

There was a second, smaller terminal by the saw, and again Billy scanned his chip for clearance.

"Have a look, Chase." The back wall rose up, and behind it were thousands of arms in a huge pile.

Billy explained, "In order to keep our numbers down from the unsuccessful experiments, we cheat and cut off the chip arms and store them indefinitely. We log them as lifers and eventually list them as dead from natural causes. Also, we don't allow visitors to the lifers anymore."

Chase was surprised at the size of the pile. Even Billy looked a little shocked as he said, "Wow, there are more arms than I remember back here. See, you were correct about the experiments and deaths."

Chase swallowed the lump in his throat. He hadn't wanted to be right. "Almost every time I was at the prison when I was a kid, someone died from an experiment. As soon as Sam got his first award for humanity, I knew it was bullshit."

They stood in silence for a while, then Billy said to Chase, "Look at those nails. Isn't it weird that some things keep growing after you're dead, like your hair and those fingernails right there?" Chase simply nodded. It was an odd observation, but he assumed that's how Billy allowed himself to forget the mass murders, by thinking of mundane things. Clearing out the bad stuff or shoving it way back. "Okay, let's go. I need to get you back to your cell before anyone finds out what we're doing." They closed the door and walked back down the hall.

"This new zone is cool, Billy, but you know, I would have found it anyway back in the day." Billy grinned, and they kept walking.

They passed by a door that was painted red. "Why is this one door painted red?" Chase went to open the door.

"Stop, Chase, don't open that door!"

Because the last person had not closed the door all the way, Chase opened it without the security scan. A burst of cold air rushed out. When the fog cleared, he saw a cross structure with Phillip's body attached to it. His eyes were closed, but his body twitched a little. There were wires and tubes connected all over his body.

"Oh my God, what are they doing to him?"

"Chase, let's go. You were never supposed to see this. Let's go."

"No, I want to know what's going on. Is that really him…or…or some kind of droid replica?" Chase stammered. His heart had sunk, and he could barely think or breathe.

"That's Phillip. They're trying to successfully perform the ultimate experiment, which is bringing someone back from the dead. The owners—or in this case, your father—would be beyond wealthy."

Phillip's skin was blue, and he wore a medical gown. He smelled horrible, and his hair was long.

"He looks terrible, nothing like I remember him; and it doesn't seem like the experiments are going well. They should just let him rest in peace."

"I agree with you," said Billy. "They have pumped in so many drugs and products over the years that I'm surprised the body has been sustained."

Chase was incredibly saddened by the scene, and he just shook his head. Billy said, "Let's go. You weren't supposed to open that door."

Chase wished he hadn't.

Chapter Fourteen

Sam Applegate stood in the main guard tower and gazed at the yard. He asked his technology sergeant, "How is it that you haven't cracked the code on those prisoner's chips? How can they still be scrambled?"

"We're making inroads, sir. For example, we're pretty sure it was prisoner eight-nine-seven-six-five, the one named Julian, who scrambled the chips. He's pretty smart."

"I'm sure he is, but I pay you to be smarter, right? Are the basic vitals normal, or did he modify other human functions?"

"We're not sure, since we cannot scan the ports. Everything is scrambled."

Applegate snidely responded, "You know, years ago people didn't have ports and chips, and they somehow found a way to give a basic physical." With visible irritation, he stared out the window, looking at the crowd of women prisoners. "Isn't it interesting how the men and women always separate in the yard?" The technology sergeant nodded.

Kay sat at a picnic table for a moment, and then stood up. Applegate did a double take. "Look at her stomach. She looks pregnant! Have you checked her or given her an exam?" he asked the sergeant.

"I told you, sir, we cannot scan their ports."

Applegate yelled, "You don't need a fucking port to tell if a woman is pregnant! You're fired. Get out of my way."

An emergency alarm sounded in the yard, and a voice over the loudspeaker instructed all prisoners to return to their cells for a count. The guards ran into the yard, rounded up the prisoners, and directed them to their cells. Thirty guards led Kay and Maggie, and their magnetic force increased to ten. Julian noticed and quickly told Chase and Sean that something was going on. They started toward the girls, and the guards pressed a button, and Julian, Chase and Sean flew through the air and slammed against a wall.

"You're not going anywhere," said one of the guards.

As the rest of the prisoners left the yard, the guards watched over the three who remained stuck to the wall.

Billy was one of the guards, and Chase heard him tell the others he was going to see what was going on with the girls.

Two hours passed, and the three could not move. In the sky, a class one military ship descended and landed at the prison. Julian looked at the other two and said, "I wonder why the military ship is landing here?"

"Guards," Sean said, "can I ask what is going on?" The guards ignored him.

Shortly after, they heard the military ship fire up its engines, and the wall they were stuck against shook. They looked up again to see the ship lifting off.

The head guard got the message that Sam Applegate was entering the yard. The guard pressed his button, and the three prisoners fell to the ground. After a moment, they stood.

Applegate entered with ten additional guards, a smug look on his face. He approached the three and stood as he often did while gathering information from the family council. He tapped his port and answered, "Yes, they are all secure…Okay, I will take it from here." Applegate looked at them and tapped his port in Record mode.

"Okay, dirt bags, pay attention. We are now on the record and connected with the council of the Sixteen. Lead Councilman, it has just been discovered at Applegate One that two of the female prisoners, numbers three-three-three-two-two and three-three-three-two-three, are pregnant, which of course is very unusual and highly illegal. Furthermore, we have reason to believe that, because of the close relationship between the parties present, they are all responsible for this crime. Prisoners, for the council record, how do you all plead?"

He paused for a minute, and none of them spoke a word. Applegate was also silent as he read his eye screen for direction.

"Very well. Based on your silence, the family council of the Sixteen has found you guilty. This crime of which you have been found guilty is punishable by death. This order calls forth that Warden Samuel Applegate will determine the date and time of the execution and manner. This concludes this criminal proceeding. Thank you, council. Over and out."

Applegate turned to his guard in charge. "The women have already been removed from the prison, and I'll make arrangements for the deaths of the three convicts. Guards, bring them back to their cells and cease all food and water. They are now officially entering the pre-punishment death period."

The guards surrounded the prisoners, and they started walking. One of the guards yelled at Julian to speed it up. Julian moved only slightly faster, and the guard switched his laser gun to its lowest setting and shot Julian in the leg.

Julian screamed, "My leg!" and fell to the ground. His bone had broken through the flesh, which had caught fire from the laser. They put the fire out, and Julian lay on the ground.

"Move it along," the guard yelled, and Chase and Sean started walking again as a large guard dragged Julian through the dirt. Another guard stomped on Julian's injured leg. Julian screamed again. Chase shut his eyes in anger and read the program to loosen his ankle cuffs. The guard who stepped on Julian was laughing and joking with the other guards when Chase dashed over and kicked the side of the guard's knee hard enough that a snap echoed through the area.

The other guards jumped on Chase. Eventually, they got new ankle cuffs on him and moved them into their cells. That night, everyone felt discouraged and defeated and wondered where Maggie and Kay were being held, assuming they were even alive.

Three days passed very slowly for the group, especially without food or water, and Chase, Sean and Julian never left their cells. On the fourth day, at three o'clock, guards approached their cells.

"Okay, boys, it's time to go on your field trip." The guard rounded up the prisoners and placed them in a single-file line. Julian's leg looked infected, though he received no treatment and was given only an old-fashioned crutch to use. "Follow us in a straight line and don't talk."

Sean asked Chase, "Do you think this is the end?"

A guard hit Sean with the tip of his gun. "I said shut up!"

They walked to the main entrance of the prison and entered the large room for scanning. While the scanners buzzed, the guards talked amongst themselves.

"Guess we won't be seeing these guys around here again."

"That's true. Hey, did you know that the collective once calculated that the one guy over there, Chasten Applegate, was estimated in the future to be the world's most likely disrupter?"

"Really? Well, not anymore."

They were moved to a holding area, their flak jackets charged to one-hundred percent for safety and control. Outside the prison, it began to pour, and one guard received a message that the transport ship was close by and landing.

"Let's go, boys. Your ride is here."

The guards put their hoods up and led them into the acid rain to the front gate. Watching the ship's lights in the sky, they waited next to the gate while it landed. The ship's powerful thrusters drove the rain, so it felt like they were in a hurricane. Chase looked over and saw a guard run out from the prison and approach the supervising guard. It was Billy.

"Johnny, if you don't mind, I would like to walk Chase onto the ship. Is that alright?"

"No problem, Bill. I know you were fond of the kid. I'll get clearance immediately."

The guards walked Julian up the ship's ramp first, followed by Sean. Chase went last, escorted by Billy.

"Chase, it has been a pleasure knowing you all these years, and I'm so sorry it had to end this way."

Chase didn't know what to say. He didn't feel much of anything, but he had appreciated the guard. He told Billy, "No, my friend, the pleasure has been all mine."

Once on the ship, Billy walked him through the scanner for the last time. He nodded at Chase then moved into a line with the other prison guards. They made a straight military line, turned, and walked off the ship.

The prison guards exited the ship and stood by the main gate as the ship's boosters fired up for takeoff. The rocket thrusters kicked in, and all the guards moved back simultaneously, except Billy. The ship rose up, and Billy just watched, with his hair blowing in the wind.

On the ship, the soldiers immediately utilized the magnetic flak jackets and stuck the inmates to the ship's wall. Although the prisoners couldn't move, they could still see the ship's main screen. The military feed displayed an update regarding the extermination of unnecessary humans. It stated that sixty-two million people had been exterminated in the previous week. No one said a word at first, as they were amazed at the sheer number of killings.

Sean looked at Julian and his leg; the injury was turning green. In a low voice, he said, "How's your leg feeling? It doesn't look good."

Julian shook his head. "I can't feel anything, t's numb."

None of them knew exactly where they were being transported. Chase checked the ship's coordinates on his eye screen and recognized the zone they were in. The ship was flying near his hometown. As the ship descended, he looked at the main screen and noticed a few familiar landmarks. The ship made a circle around the city and began to lower toward a large building. Chase and the others quickly glanced again at the main screen and saw the big H on the roof. All three looked at each other, wondering why they were landing at a hospital. They could see lots of military soldiers and drones around the hospital's perimeter.

As they landed, it appeared as though there was a small army on the building's roof, awaiting their arrival.

Once the ship landed, the doors did not immediately open, and the soldiers awaited their orders. On the screen, Chase could see the military was hard at work outside, placing large wall magnets from the ship to the hospital door, to prevent any chance of escape.

Once the walls were in place, the door of the ship opened. A general walked aboard with a team of additional soldiers. All of their weapons were aimed at the three prisoners, awaiting orders.

The general said to the ship's sergeant in charge, "So these are the three, right here?"

"Yes, General."

"Release the magnetic field." The sergeant did, and the prisoners fell to the floor. They were so stiff from not moving, they lay, unmoving, in pain.

The general yelled out, "Stand up." Sean and Chase got right up, while Julian struggled but managed to get to his feet.

The general looked at Julian's leg for a second, then said, "I want ten soldiers in front to lead them and ten behind them." The soldiers marched to the door. They walked off the ship, and at the beginning of the magnetic wall, they were stopped.

"Lieutenant, test the new wall." The lieutenant pressed his port, and the prisoners immediately went airborne and hit the wall. It was working.

Chapter Fifteen

Soldiers led Chase, Sean and Julian into the hospital and through the hallways. There were no patients in the hospital, only military personnel. The walk was slow since the soldiers were ready to shoot on command.

Finally, they approached a large room, lined with the magnetic walls. The lieutenant stopped them again at the entrance as he awaited his orders.

Then he said to them, "Go inside."

No one moved, not knowing what type of chamber they were walking into. After a minute, the general yelled out, "Let's go. Get moving, or I'll turn the mag field up again." All three of them walked into the room. They were moved to the far side, and a magnetic field was set up as a barrier, so they could only stay in one small area.

The general connected with Sam Applegate. "Sam, we have them all detained and secured. I'll connect you with the room speaker and put you on the record beginning now."

"First of all, to the hard-working men and women of the military, good job. As you are all aware, the five criminals here today have conducted numerous crimes against the world and have been convicted in a court of law for these crimes. Today these crimes will be punished accordingly, beginning with the illegal pregnancies and followed by the deaths of all. Proceed."

The hair on the back of Chase's neck shot up and his heart raced. Applegate had said "the five criminals here today," yet Chase couldn't see Maggie or Kay. He hoped that perhaps Sam was mistaken. Maybe it was only the three men who were there. Maybe the women were safe.

The general tapped his port, and the soldiers exited the room. When the last soldier left, he slammed the metal door, and the magnetic locks engaged.

Chase anxiously waited for something when the wall next to them began to rise. Behind the wall was a bulletproof glass that looked into a hospital room. The room was pitch black and hard to see into. Slowly, lights illuminated the room, and there were two operating tables onto which Maggie and Kay lay, strapped down.

Chase, Julian and Sean went ballistic, banging on the glass with their electronic cuffs and Chase yelled out, "You fuckers!"

On the right side of the operating tables was another window. It opened into a smaller room for the human and AI technicians who controlled the procedure. They could hear the technicians on the speaker talking about the procedure.

One technician said, "This is the only operating room set up for births or abortions these days. It has been a long time since anyone has performed either, so let's take our time and get it right. Odd that they very last human being born naturally was born in this room and now we are aborting his baby."

Chase lost all control of his anger and he repeatedly beat his arm with the magnetic brace against the thick glass. Sean did the same as doctors entered the girls' room. There were no human doctors in the operating room, only AI droids. A humming sound began, and two robotic arms lowered from the ceiling to scan the girls' stomachs, moving back and forth. Sean and Chase banged on the glass as Julian put his hands over his face. When the scanning was complete, the droids used an instrument to mark a red illuminated box on the girls' bellies for the operation.

A military doctor entered and said, "Let's start with the one girl, then move to the tattooed freak last."

One of the droid doctors asked, "Did you decide to use any pain-med injections?"

The military doctor responded, "What's the point of that?"

The droid answered, "In case the screaming decibel reaches a dangerous level for your hearing."

"Don't worry about that. We can soundproof the room if it gets too loud. Plus, this won't take long. They'll be dead soon enough. Sam suggested the abortion as an additional punishment. He seemed positively gleeful over the fact that the parents would have to witness the death of their children before they met the same fate. Let's get started."

Maggie squirmed and tried her best to loosen her metal straps, to no avail. The robotic arms lowered just above her belly, directly over the red box. One robotic arm had a white beam of light on the tip, which got brighter and brighter. The straps got tighter, and Maggie squirmed, but otherwise, couldn't move much.

Chase and Sean banged harder on the glass. "Let me out of here. I'll fucking kill you," Sean screamed.

The white light got so bright Chase and Sean couldn't look directly at it as it maneuvered over her pregnant belly. The beam started to cut the skin of Maggie's abdomen, and the smell of burning flesh was so pungent, it wafted through the room. Maggie screamed, and Chase felt like a caged animal, running from wall to wall and smashing anything he could, wailing, "No, no, no!"

Sean banged as hard as he could on the glass, while Maggie screamed. Julian kept his eyes closed, trying to block out everything.

Chase ran to the glass in a rage, frustrated he could not stop time or move into another dimension at will. As he placed his hands on the glass, the veins in his neck protruded. He shut his eyes and wished he were dead. The sense of helplessness and anger boiled over, and he began to shake.

Suddenly, with his hands still on it, the thick glass smashed. Time seemed to pause, with the shattering glass frozen midair. He looked around, but no one else moved. Chase knew from experiencing this phenomenon before, that he had moved into another dimension. It seemed like a parallel dimension very similar to his normal life, but with distinct differences. It had to be another world.

He stood for a moment and observed the thirty people standing around the operating room. He observed everything. The images of the people were transparent, and he wasn't sure who they were. Some were just stood there, while others moved around. He looked closer and recognized, though he had not met her, Maggie's dead grandmother, who stood next to Kay's father, whom Chase had also never met, who had died from cancer two years ago. The recognition of people he'd never met was odd, but he wasn't scared. He felt at peace.

Chase was confused by seeing the passed away relatives and understood that this must be where human sprits go after they leave their bodies. He wondered for a moment if he had actually died. Still filled with anger, Chase ran to the operating room. Maggie and Kay had their mouths open, in mid scream. He ran to the robotic terminal room and placed his hands on the motherboard. Under his focused energy, the motherboard began to melt. Once he disabled everything, Maggie's grandmother smiled at him. He disabled Kay's abortion robot, and her father gave him a nod of approval.

Chase felt an odd force field as he moved throughout the room with the others. It was as though he were walking in a yellow haze. He realized he was in a universe parallel to Earth. There seemed to be more energy in this dimension, and he tried to move between the dimensions. He wasn't sure if it was working, but he saw the military doctors and the droids in the original dimension started to slowly move again.

Once he disabled the entire operating room, he went back up to the roof of the military ship and programmed it to take off. On the ship, there were a limited number of soldiers, but they were all frozen in their dimension. He removed the guns and placed a magnetic jacket on each soldier. The ship's engines fired up for takeoff, and Chase was at the helm.

As the flight continued, he noticed that some of the soldiers in the human dimension were confused and beginning to move slowly. Somehow, Chase was in two separate dimensions in a multiverse. He didn't know how, but he was able to exist in both at once. Chase noticed that things moved about ten times slower in Earth's dimension. Not only could he see them move slower, but he could also hear them communicate.

"Sergeant John to Lieutenant Rex, what is going on? How did that bulletproof glass break, and why has the abortion stopped? What is going on?"

"I'm not sure, Sergeant."

Before more than a few sentences were spoken, Chase was long gone on the government's military fighter ship.

"Ten-four, Lieutenant," said the sergeant. "I think we're under some kind of attack. The fighter ship on the roof is gone, and we're having a hard time tracking it. It is as if it disappeared."

"Sergeant, I am sorry to report that Chasten Applegate is also missing, and all the robots in the operating room are disabled. He must have found a way to hijack the ship with another underground army. We will track him down with the collective."

Back on the fighter ship, Chase was alone, sad and angry. He felt it was not worth living like that. He couldn't erase from his mind the image and the fact that the collective and the family council would kill his unborn child and make him watch.

As the ship flew at warp speed between dimensions, he heard the lead councilman speak on the military feed.

"Find Applegate at all costs. Use whatever weapons necessary, including nuclear, fusion, or gamma, to destroy him. I am officially granting clearances to fire these weapons no matter the consequences. We feel he is heading directly to the collective's main center, and we are sending reinforcements for a battle. Furthermore, the collective has finally unscrambled his chip, so he'll not be able to enter the underground collective facility. The collective is calculating every possible move he may choose. Let's get him quickly, again through any means necessary. Over and out."

Chase was surprised that the collective had unscrambled Julian's programming. He immediately changed the coordinates of the ship and made a steep turn to change directions. Julian had always told Chase that the collective's supercomputers were amazing at calculations, but their one flaw was the unpredictability of human nature. He tried to think. Where would they calculate he wouldn't go? He programmed the ship with new coordinates.

The ship made another big turn, and a few soldiers slammed against the wall. Because of the magnetic flak jackets, they were stuck. Chase pressed a button at the helm, and the remaining soldiers slammed against the nearest wall. Now they were the prisoners.

Soon the ship was descending and preparing to land. The autopilot brought the military ship in for a smooth landing at Applegate One. When the door of the ship opened, Chase noticed the yellow haze was breaking up, and it was clearer outside the ship. He now knew that he was about to walk back into his earth's dimension. He would be in the same time and space as everyone else in the prison. Quickly, he got into the prison before he was completely out of the dimension.

He felt as though he had a pretty good head start and immediately went to the secret hallway Billy showed him. He stopped in the hall, thinking of his next move, reviewing his calculations. With time returning to normal, he hoped Maggie would be okay.

The door that housed the forgotten arms and chips of the dead prisoners was just ahead. He walked in and closed the door.

He tapped his port. "Julian, are you there?"

"I am. Holy shit, where are you? The glass wall broke, and the soldiers are running all over the place."

"Be careful."

"I am. I'm sending you these messages from my eye screen.

They still haven't decoded it. Good news, the robotic arms stopped cutting. Something happened to them."

"Where's Maggie?"

"She's still strapped down. They're not sure what to do. It's crazy here. Where are you?"

"Jules, I'm fine, but I'm done with all of this. What's the code?"

Julian didn't say anything at first, but after a few seconds, Chase heard him speak. "You want the code?"

"Yes, the one that overrides everything with the collective and the weapons of mass destruction."

"Are you sure you want the code, Chase? It… it's capable of destroying it all. Everything," Julian said.

"Yes, I am."

Julian paused again, then said, "Okay, my friend, here it is. Be very careful."

"Thanks, Jules, and hopefully I'll see you again someday."

Chase wrote the long sequence of numbers and symbols on his right arm in ink, from a pen he found in the arm room.

A loud ear-piercing sound blasted. "The prison is on lockdown. The prison is on lockdown." Chase knew they must have seen the ship take off or land. He had little time. He took the circular saw mounted on the wall and turned it on. He found a wire on the floor and tied it around his left arm just above his port. He picked up an old rag from the table and stuck it in his mouth. Then he walked over to the saw, closed his eyes, and sunk it into the flesh of his arm.

As the saw reached his bone, he let out a loud scream, and blood gushed everywhere. In excruciating pain, he swore to himself, "No one will ever track me down again." He pushed harder on the saw blade, and it made a clean cut.

The lower half of his left arm fell to the floor, and he used the cauterizing robotic machine to stop the bleeding. He threw the arm in the pile and staggered out.

He knew that section of the prison was soundproof, but he also knew it was only a matter of time until they found him. Down a side hallway, he noticed the mechanical transporter they had used to move him around when he was in the block of metal. Chase fiddled with the terminal, fumbling with his single hand, and quickly figured out how to run it. He jumped on the transporter and drove down the main hallway into another section of the prison that Billy had shown him. It was the place Billy hadn't wanted him to go to. He jumped off the transporter, looked at two doors, and picked one.

When he opened the door, a rush of cold air came out, and he turned the lights on. Propped up with even more wires than he remembered was Phillip's body. He ripped off the wires as quickly as he could and removed the body from the cross-like contraption they had tied him to. Chase struggled but finally lifted the body onto the transporter, drove to the cargo elevator, and pressed the "close" button repeatedly.

The elevator door closed, and a sign inside flashed, "Lockdown—Code Red."

As the elevator rose to the roof, he heard the commotion of the guards. It was a race to get to the ship before the armed guards did. The door opened, and he moved out with Phillip as quickly as he could.

Because he used the cargo elevator, it brought him to a different portion of the roof. Worse yet, to enter the main roof where the ship was parked, he would have to open a door that required a passcode.

Chase knew there was a universal passcode, from when he was a kid, but that had been a long time ago, and he couldn't remember it. He heard someone coming behind him, and he tried passcodes as fast as he could, hoping to get lucky, still struggling with only five fingers. He looked back and saw a guard running toward him. He turned and kept punching in passcodes, until suddenly the guard grabbed him by the shoulder and yelled, "Chase, look out." It was Billy.

"Look out, they're coming." Billy punched in the passcode, the door opened, and they jumped on the transporter. They drove as fast as the transporter would go toward the ship. The ship's door opened, and the ramp began to lower, but not quickly enough.

Billy yelled, "Come on, come on!"

Finally, it was down, and Chase drove Phillip's body up the ramp and onto the ship. Chase jumped off and said to Billy, "Do you want to come with—"

Just then, the main roof door opened, and guards came out shooting their laser guns, and Billy was hit repeatedly. They blasted hundreds of shots into his body as well as into the side of the ship. Billy's flesh and blood flew everywhere as ship's door closed.

The military ship took off, and Chase plugged in the coordinates for the collective's ground-zero base; Edgewood, New Mexico.

As the ship took off, a great explosion jolted it. Chase watched from the main screen as the prison exploded. It wouldn't be long before the family council's military ships would close in and attack.

On the other hand, he was in one of the largest and most advanced military fighter ships. Chase plugged in the automatic fight-and-destroy feature and went full throttle toward the collective.

The fighter ship was as high tech as they came, but Chase wasn't impressed. He pondered everything that had happened in his life. He looked over at Phil's body. "What a shame," he thought. "He looks worse than a zombie."

As Chase was lost in thought, the ship shot ten quick blasts off, and snapped him out of his daydream.

The ship maneuvered and was shooting at other ships before Chase even realized they had caught up to him. The fight was on, and the ship was hit. It jerked downward. Fortunately, it was not a direct hit, and the ship regained control.

He kept the ship moving forward and then looked at the screen and saw four of the same F-99 ships he was piloting approaching fast.

He was about three-quarters of the way to New Mexico, but he would never fight off four F-99s. Another missile flew by the ship and narrowly missed. The other ships started firing at random, desperate for a hit.

The automatic fight feature was firing nonstop, and the ship spun and rolled with maneuvers. He had to get into the other dimension or he would certainly be shot down. The F-99s moved in closer, firing shots, and Chase's ship went into a continuous barrel roll to avoid getting hit.

Suddenly, the ship leveled out, and things got quiet. Then the blasts stopped. The air felt lighter, there was a slight ringing in his ears and that inexplicable glow illuminated the ship.

I'm in the parallel dimension again, but how? he thought. At this point it didn't matter. He bee-lined for his destination.

On the military feed, he heard the other ships' commanders questioning where Chase had gone.

Chase made it to the coordinates of the collective's central system. On the ship's screen, he saw a massive military presence. Fortunately, they couldn't see him, at least not yet.

Each family from around the world had sent gunner ships, fusion destroyers, or whatever weapons available to destroy him and protect the collective.

He knew only original members of the sixteen families could open all the locked passages to the collective. There were no other ways into the tunnels that led to the collective's brain. His chip was not only blocked but also sitting in the pile at the prison.

Perhaps the families had never turned Phillip's chip off.

The ship landed, and Chase jumped on the transport machine with Phil's body. When the door of the warship opened, he noticed the thick yellow haze and feared he would be returning back to the earth's dimension very soon.

He took a deep breath and staggered through the haze to the underground tube's main entrance. He programmed the ship to take off, and while he was heading to the elevator tube, he heard a loud blast as the ship passed through the sound barrier, then into the earth's dimension. The ship flew at warp speed through the night sky. It wasn't long until there was a massive amount of shooting and explosions in the distance.

Then a great explosion shook the ground, and Chase felt a huge gust of wind. There was a black cloud in the sky, and he assumed the collective and the Sixteen had finally destroyed the ship.

He regained his composure and moved to the main entrance. He twisted Phillip around the best he could, in order to get him close to the lock scanner. After a few failed attempts, Chase held Phillip's port arm next to the scanner and hoped for the best.

Nothing happened. Chase put his head down. Then the door opened. "Yes!" he said to himself. They never deleted Phillip's chip, and for the first time, Chase didn't feel bad for cutting off his own arm.

It wouldn't take long for the collective to notice that a family member had entered the main headquarters. Chase moved as quickly as possible. The tubes were fast, and got narrower the deeper they went into the earth.

As he reached another level, it was becoming impossible to move. He had a hard time moving Phillip's body into position to scan another lock. A buzzing sound—as if from a swarm of angry bees— started in the distance.

Chase turned and looked down a long hallway, from which hundreds of bird-size drones were coming.

He struggled, but finally hit the release buttons on the transport machine and moved Phillip's body around to better access his port. He scanned the elevator tube and the door began to open.

Chase yelled out, "Come on, come on." He maneuvered in with Phillip's body and pressed the button repeatedly. "Close, close, close!"

Just as the door closed, the drones hit the outside of the door, like bullets sprayed from a machine gun. Inside the elevator tube, the light flickered. Chase took a deep breath and then let it out, closing his eyes. He felt a strange force coming over him and at that point, didn't even know what dimension he was in.

When he opened his eyes, Phillip was gone.

The door opened, and Chase just stood there, still in shock, looking around. With no time to waste, he quickly ran to the big entrance of the council chamber. To his surprise, the door was open. This was the heart of all the world's connected supercomputers and intelligence; this was the collective.

He figured this was going to be the hardest challenge of all, and the door was strangely wide open. Where am I he wondered, am I dead or stuck somewhere? Before entering, he stopped just outside the large door and prepared mentally for what was inside. He figured that, as before, the council members would be in the main room, guarding the collective, and would apprehend or kill him immediately.

Chase cautiously entered the room that was empty except for a four-foot-tall command system in the middle: the brains of the collective. It glowed a reddish color.

Chase walked up to it thinking about all the cruel things that were happening in the world. While at the same time looking over his shoulder.

He started to program the command control system with the sequence code, in the exact order Julian had described. He scheduled all the world's global weapons to target each of the sixteen families' epicenters. All remaining weapons of mass destruction were then directed to target the collective—exactly where he stood.

As Chase continued, warning alerts, bells, and loud messages began sounding everywhere. All the screens in the room displayed the word and sound "Danger, Danger" continuously. The entire round terminal system blinked red. Chase kept going and kept hitting "Continue" and "Yes" when the question "Are you sure?" kept appearing.

At the end of the programming, the terminal system simply said, "Enter the password sequence," and the warning pitch in the room became louder. All the wall screens also blinked "Danger."

Chase paused, wondering what had happened to Maggie and everyone at the hospital as he looked at the sequence code he wrote on his arm. After a moment, he typed in the code.

The control system's screen on the terminal read, "Entered successfully," and two electronic circles appeared. A green "Go" and a red "Stop" circle filled the screen at his fingertips.

Chase paused for a moment and thought again of all the greed and human suffering he had experienced. Then he smashed his fist on the green button. A loud beeping sounded, and red lights flashed in the room.

The loud beeping quickly changed to a monotone voice that said, "The weapons entered will fire in thirty seconds."

The largest wall screen in the room displayed the numbers 29, 28, 27.... Then the screen scrambled, and an image appeared. It was Mrs. Applegate.

"Chase don't do this. You're going to kill everyone."

Chase was surprised. "Mom, what are you doing?"

"Chase, I'm trying to stop you from hurting and killing everyone. Please. Give us a chance to make this right. I've already met with the family council leaders, and they want you to have the vacant seat. They think your views are really important. Chase, my baby, please don't do this. You know how much I love you, and please give me the chance to make this right."

All the walls became screens and they continued with the countdown: 10, 9, 8…

Chase closed his eyes, thinking, while the display read 3,2,1…

He opened his eyes and slammed the red "Stop" button. He took a big breath as his mother cried emphatically.

"Thank you, Chase. Thank you." The screens went black and she was gone.

He let out another sigh of relief, while he looked down, exhausted, with so many emotions flowing through him. When he looked up, to his surprise, the room was filled with people who had a yellowish-white glow around them.

In the main upper section of the chamber where the sixteen family members had once sat, were sixteen new images of people. However, they were glowing and seemed almost translucent. All were dressed oddly, and their faces were illuminated almost a pure white. For some reason, he felt safe.

Glowing the most was the figure of a man seated in the center. He wore a robe and had long hair and a beard. It reminded Chase of what Jesus Christ would have looked like, if he had ever met him.

The beings communicated telepathically, and Chase understood what they said and thought.

Where am I? Chase wondered.

"You are home," the image answered in a peaceful voice. "You did your best, and everyone here supports you."

"Who are you?"

"We are the elders of this universe. I am the facilitator, but we speak as one. I am sorry to say that you were placed in an opposite dimensional plane in which you did not belong. It was an anomaly of sorts."

"I don't understand," said Chase, "am I in heaven or hell?"

"Heaven and hell are earthly concepts and you can use these labels if you wish, but all of our energy in the universe is cosmically connected and we are all one. The energy particles in each of us can influence others over great distances. The state of one energy force may be the opposite of the other energy force or particles, and yours became inverted.

"My energy got inverted? I still don't understand," said Chase."

"Basically, you ended up in an earthly dimension that was the opposite of where you belong. You're a great positive energy force, Chase, and you belong in such a plane, where people are kind and work together to better everyone. The dimensional plane you were on is riddled with greed and ego, where people take advantage of others for their own gain. The human race in that dimension is at best growing at a snail's pace and is in danger of going backward."

"What do you mean?" Chase asked.

"The universe is made up of many dimensions, which you

experienced on a small level. In fact, because of Applegate's greedy experiments, you were one of the first humans to have the ability to shift dimensions. The human body you were in is made up of energy and when that body dies, the soul or energy moves to an alternate dimension, sometimes a parallel universe. You're in one now."

"I died?" Chase asked.

The facilitator looked at a glowing energy to his right. She was a beautiful female figure with long, silky, flowing hair. Even though they were communicating telepathically, Chase could feel that she had a loving, soothing voice.

"Chase," she said, "you died in the car accident, along with Phillip. I let you go back and forth from the earthly dimension to this one in order to give you as much help to save the earthly world as possible."

With a smile, she said, "You did a wonderful job trying, my dear. I'm so proud of you; we all are. We are all loving energy, and we chose to appear as humans to allow you to adjust. In time, this won't be necessary, and you will become pure energy in whatever image you prefer."

"So where are all the other people on the earth dimension right now?"

"They are still there. Because the dimensions are parallel, you can look back any time and see for yourself.

"What about the new technology, the sixteen, religion, is all of that still there?" asked Chase.

Another energy force sitting next to the facilitator smiled and said, "I love his vigor and determination, don't you?" Some of the others grew brighter.

The facilitator said, "These are all free choices."

"How is that? Who's choices?" Chase asked.

"In other races and dimensions, if technology affected five percent of the population negatively, the leaders would simply increase what you call the draw by five percent to help the needy recover and prosper. However, on the earth plane, that race chose greed and used it only to benefit a few at the top and eliminate the rest. These are all choices. The sixteen families had just begun the process of eliminating the poor and the nonbelievers. They were forming a new religion that worshiped themselves. We have seen this before with past infant worlds. Most religions start out well intended, but free will, greed, and deception creep in. It never ends well."

"So, which is the correct religion?" Chase asked.

The facilitator answered, "As humans define it, there is no real religion. We all are governed by nature, energy, or the universal truths."

"What truths?" he asked.

"The only truth in the universe that you would be able to understand is that we are all one. Everything begins with energy and energy is in everything. In addition to energy, you may understand these truths as love, compassion, and math."

"Did you say math?"

"Yes. Math is one of the universal languages throughout the galaxies."

Chase was confused.

"If three alien ships hovered over an earth city, there are only a few absolute truths that matter, and they are universal. Every conscious species in the universe will comprehend the two most important truths.

"Is the alien ship friend or foe? The friend is love, or the foe has no love. The second thing they will comprehend is the number of ships, which is what you call math. Everything else that you are aware of is built around these two truths.

"Love is made of compassion, pride and positive conscious energy. The opposite is pain, greed, and negative energy. Your concept of math is a universal language. Number sequences of energy make up the universe. These sequences of particles make up everything, including the DNA and genetic codes in your body. Nature itself is made up of Fibonacci numbers, computers of quantum energy, and even dark energy, which you cannot yet comprehend, but you will soon enough."

Chase said, "I understand love and energy, but I'm a little surprised at math."

The facilitator turned to a glowing force that had no human features and said, "Zero, perhaps you can explain better."

The image illuminated and said, "The race you experienced may be slow, but they are making strides with quantum physics and similar discoveries that they call science. Even when the scientists of old discovered a breakthrough, you will recall they completed long math formulas on their ancient chalkboards. Those calculations create the universal language of everything. The quantum computers and the technology they called the collective are all ultimately energy calculations."

"That may be true," Chase said, "but look what the sixteen

families have done with that technology and how they have brutalized the majority of the people. I feel like that is the real truth!"

"Yes, you're right. The other end of the spectrum of love is greed, ego and discrimination. Chase, you will realize that in addition to energy, either love or numbers control everything. Most intriguing to me," said Zero, "is how humans, more so than other races, use math to gain an advantage or profit at the expense of other less fortunate humans. There are many sad examples of this, but my favorite is the earthly concept of the gambling casino. Did you realize, that on a roulette table, if a human bets the green double zero, there is only a one in thirty-seven chance of winning? Slot-machine odds are worse, and humans target their own elderly and less fortunate population to profit. This is all very interesting to us, but then again, it's always interesting when some deceased energy souls from the earth plane enter and ask for seventy-two virgins."

The facilitator interrupted. "It's time to proceed."

Chase turned to the facilitator very attentively, not knowing what to expect.

The facilitator continued, "Chase all the energy in your being is still entangled and connected and you will be returned to your rightful place. The dimension to which you rightfully belong is filled with love, compassion and goodness. There are sixteen families there as well and the population competes to achieve that level of extreme virtue and moral excellence towards others. The environment is beautiful, and the technology is also beautiful, as it benefits all. The massive positive energy force and the culmination of everything wonderful there is called "The Human Collective" and you will experience it all. The dimension you knew of will be destroyed once again from a sequence of massive CME solar flares. They have already started. Eventually, that earth plane will have an opportunity to start over once again.

Chase spoke out, "What about Maggie and the others?"

Just then, the facilitator pointed to his left and in a glowing form of white energy appeared Maggie, Kay, Sean and Julian.

More astonishing for Chase was the image of himself standing right in front of him.

The facilitator spoke, "Chase this is the true energy of yourself".

Speechless, Chase felt the most comfortable, peaceful and awakened feeling as he slowly moved towards his image. Melting into one, Chase felt immense love and freedom for the first time. The five held hands and walked into the bright white light of nirvana.

The Dark Side of the Moon Casino was in rare form that night, celebrating the opening of the 100th location on the moon. Partying was brought to a new level. Jared was out of control. He decided to work the floor as a naked dealer. Guests were taking turns throwing knives at him. This was in addition to the drugs, hedonism and every other vice imaginable to man.

A group of drunken new guests rode motorcycles through the casino, and one smashed through a large glass wall. The casino erupted with cheers.

Suddenly, another guest yelled, "Holy shit, look at that big flash!"

At that moment, the casino violently shook, and everyone looked up at the giant screens depicting the earth.

Jared was the dealer at the roulette table, and he tapped his port to turn all the screen's video to Earth. Everyone was in shock. The earth was one huge fireball.

The casino violently shook again, and this time they felt the heat from the blast. For a moment no one spoke. No one knew what to do.

Then almost at the same time, people started crying and screaming, and someone yelled out, "We're stuck here. We're stuck here. How are we going to get back?"

Another person yelled out, "Get back to what? Look at the fire. There is no back. There is no Earth!"

Everyone was stunned, looking around at one another, unsure of what to do.

Jared stood on his chair and yelled out in his loudest voice, "Attention, everyone. I knew this day would come eventually. We have no home anymore, so we might as well have fun until one of those blasts hits this side of the moon. Who's with me?"

Just then it felt as if an earthquake hit the casino, and Jared fell off his chair. He got up and said, "Quick, we don't have much time!"

He ran to the roulette table. A man sat by himself as everyone else was screaming and running in panic.

Jared asked him, "Would you like to make a bet, sir?"

"Yes, I would." He pushed his big pile of chips toward Jared. "I'm betting it all on green double zero."

Michael Anthony Lang has truly lived a rags-to-riches life. Growing up with humble beginnings in a small Hudson Valley community in New York inspired him to work hard. He developed one of the largest independently owned media companies in New York state, creating and installing thousands of out-of-home media displays, including for the Times Square district. Valuing fairness and balance like a true Libra, he has encountered everything from corporate greed to near death experiences. While working with Fortune 500 companies, he became a certified psychic and attended hundreds of spiritual séances to balance his hectic life. After he sold his media company and retired at 49, he began meditating and within a few months wrote *The Human Collective*, his first novel. Today, you can find Michael consulting for one of Wall Street's largest firms, working with psychic mediums or assisting at his kids' lemonade stand.

For additonal content from your
other favorite authors visit
www.OverlookPublishing.com

Don't overlook the obvious...